SOME ONE'S THERE

DIANE SAXON

Boldwod

First published in Great Britain in 2020 by Boldwood Books Ltd.

Copyright © Diane Saxon, 2020

Cover Design by Head Design

Cover Photography: Shutterstock

The moral right of Diane Saxon to be identified as the author of this work has been asserted in accordance with the Copyright, Designs and Patents Act 1988.

A CIP catalogue record for this book is available from the British Library.

Paperback ISBN 978-1-83889-262-3

Large Print ISBN 9781838897048

Ebook ISBN 978-1-83889-263-0

Kindle ISBN 978-1-83889-264-7

Audio CD ISBN 978-1-83889-260-9

MP3 CD ISBN 978-1-83889-701-7

Digital audio download ISBN 978-1-83889-261-6

Boldwood Books Ltd
23 Bowerdean Street
London SW6 3TN
www.boldwoodbooks.com

To my dad, William John Saxon, who would have been 100 on 26th February 2020, the month Someone's There is released. A master storyteller himself, it was only in the years after his death we discovered his tales were mainly true recollections of his time in World War II and later as he continued his career in the RAF. Thank you for never putting the brakes on my imagination.

1

Dark laughter bubbled up from the depths of his blackened soul and reverberated around the four walls of the single-accommodation concrete cell in HM Long Lartin prison.

He blinked in the dimness of the grey light that was never quite dark enough as he slipped the burner phone from his pocket. Odds were it would be confiscated within a couple of days, as soon as the prison guards did their next sweep, but it wasn't difficult to hide a SIM card. Searches weren't always as thorough as they should be, especially if the guard was a lazy arse. They got that way when you nurtured them, lulled them into a false sense of security by behaving well enough until they trusted you.

He depressed the side button for a moment before he let the basic retro 'dumbphone' kick-start. With a battery life of almost a month, the phone was easily disposable and cheap to replace, provided he could persuade one of the new boys to pick it up from where his mate lobbed it over the wall. It was never an issue, provided he also persuaded him to put a few tabs in with it as a reward for the collector.

A quiver buzzed through his warmed blood and he stifled the excitement before it turned to a raging torrent of uncontrollable exhilaration.

He clamped his jaw closed, air hissing through his clenched teeth as he shaded the overly bright screen with his meaty fist and squinted at the single text. It didn't matter if the number was blocked. He had no intention of replying. He didn't need evidence of a link between them, but the connection would be more than obvious.

His lips kicked up at the sides. Another evil chuckle escaped him as he scanned the single word.

Soon.

2

The orange glow of street lamps flickered through the windows of the Uber car as Marcia Davies reclined in the rear seat, her head a gentle fuzz of alcoholic anaesthesia. Not sufficient to excise the pain of her broken heart, just enough to dull it for a short while.

She swiped her finger right over her phone to reject yet another hopeful candidate on Y'ello, the dating app she'd recently downloaded and soon regretted for its useless addictiveness.

She raised her head to stare out of the window at the insipid rain she knew still wept the icy winter's chill that seeped bone-deep. She went to swipe again and clenched her jaw at the sight of the vague tremble in her fingers. Dammit, it wasn't like her to be a coward.

She was strong.

She'd withstood so much. Rejection, humiliation. She could continue to withstand the intimidation, the menace.

Her chest expanded as she drew in a long breath and then blew it out again. She could do this. She had to do it.

She didn't have a choice.

As the Uber drew up outside her compact two bedroom terrace house in Lawley, a ripple of fear threaded through her. Fear of what she'd find this time.

When she and Ray had bought one of the brand new homes in the Telford expansion phase two years previously, she'd lavished her love on the place and him. On the outer edges of Telford, it was a short hop to spill over into Ironbridge and beyond to Much Wenlock. An idyllic village lifestyle located so it was just as easy to reach the M54 as it was the farmers' fields.

Instead of sharing space with Ray's mother and stepfather, as they had for several years until they'd saved the deposit for their house, she'd taken pride in furnishing her own space. Delighted that for the first time in her life she had something that would reflect her taste, her style.

Unfortunately, Ray had not been of the same mind. He hadn't even had the decency to leave her for a younger woman. Not that he could have found anyone much younger than Marcia when he'd met her. She'd been seventeen. Eighteen and still at university when they moved in with his mother and stepfather together. Once qualified, she'd thought the world was at her feet and within the span of a few short years, the prospect of promotion had been a viable one. They'd lived the golden life.

The peace and tranquillity of a suburban lifestyle with the security of neighbours she'd barely had the chance to get to know as everyone worked. Her shifts at The Princess Royal, Telford's main hospital, rarely afforded her the opportunity to make friends outside her own circle of work colleagues. She'd been happy enough with that arrangement. Until recently. Until she'd been ostracised by half of her work colleagues and the other half treated her as though she was about to break apart. She was.

She stared at the 'For Sale' sign in the neat patch of a front garden as it dripped with rain and misery.

The security she believed she had disappeared in a wisp of mist as she glanced at the house that no longer felt like her home. Not since Ray had left.

The fast clench in her stomach had her gripping the phone to her chest.

He may have left, but she'd been unable to stop him from returning.

'You all right, bab?' Powerful Birmingham laced the driver's words. The gentle term of endearment pulled her back to the present while she stared blankly at the taxi driver, her gaze meeting the watery blue of his in the rear view mirror. She remembered where she was. Embarrassment surged through her to nudge away the blur of alcohol. She fumbled as she dipped her hand hastily into her purse for the fare while he turned in his seat to face her.

'You're all right, bab. He already paid for you.' At her vacant stare, the driver nodded. 'Your young man, back there. He paid.'

Not her young man. Never likely to be. She zipped her purse closed, snapped her phone off and slipped it into her pocket, her gaze pulled back to the dark foreboding of the empty house.

A sliver of dread prickled her skin at the prospect of getting out of the safety of the car. Ray had done that to her. Made her scared of her own shadow, with his sly insistence that she'd lost her mind. The irony of it was, she had succumbed to the insanity of his mind games. His clever little tricks to make her frightened in her own home.

Marcia squeezed her eyes closed and gulped down the scalding acid threatening to bubble up the back of her throat into her mouth. She touched trembling fingertips to her lips and breathed in through her nose as the heat of the Uber pressed in on her, thick and claustrophobic. She dragged in another breath, almost choking on the sweet, cloying scent of the cherry shaped air freshener which dangled from the driver's rear view mirror and gave an erratic sway as the driver hefted his large frame out of the car and moved around to yank her door open.

The fast rush of cold draught had her eyes popping open as she heaved in a quick gasp of refreshing air while the biting wind ripped at the thin layers of clothes only suitable for a date in a warm, cosy restaurant, not a late night walk, even if it was only to her front door.

Icy fingers of panic stole along her spine as Marcia shot her gaze up to the darkened bedroom windows in the fear of what Ray may have done while she'd been out. Had he sneaked in to break another cup, move a precious lamp, take away a kitchen appliance? He'd already had the television, leaving her with nothing but her laptop to watch programmes on.

A shiver took a hold of her and she clenched her teeth, her jaw popping in her ears.

'C'mon, now love, you've had too much to drink. I wish you girls would take better care of yourselves.' An edge of iron had crept into the driver's voice as he held open the door, his face set in disapproval.

'Sorry. I'm so sorry.'

Embarrassed, Marcia stumbled from the taxi, muttering a 'thank you' as she tripped along the neatly edged pathway, desperate to escape her humiliation.

Not so desperate she didn't hang onto the door frame, reluctant to enter the house as her world spun. She should never have drunk so much. She stabbed her key into the lock, only succeeding in inserting it on the third try, aware of the presence of the Uber driver as he waited at the end of her pathway, his engine running. It should have made her feel safe, but the danger wasn't so much outside where the street lamps cast puddles of light onto the wet pavements. Her fear came from the silent stillness of her own house.

With her back to the lawn, she refused to turn around and look at the single word Ray had burned into it with weedkiller. She didn't have to look; it was etched on her mind.

Bitch.

As though she'd been the one who'd cheated, and he wanted all the neighbours to know. Well, they thought they knew, and oh, how they judged.

She lowered her forehead to rest it against the chilly glass in the front door as the insistent drizzle seeped through her thin coat to send goose bumps chasing over her flesh. With a quiet sob, she raised her head, turned the key and stepped inside.

As she paused in the open doorway, more than willing to absorb the comfort she'd always taken from the house, a swift rush of fear washed over her to make her flesh crawl.

Without looking back to check if the driver still watched, Marcia slipped inside and snapped the door closed. Her fingers trembled as she pushed the door handle up and turned the lock, engaging the five-lock mechanism.

She glanced up the darkened stairwell, her heart thundering. The silence pressed down.

Disgusted with herself for allowing her imagination to run roughshod over her, Marcia straightened her shoulders and raised her chin. It was rubbish. Whatever the hell Ray thought he was doing, he wasn't going to intimidate her. The creaks and bumps she'd only heard in the last few days since he'd sent a solicitor's letter the week before demanding she sell the house. It was on the market. It wouldn't sell any faster just because he was trying to strong-arm her.

It was his fault the last couple simply drove off after seeing that word emblazoned over the front lawn.

Did he even regret his impulsive action in a fit of temper a couple of weeks earlier when they'd argued over the sofa? She'd refused to let him have it, showed him proof that she'd paid for it and threatened to report him to the police.

Just to prove he could, he'd returned once she'd gone to work. Left the box of weedkiller on the bench. It was a few days later it dawned on her what he'd done.

He may have damaged the lawn, but there was no way he'd physically harm her. Surely?

He'd loved her once.

Hadn't he?

Emotions rocked wildly with the adrenaline shot of alcohol, sending her from the edge of tears to anger, frustration, fear.

The sheer cruelty of it almost brought her to her knees as grief struck her in a violent blast.

Infuriated with her uncharacteristic weakness, she ground her teeth as she strode through to the kitchen, dipped her hand into her pocket and tossed her mobile phone onto the smooth wooden counter next to the almost empty bottle of wine she'd managed to consume before she'd gone out.

She frowned as she tried to remember where she'd left the glass, sure she'd brought it from upstairs when she was about to leave for the evening.

She opened a cupboard and snatched out a clean glass, spilling the wine over the side as she sloshed the last of it from the bottle.

Tears pricked the back of her eyes as she took a deep slug and allowed humiliation to flow over her.

She'd made a mistake.

She wasn't damned well ready to date. Three months. It was hardly a lifetime since Ray had left. Barely a blink since he'd announced he had another woman. Even less when he told her last week that his new woman was pregnant. Another hard blow in a long string of them.

She stripped off her damp coat and slung it over the back of one of her kitchen chairs.

She hadn't the blindest clue why she'd gone out for drinks with the young police officer. Other than the girls at work telling her to get back out there – enjoy herself. Enjoy! As if that was about to happen. Feel like an attractive woman again, they'd told her, not the piece of unattractive shit Ray had made her feel like.

She thought dating a police officer might make her feel safe. Just for a short while.

She placed her hands either side of the small kitchen sink and hung her head low.

Even that, she couldn't get right. He hadn't wanted her either. She'd read it in his eyes within minutes of their meeting. Pity had lurked there as she drank too much, talked too loud, sounded a little too desperate. Pity and rejection.

Rejection. It was the last thing she'd needed tonight. If only he'd been a little more interested and a little less noble. Noble he may have been, but he'd lied about his age. She hadn't minded a younger man. He'd told her he was twenty-five. From his baby-face features and skinny frame, he'd been nowhere near that age. Twenty-one at the oldest. She could hardly hold it against him, though. She'd lied too. She'd claimed she was twenty-five when she was pushing twenty-eight. It just went to show what a soft focus camera, subtle make-up and a naïve mind could achieve when dealing with the dating app community.

A quiet moan slipped from her lips and then stuck in her throat as she raised her head and held her breath to listen. Her own watery reflection stared back at her from the rain splattered kitchen window she'd yet to close the blinds on. She never did. Why would she? It only overlooked the barren wasteland that was about to be built on. No neighbours beyond their small garden yet.

Still, the pitch black closed in.

She reached out a hand to yank them down, then halted. Eyes narrowed, she watched herself as she tilted her head and concentrated, sure the muted sound she'd heard came from upstairs. A sound she'd heard a number of times over the last few days. A breath, a movement. A quiet shuffle. As though someone was up there.

Watching.

Waiting.

Goose bumps pebbled her forearms, making the fine hairs stand on end, the stroke of feather-light fingers drawing a line along her spine to make her flesh tingle and crawl.

She blinked eyes awash with tears while she waited and listened, letting the rhythmic tick of the kitchen clock fill the silence in the room and mark time as it slipped away. She was working too hard, doing too much. She had so much more to do, living alone. Her twelve-hour shifts left her exhausted.

She breathed, her dizzy mind whirling.

Ray still had his own key to the front door. Had he slipped in? Was he up there, trying to frighten her?

The low-life bastard. She should have called the damned police. Instead she'd tried to date one. To bring her sanity and protection. It had brought her neither, just a sick sense of shame. Poor boy.

She'd contact the police tomorrow. Report Ray. He was an arse, but an arse who had escalated his attempts to intimidate her. And he'd succeeded.

Bitterness curdled her stomach.

She hitched in a desperate sob. She took another healthy gulp of wine and watched her eyes harden in her mirrored reflection.

An elusive trail of evidence of his visits greeted her each time she came home. The mean pig. Subtle insults, as if leaving her wasn't enough of a blow. Her favourite bone china mug, the one he'd bought her from Royal Worcester in happier times, in the cupboard, the handle shattered into several pieces. At first, she thought it had been an accident, perhaps she'd caught it with another piece of crockery and not noticed. But the build up of incidents negated that. Missing underwear, her newly ironed uniform in a heap on the floor, an entire roll of toilet paper dropped down the loo, the radio left playing.

He'd taken the TV, the thoughtless moron. He'd bought it for her the Christmas before last. It belonged to her and he'd taken it.

Annoyance whipped through the self-pity. She'd bloody kill Ray if he'd decided to sneak around the house, the thoughtless little prat.

She listened.

Nothing but silence greeted her.

To the count of ten, she let out her breath. In, to the count of five.

Overwhelmed by a multitude of emotions, she squeezed her eyes closed. She was going to her mum's.

The soft whisper of a breath stroked over her consciousness. Her eyes flew open and she reared her head back. Her heart stumbled to a halt, then thundered violently, the wild thrum of it lodging in her throat to choke off her breath mid-stream.

A ghostly shadow reflected in her window stood in the kitchen behind her.

Marcia whipped around. That weasel of an ex-boyfriend.

Confusion chased every coherent thought from her alcohol infused mind.

Dread crushed her chest until she could barely draw a breath.

She opened her mouth and her voice cracked on a desperate gasp.

'You're not Ray.'

3

'Who the hell are you?'

He angled his head to one side to better study her, curious to get a closer look after so many days of observing with the quiet thrill of knowing he'd made her doubt her own sanity.

The alcohol he'd seen her drink earlier in the evening had slowed her responses but not dulled eyes that sparkled with tears, nor taken the shine from her cherry-red nose she'd blown all too much while she sobbed the last few days away.

It had been priceless to watch as her stupid, thick-headed ex had told her about the pregnancy. She'd broken then.

The man had denied everything, accusing her of losing her mind. She hadn't lost her mind. She was right. Her mug had been broken, things had been moved, underwear taken. But it hadn't been her ex. He hadn't even been in the house, the coward. The only thing he was guilty of was the writing on the lawn.

Eyes wide, mouth slack, she stood frozen to the spot.

Poor, pathetic soul. He thought he'd lost her when she went out. Dressed to kill. Obviously on the pull. She'd already had too much to drink before she left. A cheap bottle of red wine. Not to his taste. He'd taken a sip from her glass before he remembered DNA. He'd scrubbed it clean and then placed it very carefully in the wrong cupboard, just to see her reaction, but she'd not looked since she'd returned.

Dutch courage, she'd told her friend on the phone just as she went out. Dutch courage. She'd need more than that now.

She'd returned earlier than expected. He'd still been in the kitchen, but he'd soon shot up the stairs to wait.

He'd been prepared to sneak back up into the attic space above the spare bedroom where he'd been waiting and watching for the past few days. If she'd brought someone home with her, he'd have had to brave the chill of her attic once more, but when she'd stumbled from the cab all alone, her distressed sobs echoing up the stairwell, he'd considered his options and decided the time was right to carry out the next phase of his plan. A little earlier than anticipated, but he had all the equipment he required with him. He'd stashed it in the attic.

Anticipation fluttered through his stomach as he took his time to study her.

Her haunted eyes sent out a desperate appeal. An appeal he was willing to help her with. She didn't need to suffer from a broken heart. Not for long. Pitiful little woman.

He leaned his shoulder against the door frame, effectively blocking the one and only exit from the room. As he crossed his arms over his chest, he schooled his features into friendly, approachable. He forced his lips into a wide grin and a sharp thrill raced through his veins as her eyes widened and her sluggish brain evidently caught up. He could only hazard a guess at what she thought of the stranger in her kitchen dressed in pure white personal protection equipment.

From the fear slashing over her features, she had an idea. It didn't really matter what his face portrayed, the outfit said it all. She wasn't stupid. He didn't want stupid. Half the game was the taunting, the teasing, the breaking down of the spirit so once he made his move the game was already well under way. The thrill was in the chase, the hunting down of the prey. The cornering of the victim.

When she recognised him as her executioner, the game would truly begin.

She swayed, a drunken rolling lurch, and reached behind her to lean her hands against the kitchen bench to steady herself while he waited and snapped out a smile.

She found her voice at last, recognition slashing over her features. They hadn't met, but she knew him. 'What are you doing here?'

He squinted at her and then pushed away from the door frame, heart soaring with excitement. Years of study, plotting, planning, fell perfectly into place. Narrowing down his prey had only taken a matter of a few weeks. Y'ello had provided him with so much information. Too much. It was so easy to prise personal details out of people. Flattery went a long way, when someone was lonely. Sad.

His lips twitched into a genuine smile this time. 'You have the most beautiful hair, Marcia. I've told you that before.'

A brief flash of confusion flickered through her eyes before the fear dashed it away as he brought one of her kitchen knives from behind his back, the white light of the kitchen flashing across it.

Only four paces in front of him. The scent of her heady perfume wound through his senses. The perfume he'd come to enjoy, the one he'd take with him for the memories the aroma would invoke.

Yes, this was right. It was all perfect.

4

Darkness engulfed him disguising the tremor in his hands. He'd never killed before. He'd dreamt of it, imagined his hands around a woman's throat. Tested it from time to time on various girlfriends, the thrill shooting through his veins like liquid nitrogen, making him an all powerful being. A god.

Not that the two girlfriends he'd tried it on had enjoyed it. The experiment had been short lived, as had the relationships.

This had been nothing like his previous experiences.

For a start, he'd never expected so much blood. The warm explosion of it had still managed to penetrate through his thin nitrile gloves.

Nausea clenched his stomach, pushing hot bile into his throat.

Hands on hips, he lowered his head and panted out short bursts of breath, his lungs burning as his chest tightened.

He swiped the back of his hand over his dry lips. A ripple of pride pulled him back from the edge to gain a better grasp of control. Control was what he needed. He'd almost lost it for a short while.

His first kill.

It hadn't been strangulation, but something much darker, more final. Once the single, vicious stab of the knife had been made into her throat, there was no opportunity to turn back, no relaxing of his fingers against the fine line of her throat. No redemption.

It hadn't been a clean death. He could see that now, would know what to do next time. He'd not plunged the knife deep enough into her throat to make it a swift end. He'd fudged it. No matter how much he'd studied, he'd been unprepared for the reality of it. It should have been a deep slash, ear to ear, rather than a stab and pull. He knew that now. Next time would be cleaner. More efficient. Despite his plan, it had all been too rushed.

He wiped the blood from her kitchen knife and placed it neatly on her countertop as he stared down at her.

He'd not anticipated the terror that had her rushing towards him, spoiling the whole plan of controlled fear.

With one punch to the face, he'd stunned her. That's where he'd made his first mistake. He should have gagged her, tied her up straight away and then taken his time. He could have used one of the two ladder-back kitchen chairs from around her small drop-leaf table in the corner. She'd have been in position then. He could have used her beautiful red hair, wrapped it around his fist to pull her head back and expose the whiteness of her throat. Instead, adrenaline still boiling in his stomach, as she dropped to her knees on the floor in front of him, he had shoved the knife straight into her throat.

Eyes wide with shock, she'd wrapped her hands around her neck to staunch the flow.

When the blood spilled, thick and glutinous, soaking its heat through his gloved hands, he'd panicked, never imagining blood had the power to spread with such energy. Not a thin trickle, but short, hard spurts of crimson liquid straight from the carotid artery.

Worse still, no one had ever described the sound. The desperate gasp and bubble which filled his head. The accompanying gagging from her as she struggled to draw in that precious last breath of air while her lungs filled to drown her in her own bodily fluids. The hopeless struggle as she thrashed against the cream tiles of her kitchen floor, sending blood splatter in a pattern up the kitchen units and across the magnolia tiles of her perfect, pristine house.

As she crumpled to the floor, he'd stepped back, out of reach of the spray of blood, fascination chasing away the nausea while the woman's limbs slowed their frenzied grasp on life as she dug her heels down to gain purchase on the slippery floor. The last of her blood pumped ever slower to soak through the thin man-made fibre of the dress which barely covered her.

He hunkered down beside her, leaning his head close to hers to engage in the last precious seconds of her consciousness before the desperation in her eyes faded to leave a bleak emptiness, regret and sorrow sliding away to nothing.

Curious, he leaned back on his heels to observe while her right foot gave one last twitch, then all movement ceased. Bright copper hair, matted in the stickiness of her blood, pooled out in a halo around her angled head.

Distracted with every feature of his kill, he studied her inch by inch. Her position on the floor, the way the pool of blood bloomed like an opening rose and then dribbled in straight lines where the grout formed grooves. His purpose slipped away as he absorbed every interesting detail.

With a jerk, his brain engaged again. A zap of static kick-started his thought process.

He straightened, stretching out the taut muscles in his back, the crack and grind of them reminding him he'd taken so much longer than he intended. Long enough to have forgotten his next move.

He strode to the kitchen window, jerked the blind down, not that the house was overlooked, but just in case.

He blew out a breath and turned to face the scene.

Never to lose sight of the purpose. He twisted his lips, a lick of irritation tightened his chest. He'd lost sight easy enough. Straight into a dreamworld of crimson pools and gaping wounds. But he was back.

With a careless swipe, he smeared the blood from his nitrile gloved hands onto the trouser legs of his white PPE suit while he gazed around at the literal bloodbath she'd created with her messy death. His heart still hammered hard against his ribcage despite his attempt to control it.

He needed to get a grip, clean up the mess. A mess far worse than he could have imagined. Stupid of him not to have realised. The volume of blood in one body contained between eight and twelve pints.

Looked like she'd pumped out all twelve pints of hers with all her thrashing around, her hands grasping at her own throat to staunch the flow that wouldn't be stemmed. Who'd have thought it would leach so far?

He blew out a breath in preparation of phase two of the job. The clean-up. He knew exactly what he needed to do. He just had to move. Legs heavy, he acknowledged the shock had hit him harder than he'd believed, the drop from the adrenaline rush left him weak and empty.

He glanced down at the white shoe covers he'd pulled on. Crimson streaks daubed them, but despite the amount of blood on the floor, he had relatively little splashed on his PPE.

With a twitch of irritation, he moved to the kitchen doorway, swiped off the left shoe cover first and replaced it with a fresh one, careful not to place his shoe directly on the floor. Once he'd replaced the cover on his right foot, he made his way up the dark stairs, conscious of not switching on a light, familiar with the place after three days of scoping out the tidy little house while she was out. He cruised his gaze around. He'd miss the place, miss lodging in her compact attic. Miss the little tricks he'd played on her. It hadn't been difficult to gain entry. Her little key safe hadn't taken much to figure out. Year of birth. Why weren't people more inventive?

She'd drawn the curtains in her bedroom before she left, and the soft glimmer of the bedside lamp cast enough of a glow for him to find what he wanted. He opened the second drawer down in her bedroom chest and pulled out the neat, ironed uniform. The memory of the original etched deep in his mind, disappointment had his lips turning down at the edges. The practical green scrubs were hardly a close comparison to the old-school, pristine blue uniform with the matching cap and little white apron.

He glanced at the time, speeding by faster than he realised. He needed to press on. He knew what the format and procedure was, he'd paid close attention, but the actual execution of it had been far beyond his expectation.

The whistle of air streaming in through his nose in panicked gasps stilled him. He clung to the uniform, spread his arms wide and invited energy in from the universe, tossing his head backwards he parted his lips. Muttering soothing words under his breath, he drew in measured air to expand his chest.

There.

One. Two. Three.

He pursed his lips and blew out, his eyelids flickering as bright golden lights sparkled behind them, pulling energy from around him.

The control was back.

Time. Time was his enemy, therefore he wouldn't allow himself to be controlled by it.

Without consulting his watch again, he dashed downstairs with the uniform tucked into the top of the brand-new holdall he'd left at the top of the stairs.

He chewed his lip as he stared at the dead body sprawled on the kitchen floor in a wash of blood. The loss of dignity in her death didn't escape him. He'd meant it to be a humiliation, a ripping away of all respect.

With lips parted, he dragged in the overriding smell surrounding him. Tannic undertones coated the back of his throat with metallic wisps burning his nose.

Sensations bombarded him while he settled down to clean the scene.

A step-by-step guide to covering your own footsteps, cleaning your DNA. Deniability was the key. Leave nothing and nothing could be proven.

The gloves crackled as he rubbed his hands together and then reached into the holdall for a thick, black bin liner. Each item thought out, planned.

A quiet thrill chased through his veins to heat his skin. He appreciated the total silence as he took a moment to study her before he reached into his holdall and took out a thick length of rope. He rolled out a clean sheet of plastic and lifted her onto it, so she no longer lay in her own oozing blood.

It was all an exercise. An experiment.

Affording her no dignity in death, he took the knife from the counter and slashed the flimsy dress from her body. He soaked a bundle of tea towels in diluted bleach. He angled his head as he cleansed her body, wiping away the blood with swift, efficient strokes, her flesh wobbling under his ministrations. He curled his lip.

'Distasteful little liar. You're much bigger than you claimed on Y'ello – by at least a whole dress size. Possibly two. And older. By a good five years. I found that out when I stalked your Facebook.' He leaned in closer. 'Yeah, not so obvious until you get up close and personal.' He chuckled to himself.

With meticulous care, he stroked the bleach dampened towel over her body to remove all traces of blood. He swiped at her neck, irritated as blood insisted on bubbling again and again where he removed it, no longer pumping, just seeping.

Practicality filtered through a mind cluttered with the death of her, his first victim. He fished the thick brown tape from his backpack, tore off a long strip and wrapped it around her neck, then continued until her body was clean of all traces of blood.

He gave her skin a brisk rub with one of her dry towels he'd stored in his holdall and then yanked her uniform on, tutting as inevitable smudges of blood smeared over it.

He lay her down, her shoulders slipping from his grasp. The wet thunk of her head hitting the floor invoked a deep satisfaction. His belly warmed as he grinned down at her. Better dead than the pathetic being she'd become. He'd done her a favour, putting her out of her misery.

He dragged one of the chairs closer, then lifted her body from the floor and positioned her on the seat. The dead weight of her flopped forward, but he arranged her, using her hair to gently pull her head back, stripping the tape from her neck so both the gaping wound and her eyes stared vacant at the ceiling, her shoulders slumped backward over the wooden frame.

He took the palette of make-up from his holdall. Dipping his gloved finger into the blue eye make-up, he smudged it over the bronze she'd applied earlier. Not as neat as he wanted, he dragged his thumb over it, but only succeeded in smearing it with the nitrile glove. Her slackened lips wobbled as he applied the crimson lipstick.

Little quivers of excitement pulsed through him to speed his heart rate.

Next time, he'd extend it. Torture the poor soul as he'd originally planned. Irritation circled as he considered the cat and mouse game he could have played out, keen to observe the fear and the pitiful pleas for mercy. The begging wouldn't bother him. It interested him. The human mind.

He combed his fingers through her blood-soaked hair to try and put it in some semblance of order before he held her head, one hand on the back, the other beneath her chin, and tipped her forward. He slid the hand from under her chin and let it touch her chest. He stepped back and gazed down at the thick layer of blood surrounding the chair.

He needed to clean up. He couldn't leave it in the state it was. After all, the original had been cleaned.

With meticulous care, he stroked the bleach dampened towel over her body to remove all traces of blood.

Anger simmered beneath the surface as he couldn't resist checking the time. He'd thought it was easier than this, hadn't imagined how difficult it would be, how much effort he needed to put into the clean-up process. How time consuming. He'd far rather have left the body where it lay. He'd had the satisfaction, now the killing urge had gone to leave him empty.

He wiped his forehead with the back of his wrist and then stared at the sweat beading on his skin. Tempted to use the second cloth to wipe it away, he hesitated and then smudged his exposed wrist on his PPE

DNA.

He should never leave any DNA.

He huffed out a disgusted breath. It was damned hot in her house. She'd kicked the heating up high and he was about to suffocate. Why couldn't she have switched it off?

He stared at his own exposed wrist as the thought swirled around his mind that he may already have dropped a bead of sweat.

'Too late now.'

A thin slice of panic wormed its way through the control. What if he left a hair behind? A droplet of sweat? His DNA would be in evidence. He'd be found out.

With determined resolution, he cut off that line of thought, yanked the sleeve of his jacket down and covered the offending exposed flesh.

'It's not too late. I've not dropped any sweat. There are no stray hairs around.' He turned in a circle. 'I'll clean up.'

The acrid scent of bleach burned his nostrils as he poured almost the full bottle into her mop bucket. He wrinkled his nose against the temptation to sneeze. Soon. He'd be finished soon, and the discomfort would be worth it.

On his hands and knees, he rolled the plastic sheet as tight as he could and pushed it into a plastic bag, then inside his holdall, then he scrubbed the mop over the smooth surface of the tiles, time and time again. He changed the water in the bucket for the fourth time, slipped the covers from his feet and applied new ones.

Deep satisfaction filled his soul. The last part was the best. There. Breathless, he slipped the mop and bucket back into the corner and surveyed the scene. That was how it should be. The effort had been worth it. Perfection.

His lips curved up in a satisfied smile as he contemplated his workmanship. There wasn't a thing out of place, not a speck of blood to be seen by the human eye.

Proud of his work, he stepped back and snapped a photograph with the little burner phone he'd stowed in his backpack. He hesitated, his thumb hovered over the send button before he backtracked. He tapped in a few words, his lips curving in a satisfied smile as he pressed send to the only number that was on the phone, and then slipped it back away.

He inspected the place. Satisfied.

Leave no evidence and they'll never catch you. He grinned. It should be his motto. He could write it across the countertop in lipstick. But then the very thing he was wary of would become a truth and he'd have left evidence.

Ego. That's where they all went wrong. When they allowed their ego to surface.

He slipped the remaining items inside his holdall and made one last check of the room before he stepped outside the back door and stripped off the PPE gear, stowing it alongside the plastic sheeting. He removed his generic black hoodie from a separate polythene lined pocket in the bag and yanked it over his head, pulling the hood up to shadow his face. No brand names, nothing identifiable.

Soft drizzle settled around him and washed away the heat of her house but wasn't enough to rid him of the scent of blood and bleach. He drew in several long draughts of rain-fresh air, expanding his chest until his lungs burned with the joy of it.

Despite his misgivings, he'd done it. Totally on his own. No one would ever know.

The next time, it would be easier. He'd know what to do, it didn't matter how many times you went through it in your head, until you physically made the kill yourself, you could never know. Never understand the sheer perfection of it.

A shiver of delight flowed over him. Such deliciousness.

He cracked open the gate and checked each way before he slipped out, striding down the alley at the side of the house, his head lowered to avoid anyone seeing his face.

His heart soared with power as he considered the next victim on his list.

5

Dark satisfaction coiled snake-like in the pit of his stomach.

Nostrils flaring, McCambridge drew back his lips and sucked air in through his teeth.

He shielded the bright light of the screen with his hand as he cruised his gaze over the words.

The first of many.

Far from the pure thrill of carrying out the execution himself, he'd have to satisfy himself with the vicarious pleasure of someone carrying the job out for him.

He touched the tip of his finger to the screen as pleasure heated his blood, anticipation coursing through his veins while he waited for the image to appear.

Vicarious it may be, but each time she died, satisfaction seared his soul. His hands were quite literally tied. His incarceration preventing him from carrying out the deed himself.

A slow smile slid across his features. No worries. This was the next best thing.

His work continued under the guise of another, but it was his mark on it. His style. His revenge.

Revenge on the woman who'd stolen his life with her self-centred thoughtlessness.

His mother. A nurse. Why hadn't she known better? Known what would happen to him when she took her own worthless life. The selfish bitch.

He closed his eyes and let the anger surge up to close his throat and choke him. The vivid image of his mother's limp body slumped forward in the kitchen chair, a river of blood washed over her uniform and splattered on the surrounding tiles. The short, sharp kitchen knife protruded from her neck where she'd slammed it into herself, blood still pumping from the carotid artery.

'Mummy! Mummy?' The little boy had grasped her head, pulling her face up to meet his. The smudge of blue tears streaked her face, the reek of gin filled his lungs.

Drugged eyes flickered open. Empty. Soulless. The flutter of a breath hovered on her lips for a brief moment before her dead eyes closed, her crimson, bloodied lips slackened.

He'd learned later that it barely took minutes to bleed out from a slash to a main artery. Her death had been quick, if messy. And she'd left him with a whole lifetime of bitterness. A seven year old boy put in the system, pushed from pillar to post, abused, neglected, all because his mother hadn't loved him enough to live.

His fist enclosed the small phone. Four bars registered. Plenty enough for an image to download.

Far into the night, he waited with the dull glow of the screen turned to his face. His blood simmered, anticipation turning to fury.

The first of many.

But where was the image? Where was the *fucking* photograph?

6

Detective Sergeant Jenna Morgan leaned her elbows on her desk and pressed the heels of her hands as deep into her eye sockets as she could without popping her eyes out of the back of her head. If she did, it would only be an improvement on the pain of a hundred woodpeckers stabbing into her brain through her left eye.

The low level buzz of bright electric lighting in West Mercia's Malinsgate police station jackhammered through her head and stabbed at her eyes.

'Night on the town?'

With reluctance, Jenna raised her head to squint at her partner. A pitiful groan squeezed its way from her lips.

Detective Constable Mason Ellis shot her an evil grin as he dumped his tall frame into the typist's chair opposite and wheeled it to the desk, bringing his head in close to hers.

Unable to focus on him at such a close range, Jenna bowed back and swallowed the heave of nausea. 'Girls' night in.'

'Ooooh, do tell.' He leaned his chin on his hand.

'Just me and Fliss.'

Barely discernibly, his eyes flickered at her sister's name, then he grinned.

'Well, you look like shit, boss.' Only he could get away with speaking to her like that. He'd known her too long and any sense of propriety had long since evaporated, except when in the company of other officers.

'Thanks for that.' She screwed her eyes shut and raked her fingers through her thick, choppy hair. She felt like shit, she knew it, what was she thinking of on a school night, and the start of a twelve hour shift? She'd barely been able to drag herself out of bed. But really, she didn't need Mason to tell her. All would be well if she could lie down in a darkened room, pull the covers over her head and sleep for twenty-four hours. Oh God, she should never have had so much to drink. Her head still spun, but worse than that was the acid burn in her stomach.

Saliva filled her mouth and she pressed the fingers of one hand against her lips and leaned her forehead on the other hand while her eyelids fluttered. 'It was the Prosecco.'

'Prosecco?' Mason quirked his dark eyebrows.

'Yeah.'

'You don't drink Prosecco.' He sat back and squinted at her, pulling at his earlobe. 'You've always said it's a trend for people who pretend to be what they're not.' He clicked his fingers as the correct word came to him. 'Pretentiousness.'

'Gah, well, I was pretentious. I pretended to be what I'm not and look where it got me.' She peered at him from between her fingers. His face swam in the mist of her eyesight. 'I should have stuck to gin and tonic.'

'You drank gin and tonic too?'

'Only at first. Then Prosecco.' The memory of it bubbled in her stomach and she caught herself just before she heaved.

'Bleh. Not a recommendation. You should never mix your drinks. I thought you were seasoned enough to know that.'

She was. She thought she was.

She covered her wide yawn with her hand and shook her head at him. 'We really didn't eat much last night.' She breathed in as she tried to recollect. 'Olives.' Her stomach churned. 'Prosciutto and sun-dried tomato bread.' Her lips tightened at the memory. 'We were going to make lasagne, but...' She gave a vague wave of her hand. 'I don't suppose you have access to a cup of coffee and a bacon sandwich?'

Spreading his empty hands wide, he shot her an unsympathetic grin as he leaned back in his chair while it creaked its protest. 'Sorry, I can't oblige.' He squinted at her. 'It's not like you to drink midweek. What were you celebrating?'

'Fliss.' Again, the quick flash of awareness at the mention of her sister's name. Jenna's hangover fuzz cleared a little and she paid closer attention to him. 'She's been offered a new job.'

Surprise raced over his features. 'I didn't know she wanted a new job. You never mentioned it.'

'Yeah. She's not settled since she was...' she hesitated over the word, still finding it difficult to acknowledge what had happened to her younger sister, '... kidnapped.'

Heat rushed over her, less to do with the memory of the incident than the acid churning in her stomach. She rubbed the back of her aching neck and swallowed the excess of spit in her mouth.

'She says she's not sure she can cope with the constant sympathetic glances she keeps getting from people at school who weren't even her friends before. She feels she needs a change. Perhaps teaching elsewhere would help.'

Mason gave a solemn nod. 'I can understand that, but with the exposure she got in the press, it's unlikely she'll get away with anonymity, no matter where she goes. It hit the papers nationwide.'

Anger unfurled in her, temporarily overriding the nausea. 'Bastard press with bastard Kim Stafford. Who the hell keeps leaking shit to him?'

'Dunno, but when Inspector Gregg finds out, he'll rip their intestines out.'

'Hopefully, he'll rip Kim's out soon. He's not helped the situation with Fliss. I don't know if she's making the right move, but maybe because they won't know her, they won't feel entitled to give their opinion. Yet.'

He leaned forward to rest his elbows on the desk. 'Where's she thinking of going?'

'Wolverhampton.'

'Really? That's a fair commute. That's going to be tough on both of you.'

Tears grabbed Jenna's throat and squeezed tight. She should never have had so much to drink on a work night. The desperate hangover allowed her emotions to spill over. She hoped she wouldn't become a blubbering mess. Especially not at work. 'She'll probably move there, if she accepts the position.'

'Oh.' The one flat word reflected his opinion and hers.

'Yeah.'

'You'll miss her and that furry fiend of hers.'

'I'm not so sure.' Filled with bravado, she forced further words from her throat, knowing if he pressed too hard, she'd be in floods of tears and he'd be mortified if she cried over the Dalmatian. 'Domino's a pain in the arse. You'd have thought he'd have learned a lesson, but no, he's just as exuberant as ever.' She sucked in her upset for the sake of the man opposite.

More comfortable with hitting people, feminine tears destroyed Mason.

She was destroyed herself. She couldn't imagine her life without Fliss and the gorgeous Dalmatian. She'd held her close – both of them close – ever since they'd been attacked. Domino left for dead and her sister abducted. She'd probably overprotected her. Stifled her, as she allowed her to do whatever she wanted, just as long as she was safe. Her beautiful Dalmatian dog, Domino, so severely injured, now slept on Fliss's bed where he'd never been allowed before.

Jenna had thought that was the way their life was to continue. When Fliss had brought two bottles of Prosecco home, Jenna had put on a brave face, smiled, celebrated with her little sister while inside her heart had broken. Which was why she'd allowed herself to drink so much. Less a case of celebration and more drowning her sorrows.

Mason raised his head and stabbed his forefinger on the table. 'She's making a mistake. You need to tell her to stand her ground.'

Amused at Mason's opinion that she had any sway in Fliss's decisions, Jenna mustered up a weak smile. 'She's a big girl now, she needs to make up her own mind.'

Mason shuffled in his chair and grunted just as Jenna's stomach served to remind her it still needed to punish her for her excesses of the previous night. If only she hadn't consumed that gin and tonic before Fliss had got home.

The wild sway in her mushy brain had her clutching the sides of the desk so she didn't crawl over the ceiling.

Determined to centre herself, Jenna studied him through narrowed eyes as she could only imagine what thoughts zipped through his mind.

'So, how's the dog-walker working out?'

Surprised he'd remembered the plan Fliss and her had put into place to have Domino walked on the days both of them were at work, Jenna shrugged to cover the little glow of delight. 'She's good. Very caring. Pip Lovell.'

'Can she handle him?'

'Him and two others, she literally has them eating out of her hand, walking at heel and virtually dancing on their hind legs.'

'That should keep him out of mischief.'

'If you mean it should keep him from eating any more of my kitchen, that is the idea.'

Mason chuckled then fell silent, his gaze turning serious.

'You know...' With thumb and forefinger, he tugged at his bottom lip as his gaze skittered over hers and then away.

'Yes?' She wasn't sure she had the patience for his hesitant intimations. Couldn't he just get on and spit it out?

He pushed the chair away from the desk, almost came to his feet, and then slumped back down again. 'Would it be weird if I asked your sister out?'

At last. It had only taken him several months to voice what Jenna had known was coming. She hummed a soft sigh as she leaned back in her chair, her gaze directly on Mason's slightly pinkened face. 'It would be about time.'

'Sorry?'

'Mason, how long have you wanted to go out with Fliss?'

'Well, forever.'

'Yeah. And how long have I been a detective?'

His lips twitched. 'For about the same length of time.'

'Right. So how long do you think I've known that you have a thing for my sister?'

'Shit.' This time, he rolled all the way to his feet and paced away across the room. When he swung around on his heel, his eyes had narrowed. 'So, why haven't you ever brought the subject up?'

'Because she had a boyfriend.'

'He was a wanker.' He'd have loved the opportunity to smack him one in the mouth, she knew.

Jenna smiled. 'Indeed.'

There was no denying Fliss's ex had been a complete moron and caused indescribable damage to her self-confidence, but it was being attacked and incarcerated in a small, damp cellar for several days that had caused a huge change in her younger sister. She'd become more determined, more single-minded and less sociable. It was time for her to get out, to establish new relationships and Jenna could think of worse people than Mason for Fliss to establish a relationship with.

She glanced up at him and blew out a long breath. 'Look, ask her out. Don't, for the love of God, tell her you asked my permission. And, Mason?' With a malicious grin, she locked eyes with him. She knew how to wipe the look of relief from his face.

'Yeah?'

'You hurt her, and I won't kick your arse for you.'

The little glimmer of hope was pitiful. 'No?'

No.' With a flat expression, she stared him down while she dealt him more truth than he would ever know. 'I will bury you. Alive. Where no one will ever find you. There will be no witnesses. There will be no evidence. There will be no forensics. And there will be no one there to rescue you. You will die alone and petrified, having pissed your own trousers several times, because it will be a long drawn-out death.'

His eyes widened with each statement she nailed home. 'Sheesh, Jenna, do you have to be so bloodthirsty?'

'I investigate crimes every day. What do you expect?'

The look he sent her was pitiful. 'A little compassion.'

'You have as much compassion as you need, you know I don't do fluffy bunnies.' She pointed her index finger at him. 'Hurt my little sister and you're dead meat, pal. In the very worst sense of the word.'

Mason jiggled his shoulders. 'Dead is dead. Anyway, she may not agree to go out with me.' Thoughtful, he tapped his fingers against his chin. 'Do you think I'm too old for her?'

Age wasn't a particular issue for Jenna, nor did she think Fliss would think so. 'No, I don't. She may, but you won't know if you don't ask.'

Mason smiled, relief washing over his face. 'Good.' He nodded and broke into a grin. 'Great.'

Distracted by the glimpse of a familiar figure, she stared past Mason at the young detective lolloping towards them through the main office of Malinsgate Police Station. Detective Constable Ryan Downey, the son of Jim, their senior forensics scientist, seconded to her team when her sister went missing. His enthusiasm and intelligence had led to his position being made permanent, much to her delight.

His loose-limbed swagger became overexaggerated as he made his way past the new blonde administrator, who never even spared him a glance.

Jenna narrowed her eyes as his gaze caught hers. She jerked her head in a 'come over' motion and curved her lips in a friendly smile.

Like a deer in headlights, the young man hesitated mid-stride, his gaze darting from side to side as though looking for an escape route.

Mason glanced over his shoulder to see who she'd pinned with a look, kept his voice down low and mumbled out of the corner of his mouth. 'Would you stop baring your teeth at the poor lad. He hasn't a clue what he's done. It only quarter to six. He's early for God's sake.'

The smile zipped off her face. 'I wasn't baring my teeth.'

Mason quirked his lips in disbelief.

Offended, she snapped upright in her chair. 'I was smiling.'

Mason snorted out a burst of laughter, half relieved, she suspected, to have the attention off him. She'd lost interest in any case. There was nothing further to discuss. Mason would ask her sister out. Fliss would most likely say no and Jenna would have to tolerate the pitiful heartbroken eye-rolling pettiness that would ensue.

Not unlike how she felt about Adrian Hall, the Chief Crown Prosecutor she'd spent so much time with when Fliss went missing. If the situation had been different, she may well have made moves on him. But timing had been the issue and her sole focus had been her sister. Once that focus had changed, she'd have quite happily ripped his clothes from his delectable body. She'd barely moved past the change of focus when she found out he was married. Off limits. That was her rule, a one she'd never strayed from. Married men held no interest for her.

She pushed all thoughts of Adrian from her mind, just as she had when she received a text from him that morning, acknowledging her drunken message from the night before. It wasn't altogether cringeworthy, she'd asked him when he'd be in the station again. He'd not answered her the night before, but by the time she arrived in work, he'd replied, asking when she was available for a quick coffee.

Coffee was all she could allow herself with him.

Right now, she had more interest in the approaching Detective Constable. Her avid gaze zoomed in on the items the young man clutched in his bony, over large hands.

She leaned forward to get a better look. 'What you got there?'

Newly appointed to the team, DC Ryan Downey bobbed his head a couple of times, racing pigeon style, and cast Jenna a sheepish grin. 'Bacon and egg baguette and a Venti caramel shortbread latte with extra cream, Sarg.'

Mason blew out a breath and flung himself back in his chair. 'A fucking, what...?'

Jenna's stomach flipped over and threatened to throw up the biley contents at the thought of so much cream. She covered her mouth with her hand and squeezed her eyes closed as her stomach rolled over, then did a quick backflip to make her gag.

In the silence, she sucked air in through her teeth and coaxed her eyes open, relieved as the rush of nausea subsided.

With a depth of maturity and command she didn't quite feel, she lowered her eyebrows and pointed at the baguette he held in his left hand. 'Gimme.'

'Excuse me?' His eyebrows shot high in his smooth, unwrinkled forehead.

'Gimme.' She wriggled her fingers, beckoning him towards her, and then reached inside the top drawer of her desk with her other hand to pull out a ten pound note. Desperation made her generous. She'd have offered him a bar of gold if she'd had one. 'I'll give you ten quid for it.' She hoped her voice sounded more business like than wheedling. If he scented her wretchedness, Ryan would have the upper hand. Sweetheart though he was, Jenna couldn't afford for him to choose now to find his confidence.

Mason snorted.

'But it's my breakfast.' Despair tinged Ryan's voice and he ended the sentence on a high pitched squeak.

'Mine now.' She wriggled her fingers again.

His huge brown eyes drooped at the edges and she could have sworn tears started to form. She relented and reached inside her drawer for another ten pound note. 'Twenty quid, Ryan, and I'll let you go and get another one right now. If you're quick. But I want that one.' Self-preservation was all that mattered. The young man was never without food. He'd find more.

Mason groaned and dropped his head into his hands 'Pathetic...' he muttered under his breath. 'Truly, pathetic.'

Pathetic didn't quite hit the mark. She'd have crawled over broken glass to get that baguette. It was the magic cure for her hangover.

'Here. My need is greater than yours. You can go back.' She waggled the money at Ryan, knowing she had him. 'While you're there, I'll have one of those huge cups of coffee – black – lots of sugar.'

'Venti.'

'What's empty?' Confused, she stared at him, the murkiness of her hangover fogging her mind.

'Not empty. The size of the coffee. It's Venti.'

What the hell made him think she cared. She didn't care. She only cared about coffee. Now. 'Good enough. Get me a Venti. Triple shot of espresso'

His gaze darted between her and the baguette, his skinny chest appeared to deflate, and then he handed it over, exchanging it for the money.

His head drooped, his shoulders rolled in and he reverted to his teenage-boy stance, one that still amused her even through the pain.

Smug in her victory, she honoured him with another one of her smiles. 'Make it quick. You've got fifteen minutes, or you'll be late for work.'

His eyes almost popped out of his head as his chin shot up and his skinny neck stretched taut, his shirt collar leaving so much room, he reminded her of a surprised tortoise, before he wheeled around and made off in the direction he'd come.

'Ryan,' Mason called before the young officer had even taken three steps.

His shoulders drooped again in defeat and he slouched back around to face them. 'Yeah.'

Mason shot him a shark's grin. 'I'll hold onto your Venti caramel shortbread latte with extra cream until you get back.' He dropped a fast wink. 'Keep it safe, so to speak.'

Not to be conned twice in a row, Ryan's gaze sharpened; a crafty gleam entered his narrowed eyes to show exactly why they'd chosen him for their team, his bright mind already calculating. 'How much?'

'What?' Mason's forehead crinkled with confusion.

'How much will you give me for it?'

Mason flopped back in his chair, a benign smile on his lips. 'Cheeky bugger. How much did it cost you?'

Ryan sniffed and glanced at the cup he still had possession of. 'Six quid.'

Mason chewed on his lip. 'Would that be your answer if you were under caution?'

A delicate flush spread up Ryan's skinny neck, but he stood his ground. 'I'm not under caution. The Sarg gave me twenty quid for her baguette and a triple Venti espresso.'

Mason squinted up at him. 'Sergeant Morgan has more money than sense this morning. I'm pretty damned sure if she wasn't in such a delicate condition, she'd have thought this through a little better.' He slid her a sly look, before he turned his attention back to Ryan. 'So, you leave that drink with me, son, and go and get yourself another one with the twenty quid you were given.' He reached into his pocket and pulled out a few coins. 'And while you're there, pick up a bacon and egg baguette for me too. Grab some brown sauce with mine.'

Ryan's lips twisted, but he snatched the money from Mason's palm, slapped the drink down on the desk and marched off through the office muttering, 'You're not the boss of me.' Under his breath.

Weak with laughter and lack of food, Jenna held her tender stomach. She wiped her eyes and picked her baguette up, took a huge bite and relaxed back into her seat. All she needed was food in her stomach, the giant coffee, fifteen minutes for it all to process and she'd be cured. Please, God, let her be cured.

She eyed the cup Mason raised to his lips and her stomach clenched enough to have her lowering the sandwich into her lap, a quick wave of dizziness spinning her head.

'How the hell can you drink that shit?'

Mason grinned, raising his head away from the cup to leave a thick, white moustache on his upper lip, so she almost threw up anyway.

'That's disgusting.' Jenna glanced away. What she held in her hand was a cure-all. A bacon and egg baguette was the answer. Always. Regardless of the question. She took another healthy bite and shook her head as the fuzziness cleared momentarily. 'I've changed my mind, you can't date my sister.'

He stared at her over the rim of his cup, the deep blue of his eyes turning steely. 'Too late. You already agreed. I've got it recorded. Besides...' he lowered the cup and swiped the cream off his top lip with his tongue and made her belly roll again. 'You know you'll love having me around.'

Poker faced, she stared back at him. It didn't warrant an answer. He was yanking her chain. She hadn't given that a thought. Did she really want Mason hanging about in her house? Her stomach rebelled and threatened to chuck its contents all over the desk in front of her.

If Fliss moved out, it wouldn't be an issue. She'd barely see either of them.

Before she allowed those thoughts to consume her, she deliberately turned them off.

With a valiant effort, she swallowed the mouthful of bread, knowing it would line her stomach against the punishment she'd administered to it. She pressed the heel of her hand to her eye to stop the jackhammer from slamming it out of her head, took another bite of the baguette and chewed. It would do her good. It had to.

With slow, deliberate movements, Jenna reached back into her drawer and picked out the battered remains of a paracetamol blister pack, almost kissing it as she noticed two left. She popped them out of the packet, threw them to the back of her throat and, in the absence of any liquid, took a small bite of her baguette and swallowed.

Satisfied it would go part of the way to resolving her hangover, she rootled around in the bottom of her drawer again and came up with two white-coated tablets. She shot them into her mouth and dry-swallowed, hoping that the bread she fed in after would push them down quickly enough to avoid them burning a hole through her gullet.

Mason screwed his face up. 'That's disgusting, they could have been anything.'

'Nope. I gave DI Taylor some the other day and two dropped out into my drawer. They're the last two. I know they're ibuprofen.'

He snorted, looking at her from under lowered eyebrows. 'Are you quite sure? You've interviewed a couple of addicts lately. You never know what they may have slipped into your drawer when you were looking the other way. Planting evidence, so to speak.'

No, he wasn't going to get her on that. There was no way she was about to doubt what she'd already swallowed. It was too late. She knew for a certainty they were ibuprofen. She thought. If she started to see dancing pink elephants, she'd maybe admit they weren't what she believed them to be.

She spared the open drawer a momentary glance and then dismissed his suggestions from her mind as she opened her mouth to take another bite and stopped with the baguette almost touching her lips as her radio crackled to life.

'Sarg, are you there?'

Jenna picked up her Airwaves, not recognising the voice. 'Sergeant Morgan, go ahead.'

'Sarg, its PC Dodd here. We have a body. Life extinct. Suspicious circumstances. Duty acting inspector is on his way. The scene has been preserved, Sarg. The ex-boyfriend is in the lounge, Sarg, he discovered her. He's an emotional mess.' Static filled the silence for a long moment before PC Dodd's voice whispered down the line, 'I can hear him sobbing.'

Jenna depressed the button on the radio, her gaze connecting with Mason's as her brain clicked into gear, fresh and bright, as though it had never been hindered by alcohol. 'Is anyone else there with you, PC Dodd?'

'No, Sarg.' Now she heard the wobble in his voice and her stomach gave an instinctive heave. 'Duty acting inspector's on his way,' he repeated. 'He told me to contact you.'

'What happened to the victim?'

The radio crackled before he answered.

'You've got to see it to believe it.'

7

The hitch in his voice had her surging to her feet. Her gaze locked with Mason's as she waved the remains of her baguette at him in a wordless bid to make him understand the urgency.

'I'm on my way. Keep things in order until I get there, PC Dodd.'

The metal slid back into his voice. 'Yes, Sarg.'

She was already taking the back stairs down the building as she shoved the last of the baguette into her mouth, aware of Mason on her heels.

Of all the days when a murder hit her desk, it had to be midweek when she'd overindulged. The bread settled heavily on her stomach and she could only hope it lined it well enough to keep the contents in place.

The wind whipped at her coat the moment she stepped outside the glass and brick building, making her regret her decision to wear a lightweight mac instead of her winter woollen overcoat. She'd mistakenly thought spring was on its way. She darted a glance up at the dark clouds rolling over one another as they scudded across the grey dawn sky to dip the temperature another two degrees, a deep shroud of fog threatened for the rest of the day.

She trotted across the concrete bridge over the moat surrounding the police station, making it more of a fortress than a sanctuary, dashed into the car park and yanked open the driver's door. She stared at Mason over the roof of the car and then tossed him the keys, aware of the swirl of alcohol still in her system.

'You'd better drive.'

She slipped into the passenger seat of the Vauxhall Insignia while Mason made the car jiggle in his enthusiasm as his backside hit the driver's seat. He spared her a brief glance as he fired up the engine and pushed it into reverse.

'What about Ryan?' Jenna heard the mild whine in his voice and knew he was less concerned about the young police officer than the food he'd promised to bring.

She ignored his silent plea, briefly mourning the loss of her own enormous cup of life saving caffeine when there were more important matters to consider. 'We'll brief him when we get back.'

Mason fell into a quiet sulk as he concentrated on manoeuvring the vehicle backwards before he put it in first gear and drove it out of the car park, turning left onto the main Telford town centre thoroughfare. The bright headlights cut a wide swathe through the mist.

Jenna leaned forward and plumbed the address she'd been given into the satnav.

With a squeak of enthusiasm, Mason shot upright in his seat, pointing a finger as he accelerated. 'There's Ryan. I'm going to stop. I have to stop for him.' His palpable excitement almost bounced the car from the road as he wiggled in his seat. 'We'd hate for him to be late!'

If it hadn't been for the giant cup of coffee Ryan balanced in his right hand, she may well have instructed Mason to drive past, just to piss him off. But there was no point punishing herself. After all, she'd paid twenty quid for the luxury of a bacon and egg sandwich and a coffee. She was damned if she'd pass up that opportunity when it was within touching distance.

With a flick of his indicator and a quick glance in the rear view mirror, Mason slewed the vehicle to the edge of the road alongside

Ryan. He lowered the electric window and bellowed, 'Get in, quick,' as he flicked off the automated door lock with a dull clunk.

Wind exploded into the car as Ryan flung open the door, almost taking it off its hinges with the howl of the February gale. Jenna sucked in her breath and resisted the urge to yell at him. If it was her own car, she may have chucked him out and driven off. As it was, forgiveness was easy as he leaned forward from where he'd flung himself on the back seat with a wide grin and handed the giant coffee cup to her.

'Where are we going?' Youthful enthusiasm vibrated from him. Give him a few years and the Force would wipe that out.

Cynicism sneaked through as Jenna took a slug of scalding coffee and closed her eyes, allowing the pleasure to soak through every taste bud in her mouth. The best coffee ever. Not coffee. Ambrosia, the nectar of life. One sip, and the taste of it tweaked her from the depths of self-indulgent pity, enough so she could answer him.

'Sudden death. Domestic. Possible murder. We'll find out when we get there,' Mason answered for her before he chomped down on the baguette, then put the car in gear and pulled away from the kerb. He fell silent while he negotiated the vehicle one-handed around the curve in the road, probably contemplating how to ask Fliss out without making a balls-up of it.

Jenna took another gulp of coffee before she cradled the cup between her hands, absorbing the heat into her chilled fingers.

Mason negotiated his way around the Telford Retail Park, taking the quickest route over three roundabouts and along the new road to Lawley. An easy drive through a ghost town at that time in the morning, which allowed him to stuff the baguette into his mouth before they reached their destination, while Ryan chomped happily on his own breakfast.

Jenna stared out of the side window while she contemplated whatever the hell they'd been called to, instinct letting her know it was going to be a long day.

8

By the time they arrived at the address she'd punched into the satnav for Mason, the triple shot of caffeine, paracetamol and sugar coated ibuprofen had joined the bread to settle her stomach. A swift kick of energy surged through her veins, giving her vision a brightness at the edges. She glanced over her shoulder at the top of Ryan's bowed head as he scrolled through his phone. She might be twenty quid lighter when it wasn't even 7 a.m., but she'd be eternally grateful to him for the life saving breakfast baguette and coffee.

She turned back to stare out of the side window, the insistent drizzle of rain coating it to blur the passing images and fuzz her vision.

God, why had she given in to a midweek drink?

She puffed out a breath. Because it was Fliss. Because she'd almost lost her and, every day, she sent a silent prayer of thanks that her sister was alive and well, if just a little damaged. The scars weren't visible like the ones Domino had suffered, the rip along the whole length of his side, like a zipper, but they were there all the same. And she may be about to lose her again if she decided to take the job and move house. She'd be almost an hour away. Not far in some people's minds, but too far for Jenna.

With a sigh, Jenna pushed her dark thoughts to one side as they pulled up outside 5 Brook Avenue, Lawley. The address she'd been directed to. Mason switched off the engine while she kneaded her finger against her forehead, smoothing out the frown. A dead body. Of all the days for a dead body to appear on her patch, it had to be today.

Jenna slipped from the car, squinting at the activity outside the small, two storey, semi-detached house. Newly built, quiet neighbourhood, just above the steep drop of Jiggers Bank into the Ironbridge Gorge. Absolutely no reason for a problem. The occasional domestic, nothing major in a nice neighbourhood.

Still early, dark out, the neighbours hadn't yet been alerted by the arrival of CSIs. It wouldn't take long, though. Not once people stirred for the day. When they walked their dogs, put their bins out, stepped, yawning, to their cars to start their early morning commute into Birmingham. The M54 was supposed to have made life easier, but Jenna wasn't sure in which realm that counted. Under thirty miles could take up to an hour and a half regularly. A commute she wasn't willing to take.

Jenna glanced at her phone: 6.20 a.m. Yeah, anytime now. The dog walkers would already be out and about. Curtains would twitch, elbows would nudge, texts and WhatsApps would be sent.

Not her problem, but once the press, especially journalist Kim Stafford, got wind of it, he'd be on their tails, sniffing out a story he could twist until it barely resembled the truth.

Ambitious and ruthless, Kim should have gone to one of the big cities to make his fame and fortune. London, Birmingham, Manchester. Instead he'd stayed, for whatever his reasons were, and the bitterness of a small-town journalist poured from him to make him a dangerous adversary. One who already hated her from their schooldays when Jenna had punched him on the nose for snapping her bra strap undone in assembly. If the head teacher hadn't caught her flying fists and fast knee, she probably could have done a lot more damage. Regret rumbled through her every time she thought of the sleazy little man.

She scanned the area. No one there but their own people.

Her gaze skimmed over *Bitch* burned in the lawn, neatly cordoned off already. 'Charming.' She'd return to that. It wasn't about to go anywhere.

She offered a smile to the officer who stood at the outer cordon. Not recognising him, she flashed him her badge. 'DS Jenna Morgan, this is DC Ellis, and DC Downey.'

'Morning Sergeant. PC Dodd.' He blew out a breath and waved his hand to a pile of white overalls. 'CSI insists. It's not good in there. Bloody awful mess in fact.'

As the three of them yanked on their personal protection equipment, Jenna glanced around at the other two. 'Ready?'

At their nods, she drew in a breath. Used to facing horrific crimes, she stepped inside the house, following the sound of quiet, respectful activity into the kitchen. She kept her own approach quiet and respectful. If someone had died, she wasn't about to disrupt proceedings by storming in as she'd witnessed some senior officers do. It wasn't her scene, they weren't yet her victims.

Jim Downey, the West Mercia Police Senior Forensic Scientist, engulfed in a pale blue PPE suit, barely raised an eyebrow in acknowledgement of her as she slipped into the compact kitchen. Used to his level of concentration when he was engaged on a job, Jenna didn't take insult but simply waited him out until he raised his head. His solemn grey gaze met hers over the slumped body tied to a kitchen chair amidst a scene of tranquillity.

Mason leaned his shoulder into Jenna's back as he shuffled to gain access to the room, while Ryan turned sideways and slipped his skinny frame through the doorway past them. With loose casualness he loped around the chair and stood shoulder to shoulder with his father to squint down at the body. His whole posture and attitude so like Jim's, it would have made Jenna smile if the circumstances hadn't been so grim.

'What happened?'

Jim's fine nostrils flared as he cast his son an impatient glance and then addressed Jenna directly.

'Sergeant Morgan. I won't wish you a good morning. There's very little good about it, I'm afraid.' The grim crack in his voice drew Jenna closer, so she stepped ahead of Ryan to stand next to Jim in front of the victim.

Jenna angled her head and narrowed her eyes, a lick of discomfort unravelled in her delicate belly. This wasn't an impassioned domestic. This had the marks of a controlled, contrived killing. 'Tell me what we've got.'

Jim tapped the end of a pen against his pursed lips, and then dropped his hand down to point at the victim. 'I'm not entirely sure yet, but I have a suspicion. You're just in time. I've noted my initial findings, taken photographs and we're just about to touch the body for the first time.'

Jenna moved in.

First impressions. The victim, tied around the waist to a chair, slumped forward so her face almost touched her closed together knees, but not quite, the restraint holding her in place. Her feet placed wide apart, naked toes turned inward. A mass of auburn hair covered her face and spilled onto her thighs. Her arms dangled loose with relaxed hands, fingers almost stroking the floor.

A sense of unease unfurled inside Jenna's chest as her mind grasped at a vague familiarity but couldn't quite comprehend the connection.

With a reverent gentility Jenna had the utmost respect for, Jim stepped forward and placed a careful, gloved hand under the victim's chin and raised her head, straightening her upper torso with a degree of strength and studied control. Her hair fell back in a satin curtain to reveal the first glimpse of her face and the gaping slash across her neck.

'Fucking hell.' Ryan fell back a step as the words exploded from him. He slammed one hand over his mouth and the other across his belly, a plaintive groan ripped from his throat as he gagged.

Without so much as a twitch of a muscle, Jim addressed his son over his shoulder. 'If you contaminate my crime scene, I will rip your head from your shoulders, young man. Leave now.' Authority laced the words and brooked no argument.

It wasn't a command reserved especially for his son, Jenna had heard Jim use it frequently, the preservation of his crime scene paramount to the senior forensic scientist.

Ryan spun on his heel and made for the door, skidding around Mason as he staggered away, almost doubled up by the time he reached the hallway that ran parallel to the kitchen.

In an effort to overlook her own queasy stomach protesting, Jenna bent at the hips to study the young woman's stiffened face and tried to ignore the churning of Prosecco and bacon and egg baguette.

'Rigor mortis.' Jim's soft voice encouraged Jenna to move in, study the signs to a closer degree. 'See here.' He scrolled his finger in front of the woman's jawline, the deep brackets either side of her mouth, the indentations around her nose. 'For want of better phrasing, this is moderate rigor mortis. She's possibly been dead three to four hours, her face has stiffened. There's still warmth in the body.' He nodded his head in invitation and Jenna reached out with her gloved fingers to touch the victim's exposed skin on the side of her neck, cautious not to come into contact with the deep gash. 'She's not entirely stiff yet.'

Jenna withdrew her hand. The body felt like ice to her, but she trusted implicitly in Jim's experience.

Without taking his gaze from the woman, he continued to murmur his findings out loud for their benefit. 'Time of death could be deceptive, though. The radiators were almost bouncing off the walls when we came in. They'd been left on "constant" instead of "timed".'

A parody of make-up smeared across the young woman's face and recognition welled again. Jenna leaned in. She'd seen it before. Bright blue make-up smeared over closed eyelids, not something any young woman would necessarily choose. More of a child-into-teenager choice. Cheeks rouged with blusher in messy circles. Vivid scarlet streaked haphazardly to distort the shape of the woman's lips. Blood from the gaping wound on her throat soaked the front of her green nurse's scrubs.

Jenna blew out a gusty breath and came upright, her mind reeling as she searched for the recollection just beyond her grasp. The light of memory she recognised in Jim's pained gaze. His mouth a tight line, he smoothed his fingers over the victim's hair with a tenderness that caught the breath in her throat before he lowered the woman's chin back onto her chest and slipped his hand away, allowing her hair to curtain her features once more. The victim's body remained upright, portraying all the symptoms of the early rigor mortis Jim had spoken of where the main muscles had started to stiffen, enough so that she didn't simply flop forward but remained where he placed her.

Jim's head came up. 'Do you remember?' He pinned her with his gaze.

She squinted at him, sighed and then shook her head. 'No. I don't know. There's something.'

'I'm not sure you're old enough to know the case. I think it was before your time.' His lips twisted in a rueful smile as he stepped away, stripped off the make-up and blood contaminated gloves and bagged them in a disposal bag before snapping on a fresh pair. 'I reckon around nine years ago, possibly a little more.' He linked his fingers together, his forehead creased with a vertical line between his eyebrows as he recalled the case. 'Three young women.' He nodded at the victim. 'All nurses. All redheads. Same pose. On first inspection, same make-up.'

'I do remember.' The memory burst through as Jenna stared at the top of the young woman's head. 'I'd just joined. Only been on the force a week when the third murder occurred. My sergeant wouldn't let me go into the crime scene. Said I was too young and too green to have to witness something so debased.' Regret tinged her words. 'I probably shouldn't have let Ryan in.'

'Ryan isn't too young or green. He's grown up with this in his life.' Jim shook his head, his lips in a straight line. 'He's been on the force almost a year now, Jenna. I'm surprised he reacted the way he did, but different situations affect us all in different ways.'

'It would be the caramel shortbread latte with extra cream.' Mason's lips kicked up in a rueful smile as he never hesitated to dob in his own young colleague to his father.

Jim's grey eyebrows shot up. 'Dear God, anyone who drinks that muck at this time in the morning gets their just desserts.'

'Twice.' Mason quipped as he squatted in front of the body, steepling his fingers in front of his mouth while he took in the scene, his intelligent gaze sharp. 'Why the pose, Jim?'

Jim hunkered down beside Mason and, with a tenderness that stirred Jenna's admiration for the man, took hold of the victim's left hand and gently scraped under her fingernails. 'We never released it to the press. This.' He nodded at the girl again. 'All those years ago. The pose. The whole make-up thing. We had to admit that nurses were being targeted. That was enough to send the county into a wild spin. Jeez, every single nurse prayed they weren't the next victim. But it was tighter than that. The MO was a certain age group.' His lips tightened. 'Redheads.'

The weight of fear pressed on Jenna's chest. 'But we caught him. Didn't we?'

'We did.' Jim nodded as he straightened and carefully inserted the swab into a small phial, screwing the lid on and, with meticulous precision, he labelled the sample. 'I can't believe he's been released. Who in God's name would let a monster like that out – ever?'

'Can you remember his name?' It would save her a great deal of research if she could pick Jim's brain for the information.

Jim stared out of the kitchen window and Jenna followed his gaze to centre on his son. Ryan, crumpled on the lawn, his forehead pressed against the grass, his arms wrapped around his midriff, his lips moving in silent prayer.

'See to Ryan. This is not like him. He needs help.' Jim rubbed his forehead with the back of his gloved hand. 'Paul McCambridge, if I remember rightly. Nasty piece of work. I can't remember all the details.

During the trial, he showed no remorse, just a sick sense of superiority. I'd say a true psychopath.' He hunkered down next to the victim and took her right hand in his, repeating the swabbing procedure as he spoke over his shoulder. 'Jailed for life. No consideration for release for twenty years, or so I thought.'

Surprised at his sudden full recollection, Jenna hauled herself back from her contemplation of Ryan. Vague memories of the case raced through her mind. She'd been assigned some stupid menial task to keep her from the scene, trawling through car registration numbers if she remembered correctly. 'Surely it can't be him?' It would be her first line of enquiry. Had he been released? Had he escaped? If so, why the hell hadn't the prison service informed them?

Mason rose to his feet. 'What about the boyfriend?'

Jim shrugged. 'In the living room. I haven't spoken with him. Duty Acting Inspector Evans put a PC with him while he does all the groundwork, door-to-door. You'll find him out back somewhere if you need him.'

'Okay. Thanks, Jim.'

She cast Ryan another brief glance, turned and then whipped around again to stare at her young DC. His tortured gaze clashed with hers and she squinted out the window.

'Mason, keep the boyfriend on ice until we're ready to question him. I haven't seen Acting Inspector Evans. Find out if he needs any assistance with setting up teams, door-to-door, admin backup.' She knew he wouldn't, but keeping up to date on his procedures would be vital to the case. 'I'm going to check on Ryan.' There was something wrong, far worse than any glut of overwhipped cream on top of a sickly drink.

She swung on her heel and headed straight outside, skirting around the patch of vomit soaking into the lawn. The wind whirled around, clearing her head as she strode over to Ryan and squatted in front of him. 'What's up?' She drilled her gaze into his to make him understand she wanted his attention. There was no caramel latte shit could do that to anyone. There was more to it than that.

He sucked air in through gritted teeth. 'I know her.' He shuddered that breath back out again, his whole body quivering with aftershock. 'I don't actually know her.' His agonised gaze held onto hers as confusion nagged at her thoughts. 'I dated her. Last night.' He closed his eyes and his long blond lashes fluttered against his pale skin. 'I'm one of the last people to see her alive.'

Cold from the inside out, Jenna stared at her apprentice. 'Ryan.' He opened his eyes. 'You need to go to the station.' He nodded. 'I'll have to question you.' Again, a small nod. His soft mouth tightened. He understood. He wasn't stupid by any means. He'd already known exactly what was required. She didn't need to spell it out to him.

She straightened, her knees creaking from the cold and damp seeping into her bones. She held out a hand to him. He took it and she dragged him up, taking his weight easily. Her hand linked with his, she held on, her firm grasp a silent declaration that she knew without a doubt he'd done nothing wrong. Nevertheless, they had a process to follow and every nuance of it had to be recorded.

She pulled out her radio and waited while the duty sergeant answered her call, relieved when she heard the familiar tones of her old sergeant from when she was in uniform. A good, solid man.

'Hi Gerry, I have DC Ryan Downey with me.'

'Jim's son?'

'Yeah. We're at a sudden death and turns out Ryan saw the victim last night.' She wandered away from Ryan, dipping her voice to a whisper, 'I'm going to send him in to you. He's a little shook up, Gerry.' She didn't mention the projectile vomiting, there was no need to strip away his dignity when he already had enough to contend with. 'Would you look after him for me, put someone with him?'

'You need to question him?'

'Yeah. Afraid so.'

Gerry knew the form, he'd do the right thing. 'I'll contact one of our reps. I'll check who's on.'

'Gerry, thanks.'

She clicked Airwaves off.

Jenna's gaze skimmed across the patch of garden, flitting over *Bitch* and onto the uniformed officer tripping up the path towards them, dark eyes wide with concern. A certain sense of relief at the sight of the experienced and empathetic officer settled her. 'Donna, any chance you could run DC Downey back to the station for me?'

PC Donna McGuire nodded. 'Of course. Is everything all right?' Her blue-black hair danced in the first rays of sunlight to break through, her latte skin glowed smooth and flawless.

'Yeah.' Jenna stepped in close, lowered her voice. 'Seems he knows the victim.'

'He's grey.' Donna shot him a fast glance. 'Looks faint.'

Jenna crooked a smile. Quite the mother hen, Donna would take care of him. She'd taken care of Jenna when she'd needed someone. 'The creamy latte shit he downed before he got here probably didn't help.'

'Oh, dear.' Sympathy overflowed as she gave a quick nod at two other officers as they arrived, ready for the door-to-door search Jenna assumed Acting Inspector Evans had arranged. 'I'm off to the station. I'll be back later.' She raised her chin and called over to Ryan. 'Ryan, come on. I'll give you a lift back.' She touched Jenna's arm. 'He'll be fine. I'll take care of him.'

Reassured, Jenna knew Donna would, as she headed for the squad car with Ryan in tow, his shoulders slumped, not in a teenage sulk but a deep sadness.

Mason glanced up as Jenna entered the kitchen, but Jim continued with the precise, measured movements that his job required. She needed his attention though.

'I've sent Ryan back to the station.' She knew it would knock him. 'He knew the victim, Jim. Turns out he was on a date with her last night.'

She ignored Mason's sharp intake of breath and concentrated on her CSI officer.

Jim tilted his head to one side and squinted up at her over the top of his glasses. 'He was home by eleven, Sergeant Morgan.' The edge of formality sneaked into his words. 'His mum can vouch for him. Not me, because I know what time the victim was killed. Give or take an hour or so, she was dead at around three this morning, no earlier than one.' His smile was tight, not with her, but the situation. 'Send someone around to speak with Lilian, you'll need it recorded.' He scratched his head. 'I'll let Acting Inspector Evans know what's what. I think he went out back. He said he needed some quiet space while he was on the phone.'

Admiration rolled off her at the calmness of his attitude and she reached out a hand to smooth it across his shoulder. A subtle gesture of solidarity.

He patted her hand and skimmed his gaze around the room. 'I'll brief Phil, get him to finish up in here, just in case there are any questions later. It's best I remove myself from the scene at this point and avoid any conflict of interest.' He stripped off his gloves, looked around as though he wasn't quite sure what to do next. 'We'll have Ryan's prints on file. I don't believe he touched anything in the brief time he was in here, but you'll need to verify that.' He flipped the gloves into the disposal bag and blew out a breath. 'I'll go back to the station.' He caught her gaze. 'I won't speak with him until you come back.' He placed his hands on his hips and hung his head for a moment. 'I hope it doesn't worry Lilian too much, she's not had a good time lately.'

It was an understatement, as Ryan's maternal grandmother had died a short while ago, her body ravaged by cancer. Ryan said very little, but he was close to his mother and grandmother. The hurt would run deep and the empathy for his mother's situation would put more pressure on him.

Mason held his silence until Jim left the room.

'Bloody hell, this could be messy.'

She gauged the scene. 'I don't think so. We need to stick to protocol and everything will be fine. It's coincidence.' She rubbed her icy hands together to warm them through.

Mason shot her a sour look. 'No such thing.'

'I hope to hell there is on this occasion.' She sucked air in through her teeth while she contemplated her next step. 'Okay, let's go question the boyfriend.' She glanced out of the window at the dark brown word etched into the lawn. "Bitch', sounds like a real charmer.'

'You want me to lead?'

She flashed Mason a quick smile. 'Nah, I've got this. Let's see if we have any reason to take him in to the station.' Her gaze fell on the block writing on the lawn again. 'If he wrote that, he's down the station, regardless.'

'Yeah, prick.'

Typical Mason bluntness brought a brief smile to her face, which she wiped off as she stepped into the minimalist living room, its neutral tones giving an air of quiet sophistication in sharp contrast to the indignity of the woman's death.

She took a quick glance at her notes and then stepped forward into the man's personal space as he came to his feet from where he'd been sitting on the sofa. 'Ray Horrobin? I'm Detective Sergeant Jenna Morgan, and this is Detective Constable Mason Ellis.'

Panic skittered through reddened eyes swollen with crying. 'Am I under arrest?'

Already she didn't like him as his concern was primarily about himself not the deceased woman. Mason was right. The man was a prick.

Being a moron didn't make him a killer though and Jenna shoved aside her personal opinion and deferred to her professional judgement.

'Do I need to arrest you?' Her tone was sharper than she'd intended, the personal slipping through despite her intention for it not to.

His eyebrows shot up, surprise wrinkling his forehead. He really had no concept that he could be arrested. That just by being her ex-boyfriend and a prick he'd made himself the prime suspect. It still didn't make him the murderer though.

Jenna relented and drew her expression into one of sympathetic understanding. She needed his co-operation at least. 'Ray – can I call you Ray?' She pulled the bland smile from deep down. She was a police officer, one with enough experience to have an excellent acting repertoire at her disposal.

He hitched in a breath, eyes filled with a desperate confusion she suspected was genuine. 'Yeah, absolutely. Ray's fine. That's my name.'

'Ray, take a seat.' She laced her voice with compassion as she sank into the chair next to him and leaned forward, bringing her face in close to his. 'I'm not here to arrest you, just ask a couple of questions. If we consider it necessary, we'll stop the conversation and take you to the station. Right now, I just want to establish a few facts. Is that okay with you?'

'Yeah. I think so. Do I need a solicitor? They always have a solicitor on TV.'

'That's on TV, Ray. A solicitor isn't necessary right now, you're not under arrest. We're trying to establish what happened.' If only people would stop believing everything they saw on TV. 'Ray,' She needed to get him to focus. 'What's your relationship with Marcia?'

His brow furrowed in concentration. 'Umm, I'm her boyfriend. No, umm ex-boyfriend.'

'Ex?'

'Yeah, we broke up fairly recently.' He raised his hand to his face and screwed his eyes shut. 'I can't remember exactly when.'

'Okay. That's not important right now.' They could pin that down later. 'Can you tell me where you were last night?'

'Last night?' Confusion flitted through his eyes. 'I don't know. I'm sorry. I can't think straight. I'm tired and... and shocked.'

She'd leave that for later too. Corroboration would be under caution.

'Okay. What brought you here so early this morning?'

He shook his head as though the change in direction confused him. 'Umm, Marcia wasn't returning my calls. She needed to sign the contracts for the sale of the house. She's ignored the solicitor's request for the past ten days.'

Jenna nodded, sympathised with him. She was on his side, understood his point of view. 'You have a key to the front door? Can you gain access any time you want?'

'Yes, yes of course. It's as much my house as hers. I paid half the damned mortgage, the bills, while she just lives... lived here.' His mouth turned sullen, his tone hit belligerent. 'She was being awkward. She refused to sell. I need the money.' He dropped his face into his hands and scrubbed them over his skin. 'My girlfriend's pregnant.'

Bingo. Two damned good reasons to murder your ex-girlfriend.

Jenna grabbed eye contact with him when he looked back up. It didn't look good for him. 'Ray.' She repeated his name to keep him focused, keep his attention on her. 'The writing on the lawn...' She caught the wary flicker. 'Are you responsible for burning the word "bitch" on the lawn?'

His breath juddered in. 'Yeah. Umm, she wouldn't fucking move out.'

'It's a pretty drastic message.'

'She was ignoring me, pretending it was never going to happen, but every time I came around, we argued. She'd scream at me. Like that would make me come back. The last time I came around...' he rasped his fingers over dry lips as he shook his head. 'I just needed her to let go and move. She was clinging. I've got my girlfriend, you know...'

Jenna had heard enough, she needed to caution him. If she could keep a lid on the temper she sensed bubbling just below the surface, perhaps she could have this wrapped up before the end of the day.

'Ray, we're going to stop here. I don't think you should say anything further until I caution you.'

Surprise rippled over his features. She kept her voice low and controlled as she proceeded to read him his rights.

Before she was halfway through, he shot to his feet. He towered over her, his fists clenched in white fury, his eyes blazed with indignation. 'It wasn't me. I didn't fucking kill her. You have to be kidding.'

Ice formed in her veins. She'd been here before and these days she refused to wait for the assault. So close, he restricted her from rising to her feet without coming into contact with him, Jenna took a split second to consider her options.

Before she had a chance, Ray stumbled backwards and Mason's deadpan face appeared over his shoulder, a hard glint in his eye. 'I've got this, Sarg. Mr Horrobin can tell us more at the station.' He wheeled the man in the opposite direction, one strong hand encircling his biceps, the other holding tight to his shirt collar and called over his shoulder, 'I'll meet you back at the car.'

Knees weak, Jenna melted back onto the chair, unable to get her feet under her. The adrenaline rush burned through her system, setting each nerve end on fire. She sucked air in through her teeth, desperate to control the fight/flight response. All too fresh in her mind was the knee to the face she'd suffered when her concentration had been blown after Fliss went missing. A rape enquiry which had quickly turned into an assault on her.

It wouldn't happen again, she wouldn't allow it, but training didn't matter. At the end of the day, if the guy was built and desperate, she'd learned, to her detriment, that no matter what she did, without backup, she was effectively defenceless. Too many officers had fallen foul of a bad temper and a fast fist.

She unfurled her own clenched fists. She would have given him a good run for his money, done some damage, but being a police officer was about teamwork, backup and relying on your partner. She knew with absolute certainty she could rely on Mason.

Under control once more, Jenna pushed up from the chair. The slight shake in her fingers could be attributed to caffeine overload or overindulgence the night before, but she knew better. With studied control, she made her way outside into the fresh air, passed the pool of vomit and the word '*Bitch*' to the car, where Mason waited for her with his detainee in the back seat.

She scoped out the stragglers starting to pay interest in the police presence, the familiar figure of Kim Stafford loitering on the outer edges of the cordon.

A fine buzz of irritation skimmed over her. How did he know so quickly? Was he connected to the police scanners?

Mind clear, the dull ache of the hangover long since forgotten, Jenna waited in silence as Mason fired up the engine of the Insignia and headed back to Malinsgate for what promised to be a challenging day.

9

Jenna's detective constable sat pale as death, his freckles stark against his high cheekbones. Pride shimmered through Jenna at his quiet, dignified composure, so like his father. She'd not spotted it before, but every inch of him screamed morality, from the top of his light sandy hair to the shiny bulled shoes. She chewed her bottom lip while she studied him. He should have been a copper in the sixties, he'd have been more suited to the times.

Her heart softened.

She needed to be careful how she phrased her questions. He'd give her everything. Full disclosure. He'd lay himself bare before her and every other police officer who heard the tape.

His father, Jim, sat quietly outside in the darkened hallway, his rangy body crushed into a small plastic chair. He wouldn't come in. He wouldn't ask. He was there for his son. Calm, supportive.

Jenna wished she'd had a father like him. Unquestionably, immovably on Ryan's side. Instead of the man who'd left before she barely knew him, never attempting to establish a relationship, never mind the one like Ryan had with Jim.

Never an issue before her mother died, Jenna often dwelled on what could have been with her father.

She shook off the melancholy. It wasn't about her. It was about the poor lad who'd discovered he could be integral in a murder investigation.

She drew in a long breath before she entered the interview room.

Jenna closed the door and took a seat opposite DC Downey. She flicked the digital recorder on and waited while it went through the setting up motions, the dull buzz of the machine vibrating its warning. When it finished, Jenna looked directly into Ryan's eyes and winked. She'd have leaned forward and patted his hand, but felt it was too overt a move. She was Team Ryan, too, but it wouldn't help his cause if she made it obvious to everyone else.

As long as he knew.

'Interview with Detective Constable Ryan Downey commencing...' She checked her phone for the time, '1045 hours.' She glanced down at the blank sheet in front of her and tapped her pen twice before she raised her head again, her gaze connecting with his. 'DC Downey, we've invited you in to be interviewed regarding your relationship and contact with the deceased, Marcia Davies, as we believe you may have been the last person to see her alive. You are not under arrest at this point in the investigation.' She looked up and smiled at the woman diagonally opposite. 'Currently you have Federation Representative Sandra O'Neill accompanying you and both myself, DS Jenna Morgan, and DC Mason Ellis are present. If at any time we consider the information you give us is at all detrimental or could in any way implicate you in an offence, or prejudice your position, we will stop the interview and invite you to seek legal representation. Do you understand?'

'Yes.'

He inclined his head in sharp acknowledgement. Good lad. Professional, he wanted the interview over as much as she did, but she needed every iota of information from him.

'DC Downey, could you please tell me your relationship with the deceased?'

The question had to be asked, but she hoped to hell he didn't throw himself under the bus.

'Yes. I met her on Y'ello.'

Surprised, his answer threw her. 'Y'ello?'

'It's a dating app. Relatively new.'

Dating apps were not her thing. Perhaps they should be, given her long-term single status, but she couldn't persuade herself to invest her precious time looking at profiles online when that's what she did for a living. Every man she looked at would be a suspect. She'd profile them with a cynicism that wasn't warranted on a date.

Her lips twitched as she looked at Ryan. He'd learn.

'Okay. Tell me about Y'ello. I'm afraid it's not something I've come across.'

The flash of pity almost made her reconsider joining – obviously everyone knew she was going through a dry spell. Ryan dug into his pocket, fished out his phone and placed it on the table between them. 'You can filter this app to real specifics.'

'Right. For the record DC Downey has placed his phone on the table and has opened the app for us to see.' She narrowed her eyes as he tapped the screen and a bright yellow app opened up. 'What specifics were you filtering through?'

His pale cheeks pinkened and he ducked his head in embarrassment. His voice when it came was low and husky. 'I prefer women who understand the uniform, the shift work, the commitment to long hours.' He cleared his throat as he gave the Fed Rep, Sandra, a bashful peep. 'But police officers aren't for me. I want to get away from work when I leave for the day.'

She could relate to that. Pillow talk would be forever arrests and convicts. She'd found that out pretty quickly once she joined the job and shied away from work romances.

Jenna shifted in her chair while she waited for him to continue. She knew he'd go for full disclosure, but this could shift into the realms of deep discomfort. She could only pray he didn't divulge every aspect of his sex life.

'I chose nurses. They'd understand the shifts, the personal contact.'

'Right.' She nodded. So many police officers married nurses. It was logical. There was the shared sense of shift patterns, death and humour.

'And I like gingers.'

Disconcerted, Jenna squinted at him. 'Gingers?'

'Women with ginger hair.' He stared at her as though she was mad and the soft snort from Mason verified she probably was.

Gingers? They called them gingers? Whatever happened to redheads?

'Ah.' For a moment, her mind had zoned out. She'd been on a totally different plain. Before she could gather her thoughts, he continued.

'I like the ones with brown eyes, you know the gingery ones that go with their hair colour?'

'Yeah.' She agreed. She had no idea. What the hell? Who was so precise? Didn't you engage someone in conversation, figure out you quite liked them, check out their body to make sure it wasn't repulsive, do the whole jiggy-jiggy after the third date to see if you were compatible and then go from there? She'd obviously been doing it wrong all along. Proof positive in the fact that she was currently single. Perhaps she should get the dating app.

Aware of the silence, she raised her eyebrows at Ryan to encourage him to continue. 'What else?'

'Tall – I like tall women, five eight to ten.' It sounded more and more like a crime profile. 'And... slim.' He squirmed in his seat, gave a self-conscious shrug. 'I like them slim, so I input athletic.'

She didn't want to show her ignorance, but she had to know. 'You can be that specific?' She'd rather they had a brain and a personality. Preferably a sense of humour would help. Maybe a dating app wasn't for her.

'Absolutely.'

'You input athletic and you get an athletic woman?' Amazed, she gawped at him, blown away by the fact that she had no idea. What the hell was athletic?

No one had ever suggested a dating app to her. She straightened her spine and rubbed the back of her aching neck, her muscles protesting. Perhaps no one dared to suggest it.

'Well, you select a choice. Athletic, average, a few extra pounds, and curvy.'

She glanced at her notes, circled her writing so Mason picked up on it as he glanced at the notebook. 'You chose ginger, brown eyes, tall and athletic.'

'That's right. Oh yeah, and aged between twenty and twenty-five.'

'Okay.' That didn't quite jibe but was reasonably close. Jenna flicked the page over on her notes. 'The victim was twenty-eight.'

He puffed out a breath, his cheeks taking on a flush. 'Yeah. Her profile said she was twenty-four.' His lip curled.

'She lied on her profile?' Horrified, Jenna glanced up at him. 'People do that?' Why in hell's name would you lie if you were seeking a relationship with someone?

'Yes.' His lips tightened and that pink flush deepened.

A sneaking suspicion crept in and she leaned towards him across the desk and pinned him with a direct gaze. 'Did you lie on your profile, Ryan?'

He cleared his throat before he answered. 'Yes. Everyone does to a certain degree.'

'Mmm-hmm. A certain degree. What degree did you lie about, Ryan?' A touch of disappointment edged her voice. She'd never expected Ryan Downey to tell lies. He always seemed too honest for his own good.

The fast blush darkened his cheeks. 'My age.'

Interested, she tapped her fingers against her lips as she studied him. 'How old did you say *you* were?'

'Twenty-five.'

Jenna squinted at him. Interesting, but not relevant at this stage. Except it meant that her young police officer had the ability to dodge the truth. Something she may have to consider in the future.

She ran her fingers through her thick hair, pushing it back from her forehead while she studied what she'd written. The moment she let go, her hair sprang back into her eyes. Damned if she had time to get it cut, but she'd ring Teresa at A-Head in Newport and make an appointment. Popular, though, it would be a miracle if she could grab an appointment. She should have done it the last time she'd been there. Perhaps they'd have a cancellation. She certainly wouldn't consider going elsewhere. Most hairdressers frightened the bejeezus out of her. But Teresa, she knew she could trust.

She blew out little puffs of air as she stared at her notes, dragging her mind back to the present.

'So, your profiles matched, and you decided to meet.' She stared into his eyes when she asked the question. 'Was this the first time you'd met?'

'Yes.' There was no hesitation, no avoidance of truth, of that she was sure from his direct eye contact.

'Tell me what happened.' She really didn't want to know, cringed inside a little at being exposed to the detail, but it was necessary. She didn't want Ryan's sex life in her head. Just the mere thought of Ryan naked made her brain shut down.

Aware of Mason shifting next to her, she suspected he was of the same mindset.

'We met at twenty hundred hours at, umm...' he hesitated, nerves riding high. 'The Liquor Lab on Southwater. Had a drink together.' Ryan raised his hand, scratched his cheek, uncomfortable as much as Jenna. 'She'd already been drinking. She'd had far too much and all she spoke about was the break-up with her ex. What a supreme arse he was.' He dropped his head and sighed. 'She was really nice. And wistful. I felt sorry for her. I had one drink. She had three more. Violet Unicorns.'

Jenna raised her eyebrows, she'd never heard of a Violet Unicorn, didn't want to ask. Instead she asked a relevant question. 'Who paid?'

Confusion stole over his features and then cleared. 'We went Dutch. Each round.'

'How did you pay?'

He squeezed his eyes shut. 'She paid cash for the first two rounds, and then card. I used Apple Pay each time.'

Jenna nodded, took a note and then raised her head to look at him 'Then what?'

'I noticed she was a lot older than me.' His shoulders gave a bony jiggle. 'And there was no way she was ready to move on and start another relationship. I realised straight away, but it would have been impolite to have just left. She seemed such a nice lady, it would have been wrong to have left too early.'

Twenty-eight. Hardly ancient, but he had Jenna feeling her own age.

'I felt sorry for her. She needed looking after. She didn't want a date, she wanted a shoulder to cry on. I could tell we weren't compatible, so after a decent amount of time, I decided to call it a night. I put her in an Uber and sent her home.' He blew out a breath.

'An Uber?' she questioned, a dash of hope brightening her mind. 'Who paid?'

'I did.'

An unreasonable relief rushed through her. Thank God. 'So, you have the details on your phone?'

As though it suddenly occurred to him, Ryan's eyes lit up and he slid the phone back towards him and placed his thumb on the bottom to activate it as he gushed his own relief in disjointed sentences. 'I've got it. I never thought. I was worried about her. She stumbled as I put her in. The driver said he'd look after her.' He swiped his finger over the screen and handed it to Jenna. Everything she needed was there.

'For the record, DC Downey has given me his phone with evidence of the details of the Uber journey he booked for Marcia Davies last night. A digital image will be taken and it will be entered into evidence, but, for the record...' she took a long breath in, 'it states the passenger was picked up at 2148 hrs and dropped off seventeen minutes later at 5 Brook Avenue, Lawley, which,' she flicked a couple of pages back on her notepad, 'I confirm is the address of the victim. Uber information confirms one female passenger. Registration Number of the cab was

DY17 NLM and the driver's name Trevor Lockley.' Her gaze met Mason's. 'Trevor Lockley.' Murderer, the thought flickered through her mind, or the last person to see Marcia alive? 'Let's pay him a visit. Unlikely as the perpetrator, having given all that information, but he may be able to tell us something.'

A small shudder of relief passed through her. That let Ryan off the hook, provided the driver verified what Ryan had told them.

She tapped her pen on the desk while she considered what other information she needed from Ryan.

Mason shifted, his chair legs scraped under his weight as he leaned forward and Jenna gave a brief nod of acquiescence. 'DC Downey, was this the last you saw of Marcia?'

Good call.

'No.'

Jenna's blood ran cold as she stared at Ryan. What the hell had he said? 'Go ahead, DC Downey.'

'The next time I saw her...' he blew out a breath, 'was this morning. She was dead.' His breathing became short and shallow.

Jenna glanced around to locate the nearest bin, but they no longer kept them in the interview rooms. Health and safety. In case you were coshed by one. Or tripped over it. She could only pray he didn't throw up again. The green tinge had been replaced by pink, but you could never tell. Despite this, relief flowed through her. That was it. All they needed from him to show that he wasn't involved.

He sucked in another loud, gusty breath. 'I didn't recognise her at first.'

He didn't need to say any more, but he continued regardless, and Jenna could hardly gaffer-tape his mouth shut in front of the Federation Rep.

'When we met last night, she was really pretty. She didn't wear much make-up. I'd hazard a guess at minimal.'

Jenna tugged at her bottom lip. Men had no idea. She knew some who believed their girlfriends were au natural when they had their eyebrows tattooed on, false eyelashes and fake tan, but because they didn't wear scarlet lipstick, it was considered natural. Jenna couldn't be bothered with all that shit. She was what she was. The occasional scarlet lipstick function aside.

She frowned as she studied Ryan. Perhaps he wasn't so out of sync.

'And when you saw her this morning?'

'It wasn't the same make-up.' He closed his eyes as though he could pull up her image. 'She didn't wear blue eye make-up last night. It was tawny. I noticed it emphasised the colour of her eyes. She had really pretty eyes. Melancholy, but pretty.' He nodded as though he confirmed it in his own mind, his mouth pulling down with regret. 'Her cheeks just had that shimmery stuff on.'

'Highlighter?'

'Yeah, and a bit of bronzer.'

Turned out Ryan knew what he was talking about after all. Who knew he was a make-up guru? Who knew he had any idea what colour tawny was?

Jenna glanced sideways at Mason. His face had gone blank, his eyes glazed over. No guru there. Shades of any colour way beyond his reach.

She turned her attention back to Ryan and dreaded asking her next question. 'Anything else you feel we should know, DC Downey?'

'Yeah.' He steepled his fingers together and pressed them against his lips. 'I only saw her briefly this morning before I...'

'Had to leave the room.'

'Yeah.' He nodded his agreement. 'But she hadn't been wearing red lipstick either. She didn't seem like a red lipstick type of person to me. She was too quiet, and heartbroken. Why would she put that make-up on herself *after* she'd returned home from our date? It looked like a child had painted it on.' He gave a delicate shudder. 'It wasn't right. Like someone had slapped an insult on her face.'

Jenna leaned back in her seat, proud of his perception. 'No. It isn't right.'

Now wasn't the time to discuss the case. There would be time enough later. Right now, she needed to end the interview. She checked the time and reeled off the information she needed to bring the interview to a close.

Ryan scraped his chair back and came to his feet as Jenna switched the tape off, regret twisting his lips. 'Perhaps if I'd taken her home, she wouldn't be dead.'

Mason fell in behind him as he opened the interview room door so Ryan could go to his dad. He placed a hand on the younger man's shoulder and imparted the most chilling thought. 'Perhaps if you'd taken her home, you'd also be dead.'

10

With the few patrons in the coffee shop, it wasn't difficult to pick out his date. The washed-out strawberry blonde was hardly the vibrant redhead she'd advertised herself as on her dating app. A faded version of her photograph, skin not as milky white on first inspection.

He hesitated at the window of the little local coffee shop he'd deliberately suggested instead of meeting in Telford town centre where there were plenty of CCTV cameras scattered around.

She thought his suggestion was sweet. Sweet, for Christ's sake! Naïve cow.

He studied her for a moment longer. It didn't matter that she wasn't the exact description of what he needed. Just a dim reflection of the woman he thought he was going to meet. Still, there was something about her. A quiet, unassuming attractiveness.

Mind made up, he pushed the hood of his raincoat back and stepped through the doorway into the welcome warmth of the old-fashioned coffee shop.

The woman raised her head, pitiful hope fluttering through her eyes, and came to her feet in an instant, a vibrant smile plastered on her face. A mouth more lovely than he'd realised. He focused on it, staring hard at the curve of her lips. The things she could do to him with that mouth. The upward curve of it straightened out and hesitation flitted over her face, making him realise how intense his contemplation had been.

He took a step back, put his hand on his chest and hit her with his best boyish smile. 'Wow, I'm sorry. You knocked me sideways then. Your photograph really doesn't do you justice. What a radiant smile you have.'

Her eyes cleared, the smile kicked back up and an attractive dimple winked in.

Confident he'd turned the situation around, he stepped forward and offered his hand. 'Ellie, I assume?'

'Gareth, it's good to meet you.' Her voice held a melodious huskiness beyond the maturity of her years.

With a double handed greeting, he enfolded her icy fingers in his warm hands, all the time smiling into her pretty hazel eyes. She'd not lied about them. They were beautiful. He held on a second longer than necessary to register his interest in her, but not long enough to make her uncomfortable. Gently does it.

As he dropped his hands to his side, he glanced at the table she'd selected, and the half full cup of coffee.

With an injection of regret, he lowered his voice to instigate a subtle intimacy, not so much to appear like a creep, just a touch, enough to assess her receptiveness. 'I'm sorry if I kept you waiting, can I buy you a fresh cup?'

'No.' She fluttered her hand over the coffee. 'This is just fine. It's okay, it's my fault, I arrived early.'

She was an apologiser. That was good. Because it would all be her fault in any case.

He pulled a chair out for himself and indicated for her to sit back down.

'Let me buy you cake, at least.'

'I shouldn't.' She placed her hand on her gently rounded stomach. 'I'm trying to lose weight.'

Although she'd lied on her description – she favoured the curvy rather than athletic – it didn't bother him.

With a long, slow, deliberate rake of his gaze down her body, he raised one eyebrow and quirked her a smile. 'You don't need to lose weight. You're perfect as you are. What I'd class as a real woman.'

A pretty pink flush stole up her neck and into her cheeks.

He watched with amusement as she stumbled around for a reply, her blush deepening the pale, freckled skin.

The waitress stepped up to their table and the temptation to tell her to fuck off almost got the better of him. He pulled in a breath through his nose and picked up the pretentious little menu, with a dozen items listed, in front of him, as though they couldn't see what was under the glass counter in front of them in the tiny little excuse of a shabby shop.

'How about the triple chocolate rocky road, glazed marshmallows with the dipping pot of melted chocolate sauce and a hint of chilli?' The glow in her darkened eyes told him he'd hit the mark. Women and chocolate. It made temptation easy. 'And I'll have the lemon drizzle with raspberry jus.' He couldn't resist giving them their full description as laid out on the menu.

Attentive, he leaned closer to Ellie, the scent of her freshly washed hair wafting over him, sweet and heady. 'What would you like to drink?'

'Well...'

'Go on, be a devil.' He kicked out a husky laugh. 'Have another. It won't kill you.'

She raised her hand and tucked a lock of hair behind her ear. 'I'll have a latte, then. Just a small one.'

He closed the menu and without looking at the waitress handed it to her over his shoulder with a dismissive flick of his fingers as she took it from him. 'I'll have a cup of Earl Grey tea.' He hated the stuff, but to keep up appearances, he'd swallow battery acid.

Ellie fluttered with pleasure while he refused to take his gaze from her. He forced his muscles to relax. Turning slightly sideways in his chair, he draped his arm over the back and crossed one leg over the other to create a casual appearance.

Not difficult to engage her in conversation, he managed to allow the bullshit that came from her mouth to go over his head as he waited a terminally long time for the fucking waitress to get her arse in gear. She just needed to serve fucking tea and cake on the second-hand mismatched plates, cups and saucers and not treat them like they were fucking antiques, instead of her dead grandmother's rejects. Instead, she tucked long wisps of grey hair into her preposterous white bonnet and washed her hands twice before she dried them on the pretentious tea towel, cross-stitched with dozens of bloody ugly hens. Her swollen ankles spilled over flat black shoes, she shuffled along the floor as her drab black skirt wafted around her calves and the smell of lavender permeated the air with every slow move she made.

Temper rising, he clenched his jaw as he waited for the ageing woman to serve them, all false smiles and lame conversation he couldn't be bothered to engage in. He leaned away from her and forced an indulgent smile for the sake of Ellie, who chattered some nonsense about the weather to the slag of a waitress like she meant something to her. Why didn't she let her get on with her job and serve someone else? No wonder it took so fucking long.

As the waitress eventually sauntered off, like she had all the time in the world, he took up the ostentatious little cake fork and weighed it in his hand, surprised at how heavy it was. He flipped it over, registering the silver mark embossed in the handle.

'Nice.' Difficult to give up the habits of his former life, he considered slipping it into his pocket as he walked out, but instead smiled at the woman opposite. 'Classy.'

'Isn't it? I'm so glad you asked me here instead of to one of the soulless chain coffee shops.'

He kept his elbows off the table as he took a slice of lemon drizzle cake and forked it into his mouth, almost melting with pleasure as his taste buds popped. 'Oh God.' He closed his eyes and swallowed. As he opened them again, she watched him from across the rickety little table. 'That has to be the best cake – ever.'

She giggled as she took up her own fork and speared the sliver of chocolate cake she'd sliced off. As she opened her mouth to take a bite, a rush of heat built, and his instant hard-on turned painful. Unexpected, he puffed out a breath, surprised at how fast the sight of her long elegant throat swallowing had him lathered up.

He clattered his fork onto the delicate china plate and swiped up his cup to take a long gulp of the hot tea, letting it scorch its way down his throat to put out the fire inside.

A fine sweat broke out across his upper lip as he lowered the teacup back onto the saucer and searched his mind for something to say to distract himself from the overwhelming urge to strip her naked right there and force her to take him into her mouth. The fucking bitch. She was probably dying for it too. She would be dying for it when he got hold of her. Literally.

He sliced off more cake and shoved it in his mouth, remembering to chew before he swallowed.

'So, tell me, Ellie, what have you got planned for the rest of the day?'

She turned her head to stare out of the window at the grey drizzle, the white column of her neck perfectly displayed for him to stroke his gaze over and contemplate getting his hands around.

She screwed up her nose, her rosebud of a mouth tightening. 'I have work at 2 p.m.'

'Ah, yes. You're a nurse, aren't you?' Clever girl, she'd obviously incorporated an exit plan into their meeting in case it went tits-up. Coffee, cake, chat. Leave.

A tiny speck of chocolate sat at the corner of her lips and he found he couldn't take his gaze from it. He swallowed the next forkful of cake and choked as it lodged in his throat. He took another swift swallow of his tea, furious as she grinned at him. Stupid cow. If they were alone, he'd grab that long, lacklustre hair and smack her face into the table until her nose bled and her perfect lip split open to pour blood...

He rammed on the brakes of his wild imaginings and rooted in his pocket for a cotton handkerchief just to distract himself. That line of thought was destructive. He needed to keep a grip on reality, not ruin things by getting ahead of himself. It was essential that he keep a lid on the roiling anger vibrating just below the surface.

He shot her a smile. 'It's my day off.'

'You're a telephone engineer?'

'Yeah. Spend most of my days climbing trees and houses.'

'Every boy's dream, I imagine.' She laughed and he took another forkful of cake and looked out of the window.

'Not today though. It's my day off.' He repeated so he could direct the conversation the way he wanted it to go. He had a plan he needed to stick to. It required control. He felt it slip back into place.

'Nice.' She finished off her cake and laid the fork on the little plate. 'What will you do with yourself for the rest of the day?'

'Oh, something exciting and glamorous, I imagine.' She grinned again and had him leaning in closer as he scooped up the last piece of his cake, holding it on his fork for a moment while he continued to talk. 'I'll do a shop in Aldi for my mum, take it around to her.' He popped the last morsel into his mouth and chewed. Then he nudged the right button, knowing as a nurse her primary one would be compassion. 'She had a hip replacement a couple of weeks ago, so I check up on her all the time.' The sympathy flitting over her face had him elaborating to draw her in. 'It hasn't been easy on her.' He pushed his empty plate into the centre of the table and sat back, resting one hand on the table in front of him. 'We lost my dad just before Christmas.' He held his breath and nodded in response to the hand she patted on her chest, kept his voice low and intimate. 'Cancer.'

Her eyes turned to liquid.

He could feed her any kind of shit he wanted, and she'd fall for it. Gullible woman. 'It's been a long, hard journey.' He didn't know who his dad was. His mother died of an overdose twenty years previously and he couldn't give a flying fuck. He'd hated the old prostitute. She'd sold his arse before he was even ten. Left him bleeding in the gutter while she collected her money from the wrinkled old shit who'd just sodomised him.

He rubbed his fingers over his lips, tamping down the fury that threatened to bubble up, hearing his counsellor's voice in his head. *'Calm. Keep calm and you'll always be in control.'* Control was exactly the position he favoured at present.

She placed her hand on top of his and gave it a light squeeze. His heart stumbled and the breath stuck in the back of his throat. He barely resisted the temptation to whip his hand from under hers as her soft compassion struck a chord of fear in him. The human touch almost too much to bear. Panic sliced through him, the need to escape uppermost in his mind.

As his phone bleeped to indicate an incoming message, he jerked, taking the opportunity to slide his hand out from under hers. He grabbed the phone and stared at the screen. An email advertising 20 per cent off if he ordered walking boots before midnight. He blew out a breath and raised his gaze to meet hers, composing his face into a pained expression.

'I'm so sorry. It's my mum. She needs me.'

Disappointment rippled over Ellie's face, but she smoothed it out into a sympathetic smile. 'No worries.'

He knew he should reach out and touch her, reciprocate the contact, but he still hadn't got his breathing under control. Instead, he garnered a smile and pushed a little enthusiasm into his voice. 'It would be great to meet again. Perhaps for dinner next time?'

She nodded her enthusiasm as he came to his feet. 'That would be lovely.' Her gaze caught his and held on.

'Yeah. Why don't you message me, and we'll arrange a date?'

As he opened the door to the coffee shop, he slipped his hood back up and sauntered down the road, his chest vibrating with a low chuckle as he stuck her with the bill.

11

He melted into the shadow of the doorway to watch Ellie walk by as she left the coffee shop, her face tight with disappointment. He grinned. Priceless. She'd not even seen it coming, his timing was perfection, leaving her to pay. Magical. It may not have been as much as he'd liked, but she'd fallen for the whole ruse. Sucker.

He wouldn't block her number on his phone yet, in case things didn't quite go his way and he needed to backtrack, although he was confident they would as he slipped from the doorway and followed her down the street from a distance.

The bright green little Fiat 500 suited her. He crossed over the road to the far side and lengthened his stride to get to his car before she drove away. He glanced over his shoulder and grinned as she slammed the door behind her and started the engine.

As he slipped into the car he'd borrowed from his housemate in the scruffy little two bedroom flat he rented, he hit the send button on the message he'd composed while he'd waited for her to pay the bill and leave the coffee shop.

OMG, I can't believe I just left without paying the bill. I'm so, so sorry. I was so struck by your beauty, I lost my brain. I hope you're going to let me take

you for that dinner I promised to make up for my completely asinine
behaviour?

He turned the key and waited for the old engine to turn over,
hoping the bloody thing wouldn't die on him. The engine rattled to life
and he revved her up, waiting to see which way Ellie went.

As he tracked her, he pushed a CD into the player and waited for
Robbie Williams to bang out 'Angels' so he could sing along. About the
only song he knew word for word. It was all he'd had in prison with no
one who cared enough to send him anything more contemporary.

He kept his distance along the Queensway dual carriageway and
then pulled off at Ketley Interchange to curve around the bend which
took them up the hill to the Avenues. A slash of unease turned his
stomach. It was where he came from and not somewhere he cared to
revisit in a hurry.

Her little car dashed along the narrow lanes and turned right,
pulling up outside an old white cottage that looked out of place in the
Avenues, as though someone had lifted it from farmland and deposited
it right in the middle of a 1960s dilapidated housing estate.

He cruised past and stopped a little further along the street, did a
three point turn and settled next to the kerb along from her house.

Information gathering was the objective. Did she live alone? With
others? Mother? Father? Child? Did she have animals? A cat? A bastard
dog? He hated those little fuckers. There was no alarm box on the
outside of the building. Chances were she didn't have one.

Heavy eyelids drooped down. It didn't matter. She'd be a while if
she wasn't at work until 2 p.m. She had two hours to get ready and
drive in.

He hunkered down into the seat and closed his eyes. Forty minutes
was all he needed to refresh himself. His eyes drifted closed and the
sweet smell of Ellie's hair soothed over him, taking him further down
into his fantasies.

12

Used to breaking and entering, he slipped in through the back door of Ellie's small cottage with ease. He'd thought he might have to jimmy the lock, but the stupid little cow had left the spare key under a small garden ornament. It had taken him a few goes to find the right one, but he'd known it would be there. The ugly little gargoyle she probably found cute.

Predictable.

He snicked the door closed behind him and listened for any sound or movement. Nothing. No electronic beep to indicate an alarm.

Loser that she was, he'd suspected she lived alone. She'd not called over her shoulder as she slipped out the front door.

He wiped his shoes on the mat just inside the door and then checked them for evidence of dirt. He didn't need to take them off, it would be a dead giveaway if he left them by the back door and she returned.

In a check for evidence of a solitary life, he opened cupboards one after the other. A four place dinner service. Two 'nice' wine glasses. Sweet little herb pots on her windowsill.

No dining table.

He sneaked a peek in her fridge. Nothing you'd feed a grown man.

Lettuce, tomatoes, cucumber. He picked out a clear plastic bag and curled his lip at the contents before he dropped the bag on a different shelf with practised deliberateness. Green shit. No one in their right minds should eat it.

He scanned the next shelf down. Greek fucking yoghurt.

He reached inside to pull out the packet of gnocchi.

Yeah, she was a loner.

He placed it back on the shelf above the one he'd taken it from again, just to mess with her mind. He let the door close, but not quite all the way, leaving it open a crack so the warmth would get in to spoil the food and turn the milk. If he could just see her face when she found it after a twelve hour shift. Confusion. Had she done it? Had someone moved things about?

Next, he opened a cupboard beside the fridge.

The woman had a shitload of individual pods for a coffee machine.

He leaned in, took out a macchiato latte and fed the two pods into the machine, sliding a cutesy mug underneath. The loud smacking the machine made would have woken the dead and he figured if anyone was going to investigate, they would have by now.

He weighed the short bladed knife in his pocket for reassurance.

With the mug cradled in his hands, he wandered through the house, tidied a couple of items of crockery she'd left in the living room, rearranged her flowers.

When he made his way up the stairs, he paused to draw in the scent of the house. A feminine, fresh smell, like she'd just washed the bedding.

On the short landing, he plucked the bamboo sticks from the diffuser and made his way into the bathroom to throw them in the bin. He held them suspended for a moment, and then took them back. It was too much for a first-time visit. The changes needed to be subtle. Nothing so overt that she called the police in the first instance. Just enough to spook her. Make her wonder if she was losing her mind.

He sipped his macchiato as he scanned the small, neatly put together bedroom, reluctant to leave. Warm hues of burnished gold and cream invited him in. He placed his mug on the bedside table and crawled onto the soft duvet covering a double bed. He laid his head on the pillow and closed his eyes, ecstasy and comfort combining. He'd already had a nap in his car, but his insomnia was bad. He'd not slept properly at night for weeks. His muscles went weak as he breathed in her sweet scent and relaxed.

When he opened his eyes, the light had changed and dread slammed in for one long moment as he reared up and took a look around. He checked his watch. He'd been asleep for just over two hours.

Panic set in as he leapt from the bed. His original plan had been to scope out the house, move a couple of items, get the hell out of there.

Already he'd failed as the light turned to dusk and he could barely see in the small cottage.

He grabbed the cup of cold coffee and strode for the door. Instinct had him sliding to a halt. He turned to look at the rumpled covers on the bed and backtracked, heart thrumming in his chest. He needed to get out. He'd spent too long. Someone would have noticed his car, if it was even still there and hadn't been nicked by one of the locals.

He glanced at his watch again. Calm. He needed to be calm. He still had just under an hour to get to his parole officer. Plenty of time. But if he was late, she'd give him a bollocking and a mark against him. She'd watch him too closely, the stupid cow.

The duvet cover took little to tug into place and then he made for the door. He paused in the bathroom doorway and couldn't resist peering into the laundry basket.

Old habits die hard and despite his retraining in prison, the temptation proved too much. He dipped his hand into the basket, hesitated. He drew a long breath, then another as he tried to get his breathing back to normal. The excitement coursing through his veins ran hot and unchecked for several minutes and he whipped a black pair of knickers from the basket, barely pausing before he held them to his face and breathed in her scent.

What could it matter, a little diversion from the main plan?

He inhaled the sheer female aroma, his eyelids fluttering as pure lust raced through him, igniting the heat in his belly so it coursed down to harden his dick.

Voices outside cut through his delirium and his eyes sprang open. The kids would be coming home from school, those of them that went. He needed to shuffle off and make himself invisible before someone noticed.

Reluctant to return the knickers to the laundry basket, he wadded them into a ball and slipped them into his pocket. He tried to ignore the fact that he'd wank over them later just so his heartbeat could return to normal, but the sly temptation of them in his pocket warmed his flesh and had a spark flickering through his veins.

Annoyed with himself, he almost left the small mug behind but noticed it just in time, swiped it up and made for the stairs.

The light had turned dull and miserly again as he made his way through the kitchen. He threw the remaining coffee down the sink and made quick work of rinsing the mug, trying to remember exactly where it had been placed on the shelf.

His lips stretched in a straight smile. It didn't really matter. Let the games begin. She'd soon know there was something amiss in her house. He wanted her to know, wanted her to feel his presence long before she knew he was there. Long before he killed her.

He slipped out of her back door, pocketing her key after he'd locked it. She'd never notice it was missing. He'd have a new one cut, and by the time he returned the original the following day, she would be none the wiser. Why would she? Most people never even looked again at the emergency key kept under the mat, or a gargoyle. It cost thirty quid to buy one of those key safe things, not so very difficult for him to get into, most people used pretty predictable codes, but at least it was an attempt at security.

He grazed his fingers over her knickers as he opened the back gate, a tremble of excitement warming his blood. The things he would do with those knickers when he got back to his flat. He'd lie on his piss-poor second-hand single bed and breathe in the scent of her, while he wanked himself, sliding the silky scrap of material down his body to wrap it around his rock-hard cock.

He peered around to make sure no one noticed him coming out. This was the kind of neighbourhood where they were all nosey bastards. He flipped up his hood and ducked his head as he rubbed the material between his fingers and the adrenaline kicked up once more, sending his nerves spiralling in ecstasy.

The bitch of a parole officer would be waiting for him and she'd never know the hard-on he sported wasn't for her but for the little red-haired nurse whose knickers he had in his pocket.

13

'He didn't do it.' Conviction carried through in her voice.

'He didn't do it,' Mason agreed. 'Wanker maybe, but Ray Horrobin is not a murderer.'

Jenna twined fingers through her thick hair and yanked on her roots, frustration grabbing her by the throat. She couldn't agree more, but where the hell did that leave them?

Ray Horrobin may have been in shock, but he'd wasted several hours of their time when they could have been pursuing other avenues. They needed to start again. Back to basics.

Jenna bumped the heel of her hand against the incident room door, making it swing open. She found members of the team awaiting the debrief, Acting Inspector Evans, PC Donna McGuire, Sergeant Chris Bennett, the inseparable Salter and Wainwright. So many more familiar faces from the extended team who'd been drafted in from other shifts when Jenna's sister, Fliss, had been kidnapped. PCs Dodd, Scanlan and Massey, the dedicated PC Sabrina Wallis, and the overly cocky PC Gardner.

She recognised them all. Recognised also the concern reflected in each of their gazes.

Jenna's heart gave a fast thump against her ribcage in a cruel reminder of that time, a mere few months before, when they'd gathered in such a large group to be briefed about the disappearance of her own sister. The news hadn't been good then, in fact it had been devastating when they discovered Fliss had been taken by the same man who'd left the naked body of a woman and a baby on the hillside of the Ironbridge gorge.

Now they were eager. Anxious. Keen to hear they'd got a result and Ray Horrobin had been arrested for a horrific murder. A quick result. That breath-holding moment when they wait to be told they can stand down.

As Jenna made her way to the front of the room, silence descended. She was about to disappoint them. There was no quick result.

Acting Detective Inspector Evans stepped up beside her. The last thing he needed was a grisly murder when he was covering for DI Rous, who was off long-term sick, and DI Taylor, who was on annual leave. This was the kind of case to make or break a stable career, never mind the career of a man who only had one foot on the rung of the promotion ladder.

She cast him a weak smile. He wasn't someone she particularly knew. He'd come from Kidderminster Station recently, with barely any time to get to know his own shift. Still, he'd stand or he'd crumble, but Jenna was damned if she'd let that affect her case.

She ran her gaze over the notes in front of her and, when she was ready, she raised her head just as young DC Ryan Downey slipped into the back of the room. Ignoring her advice to take the rest of the day off, he'd been home, changed, probably rested, probably let his mum fuss over him until he could stand it no more, and then he'd made his way back into Malinsgate. Her lips twitched up in a smile of admiration. There was no keeping a good man down, and Ryan Downey was, without doubt, a good man.

She cleared her throat and made a start.

'I'm going to begin halfway through and work around.' She nodded at the buff folders she could see. 'You all have your brief, but this is the latest update. At approximately 0615 this morning, the body of Marcia

Davies was discovered in her own house. The doors were locked, no sign of forced entry. She was tied to a kitchen chair, her throat slashed. On first sight, we believed there was a resemblance to murders committed some time ago. However, we had every right to believe the ex-boyfriend, Ray Horrobin, who claimed to have discovered the body, may have been involved in her death.'

She raised her head and acknowledged the nods from the attending officers, knowing she was about to dash that glimmer of hope.

'DC Mason Ellis and I have literally just come out of interview with our prime suspect.' Her mouth tightened as she scanned the room and shook her head. 'His alibi is pretty much watertight. It looks as though Ray Horrobin is off the hook. He's in a better position now than he'd been in twenty-four hours earlier.' Regret flowed through her voice. Supercilious moron that he was. 'According to him, Marcia was a nightmare of an ex-girlfriend, who wouldn't sell their jointly owned house, despite Ray's desperation as his current girlfriend is pregnant.' Jenna shrugged. 'Marcia is now off the scene, house is in joint names, insured for each other. The perfect motive for murder.' She drew in a deep breath and blew it out again. 'Only Ray Horrobin also has the perfect alibi.' She raised her voice above the ripple of groans. 'Obviously this needs to be corroborated.' She glanced at PC Donna McGuire and caught the slight nod, knowing she could rely on the officer to follow the task through. 'According to him, from 1800 hours last night until 0600 hours this morning, he was at the hospital, where he has a job as a porter.'

Salter raised his head from taking down notes in his untidy scrawl. 'It might have been good if he'd remembered that nugget of information before you brought him in for questioning. It would have saved us several hours of kicking our heels thinking you had the perp.'

'What an idiot,' Wainwright murmured under his breath.

'Not necessarily.' Donna's quiet voice had heads turning in her direction. Her cheeks turned ruddy, but her dark eyes sparkled with conviction. 'People react in different ways to shock. Some cry, some scream, some collapse. People have been known to turn catatonic, depending on how severe the shock is. Ray Horrobin may see death every day while he carries out his job, but from the look of it...' she flicked open the folder she had on the desk in front of her and Ryan leaned in over her shoulder to get a better view, then recoiled, his nostrils turned white as he drew in a deep breath through them. Donna tapped her finger on the victim's photograph. 'That would be an immense shock to anyone.' She glanced up. 'Never mind the person you'd recently left.' She flipped over the first photograph and held up a second. The word 'Bitch' emblazoned on the front lawn. 'Guilt. Guilt mixed with shock and fear. Because when it comes out that prior to Marcia Davies' death she was ruthlessly bullied by her ex, his reputation will be dirt. More than.' She placed the photograph back down and closed the folder. She rested her arms on the top of it and fell silent as she waited for Jenna to continue.

Jenna sent her a brief nod, both grateful and unsurprised that Donna had tracked every step Mason and Jenna had taken throughout the day. 'Thank you, Donna.' Donna's cool, calm personality and depth of knowledge and commitment was always welcome. 'Eventually we coaxed the information we needed from Horrobin to show his innocence. Innocence that related to her murder, not the relentless bullying, as Donna mentioned. There's nothing we can do regarding that.' She found she couldn't be as forgiving as Donna. 'I just hope that guilt sticks in his throat for at least a while.'

Murmurs of agreement rolled around the office until she pulled the officers back again.

'Horrobin called in to see Marcia Davies on his way home from work to try and persuade her to sign agreements with the solicitor, which she'd apparently been ignoring. He found her. Very much dead already. His first instinct was to call the police. He recognised a dead body when he saw one. This body hadn't just been left for dead. It had been arranged. Posed. Hair, make-up, clothes. Attention to detail.'

'Horrobin corroborated what we've already ascertained...' she flicked a quick glance in Ryan's direction. 'And that is, Marcia wasn't one for thick, layered make-up. She'd be more subtle.' Too subtle for Ray, it appeared, as he'd left Marcia for a more mature, sharper version, from what Jenna gathered in her conversation with him. Once he started, his conversation flowed, never stopping until he'd poured it all out. She almost felt sorry for the guy. Almost, but not quite.

His worst offence was that he'd intimidated Marcia, mentally and verbally and, through his own guilt, passed the blame onto her. Unfortunately, Jenna couldn't arrest him for that. As Mason said, being a wanker didn't make him a murderer.

Jenna raised a hand to rub away the weariness in her eyes before she remembered where she was and scooped her fingers through her hair instead before she glanced at Acting DI Evans. He took his cue and stepped forward.

'Right!' He rubbed the back of his neck, a sure indication of nerves, then he skimmed his hand across to indicate the uniformed officers on the left of the room. 'We have our team ready to take over the door-to-door from the day shift. People will have arrived home from work, they may have heard something on the news, the radio, social media, but as it stands at the moment, the only thing that has been released to the press is that a body has been discovered and police are investigating.' His thick, dark brows dipped low over silver eyes, his voice dropped an octave. 'That's the way I would like it to stay at present. We don't need a panic on our hands.' He grazed his intent look over all of them, pausing every so often before moving on.

'Right, you all know what you're doing. Forensics have Marcia's phone and will be trawling through that for any indication of unusual activity. It's a painfully slow process. We're already on the follow-up with the Uber driver. Donna, can you get back to me with confirmation of Ray Horrobin's whereabouts at the time of murder?' At her nod, he continued. 'Obviously, we have a rough estimate from CSI, which will be nailed down shortly.' He turned his attention to Salter and Wainwright. 'Find out where Paul McCambridge is.' At the vague raised eyebrows, he glanced over at Jenna and she stepped forward.

'At this time, it appears that there are similarities to murders carried out by one Paul McCambridge some years ago. It's not currently in the pack as we didn't think it was going in that direction, but PC Sabrina Wallis will sort out the information. We believe he should still be in prison, but we need confirmation of where he is. Was he released? Has he escaped? Did he have a temporary pass out for some reason?'

Acting DI Evans stepped forward again. 'If you have any questions, see me. We'll regroup in the morning.'

As the team clamoured to get out of the room, Jenna closed her eyes and pinched the top of her nose between thumb and forefinger. She needed to go home, eat a decent meal and sleep. She knew the last would evade her. She yawned and blinked open her eyes. She raised her hand to acknowledge Mason's departure. Tomorrow would be early enough to analyse everything again in detail once they assembled the team in the morning. Unless some maniac ran down the centre of Lawley village brandishing a bloodied knife, it was all about grass-roots policing. A long hard slog with no shortcuts, no guesswork. She'd done all she could do for the night and she'd need to be fresh again for the following day.

Jenna glanced at her phone and swiped away the brief message from Adrian. Meet for a coffee and a chat. She needed to think about it. Technically, it wasn't a date. Her chest gave a painful squeeze. She'd reply later when she had a spare moment. If she ever got a spare moment. Adrian would have to wait.

She tucked her phone in her handbag and zipped up the closure, conscious that anyone could dip their fingers into it and swipe out money, purse, keys. Just as Frank Bartwell had before he let himself into her house and went after her sister.

She'd never leave herself exposed to such a crime again.

She wandered through to her darkened office. With a sigh, she glanced at the time and switched off her computer.

Jenna scanned the room to make sure everything was in order before she swept up the manila files she'd prepared. A little bedtime reading if she could keep her eyes prised open.

The day had turned out to be far longer than she'd prayed for at the beginning. Any memory of her hangover had been wiped away with the vicious, bloodthirsty turn of events.

She swung her handbag over her shoulder, legs heavy as she wandered through the virtually empty office. Too weary to engage anyone in any further talk, she could only hope no one stopped her.

Home was all she needed. Home, a cuddle with Domino, a hug from her sister, some decent food and bed. Of all of those things, bed held the most appeal.

14

Impatient to be off, Jenna snatched up her handbag as she scanned over the paperwork she'd been emailed. It hadn't taken much persuasion to obtain the permissions they required to gain access to Paul McCambridge once Salter and Wainwright had tracked him down. Other than information on McCambridge's whereabouts, nothing further had emerged from the early-morning brief.

She'd had to go via Chief Superintendent Gregg to the Governor of Long Lartin prison in Evesham to have it processed quickly. She glanced at her watch. It had still taken too long.

Built originally as a category-C training camp in the 1970s where prisoners who could not be trusted in an open prison resided and were offered the opportunity to develop skills so that they could integrate back into the community once their sentence was over, Long Lartin maintained the vibe of the previous war department ordnance depot, its prefabricated buildings still housing the majority of prisoners while new construction took place. Strictly category A and B, HMP Long Lartin contained some of the worst criminals imaginable. It had been the home of Cat A offender, inmate A3446RS Paul McCambridge, for the past nine years, serving a whole-life sentence with a recommendation from the Home Secretary that he die in prison.

A touch of evil skittered over Jenna's skin, so fine goose bumps broke out as she glanced at McCambridge's photograph, his dark eyes devoid of all emotion. A true psychopath in every sense of the word. She closed the folder and passed it to Mason as they took the stairs down, passing the front desk on their way to sign out the keys for the police vehicle.

'Have a look at him while I drive. It makes for interesting reading.'

She slipped into the driver's seat and tapped the destination into the navigation system, while Mason flicked through the files.

'We've got the permissions there to get into Long Lartin.' She dashed a look into her rear view mirror before she reversed out of the parking space some idiot had parked in forward. She'd check when she got back to the station and have a quick word. Rule of thumb. Always reverse a police issue vehicle into a space, allowing for a quick exit. 'I nabbed a short profile of Paul McCambridge. Nasty piece of work.'

'Mmm. Looks like he has a real aversion to authority and women,' Mason agreed. 'Which is part of the reason he's in Long Lartin.'

'The main reason he's there is because he's a psychopath. He slaughtered four women, but, yeah, I noticed the comment about him not responding well to female influences.'

'He must find it pretty hard having a female governor. All that power in the hands of a mere woman.' Mason snorted as he flicked over another page to study the full colour photograph of McCambridge's last victim. 'Are you sure you want to do this? Under the circumstances, it may have been better if we'd sent Salter and Wainwright. Or I could have taken Ryan with me instead of you.'

Not even tempted by the suggestion, Jenna shook her head. 'I'm not sure I'd want Ryan to visit Long Lartin yet. He may want some considerable experience under his belt before he does that. It's a horrible place. Gives me the creeps.'

'Maybe so, but with all due respect, Sarg, looking through this profile, I don't think you're the best person for this job.'

Jenna opened her mouth to protest, but Mason tapped the file with his knuckles. 'Really, everything about this screams that he hates women. I wonder how much money it cost for them to actually diagnose his condition, how many sessions with a counsellor it's taken to establish that the man really doesn't like women.' He flicked the file closed and leaned his head back on the headrest. 'They should have just asked the officer who dealt with the case.'

She glanced sideways at him and then pulled onto the motorway. She nodded at the file. 'DI Taylor dealt with it.'

'Really?' Engaged, Mason shuffled around in his seat to face her. 'How did you find that out?'

'I skimmed through the case notes last night. Interesting bedtime reading, all the better for giving me nightmares.' It was an understatement, she'd barely slept a wink as vile images flashed across her mind all night. She eventually drifted off in the early hours, only to be awakened to a pitch-black room as her alarm rudely reminded her it was time to get up. 'Taylor was only a DC at the time. Must have been a challenging case.'

'We could do with speaking to him about it.'

'He's on annual leave for another few days. I'll catch up with him when he gets back.'

'Can't you phone him?'

She shook her head, checked in the mirror and pulled into the overtaking lane. 'Afraid not. I think he may be in Yosemite.'

'The whatymittie?'

She knew Mason wasn't stupid, but she indulged him with a smile in any case, as he splashed a touch of humour into the mix. 'Yosemite California, I believe.'

Just to prove he had more grey matter than people credited him with, he snapped her a sharp smile. 'National Park. Sierra Nevada, to be more precise. Waterfalls, rock formations and shit. Didn't know Taylor was an outdoorsy type. I hope the grizzly bear don't get him. We could bloody well do with him right now.'

She glanced in her mirror, manoeuvred into the middle lane and let the blue lights sail by, hoping to hell it wasn't going to a road traffic collision up ahead. She could do without the delays.

'I hope they don't either, I could do with picking his brain.'

'I'm surprised Jim Downey didn't mention Taylor's involvement when he spoke about the case yesterday.'

'He probably didn't have time to think about it yesterday. He had other things on his mind, like a dead body, and his son.'

Mason just hummed in the back of his throat.

Jenna reached over and tapped the file. 'There's not a lot in there. Chief Superintendent Gregg has applied to the Governor of Long Lartin for McCambridge's psych evaluation, but we know that all takes time. According to information we have, though, McCambridge's mother, a nurse, killed herself when he was a child – only seven years old. He found her, still alive, and was traumatised, unsurprisingly. She used to dye her hair.' She cast a sideways glance at Mason and raised her eyebrows. 'Red.' He blew out a breath in response. 'With no other family on the scene, he was in a children's home. Fostered several times, never adopted. Some minor offences, didn't appreciate authority, but nothing to signpost any real problems. Until ten years ago. He met his first victim, Charlotte Goodall, through a dating site.'

'Did they have dating apps back then?'

She slanted him a look. 'There have always been dating apps, they just started in a different format. Lonely hearts used to advertise in newspapers.'

'I suppose you remember that?'

'Cheeky bugger.' She smiled as she overtook a lorry and then pulled into the middle lane of the motorway. Jenna was a mere few months older than Mason, just cresting the top of her twenties, soon to be the big three-oh, oh. That was something that didn't bear thinking about. 'The first dating apps on computers started at about the time McCambridge met his first victim. I'd just joined the force, but I was never on his case at the time. Something about Charlotte Goodhall triggered his memories and McCambridge went on a killing spree. Four women in quite quick succession over a six week period.'

'Bloody hell.'

'Yeah.' She scraped one hand through her hair. 'Let's pray this isn't what we have on our hands now.'

Mason tugged his bottom lip between his thumb and forefinger before letting it go. 'Do you think this is what we have? Another serial killer. A copycat?'

She hated to admit it. 'It stands a pretty high chance. Even though I knew in my heart yesterday that Marcia's ex didn't do it, there was a part of me that really wanted it to be him. Because then it would be over.'

'Instead, it may only just have begun.'

She nodded and they both fell silent for a moment before Mason drew in a long breath.

'We're agreed then?' he asked.

'Agreed on what?'

'That I'll take the lead on this show, so we don't rub McCambridge up the wrong way by a woman daring to engage with him on a basis other than having her throat slit, posed on a chair and make-up smeared over her face so she looks like a freakin' marionette.'

Mason was good enough to run the show entirely on his own, but she wanted in on it. 'Okay. I'll keep quiet, unless I feel a need to contribute.'

Mason slid the file onto the floor, leaned back, crossed his arms over his chest and closed his eyes.

For several miles, they sat in companionable silence, then Jenna let out a heavy sigh, which had Mason sliding her a sideways glance. 'What's up?'

She shrugged her shoulders and eased off the accelerator for a brief moment while she came around the long sweeping curve of the M6 as it met the M5 and judged the distance between the traffic. She slipped neatly in between an HGV and an Audi, managed to manoeuvre her way into the overtaking lane and then jammed on her brakes as the overhead gantries flashed up a 40mph sign.

Already weary, she rubbed her hand through her hair. 'I hate Long Lartin.'

'Who doesn't hate Long Lartin?'

She shot him a quick glance. 'Do you feel it? When you walk in. Do you feel the malevolence? Like it washes over your skin.'

Mason rubbed his hands over his face and nodded. 'Yeah. Like you say – only not as poetic. It's as though the depravation of all those criminals has been absorbed into the bricks and mortar, or the prefab walls, over the years. It sucks at you as you walk through. I hate it too. Thank God we don't have to go there often. I always think if there's a riot while we're there, we'd be the first ones dead.'

'Thanks for those reassuring words, Mason.' She reached over and patted his arm while she puffed out a breath. 'I was looking for more along the lines of "No, Sarg, you're perfectly safe there. I'll protect you."'

'You want me to lie to you? Someone broke the fucking governor's jaw last year. If she didn't have enough protection, who the fuck does?'

She could hardly argue that philosophy. Rather than dwell on it, Jenna picked another subject that had been whirling around her mind from earlier that morning.

'You ever used a dating app?'

His slow head-turn and jaw-drop told her everything she needed to know. She jiggled her shoulders, indicated and took the slip road off the M5 to join the M42. 'I don't understand why you'd select a particular type of person. Do we all have a type?'

He hummed in the back of his throat as he gave it some thought. 'I like tall blondes.'

'Hmm. But you don't meet them online.'

'I didn't say that. I said I didn't use a dating app. But you can meet women on any kind of social app these days.'

'Yeah, but I wouldn't.'

'I thought you preferred men.'

'I do. I meant meeting someone through a social app and start dating them. Seems weird to me.'

'You don't date full stop.'

She opened her mouth, ready to deny it, and then found the breath lodged in her chest. She hadn't dated for months. Longer. Possibly over a year since she'd gone out with that fitness instructor. She'd not met him online. She'd met him at the gym, all rippling muscles and glowing skin. So tied up with his own self-image, Jenna soon realised he didn't want a relationship with someone, merely a sounding board for his own looks. Someone to praise him every day and stroke his ego. It was never going to work with her. It wasn't in her psyche to stroke someone's ego.

'Maybe I should try the dating app.' Aware of Mason's scrutiny, Jenna sent him a quick glance. 'What?'

'I thought you and the Suit might have got it on.'

'The Suit?'

'Yeah, you know. Wanker boy with the black Range Rover Autobiography. Flash bastard.'

She grinned. 'You really liked Adrian, didn't you?'

He laughed. 'More to the point, I thought you did.'

'Yeah, I thought he was... interesting.'

'Interesting. Right.'

She blew out a breath. 'He's married.' She hoped it would make him shut up.

'Married. Oh fuck. How did you find out? Did you ask him?'

She snorted. 'No. I wasn't exactly looking for a relationship. I was trying to find my little sister,' sarcasm laced her voice. 'You know, that insignificant incident when she was kidnapped by our deranged intel-analyst, Frank bloody Bartwell. I was a little preoccupied at the time.'

Mason's lips kicked up at one side. 'Still, Adrian was around for a while longer after you found her. To tie up the loose ends.'

'Well, he did tie them up. Donna asked him if he was married and he told her he was. Even if I had been interested, he wasn't. And too right. Married is married.'

The traffic thinned as she hit the A435 and sailed past the slower traffic. She wasn't about to tell Mason the married man still contacted her from time to time. A little flirtatious, a little suggestive. Friends she would classify them as, coffee and cake as Adrian had suggested, but she'd put him off several times until he'd stopped texting, then she'd sent that stupid message to him when she'd drunk too much. She should never have sent it. Never encouraged him to keep in contact. She wasn't about to date a married man.

'Shame. I might have got on with him. He was sound.'

She flung back her head and let out a hoot of laughter. 'Excellent, Mason. What an endorsement. Sound. To be damned by faint praise from Mason Ellis.'

Offended, he twisted around in his seat to face her, but she kept her eyes on the straight stretch of road ahead, determined not to let him know just how interested in the Suit she had been. Finding out Adrian was married was the prime reason she'd stumbled about the last few months. A little lost. A little confused. And certainly not interested in any other men.

In silence, Jenna negotiated the minor roads.

'Have you heard from him recently?'

She hummed in the back of her throat while she considered what she should tell him. 'Yeah. He's been seconded to a major case in London. Started a few weeks ago.'

Mason settled back in his seat, seemingly satisfied with her answer, and Jenna held back any further comment. Better to remain quiet than contribute.

As they pulled into the car park, Jenna glanced sideways at Mason. 'Who are we meeting?'

He skimmed his finger over his iPad, swiped left and scowled. 'Not the Governor. She passed it on to McCambridge's counsellor,' He scanned the notes. 'Denton Harper.' He snorted. 'Denton freakin' Harper. Made up name if ever I heard one. Got to be.'

'Nice name,' she disagreed. 'Strong.'

'Yeah, strong. Like James Bond.'

'Like Mason Ellis.'

'Hey, there's nothing wrong with my name.'

'No, there's also nothing wrong with Denton Harper – or James Bond.'

'Right.' The loud clap of the passenger door slamming after him put an end to that conversation and Jenna peeled herself from her own seat, taking a moment to stare up at the ugly façade of Long Lartin Prison with its 1970s architecture flat-fronted entrance. Foreboding and miserable. She hated the place. Her worst nightmare was to be caught in lock-down with the all male A-class convicts. Some of the hardest in the country.

Her neck cricked as she rolled her shoulders and started forward.

15

When Jenna walked through the heavy glass entrance door, Mason turned to hand her a visitor's badge before he followed the prison officer into the first of the locked down areas for authorised personnel only. She raised her arms, breathed long and slow as she waited for the officer to complete his swipe with the wand over her body.

Last time she'd been, it had been a full body search. Times had changed and changed quickly. It was more like airport security. No touching. No intimacy. Which was just as well as she'd developed a distinct dislike for the full hands-on variety body search.

Good to go, she gave the prison guard a reserved nod and followed Mason through the next set of lock-down gates, ignoring the catcalls and whoops from prisoners who had no idea who was there. They wanted the visitor to know they existed. To instil fear in them as they lived with fear every day.

She appreciated Mason's deference when he stepped back to allow her into the hallway first. She'd worked with Mason for so long, they were comfortable with each other's rhythm, and the respect he showed for her rank in front of others, despite their familiarity, was evident.

A prickle of discomfort raised the hackles on the back of her neck as she strode, stiff-backed, through the dilapidated corridors, the oppressive atmosphere pressing down as a wall of overheated air closed in around her.

She raised her head and angled her chin.

Silent, their group came to a standstill outside a locked iron door leading to the close supervision centre. Jenna pretended patience as she waited for the guard to unlock it and swing it wide open.

Paul McCambridge, handcuffed to a guard, slouched back in a red plastic chair, his huge, muscle-bound shoulders pressed against the wall. Eyes of a shark narrowed as he tracked Jenna's progress into the room with a sly stare. His lips twisted with the slash of a scar through them, lacing outwards across his skin in thin white lines to map a broad face squatting on a bull-like neck.

Taken by surprise at the man's stature, Jenna hesitated as she entered the room. The photograph on file depicted a tall, rangy man with wide shoulders and broad chest. The one who'd been caught, convicted and incarcerated. The prisoner before her had evidently thrived. Bulked out, his muscles pushed at his veins, so they strained against his skin, a sign of the anabolic steroids he'd clearly had access to. The broad chest had barrelled, his thick neck sitting on muscle-bound shoulders.

Jenna made a fast assessment of the prison officer McCambridge was cuffed to. Not a small man by any means, but his slack belly and narrow shoulders didn't fill her with confidence that he'd be able to restrain McCambridge if the need arose. She could only hope it didn't.

Dark malice swirled around the room to make her skin prickle a warning. There was nothing she could do to change the atmosphere in the room. The entire prison was steeped in sinister darkness, decades in the making, but this particular man stifled any atmosphere that may have existed. As his physical presence dominated, so too did his seething aggression.

With a sense of unease, Jenna turned her attention to the man by McCambridge's side. Clean shaven, wearing navy suit trousers with an open neck shirt, he came to his feet and without hesitation held out a hand, first to Jenna, then Mason.

'Morning, I'm Denton Harper, this is Paul McCambridge. I'm Paul's counsellor. I hope we can help you with your enquiries.'

A clear blue gaze lit with bright intelligence met hers. The firm handshake he offered was quick and professional, while his straight lips kicked up at the edges in a welcoming smile.

Jenna withdrew her fingers from his and grasped the folder she carried with both hands. Pleasantly surprised by the calm openness of the man, Jenna cleared her throat before she spoke, mild relief at the sense of control from Harper. 'Detective Sergeant Jenna Morgan and this is Detective Constable Mason Ellis. Thank you for seeing us at such short notice.'

Her gaze flickered over McCambridge, she didn't bother offering her hand to him, not trusting him to be quite so polite. Instead she met his intense stare for a brief moment before she broke eye contact and gave a brief nod. Depravity lurked in the churning depths of his eyes. She recognised it immediately and chose not to challenge it. Their decision to allow Mason to take the lead had been the right one.

She'd not had anything to do with his case years ago, but from the file she'd scanned briefly the night before, she knew for certain McCambridge would never be released. Intelligence showed her the wicked crimes he'd committed. Instinct screamed that the depraved state still brewed within.

Mason had no such qualms. He leaned in after shaking Harper's hand and offered it to McCambridge, who curled his lip up in a sneer and folded his arms over his huge chest, dragging the guard's arm close in a display of power. If his eyes could turn darker, they did, while the prison officer's gaze skittered around the room as he gave a nervous lick of his lips.

Harper pulled a plastic chair away from the small table and offered it to Jenna. As she took her seat, McCambridge kept his hard gaze on her. 'So, to what the fuck do we owe this pleasure?'

She kept her smile benign and glanced down at her notes, breaking eye contact with him for a second time. No need to aggravate the man before they started. They needed information from him. The last thing she was looking for was for him to kick off.

Harper made his way back around the small table to sit next to McCambridge, while Mason took the chair next to her. His expression filled with placid amusement she knew was only for show. Inside, Mason would be on full alert.

Harper placed both hands on the white surface of the table, palms down. 'I'm sure the officers just want to make some enquires, Mac, just relax.'

'You fucking relax. I hate pigs.'

Harper sucked air in through his teeth and his lips flattened in a straight line. 'Mac. You know what we've talked about. Anger management is vital in volatile situations.' His tone, a firm warning, appeared to have no effect on the man next to him.

Mason scraped his chair as he pulled it in and, as her partner intended, McCambridge whipped his attention straight to him.

'Paul. Do you mind if I call you Paul?'

'You can, but I won't fucking answer you.'

Unfazed by McCambridge's answer, Mason gave a tight smile.

Harper linked his fingers together. 'Mac.'

'Mac.' Mason paused, waiting for some sort of acknowledgement, but this time McCambridge stared ahead, boredom reflected in his dead eyes. Mason drew in a breath and continued. 'Mac, we're conducting some cold-case enquiries and hoped you might be able to help us.'

A sharp grin slashed over McCambridge's face and he leaned his elbows on the table, his stare burning into Jenna as though it was her who had spoken. 'You mean some *bitch* was murdered night before last, and you want to know why it held similarities to my MO?'

Shock rippled in small electrical pulses through Jenna's veins and it took all her effort not to let it show. She removed the lid from her pen and wrote McCambridge's name at the top of her pad. Date. Time. She kept her eyes downcast in order not to engage the manic interest brewing in the inmate's eyes.

Mason's fingers spasmed in surprised response, and then immediately relaxed. If she hadn't had her gaze down, she would never have noticed and only hoped McCambridge hadn't. They didn't need to supply him with any more power than he already exerted.

McCambridge wasn't supposed to know. How the hell did he? Theirs was an information gathering exercise about his past crimes to establish if the similarities were a coincidence or merely the perpetrator's attempt to emulate them. The details of their visit hadn't been given, not even to The Governor of Long Lartin. McCambridge should have no knowledge. The details of the victim, the crime, the murder, were all still under close wraps. The press had only been told the basics. Unexplained death, female victim, police investigating.

She waited in the silence for Mason to continue. They'd agreed she shouldn't say anything unless absolutely necessary. McCambridge's reputation as a woman-hater could prove flammable.

A thin line creased between Harper's eyebrows and confusion flitted across his face. 'What's going on?'

Mason cleared his throat and drew their attention away from her once more. 'We're here to investigate historical cases, Mac, but if you have any information you think will assist with a current crime, we'd really appreciate it if you could help us.'

'Current? You couldn't get any more current. I bet her blood was still fucking warm.' His yellowed teeth flashed from behind tight lips. 'What time did you discover her?'

A frisson of shock skittered through her veins. Where the hell did he get his information from?

'Yesterday morning. Around 0630 hours.'

'Yesterday morning? Early. Fresh. Although not as fresh as I would have expected. You took your time getting here.' He leaned back, his face flushed with eager enthusiasm. 'Someone identified the modus.' Full of arrogant pride, he banged his hand on the table. Other than a sharp blink, Jenna never moved a muscle. 'What was the hold-up – paperwork?'

Jenna bowed her head and he slapped his hands together, rubbing them vigorously in barely contained excitement. She wasn't about to explain they'd lost time chasing the wrong perpetrator.

'Excellent. Tell me...' He leaned forward across the table, not even attempting to disguise the manic glint of fanaticism which swirled through his expression. 'How was it for you?'

Unable to resist, she raised her head, so her gaze clashed with his. Jenna scratched her nose. He hadn't engaged Mason at all, despite her silence, he was focused entirely on her.

Dark eyes pierced into her soul, sending sharp icicles through her veins to compel her to answer.

'A little sad, but I have my job to carry out.'

Dammit, but she hadn't meant to engage him. That was the deal, but how was she supposed to get information from him when he virtually ignored Mason and centred all his efforts on her?

'*Sad*? You found it *sad*?' His lips pulled up in an ugly sneer as he leaned back in his seat, raised his arms and scraped his over-long fingernails across the shiny baldness of his scalp, jerking the guard closer without even noticing. 'I'd say it's fucking *delicious*.'

Ripples of dark fear coursed through Jenna's veins. She'd come across levels of evil in her career, but the deep psychotic darkness of this man's soul hit a note so visceral, her fight/flight response kicked, until every nerve ending vibrated with tension.

She clenched her jaw so hard, she heard the crackle and punch of it in her ears.

Through gritted teeth, Jenna spoke directly to McCambridge. 'A woman was murdered the night before last, Mr McCambridge. Would you like to tell me how you got your information about this crime?'

McCambridge grinned, lowering his bald head as he leaned closer across the table, the puff of his warm breath stroking her cheek. A mock whisper edged his gravelly voice. 'Press released it an hour ago, *pig.* The guards told me you were on your way. I put two and two together.'

Not possible. It was too much of a stab in the dark and the press had no in-depth details, barely skimming the surface of information.

She narrowed her eyes at McCambridge. He knew more than he'd revealed, but there was no way she was about to divulge anything to him.

With a casualness she didn't feel, she leaned back in her chair, as far away from him as possible, the acrid stench of his breath too much to bear. She took a calming breath and glanced at Mason, hoping her silent message that she would take over was received and understood. At the vague rise of his eyebrow, Jenna took a long breath. The interview had taken a turn neither of them had expected.

She welcomed the ice that froze her feelings, effectively locking McCambridge out so she could achieve what she'd come to do. Interview him. The change in direction may have taken her by surprise, but they needed every piece of information he could give them.

She stared at his name where she'd written it on her pad. That's all she had, the only lead. When she was ready, she raised her head.

'Mac.' His eyes gave an unnatural glow the moment she spoke. 'As you've raised the subject, can you tell me if you have any information regarding the murder of a young woman in Telford the night before last?'

'No.' The manic grin he shot her squeezed at her control. 'And if I had, I'd not tell you pigs a fucking thing. Can't get me on that one. I'm covered. I've got a great alibi.' He leaned back and punched Harper's shoulder, almost shoving him off the chair.

Harper shuffled himself back on the chair and ran his fingers through thick blond hair as he concentrated on a spot on the table in front of him.

From the frenzied gleam of interest, though, McCambridge was engaged. He knew something. They'd been right. It was a copycat killing and pride bounced off him as though he'd committed the murder himself.

If she could feed that ego, she may get more from him.

She slid the manila file she'd brought with her into the middle of the desk and turned it around so anything she showed him would be facing him. She flicked it open, turning over the first couple of sheets of paper to a photograph in full colour. She ignored the shocked intake of breath from Harper while she waited for McCambridge's response.

'Hmmm.' He angled his head to better study the photo. 'One of mine, I believe. Number four, if I'm right.' The gleam of excitement flushed his ruddy skin. Jenna's stomach clenched in a hard spasm, but she kept her features composed and tapped the page.

'Yes, one of yours.'

'How disappointing.' He exposed his teeth in a feral grin. 'I hoped this was going to be a case of *I show you mine, you show me yours.*' He pulled air in through his bared teeth to make a soft whistling sound and Jenna's flesh broke out in tiny goose bumps.

She forced a smile and concentrated on the image between them. 'I think we could manage that. I've shown you yours from years ago, what can you show me?'

As though to demonstrate his power, he raised his arm to scratch his head and yanked his wrist closer, so the guard emitted a deep, pained grunt as his smaller frame was almost hauled across the table.

'Shame on you, Detective *Sergeant* Morgan, I would have enjoyed seeing that. I'd like to see the job they've carried out. Judge their... effectiveness, so to speak.' He stretched his arm towards her and came up short once more against the restraint linking him to the prison guard at his side, who managed to anchor himself this time and barely budged. Irritation streaked over McCambridge's features before he dropped his hand back onto the table close by his body, allowing the guard to fall back. His thick brows lowered over darkened eyes.

She wasn't sure she'd get anything further from him by being polite and professional.

She touched the tip of her finger to the image and traced the line of the body posed there, appreciating the intense scrutiny from McCambridge.

'I can't show you anything from this most recent case. It wouldn't be allowed. You know that.' As she stroked her finger back up the page, she swirled her fingernail over the thick wash of auburn hair on the photograph. 'There   are   similarities,   but   there   are   many inconsistencies.'

His lips tightened, the heavier bottom one plumping out in a petulant pout, and Jenna knew exactly how to work him to gain information. 'It took you until the fourth victim to achieve any kind of finesse, *Mac*.' She narrowed her eyes to watch closely as his eyes opened wide enough to pop out of his head, the manic glint of anger a glowing ember.

'I was good straight away. There's no one better than me.'

Jenna resisted the urge to grin, put the palm of her hand over the photograph, obscuring it from his view, and scraped it back over the table towards her. She closed the file and laid both hands on top of it.

'What can I say? You had a lot of practice before you managed to achieve what you wanted. And then you were caught. And you have to spend the rest of your life here, behind bars.' She clucked her tongue on the roof of her mouth. 'Clumsy.' She let out a derogatory snigger. 'The one time you got it right, you mucked up, Mac. Isn't that right?'

She held her hand out for the second file Mason had. As he placed it in her hand, she never took her gaze from McCambridge's flushed face, his shiny pate turned a florid red.

'Four goes and you slipped up. Got caught. How was it they managed to get you?' She tapped her forefinger against her lips in an over-exaggeration of her thought process. 'Oh yeah, you didn't do your research properly on victim four and her boyfriend let himself in the front door in the middle of your clean-up. DNA all over the place. Ha, yes. And beaten to shit by the military boyfriend whose fiancée you'd just killed.' She trailed her gaze over his scarred face and rested her hands on the table either side of the folder to keep his attention on it. 'Messy. Very messy, Mac. I wouldn't have expected that from you.'

As the fury boiled in his eyes, she tapped the manila file with the tip of her finger. 'This one achieved in one go what you had to practise...' she stabbed her finger on the file for emphasis, '... time after time to achieve.'

In a move that whipped the breath from her lungs, McCambridge surged to his feet, an animalistic growl of rage bursting from a throat stretched so taut, she thought the veins lacing it might burst.

Before she had a chance to react, he dived over the small table at her, his clenched fist flew towards her face. A spike of fear dashed through her as he pulled up short with the resistance of the prison officer tethered to his wrist. With a snarl of pure fury, McCambridge wrenched the prison officer from his feet and slammed him onto the table on his face with such force, the table upended and skimmed halfway across the room, together with the files that spewed their contents across the dull grey tiles.

The hot spurt of adrenaline drove Jenna to her feet at the same time Mason, in a burst of movement, leapt up and sent his chair crashing backwards. The screech of the alarm filled her head above McCambridge's wild roar as Harper punched the panic button on the wall.

'Give it to me, bitch!' McCambridge's furious howl filled her ears. 'I want to *see it*. Give it to me!'

Manic gaze centred on her, McCambridge took another lunge at her, barely restrained by the injured prison guard, who flopped around at the end of McCambridge's wrist, emitting feeble little squeaks.

With no other option Jenna could see, she raised her fists and stood her ground. Concentration centred entirely on one man, she readied herself for his onslaught. McCambridge surged forward, yanking the guard behind him and headed straight for her, a crazed bear in full attack mode.

Her veins turned to ice as she faced him head-on.

In the blink of an eye, Mason stepped into her line of sight and ploughed his fist into McCambridge's face. The man's head whipped to one side with the force of the punch. Blood exploded in a wide arc, spraying the prison officer and Harper with bright crimson flecks across their faces and chests.

Revulsion flashed over Harper's face as he raised his hand to his cheek and spun away.

A brief flash of surprise lit McCambridge's eyes before they glazed over and he dropped to his knees in front of Jenna, then toppled forward onto his face, dragging the prison officer onto the floor alongside him.

In an explosion of activity, the outer door burst open and four prison officers in full riot gear surged in. They leapt on top of the stunned McCambridge and dragged him to his feet. The attached guard was flung back and forward like a rag doll until one of the others managed to unshackle him from McCambridge's wrist.

Adrenaline pumping, Jenna unfurled her fists, stepped to one side and waited for the furore to settle as they contained McCambridge. Heart exploding in her chest, she panted out the fear while she waited, a mask of absolute stillness painted on her face. Determined not to show any weakness, she braced herself.

She forced her gaze to stay flat and emotionless while the tremor inside threatened to burst out of her chest as she hauled in her composure.

Suspended between two prison guards, McCambridge raised his head to glare at her. Blood dripped from a nose twisted even more than before by the break Mason's blow had caused. McCambridge drew his lips back in a feral snarl, blood and spittle flew from his mouth as he slavered over his words.

'I guess that's us done for the day, Detective *Sergeant Bitch*. But you can bet your sweet life we'll meet again. You may not be my type, but the next time I see you, I'm going to rip your throat out and feed off your blood.' He gobbed a mouthful of saliva and blood and spat it at her. In a fast move, she took a step back and it fell just short of his target to land on the toe of her boot.

Manic laughter followed McCambridge from the room as the prison officers dragged him out, leaving the injured guard on his hands and knees on the floor.

The man leaned back on his haunches and swiped his mouth with the back of his hand. His breathing came in shallow, thin snatches. 'The governor's going to have your badge for this.' Eyes filled with disapproval, he gazed up at her and shook his head. 'Do you have any idea how much time McCambridge has spent in counselling to get him to integrate?' He staggered to his feet. 'He's a vicious bastard and you've just set him back years. I can't fucking believe it. Wait until I speak to the governor.'

With quiet dignity, Harper stepped in between Jenna and the guard, bent and gathered the scattered paperwork she'd almost forgotten about. As he shuffled the pages into the file, Harper narrowed his eyes. 'Thank you, Elks.' He addressed the guard and then turned to Jenna and Mason, face wreathed with concern. 'Don't worry about Mac. We'll calm him down. It's a setback, but we've learned to roll with them. I'm sorry, I had no idea what the subject of your visit was about, I thought it was to ask him about past cases.' His expression turned to stone as he directed his next comment to the guard. 'Perhaps, knowing the inflammatory circumstances, we should have had him better accompanied.'

The guard opened his mouth to reply, then shook his head. He spun on his heel and made for the door, weaving across the room in a drunken stagger before he slammed through it without looking back.

Harper took hold of Jenna's arm with gentle deference. 'Are you okay?'

Falling apart inside, there was no way she was about to allow Mason and Harper to see how much the incident had affected her. She'd wanted to get a rise out of the man; she'd never expected a full frontal psychotic attack. Fear had ripped through her at the demonic glow of his eyes.

She blew out a breath and accepted the file back from Harper. 'I'm fine. I hadn't quite expected such an explosive reaction.'

'If they'd allowed a little more time, like we requested, we would have been able to better control the situation. I'm not being sexist when I say, we probably would have recommended not sending a female officer to question him. He'd consider it most inflammatory. He has a deep, abiding hatred of all women. I'm sorry you had to witness it first hand.'

Steadier, Jenna forced a smile. 'We needed to interview him, and it's my case, my questioning.'

He shrugged as he led her to the door, skirting around the upturned table and chairs. 'I'm sorry you never got what you wanted.'

16

Jenna lowered her head to the steering wheel, her mind gyrating in ever-decreasing circles as the shudder inside threatened to break her apart and the breath she tried to draw in stuck in a painful lump in her chest.

'Fuck me, you got what you wanted and some...'

Jenna tilted her head to stare as Mason flopped back in the passenger seat, rocking the whole car with his weight, and shot her a sideways grin, his face filled with blatant admiration. 'You outmanoeuvred him like a master puppeteer.'

She snorted out a laugh while she held back the hysteria. Mason amazed her. Oblivious to her not-so-subtle nuances of vibrating stress, he would never be the type to fall foul of depression. The man was too thick skinned to notice. Maybe he was the right man for her sister. Maybe not. But something about his obliviousness centred her. Brought her back down to earth.

His dark blue eyes softened as he met her gaze. 'You want me to drive?'

She slanted him another look. Was it deliberate? A contrived obtuseness because he was completely aware of the fact that she was on the edge, about to topple over. Was he that intelligent? She narrowed her eyes, regarded him steadily for a long moment before she sat upright and turned the key, revving the engine a touch too enthusiastically. 'No, I'm good, thanks.' The adrenaline crash left her weak enough to cry. But not in front of Mason. Or anyone, for that matter.

She glanced over her shoulder and pulled the car out onto the main drag and headed for Telford. She should have let Mason drive, but she'd never admit to the rawness that scraped at her since the disappearance of Fliss. Her heart had become more tender, her nerves buckled.

'We're so in trouble.'

A wicked chuckle came from deep down in his belly. 'Yep, we're in the shit. Right up to our arses.'

As she hit the motorway, Jenna floored the accelerator and kicked the speed up to just under 10 per cent over the limit, playing Russian roulette with the speed cameras again.

She squinted into the distance, ready to go home. It had been another long day, but it wasn't over yet. 'I should never have provoked him. I knew what I was doing. Who'd have thought McCambridge's reaction would be quite so explosive?'

'Who'd have thought he'd run into my fist?' He flexed his right hand and shot her a grin.

'I could have defended myself.' She needed him to understand she wasn't weak.

'You could have. But he never saw it coming from me. He was ready for you, he wanted it. Mean bastard. He's an absolute woman-hater. We established that. It may have been hinted at on paper, but I don't think I've ever witnessed such hostility. It vibrated through the room.'

Astounded once again by his perceptiveness, Jenna kept her eyes on the road ahead. Mason got it. Got everything.

'More to the point, how the hell does he know about the murder? *What* exactly does he know? We're going to have to speak with DI Evans when we get back. Maybe I shouldn't have pushed so hard. I expected a forceful reaction, but he took me by surprise. The speed and violence of it.'

Mason rubbed at his knuckles. 'The guy was a fucking bull. Why would you allow someone that big to work out and make themselves more than the killing machine they already are?'

'I guess it's in the prison's best interest to keep their prisoners healthy.'

He leaned his head back and closed his eyes. 'Healthy is one thing, but muscle tone like that doesn't come for free.'

Jenna mumbled her agreement and leaned forward to turn on some music and allow Mason to recharge his batteries in his own way. Sleep would have been her way too, but she'd put herself in the driver's seat.

She turned off the motorway and decelerated. The push of power for an hour had settled her again. She flicked a quick glance at the time and flexed her shoulders. Another shift almost finished. She could go home and Fliss would be there. If she was lucky, dinner ready, although it was always hit-and-miss with Fliss: one night it would be turkey drummers and chips from the freezer, the next it may be pain au chocolat, all depending on which way the meal train wind blew with her sister. Junk food was very much her preferred method of cooking.

Jenna massaged the back of her neck to loosen some of the tight muscles there. It would do her good to walk Domino. The dark nights were still difficult and Fliss wasn't yet ready to walk the dog on her own in the dark. It made no difference to Jenna, she'd come to appreciate the long walks with sister and Dalmatian. She'd almost lost them both.

Weary, Jenna pulled the car into the station car park just as static crackled out over her Force radio. 'DS Morgan, Chief Superintendent Gregg requests the pleasure of your company in his office the moment you return to the station.'

The short buzz of Airwaves filled the silence as Jenna reversed into the parking space and snapped off the ignition. She made a mental note to chase the person responsible for driving in forwards.

She turned her head and raised her eyebrows at Mason as he blinked open bleary eyes. 'The pleasure of my company... great!'

'Shit. Deep, deep shit.' He grinned.

Jenna raised the Airwaves radio to her lips. 'Acknowledged.' About to put it in her open handbag, she paused as it crackled to life again.

'He'd also like to see DC Ellis if he's with you.'

With an air of superiority, Jenna shot him a sadistic grin. 'Looks like I'm not taking this fall on my own.'

Mason flipped his middle finger up, his lips twisting with disgust. 'That didn't take long. We're about to get the bollocking of our lives.'

She didn't answer.

17

Side by side, they walked the corridors, took the stairs in silence and paused at the top to catch their breath. The drag of her feet more a reluctance to meet the Chief than exhaustion from the long day. Both factored, but Jenna knew which one held more weight.

Chief Superintendent Gregg's wide shoulders filled the black leather chair he reclined in and spilled over the sides. Gruff, grey eyebrows lowered over his steel grey eyes as Jenna and Mason entered his office.

Jenna's spine went ramrod stiff and she stood with a deep, ingrained respect for the man before her. It wasn't long ago he'd given her his complete, unquestionable support. Now, she was prepared for him to wipe the floor with her. It was the way of things.

'Take a seat.' He addressed them both, flicking a hand to indicate the two hard chairs opposite his desk. She suspected he'd chosen them deliberately, so people didn't make themselves too comfortable and outstay their welcome. The man was all about calm subtleties and hard-line discipline.

The creak of the chairs filled the silence for a moment before Chief Superintendent Gregg leaned forward to rest his elbows on the desk and link his fingers in front of his face. 'I've had a phone call from the governor of Long Lartin Prison.'

Jenna kept her silence, gaze direct on Gregg, and hoped Mason could keep his mouth shut for once.

'She tells me you incited one of her inmates to attack you, Sergeant Morgan, resulting in the inmate becoming injured.'

She'd had almost two hours to prepare herself to answer the accusation but found she couldn't pull a single word from her strangled throat.

'Sir...' The word exploded from Mason's lips and halted just as quickly as Gregg held up his hand and continued.

'I've lodged an official complaint with said governor for failing to provide adequate protection for my officers while they carried out their official duty under the care of Her Majesty's Prison Service and with the permission of the governor gained only this morning. Official documentation signed and filed.'

Shocked pleasure rippled over Jenna as she stared with admiration at the man opposite her. He'd never failed to support her in the past, there was absolutely no reason why she would question his support now. 'Thank you, sir.'

He raked his sharp gaze over her. 'Were you injured?'

'No, sir.'

From her peripheral vision, Mason flexed his hand and grimaced.

With a slow turn of his head, Chief Superintendent Gregg faced Mason. 'DC Ellis, I'm told you physically abused the same inmate.' He consulted his handwritten notes, good old-fashioned pen and paper. 'Paul McCambridge.'

Straight in with a reply, Mason didn't hesitate. 'Not abuse, sir, but defence.'

'Self-defence?' Hawk-like, Gregg's gaze pinned Mason to the spot.

'No, sir. Defence of my senior officer, sir.' Pride punched Mason's chin a notch higher.

Unmoved, Gregg held him with a cool gaze. 'How did that occur, DC Ellis?'

'The wanker... I mean inmate, sir, launched himself over the table at DS Morgan, dragging the poor little bastard... I mean prison officer, over the table with him. It was my belief then, and my continued belief, that he had every intention of committing physical harm to DS Morgan.'

The Chief turned his attention to Jenna. 'Was it also your belief that it was McCambridge's intention to commit physical harm to you?'

Without hesitation, Jenna confirmed. 'Yes, sir.'

One swift nod was all he gave in acknowledgement. 'How come you were the one to strike the prisoner, DC Ellis?'

'Because it was a full frontal attack, sir. DS Morgan took a defensive stance, but in my opinion, with the scrambling backwards to get away, she lost her balance and the guard was completely ineffective at restraining McCambridge. He was stronger than we suspected, a f— a bull, sir. The prison officer was down, and the only other person in the room at that point was McCambridge's counsellor. I imagine he wasn't trained in how to restrain a Class A prisoner. In my opinion, during that moment in time, no amount of restraint would have been effective. It may well have been carnage. He didn't see me coming. It took four guards to contain him once they entered the room.'

'Four?'

'Yes, sir. He's a bloody big bastard, sir.'

'Mmmhmm.' Gregg looked at his notes. 'What was it they considered an assault?'

'I hit him, sir. Once. With my fist. In his face. Broke his nose, I believe.' Mason skimmed a look over at Jenna for verification.

She grimaced. 'It looked a little skewed, sir.'

Gregg nodded. His mouth twitched at the edges. 'That's what I heard.' Gregg turned to Jenna. He stared at her from beneath a furrowed brow. 'I'm informed that there may have been some provocation on your part. What did you say to provoke him, DS Morgan?'

Jenna gave a casual shrug to disguise her deep discomfort. 'I had no intention of any provocation. I believe the mere fact that I was a woman in a position of command was all the incitement he required.

There were a number of times he... *stressed* my rank when addressing me, as though it was an insult.' She only hoped Mason kept his snort silent as she needed to get to the point. 'McCambridge appeared to have detailed knowledge of the murder, sir.'

'Already? How would that be? Don't we have a gagging order on this?'

'Yes, sir, we do have a gagging order in place. We have no idea how he obtained the information so fast. He claimed the press announced it, but I wasn't aware we'd released any information, apart from that a body had been found. Possible suspicious circumstances, but no details at this stage, sir.'

He rocked back in his chair. 'Inside knowledge?'

'There is that possibility. I need to check my facts. There may be an internal leak, we've had them before. The press seems to get hold of a little more information than I'm comfortable with.'

Gregg nodded. 'Speak with Acting DI Evans, get him to deal with it.'

'Yes, sir,' she agreed and then ploughed on. 'However, I believe on this occasion it's worse than that. I believe McCambridge may actually have received a communication with the killer. He was overexcited about the entire situation even before DC Ellis started to question him. He literally vibrated. It's the only way McCambridge could have known about it.'

Gregg squinted at her, his top lip curling up to show his teeth. 'This is not good.'

'No, sir.'

'I'm told you showed him a photograph of our latest victim and it got him overexcited.'

Jenna had learned never to give everything all at once when dealing with diplomatic situations. Throw in a little at a time, judge which way the wind blew before giving the next little nugget.

'No, sir. I showed him a photograph of his first victim. I wouldn't dream of imparting current information to a convict.'

Jenna slipped the folder onto Gregg's desk and flipped it open. The paperwork, permission slip, report, profile analysis, were all shuffled into the disorder they'd been in when Harper handed her the file. She'd not had time to organise them again, but she flicked through, a sharp slice of panic hitting her as she rifled through a second time, and then a third. A cord of fear twisted her gut.

'It's gone.' Her voice cracked as she whipped her head up and met Mason's quizzical gaze.

Gregg narrowed his eyes, his voice dropped low. 'What's gone, Sergeant?'

She craned her neck so she could see Mason. 'Did you see it? Was it still on the floor?'

His mouth dropped open as he slid the file towards him to inspect it for himself. 'It's not there.'

'Exactly what is it that's not there?' The Chief Superintendent commanded.

'The photograph, sir. The one we took with us. Not the one I showed him of his fourth victim. But the one of *our* victim. The one CSI took yesterday. We never showed it to him. It was meant as a taunt.'

Gregg's nostrils pinched white. 'And just how is it possible that it's gone missing?'

Jenna shook her head, heat surging through her. 'During the incident, sir.' She closed her eyes to conjure up the scene in her head. 'When he launched himself at me, the table was upended, the file hit the floor, paperwork everywhere.' She tapped her mouth with her fingers, then pointed at the file. 'There's no way McCambridge could have got hold of it. There was too much going on.' She recalled. 'When the guards rushed in, he had nothing in his hands, nothing on him beyond what he came in with. Nothing.'

She envisaged the upturned table and chairs and her heart sank. 'It must have skidded under the furniture. We left pretty quickly after the incident. We were all shaken. We hadn't expected him to kick off in the way he did.' She raised her hands and ran her fingers through her hair. 'The counsellor, Harper, gathered everything that was on the floor and handed it to me. He must have missed it. It had to be there, under the table, a chair. I'm sure of it.'

Grim faced, Gregg reached for the phone and tapped in a number. 'We want to pray they found it in the clean-up. We want it back, and pretty damned quick, DS Morgan, or this image is going to go viral and the stink really will be on us.'

Desperation clawed at Jenna's chest. She turned the event over in her mind and still couldn't see what could possibly have happened to the photograph.

Crushed, exhaustion hit her.

She was ready to go home.

18

A warming aroma of enticing food hit Jenna as she walked through the front door into her house.

The next thing to hit her was the enormous Dalmatian.

Instead of attempting to push past him, Jenna dropped to her knees on the floor and enveloped him in her arms. Gurgles of laughter rumbled in her chest as he pushed her onto her backside, his toenails tapping on the wooden flooring as he gave her a whole-body wiggle, delight pouring from him.

Just as delighted, Jenna scrubbed her fingers through the short silken softness of Domino's fur, savouring the texture as she buried her nose in his neck, her lips kicking up in a smile.

There was no other greeting she'd rather have.

'Hey, baby. Did you have a good day?'

Unable to stay still, he pulled back and then launched himself on top of her again so her back whacked against the front door, slamming it shut. He snuffled his nose through her hair, his toes digging into the soft flesh of her thighs to shoot sharp stabs of pain through her black trousers.

She grabbed his head with both hands and planted a fast kiss between his eyes before he had the chance to headbutt her. 'Enough. Now bugger off.'

His white eyelashes fluttered with pleasure and he slipped out a sly tongue to swipe at the tip of her nose.

The soft glow in her heart expanded as she looked up and caught her sister watching from the kitchen doorway.

'Hi.'

Abandoned by the dog in a heartbeat, Domino trotted over to Fliss, his tail a wild circular wag, his lips kicking up in a Dalmatian smile to expose his front teeth in a happy snarl. He wound his way around her legs, his feet high stepping in a proud prance, tossing a superior look over his shoulder at Jenna as she struggled to her feet.

'Something smells unusually great.' Fear of her sister's cooking kept Jenna from committing until she found out what it could be. Anything would be better than croissants.

Fliss scratched the top of Domino's head and hit Jenna with a bashful grin. 'I chucked together a casserole before I went to school this morning, popped it in Mum's slow cooker. I figured you might need it after your long day.'

'I do.' Quietly amazed, she scanned her younger sister, something she found herself doing frequently. Fliss's skin glowed a healthy pink, probably from sitting in front of the open fire with the dog for the last hour, but her eyes contained a happy glint and a ribbon of warmth curled through Jenna's stomach. Any good news was always welcome. 'Is everything okay?'

'Yeah.' A slow smile curved Fliss's lips. 'Come on through when you're ready. You can tell me about your day, and I'll tell you about mine.'

Jenna shrugged her coat from her shoulders and hung it on the coat rack beside the front door. She toed her shoes off and shuffled her feet into a pair of slippers. A sigh of pleasure slipped from her throat as she flexed her toes inside the old-fashioned moccasins. The type her mum would have approved of – it just went to show how much like her she was becoming.

The savoury scent of the casserole had Jenna's taste buds popping as Fliss served it up with a dollop of mashed potatoes and a small pile of greens and then sat down at the small kitchen table. Jenna studied it for a long moment, serious doubt curling in her stomach that her younger sister had managed to produce a real, nutritious, aromatic meal without help.

Jenna slipped into the chair opposite Fliss and smiled as Domino rested his chin on her thigh, not convinced at all by his docile attitude. Given half the chance, he'd snaffle her food from her plate.

She eyed the glass of red wine Fliss poured her and raised her eyebrows.

'We have wine? On a school night? Again?' A little snake of fear swam through her veins. Fliss was about to tell her she'd accepted the job. Jenna held on to her smile, determined to show the support she really didn't want to give. The thought of Fliss moving out, moving away, not even down the road, Jenna's heart quailed.

Fliss's smile spread wider. 'I thought I'd put you out of your misery and let you know you're going to be stuck with me a while longer.'

Jenna's heart jumped. 'How come?' She reached for her wine and took a sip in an attempt to smother her delight.

Tension tightened Fliss's shoulders as she hunched them up, no longer able to restrain her happiness. 'Because I spoke with the Head today.'

'Sally?' Jenna needed clarification that it was the Head of Coalbrookdale and Ironbridge and not the Wolverhampton school.

'Yeah.' Fliss ducked her head and stabbed a piece of beef with her fork. She raised it to her mouth and paused. 'I explained to her how I felt about moving away.' She waggled her fork around. 'And do you know what she said?'

Jenna forked up mashed potato and scooped it through the casserole gravy. 'No. What did she say?' She took a bite and closed her eyes. Ecstasy, pure ecstasy. She hummed in the back of her throat and when she opened her eyes, her sister was watching her. Jenna shrugged. 'This is too good, Fliss, just like Mum used to make.'

Fliss blinked, a wash of tears rushed into her eyes and she dipped her head. Jenna scratched the top of Domino's head and gave Fliss the moment she needed to compose herself. If there was one thing that would reduce Jenna to floods of tears, it was seeing her younger sister well up, and they'd done enough of that since their mother died. They just had to ignore each other's occasional surge of emotion, otherwise they'd be in a constant mess.

Fliss blew out a breath and conjured up a smile, but her voice still held a tinge of smokiness to it. 'Sally said it was the worst possible reason to move. Everyone already knows my business. Give them another couple of months and they won't even think about it. She said I'd isolate myself from friends, colleagues and family and put myself in a vacuum if I moved, probably withdrawing from a social life as I won't know anyone in Wolverhampton and I'll be too scared to talk about what happened to me. At least here if I burst into tears or want to talk, I can. People know. I don't need to keep a secret as though I'm ashamed of what happened.'

Jenna opened her mouth, tempted to agree with every single word the wise headmistress had uttered, but it appeared Fliss was not finished.

'She also said that Jean Deighton had hinted at retiring at the end of this school year and there would be a vacancy for her position, which would be a promotion for me if I cared to apply.' She hauled in a long breath, took a forkful of stew and held it up to her mouth as her slightly manic gaze caught Jenna's. 'I'm not guaranteed to get the promotion, but she said I had a good chance. So, what do you think?' She opened her mouth and forked in the food.

Jenna took her time to study her sister's barely contained excitement, the first flicker of interest she'd witnessed since Fliss had been abducted. If she'd known Sally had that much influence, she would have sent Fliss along to see her several weeks ago. As it was, the timing was probably just right. Maybe Fliss was ready to come out of her shell and face the world again.

She swiped her tongue over her teeth, placed her knife and fork on the side of her plate and took up her glass, raising it to her sister. 'I think it's the best bloody news I've had all day.'

Fliss followed suit and raised her own glass, clinking it against Jenna's. They both smiled and took a sip.

'Only one glass. I'm not drinking like we did the other night.'

'Nor me,' Fliss agreed, placing her glass back on the table and taking up her knife and fork again. 'I felt awful yesterday, and I didn't drink anywhere as much as you.'

'I think you did. We were celebrating.'

'I wasn't celebrating.'

Confused, Jenna frowned at her younger sister. 'You told me you'd been offered a job in Wolverhampton. You wanted to celebrate.'

'I was miserable. I wanted you to tell me not to be so stupid, that I shouldn't leave you.'

With a slow sip of her wine, Jenna studied Fliss over the top of the wine glass.

'You didn't want a new job?'

'No.'

'You didn't want to move to Wolverhampton?'

'No. Not really. I was confused.' Fliss's mouth turned down at the edges and she clattered her knife and fork back onto her plate.

Jenna lowered her glass to the table, a whip of frustration grabbed her. 'You silly bugger. What the hell did you expect?'

Fliss's voice thickened as her eyes filled and Jenna's heart gave a hard contraction. 'I hoped you'd say what Sally said today.'

Defeated, Jenna stared at her. 'I said what I thought you wanted to hear, Fliss, I was being frickin' supportive.'

A teardrop hovered in the corner of Fliss's eye and then plopped onto her cheek and raced down to the corner of her downturned mouth. 'I wanted you to tell me not to go.' Her voice cracked. Domino raised his head from Jenna's knee, his solemn eyes studying Fliss for a moment before he rounded the table to go and comfort her.

Fliss wrapped her arms around him as he placed his front paws on her leg and lay his neck on her shoulder, smooching her face with his cheek, oozing sympathy and compassion. More, it appeared than Jenna had offered.

Tears scalded her eyes as Jenna pushed back her chair, surged to her feet and made her way around the table. She leaned down and gathered both Fliss and Domino into her embrace, automatically rocking them both to comfort them. Her throat closed around her words, so they came out strangled.

'You're a soft sod, you really are.' Domino swiped a tongue over Jenna's wet cheek as though she was talking to him. 'And you are, you silly bugger.' She took Fliss's face in her hands and stared deep into her sister's pale green eyes awash with tears. 'I love you more than you'll ever know. I don't ever want you to go, but I'd never hold you back. We're family. The only family either of us have. And it's not tragic and it's not horrible. It just is. And we need to live with it, look after each other and be clear.' She placed a gentle kiss on the end of Fliss's pinkened nose, her heart swelling in her chest as it burst to be free. 'I thought it was what you wanted.'

'I thought you'd want me out of your hair.'

'What in hell's name gave you that idea?'

A ragged breath hitched in as Fliss replied. 'Domino ate your kitchen cupboards.'

Jenna's mind stuttered to a halt. She dropped her hands back down and smoothed them over Domino's satin coat, her fingers skimming over the raised ridge along his side. 'That was ages ago. A million things have happened since then.'

'I know.' Fliss nodded while she swiped the tears from her cheeks with the back of her hand. 'But every time I come in here,' she fluttered her hand at the damaged cupboard doors as her voice broke, 'there's a reminder of what he did.'

'He's a bad dog.'

Domino's ears flattened, his huge eyes turned morbid and a distinctly Dobbie, the Harry Potter house-elf, look chased over his face. Ears flat to his head, his big brown eyes turned liquid in sad appeal, wrenching a helpless grin from Jenna.

'See.' Fliss streaked a hand down his neck. 'He knows you've never forgiven him.'

Jenna took hold of one of his silken ears and gave a gentle caress and Domino tilted his head into her hand, an ecstatic groan rumbled from his chest.

'Of course, I've forgiven him. Maybe it's you who has to forgive, Fliss.' Jenna cupped his broad head in her hands and dropped a kiss on the bridge of his nose.

'I...'

'No, you haven't, and it's probably all connected to your kidnapping.'

Her sister sucked in a laboured breath, but it was about time they spoke about it again. Since the initial investigations and aftermath, Jenna realised they'd swept it to one side in an effort to ignore that it ever happened. But it had happened and if her sister was to heal, they needed to address it.

Jenna straightened and made her way back to her own chair. She picked up her wine glass and raised it once more in Fliss's direction. 'Fliss, you are the strongest person I have ever known, and that includes our own mother. You've survived a multitude of events in your life, most of them through no fault of your own, including dealing with Frank Bartwell. You escaped. With guts and determination, you got yourself out of there and survived.' She took a sip of her wine, then put the glass back down on the table between them and pointed at her sister, who still cuddled the Dalmatian. 'One thing you're not going to do now is start throwing self-doubt,' she frowned, 'and doubt of my support into the fray.'

'I didn't doubt...'

Jenna nodded. 'You did. But you're not to. It's unhealthy. I asked you if you wanted to see a counsellor and you said you didn't, but from the sounds of it, you had a good deal of counselling from Sally today and needed it.'

'I don't need counselling.' Fliss's reddened eyes blinked with offence, but Jenna rushed on determined to have her say.

'Perhaps not, but you're not to allow mind games to take over. Say what you mean, mean what you say, but don't ever believe you can manipulate me into telling you I love you and I want you to stay. I can tell you that every day of your life if you want me to. But I'm too thick skinned to understand if you're asking for one thing and expecting another. That's not the way we were brought up. It's not the way we tick.' Just to drive her point home, Jenna met Fliss's gaze, hardening her own. Whether the tactic worked or not was to be seen. 'It's the way Ed treated you, making you lose confidence, making you doubt yourself. Don't let that happen.'

Fliss sucked in a breath, insult warring across her features as her spine snapped straight with the reminder of her abusive ex-boyfriend. She held onto her breath and then released it in a swift rush. Her face fired up, but the tears dried in an instant.

Fliss reached for her wine glass and cradled it in her hand. 'You're right. I know you love me, and I don't need to seek your approval. I wasn't playing games. For a while there, I thought that might be the best solution all around, but when Sally spoke to me today, it made such sense. Everything clicked back into place as though it had all been misshapen.' She watched the glass in her hand, her face pensive as she swirled the red wine around. 'It's far more logical to stay here than it is to move away and start over. As Sally says, I've had my fifteen minutes of fame, hopefully it'll fade now, and people will forget.'

Jenna nodded. 'Eventually they will, once the court case has been heard.'

Fliss met Jenna's gaze, her tear darkened eyes filled with trepidation.

'How much longer do they need? It seems to have been forever.'

Jenna shrugged, used to the time delay between arrest and conviction, it still seemed to have dragged on.

'I imagine it'll start in the next few weeks, Fliss.'

Fliss chewed her lip. 'I just want it over and done with so I can become invisible again.'

'Your celebrity status will fade when there's nothing further to feed it.'

'It would if that arse, Kim Stafford, would stop sticking things in the paper. I can't believe the asinine information he dredges up on me. I'm surprised he hasn't printed my A level results.'

Jenna ground her teeth as she picked up her cutlery to start on her food again. She stabbed her knife at it, envisaging Kim's face. 'He is an arse, and he's letting our dinner get cold.'

Fliss tasted hers and nodded, but continued to scoop it up, filling her mouth as though she was ravenous. 'I can microwave it for you, but mine's okay. I'm used to eating my food cold at school, by the time I've got up a dozen times to sort out one of the infants or another.'

Jenna pushed back her chair and took her plate to the microwave, placed it inside and tapped the buttons, zapping her food back to an acceptable heat. She glanced over her shoulder as she waited. 'So, you're going to stay at Coalbrookdale, hopefully take a promotion, continue to live here...'

'Yeah. If that's okay.'

'Of course it's okay.'

'Only...'

'Only, what?'

'I want to pay to have the cupboard doors replaced.'

'I think I can claim them on my household insurance.' Jenna opened the microwave door and pulled the plate out, taking her seat opposite Fliss again. Steam rose and her stomach gurgled out a protest at not being fed the food it had been promised.

'That'll only put the premium up next year, and you'll have to pay an excess. It's probably too late anyway.'

Jenna shrugged. 'Don't worry about it.'

'I'm not worried. I want to clear my conscience, Jenna, and the only way to do that is to replace these bloody doors.'

Domino rested his chin on the table and his black, wet snout pulsed as it faced Jenna as though he wanted her to know he was on Fliss's side.

Jenna chewed for a while and then took a drink of her wine to wash the food down while she thought. 'Okay. You can. But the reason I hadn't replaced them was because I'm considering changing the whole colour scheme in here. I just haven't got around to putting my mind to it.' She hadn't had a moment since it had happened. Once Fliss had been kidnapped it had ceased to hold any importance. Nothing had mattered but Fliss and Domino and their recovery. Perhaps it was time to move forward.

'Why didn't you say?'

'Because we've been a little preoccupied lately and it seemed to be the least of my worries. Also, I wanted to wait until spring. It'll be easier to deal with.' She cruised her gaze around the kitchen and took in the real oak cupboard doors, which only served to darken the kitchen. 'I think I could keep the cupboard carcases and just change the doors. What do you think?'

'I think it would be a great idea.'

'Or, I could see how much it would cost to have the whole kitchen replaced.'

'Wow, that'll cost a bit.'

'Yeah, but if you're paying for it...'

Her lips twitched as Fliss turned a sickly shade of green. Her voice came out a high pitched squeal. 'I'm not paying for your whole bloody kitchen. He only ate a couple of doors.'

Jenna started to laugh as she took another swig of her wine. She drained the glass and reached for the bottle.

Fliss shot dark disapproval at Jenna. 'I thought we weren't going to drink too much tonight.'

Jenna poured a half glass and topped up Fliss's at the same time, giving a careless shrug. 'We're not. Nor are you going to pay for the whole kitchen, but you can contribute if that eases your conscience.'

'It does.' Fliss finished the last mouthful of her food and pushed her empty plate into the centre of the table so Domino didn't try for a crafty lick. She glanced around the room and then back at Jenna. 'What do you think you want?'

Jenna shrugged. 'Something light, bright, clean.' From the look on Fliss's face, Jenna knew she wasn't going to have any trouble enlisting her to do the makeover.

Settled, she pushed her own plate away and relaxed back in her chair.

All she needed was an early night, hopefully dream free.

19

Terror slid through his overactive heart as he heard the woman in the room next to him from where he crouched inside the guest room wardrobe.

She wasn't supposed to be home yet. His fucking heart beat like the wings of a frantic bird, trying to escape the confines of his chest.

Why was she home? He thought he had her schedule, but he obviously hadn't pinned it down enough. Perhaps she'd got off early.

She'd almost caught him.

He'd been in the middle of installing a tiny camera. If she'd been ten minutes earlier, she would have heard the scream of the drill as he pushed through from her bedroom wall, right next to the photograph frame above her dressing table into the wardrobe in the next room.

Sweat popped out of his forehead. If she'd heard him, he would have been forced to dispatch her without the finesse he wanted and all the fucking planning in the world wouldn't have made any difference. Weeks of wasted time, the research, the dating app contacts, narrowing down, the online schmoozing. It would have all gone to hell. It still might.

He slumped his head into his hands and breathed in deep and rhythmic until he had himself under control once more. The heat in the small wardrobe rose to stifle him, blocking his lungs until the air backed up in his throat. The taste of her gas boiler that was installed in the cupboard next to the wardrobe coated his tongue to make it stick to the roof of his mouth.

He raised his head and risked a glance at his phone, not even knowing if he'd managed to make the connection. He tapped the glass and waited while it connected to her Wi-Fi and scrolled for a moment before the image burst onto his screen.

Excitement buzzed and popped through his veins, igniting his skin with anticipation as he watched her through his phone, the scent of her deep in his nose, her closeness a sweet temptation. The risk had been worth the thrill.

He took a long pull of breath in through his mouth, pausing as she froze on the other side of the paper-thin wall.

A slow smile spread, creasing his cheeks while he peered closer. Could she hear him? Did she sense him there, right beside her?

She came close to the hole in the wall, stared straight into the camera for a second as though she knew he was there and stopped his heart altogether. Could she see the hole? He'd only had a split second to swipe away the plaster dust before he made a run for a hiding place. He almost slipped under her bed, but this was better. So much better.

When she ducked her head, he blew out a long, desperate sigh of relief and watched her jerk her head upright.

She definitely heard him.

Curiosity got the better of him and he ratcheted in a long, slow pull of breath, let it out again on a noisy gust and stared at the screen to watch her reaction.

Her eyes widened until they almost popped out of her head, but she stayed exactly where she was, frozen to the spot. She took a cautious step back from the dressing table and raised her hands to scrub them across her face.

She screwed her eyes closed as he drew in another robust breath and blew it out again, aware with every sound, she knew he was there.

That was the intention. To let her know he was there, that he had her within his sights. Designed to make her flesh crawl with his little mind games. He'd been told it wasn't about the kill, but the lead-up, the moment they went over the edge.

It wouldn't take much, she was already a jittery mess. Silly cow probably believed she had a ghost. It was more likely than an actual person, a predator, in her house. More likely and less dangerous. The dead couldn't harm you, only the living could.

He'd flipped through the contents of her bathroom cabinet earlier. The woman was a hypochondriac. Medicated to the hilt – ibuprofen, aspirin, paracetamol, antihistamine, steroids, sleeping tablets. She had the lot. Cough medicine, nasal spray, antidepressants – several different varieties. If he simply wanted to 'off' her, he just needed to pour the cocktail of tablets into her mouth, wash it down with one of the flavoured gins she had and wait for her insides to melt. But that wasn't his game.

As it was, he could think of much more interesting, fun ways of dealing with her.

As long as she didn't discover him, crouched like a frog in a drought in her wardrobe. For him, it would be the humiliation of discovery that would hurt.

His lips curved up in a long smile. On the other hand, his discovery would definitely be the death of her.

He swiped the sweat from his eyes with the back of his gloved hand and slid down the wall until he rested on the floor to watch her via the link to his phone. Stupid woman.

Face pale, she backed away from the wall and picked up the night-shirt he'd smoothed his hands over earlier, the knickers he'd fondled. She cast an anxious glance in his direction again before she closed herself in the bathroom.

He checked the time on his phone. If he left now, he could set up the next one. He needed to maintain control, keep three targets going at once and currently he only had this one. There should be three. All at different stages. Then, if one of them went tits up, got a boyfriend, moved to a new house, went on holiday, there would always be a back-up.

He stared at the screen, the empty bedroom gave off a warm white light. The bathroom door opened, and she stepped back into her bedroom, the navy-blue nightshirt hit mid-thigh and had his pulse racing. Smooth, tanned, shapely legs grabbed his attention. He'd always been a leg man. If he'd known hers were so good...

There'd be time enough.

He should have taken his chance when she was in the bathroom and left the house, but trapped as he was, he hunkered into the corner, ready to wait it out until she was asleep.

She slipped under the covers, tossed an anxious glance his way and then slid further down the bed, pulling the duvet up under her chin.

The light stayed on as she closed her eyes and his grin spread wide. The stupid woman had no idea she'd given him access to an all-night vigil if he wanted to watch her. Fear of the dark had made her more accessible to predators of the night.

Excitement prickled his skin and set his teeth on edge. He could get up and go into her bedroom, take her right now. Rip back the covers so he could skim his fingers over those long, powerful legs, hold her down, powerless, while he licked his way between her thighs, up into the warm heat of her.

He tamped down the desperate craving. It wouldn't be as good. The anticipation, the humming desire was what it was all about. Sex was the side benefit, he'd learned, not the ultimate goal.

To give her time, he scrolled through the dating app photographs on his phone for twenty minutes and then flicked back to the camera screen, curious to see what she was doing.

He couldn't have scared her that much, she was fast asleep, one hand curled tight into her cheek. She'd gone out like a fucking light. Taken the sleeping tablets in the bathroom cabinet probably. He squinted at his screen and watched the rhythmic rise and fall of her chest until another twenty minutes had passed by.

Bored, he struggled to his feet in the tight confines of the wardrobe, keeping as quiet as possible. He'd love to disturb her, but he really shouldn't. He had more work, more setting up. He needed to compile photos, evidence of his work coming to fruition.

The door emitted a soft creak as he pushed it open. He froze, listening for any noise to indicate he'd disturbed her, but the thunder of his heartbeat in his ears smothered any other sound. He snicked the wardrobe door to, holding his breath while he crept from the room, each step a pained torture.

If he disturbed her, he'd have to kill her now and all his surveillance efforts would be for nothing. He'd rather follow the plan but the anticipation of meeting her on the landing was almost worth ditching all his good work.

He made it to the bottom of the stairs before he allowed himself to look back up at her closed bedroom door. The fast hammer of his heart slowing as he controlled his breath and blew out little puffs of air. She *must* have taken the sleeping pills he'd seen in her bathroom cabinet earlier. There was no way she could have gone that deep, that quick.

Disappointment dampened the rising excitement. It would be no fun at all if the woman was drugged. The whole point was to feel her terror, experience the adrenaline rushing through her, soak in the surge of horror of the torture and wait out the acceptance of her death.

The temptation was strong to simply go back upstairs and touch her, stroke his fingers over her silky skin.

His jaw popped as he ground his teeth and made up his mind.

With one last glance up, he tiptoed along the hallway, into the kitchen and let himself out of the back door, locking it behind him and slipping the key into his pocket before his shadow slipped down the pathway and disappeared into the night.

He had more preparation to complete before he returned, but it wouldn't be long before it was her turn. He tucked his cold hands deep into his pockets and grinned. It would be soon, very soon.

20

Jenna stared at the screen in front of her until her eyes glazed over, her brain refused to engage any longer with the sheer boredom of research, forensic checks, stepping through all the reports. An entire day with no results. Wasted. The morning brief had brought nothing more to the party. It was like walking through treacle.

'Nothing.'

She raised her head and rolled her lips inwards as she peered at Ryan. 'No, nothing. Not a clue, nothing back yet on the DNA. We can't expect anything yet. Not a damned hint of evidence and yet everything points to it being planned, staged.'

'He's a ghost.'

'Ghosts don't slice open people's throats, Ryan.' She watched him lose his colour, then it flooded back again. He'd got a hold on it, now. He'd steadied. A flicker of pride filtered through the exhaustion as she stared at him over the desk.

'Perhaps we should go home. Cast a fresh eye over it in the morning.'

Relief flooded his face, but he came to his feet with reluctance. 'You know...'

She tilted her head to look up at him, kept her voice soft as he shuffled his feet. 'Yeah?'

'I feel guilty.'

'Ryan...'

'No, please let me say it. Everyone keeps telling me there was nothing I could have done to have prevented it. But I could. If only I'd seen her home, if only...'

'No, Ryan.' Jenna leaned back and linked her fingers together, resting her wrists on the desk in front of her. Sometimes, she needed to be the teacher. 'There was nothing you could do. Everyone is right. It wouldn't have made a difference if you'd seen her to the door. Whoever he is, he found his way in. Was possibly even inside her house when she arrived home. There was no sign of breaking and entering. For all we know, she knew him. Most people know their assailants.' She swept her hand over the files on her desk, the computer screen. 'Whoever the culprit is, knew exactly what he was doing. This was planned, Ryan.' She emphasised, keeping her gaze directly on his. 'If not then, it would have been another time. She was targeted. It was deliberate.'

Ryan sank back into his chair and rubbed long bony fingers over his face, rubbing the strain of the past couple of days away. 'I'll always feel like I should have done more.'

Jenna nodded. 'We always do. But to make a good police officer, you have to park that and get on with the job, because if you dwell on each time you believed you should have done more, could have helped, it will destroy you.' Now she rested her elbows on the table, sank her chin onto her hands. 'We're a special breed. Along with nurses and doctors. We deal with death on a regular basis. We need to survive, which is why we're all such a mess in the domestic field, because there are only certain types who will understand what we do, what we deal with every day.' She nodded at his phone in an attempt to inject some positivity into the conversation. 'You chose well when you decided to try and date a nurse.'

He shuffled his backside in the chair, an air of embarrassed reluctance flushing his cheeks.

'What?' She tilted her head to one side and gave him an encouraging smile.

'I feel guilty about that too.'

'Why?'

'Because she was my choice. And I still have that choice on here.' He lifted the phone, then put it down again as if it burned.

Not sure she understood, Jenna leaned forward. 'Has your taste changed?'

'No, but...'

'You'd still choose the same type?'

'Well, yes.'

'But you haven't looked at the app since it happened?'

He nodded, his lips tightened. 'No. Because...' he shrugged. 'Guilt.'

Jenna slapped her hands on the desk and rose to her feet. 'Then take my advice and park it. Get on with your life and if that means resurrecting your dating app, then do it.'

With a clumsy scramble, Ryan stood, his Adam's apple bobbed as he swallowed several times, then swiped up his phone and waggled it from side to side. 'Okay. I will. I'll look again. Maybe change my profile search.' He picked up his jacket from the back of the chair and slipped his arms into it.

'Keep it the same.' She smiled at him as he fidgeted in front of her, trying to get the zipper up on his jacket. 'It was a good choice. It was your choice. Even in our world, coincidences can happen.'

He glanced at the screen. 'There was another woman I'd been speaking with, Carla. Maybe I'll arrange to meet for a coffee during the day, rather than an evening meet-up. It won't serve as a reminder then of what's gone on before.' His voice cracked. 'Thanks, boss.' He bobbed his head several times, shoved his hands deep into his jacket pockets. 'Have a good evening.'

'You too, I'll see you in the morning.'

With long-legged strides, he shot across the room and out of the main office door.

The heavy weight of the day pressed on her shoulders and Jenna picked up her own mobile, tempted to answer Adrian's message. Coffee, cake, a chat. And she could make it clear that she wouldn't see him again, that it was inappropriate.

She swiped the screen open.

'You're a soft shit at heart.'

Jenna whipped her head around, slipping the phone into her pocket. Guilty heat rushed into her face and she covered up by raising her eyes heavenward at the sight of Mason. 'How long have you been there?'

Mason came around the desk and dumped himself in the chair opposite her. 'Long enough to hear everything.'

'You were hiding.'

'I'd call it keeping a discreet distance while you dealt with a delicate matter.'

'He's a good police officer.'

'He is.'

'With a soft heart.'

Mason nodded. 'Nothing wrong with a soft heart as long as it's accompanied by a spine of steel.'

She smiled at him and closed the file in front of her, slipped it into her top drawer to leave the desk as clear as she liked it whenever she left for the day. 'I have a good feeling he has one of those too.' Jenna ran her gaze over Mason's smart charcoal suit and pale blue shirt. 'How did your court appearance go?'

Mason scrubbed his fingers over his forehead and huffed out a weary sigh. 'Six hours of waiting in the hallway to be told the lead witness never turned up.'

'Great. Did they throw the case out?'

'No. They've adjourned it and sent out a witness summons. What a bloody waste of time.' He glanced at his watch. 'What progress with the murder?'

Jenna came to her feet and slipped her coat from the back of her chair. 'Salter and Wainwright submitted their report after they'd interviewed Trevor Lockley, the Uber driver, the other day. Nothing.'

Mason's lips tightened as she continued.

'Poor guy. Totally flattened by it. Claims he watched her let herself in her front door.'

'What's the betting the guy was already in the house?'

Proof was thin on the ground, but it was a line they continued to follow.

'Yeah, I know. Obviously, we don't want that piece of information known. Salter and Wainwright said nothing. He blames himself, poor guy. No amount of pacifying helped. Apparently, he was talking about putting his ticket in, how he was sick of dealing with drunks and druggies and couldn't tell the difference between a nice girl and a prostitute any more. Reckoned they all act the same.'

'Scary.'

'Yeah. One good thing though, Salter said he didn't have a bad word to say about our young Ryan. He didn't let on he was one of ours, because we're trying to keep certain information from the press. Kim Stafford seems to be all over it, did you see him hanging around the other day? He always seems to be in the right place at the right time. How was he there so soon?'

Mason's lips tightened. 'I've no idea, he's a slippery one. I wouldn't trust him as far as I could throw his skinny little body. We know what happened when Fliss got taken and he latched onto the fact that she was your sister. Bastard, made out that we'd used extra resources just because she was related, not because there was one dead woman and another one missing.'

Instant anger burned Jenna's chest at the memory. 'We would have used the same resources for any missing person.'

'Exactly. Pompous git.'

Jenna yawned and scrubbed her hand over her hair.

'So, what did Uber man have to say about Ryan?'

'He said he was a real gentleman. Couldn't fault him. Paid the fare, plus a generous tip after the drop-off notification, which Lockley couldn't pin down the exact amount, but it'll be logged on the app. I've asked Donna to follow up.'

'Good. So, DC Downey conducted himself in exactly the manner we would expect of him. His father will be proud.' The discipline and respect Jim Downey had taught his son was evident in every move Ryan made. The exuberant enthusiasm was of his own making.

21

FRIDAY 7 FEBRUARY, 06:45 HOURS

Sluggish rain streaked down and masked the grey day beyond Carla's window. Saskia arched her back and rumbled a satisfied purr as Carla tore the top strip from a sachet of food and shook the contents into the cat's bowl. With a delicate snuffle, Saskia sniffed the bowl with superior disdain, turned and tightrope-walked along the edge of the kitchen bench. Tail high in the air, she hit the floor, turning her head to give Carla a cool wink before she strode from the room, all attitude and condescension.

'Ungrateful wretch.' Carla placed the cat bowl on the floor, swiped the empty sachet from the bench, flipped open the lid of the bin and froze as she stared at another empty sachet already inside.

She'd lost her mind. Had to have done. She kept her foot on the pedal and dropped the sachet she held inside, then let the lid slap down. She raised her head to gaze out of the window at the red-lidded bin at the end of her drive. She always put her rubbish out at night, so it didn't lie festering in the kitchen.

Carla dragged her attention back to the small lime-green pedal bin. She'd fed Saskia when she came home the previous night, thrown the pouch in the bin and then emptied it, slipping a fresh white bin liner inside. The smell of rancid cat food never a favourite, she'd taken the full bin liner out to the bin so the stench of it didn't hang around all night to contaminate her kitchen. Then she'd gone straight to bed. The pedal bin had definitely been empty.

Puzzled, she picked up her china mug of espresso while she studied the rain and sipped at the hot liquid. The thirteen hour shift the day before had exhausted her, but not so much she couldn't remember what she'd done. It wasn't the first time in the last few days she'd felt something out of sync.

She peered around the doorway as Saskia reached the top of the stairs and stopped to stare back down at her, her golden eyes glowed with satisfied superiority. Carla sighed. She was a clever cat, but she'd not yet mastered the art of feeding herself. She also couldn't make dirty laundry disappear. Two pairs of knickers didn't just get up and walk away.

Obsessively tidy, Carla knew with certainty she'd placed her under-wear in the small, cotton lined linen basket in the corner of her room. In the habit of washing her nurse's pale blue scrubs on a three day rota, she'd throw in anything else unlikely to shrink in the hot sixty degree wash required for hygiene purposes. But her underwear had gone.

She sipped the last of her coffee, rinsed the mug, turned it upside down on the drainer and paused. Confusion stole through her mind as she reflected on the position of the mug. It had been in the cupboard this morning. Yet the night before, she'd have sworn she left it just where she had now. Where she always did when she was late in, early out.

Carla glanced around to check if anything else was out of place but couldn't be certain. No. She was just tired. Second-guessing herself.

She pulled the back door closed behind her, turned the single key in the lock and then slipped it into the inside pocket of her Lycra running shorts.

Twenty minutes of warm-ups under her lean-to shelter and she was ready to move.

The drizzle would soon soak through, but if she was to be fit enough for the London Marathon, she had to run in all weather. With one last stretch of her calves, she set off.

Her feet slapped in a smooth rhythm against the wet pavement, clearing her mind of fog and doubts. With natural ease, she allowed her body to take over, pushing aside everything but the satisfaction of her warming muscles and loosened limbs.

Her mind drifted in the freedom of the outdoors. She had a date later. Coffee with a police officer. He looked a little young, a little geeky, but it was only coffee and it wouldn't harm. Perhaps it was time to go for young and geeky rather than mature and cocky. She'd had enough of doctors. Maybe the time was right to try a police officer. Or even a fireman. Whatever, a coffee date would be good. No pressure.

She swiped a lock of rain soaked auburn hair from her forehead, smoothing it back into place without breaking her rhythm. Her goal, eight miles, would fly past as the day awakened and movement in the houses and on the road started.

She veered off, determined to keep her rhythm as she headed away from the houses, uphill towards The Wrekin. Her breath came in long, even pulls, comfortable with the speed and distance for now.

Her feet flew over the motorway bridge, as she headed around the long bend, and despite the early morning lightening of the sky, she was plunged into darkness as she edged around Ercall Woods. Never a place she cared to run through on her own, she automatically sped up to bypass it as fast as she could while she stuck to the road rather than go through the woodland. Her feet kept a comfortable rhythm while her mind broke loose and sent doubt flying once again.

She'd emptied the bin. She'd left her mug on the drainer.

The touch of something evil had her glancing over her shoulder as a ripple of fear pebbled her skin. She peered into the woodland filled with dark, threatening shadows and put on a spurt.

Spiteful fingers stroked an icy trail along her spine and sent her speeding up the hill. With lungs burning, the sharp sting of acid filled her throat.

Winded, she pulled up outside The Buckatree Hall Hotel and let the hard whip of temper ride through her as she glanced at her watch. She'd ruined her time through her fear and stupidity. How was she ever to run the London Marathon if she couldn't control her pace? She sucked in another breath, swiped her dripping hair from her face and bent from the hips, leaning her hands on her knees. Two and half miles, that was all she'd managed and she'd blown it.

She stared up at the white façade of the hotel, discreet and ladylike, nesting just beyond the woodland at the foot of The Wrekin. Lovely, inviting. If she'd had money on her, or a cash card, she'd have gone in for coffee and breakfast.

She stared down at her soaked clothes and mud streaked legs. They'd be wise not to let her through the door. Defeated, she peered up at the rain filled clouds.

There was no point carrying on. She was done for the day. Winded. Her legs had turned to spaghetti. The tremble of adrenaline rush weakened her. She dropped her head to study her feet as she brought her breathing back under control. She was an athlete. Strong, capable, intelligent.

She crouched down, retied her laces and challenged herself to look up into Ercall Wood, opposite the beautiful woodland hotel. There was nothing to fear. Nothing in the darkness to harm her.

She scanned the treeline, squinting through the light and shade of it to make sure nothing lurked there.

The pressures of work and the vile stabbing of the young nurse earlier in the week had unnerved everyone, lacing the atmosphere with unrest and whispered fears. She didn't know the nurse personally, had never worked with her, but she'd recognised the photograph in the newspaper. She knew the ex-boyfriend, Ray Horrobin, a porter at the hospital. He'd always been so pleasant. The newspapers suggested it was him. The police remained quiet. The gossips stirred up trouble.

Disgusted with herself, she shrugged off the shroud of persistent evil. She shook out her limbs, keeping them warm while she centred herself. There was nothing in the woods. She'd listened to too much gossip, allowed the fear to filter through into her subconscious. Tiredness had taken a hold and she'd drowned in a shallow lake of her own misgivings. That's what it was.

Right.

She extended her arms above her head and lunged forward to stretch her leg muscles to stop them from becoming cold.

She shoved aside the sneaking suspicion that insisted she think deeper into matters and straightened, stretching her spine upwards while she reached for the grey clouds above, flexing her fingers, warming her muscles to chase away the chill of drizzle and fear. Perhaps she'd continue her run after all, now she'd calmed down.

She challenged herself to focus her gaze on Ercall Woods again. She'd allowed tales of the place to spook her. She'd never been comfortable there.

Hidden beyond her sight was the quarry with its geological site that had scared the pants off her ever since she sneaked off as a teenager to catch a sly cigarette there with her mates. The day the drunken old man had staggered along the path and fallen off the edge, down into the quarry. The blood from his head injury stained the rocks below and she'd scrabbled down to reach him while the rest of her friends ran. Not to find help, but in fear. Fear of retribution, fear of blame.

She risked running past the quarry, but she'd never returned. Not inside the woods.

She scanned the woodland, knowing she'd see nothing.

A black shadow exploded from between the trees heading straight for her, then dodged away. Heart pounding wildly, Carla dropped her arms to her sides, curled her hands into tight fists ready to face her demon. Her stomach contracted in a sharp spasm and she took a quick step back, her gaze concentrated on the shadows beyond the single track road in search of further movement.

A black Labrador dashed through the thicket to burst the heart from her chest into a million fragments before it settled into uneasy hitches as the dog raced along the winding path opposite.

A sharp recall whistle had the dog spinning a one-eighty degree turn and zipping off in the opposite direction without so much as an acknowledgement to the woman she'd almost given a heart attack to. As the Labrador headed into the dense woodland, Carla closed her eyes and muttered a silent prayer to whoever the hell was responsible for the continued bombardment of her emotions. She was a mess.

She pressed her hand against her leaden chest and tipped her head back, little puffs of hysterical laughter coming from her lips. God, she was an idiot. Frightened to death not by her own shadow, but that of a black Labrador.

She sucked in deep breaths.

Heart still beating way too fast for someone not actually going into cardiac arrest, Carla placed her hands on her hips and blew out a relieved chuckle. She'd never been a coward, she wasn't about to become one now. It was all a figment of her overactive imagination. It had to stop.

'Carla!'

She flung her head back at the hoarse, whispered voice. Spun on her heel to search the car park virtually empty of cars.

No imagined shadow had the ability to whisper her name.

No dark visage knew her name.

She shifted her weight forward onto her toes.

'Carla.' This time the voice held a subtle threat.

Spooked, she took off as fast as her swift feet would go. She raced as fast as possible to escape her demons. Ones she was now convinced weren't imagined. Soaked to the skin, legs slicked, she ran while her heart hammered in her chest, her breath coming in ragged bursts until she stumbled up the pathway to her house. Terror pushing her onwards, breaking the record for two and half miles.

Icy fingers trembled as she pushed the key into the lock of her back door and burst into her house. She slammed the door closed behind her, turned the key and shot the bolt across. Weak with relief, she leaned on it, gasping sobs coming from her throat. She slithered down until her backside slapped on the cold, tiled floor, legs too weak to take her weight, and covered her face with shaking hands.

The sinister whisper of her name echoed through her mind.

What the hell?

Who would want to torment her? She pressed her fingers against her forehead as the memory of the voice circled around. Whoever had whispered her name had stayed hidden. Surely if it was someone she knew, they would have made themselves known, stepped out from the bushes or wherever they were hiding.

Carla got a grip again as she heaved in another breath, searching, probing her memory. There was no one she'd upset. Not a single person she could bring to mind who would be so vindictive.

The iciness of her tiled floor and rain soaked clothes chilled her to the bone. Stiff, she struggled to her feet and walked like an arthritic patient, one step at a time, until she came to the landing at the top of the stairs.

She turned her head and sucked in her breath. There. Right there she felt it. The dark gaze. Watching, waiting.

Without a moment's hesitation, she raced through to her bedroom, slung on thick tracky bottoms and a sweatshirt over the top of her drenched running gear, not pausing long enough to strip them off. She flung open the third drawer down in her chest of drawers and snatched out a uniform, leaving the drawer wide as she grabbed underwear from the smaller top drawer and tucked it all under her arm.

She snatched up a sleeping Saskia from her bed and raced downstairs with her in her arms. Before the cat had time to react, Carla had her in her cat basket. Her fingers trembled as she grabbed a plastic bag and stuffed her spare clothes inside and then raced for the front door, seizing her handbag from the newel post at the bottom of the stairs and slinging it over her shoulder.

With the door slammed shut behind her, Carla pressed the remote key for her car and leapt into it the moment it unlocked. She slapped her fingers on the lock button and fired the engine. Before she slammed it into gear, she fished her mobile from her bag and dialled as her Bluetooth connected.

'Mum? Mum? Can I come home?'

22

Dark pleasure warmed him from the inside out until he gurgled out the laughter lodged in his chest. Priceless.

The stupid woman had run like a thousand demons chased her. No style, no technique, she'd simply belted downhill, her long legs splaying like Bambi.

He tipped his head back, rumbled out another laugh of sheer delight.

The passerby's dog had been a brilliant touch. He couldn't have planned it better himself if he'd tried. Carla had almost shit herself. Who'd have known a dog, the useless bastards, could have contributed so perfectly, adding a layer of dark atmospheric fear to her.

She'd already sensed him. Her wide eyes, filled with suspicion, had cruised around before the dog had launched itself from the bushes.

His chest still vibrated with a softened chuckle. It was all falling into place.

The final touch unplanned, he'd wound down the window and whispered her name. She'd not seen him from where he watched in his car. Her attention purely focused on the woods. Even when she'd turned her head to stare at the parked cars, she'd not spotted him.

He wiped his eyes, laughed again and put the car in gear.

Patience.

The key to ultimate pleasure. It was obvious the journey was as enjoyable as the endgame. To watch the fear build, develop it into a living, breathing terror. A terror he'd managed to instil in her so she shot back home as fast as her long legs could carry her, to hide, pathetic and cowardly, in a home that could no longer offer her protection.

Pleasure fizzled over his skin, warmed his insides. It was so much easier than he could ever have imagined.

He tipped his head back and rested it on the headrest, closing his eyes for a brief moment, pleasure and pride washing over him as his plan slipped nicely into place. A smile curved his lips and he revelled in the silence of the woodland surrounding him.

Time drifted by as his muscles relaxed, bit by bit, and he floated through the labyrinth of plans dominating his mind. Plans far superior to those instigated by McCambridge. The finesse came from him. He wasn't about to get caught, he was too intelligent to allow it.

Contentment took a hold.

He rolled his head to one side and checked his watch. Work beckoned. He snapped out a grin. No hardship there, he loved his work.

23

Fog pressed thick and heavy over Malinsgate Police Station, with a light mizzle to soak through to the bones. The shallow basin of Telford town centre sucked it in so it couldn't escape. Ten minutes' drive out and Jenna knew the fog would lift and brilliant February sunshine would break through, pushing it back, but it wouldn't disperse around the station until after midday. The pea-souper blanketed the brick and glass building with its own moat, throwing the depths of it into dark misery.

Jenna dragged a hand through her hair as she studied the screen in front of her. Forensics still worked on the evidence they'd obtained from Marcia Davies' house. The post-mortem had revealed nothing they hadn't already surmised from Jim's initial observations, apart from the lovely nurse had a mild dose of the clap, which was probably why she was taking penicillin.

Mason ambled in, the blue of his eyes darkened to navy in the electric lighting.

'Where's the kiddo?'

Jenna kicked up a smile as he handed her the weak, grey dishwater that passed as the station coffee, direct from a portable machine in the corner. 'He's on lates today. Swapped with someone. I can't remember why.'

'Eh. It's Saturday. What the hell else would a twenty-one year old have to do on a Saturday night?' Sarcasm laced his words as Mason slumped in the chair opposite and leaned forward, his chin resting on his hand. 'We got anything new?'

She shook her head. 'Not so far, but we can do a round-up. There are a few follow-ups on the house-to-house calls, but nobody seems to have heard anything – no screams, nothing.'

Jenna glanced at her watch and grabbed a file as she came to her feet, leaving the thin, brown watery stuff to go cold in its plastic cup.

Mason leapt to his feet. 'Where are we going?'

'To see a...' She consulted her notes. 'Bob Mills.'

'Who is Bob Mills, and should I know about him?'

Jenna smiled as she grabbed her coat from the rack in the corner and held open the office door to let Mason precede her. 'Bob Mills is the treasurer of the Mervyn Lucas Charity. Set up to fund children with leukaemia to have an experience of a lifetime, whatever their dream is. Mervyn Lucas was a grandfather whose grandson, also named Mervyn, died of leukaemia at the age of four, having never really lived.'

Voice solemn, Mason ducked his head. 'A good cause.'

They bypassed the lift and took the door to the stairwell. 'A very good one. Which has run smoothly for the past two decades.'

'I sense a "but" coming on.'

'But the president of the association has asked us to look into the slow, insidious disappearance of approximately £24,000 over an eleven month period.'

'Eleven months. Sounds pretty precise to me.'

As they reached the bottom of the stairs, Mason turned right and leaned through the service counter to snatch a key fob for one of the police vehicles off the rack.

'Don't you dare take those, DC Ellis, without signing them out.' The authoritative voice rolled out from the tiny woman most police officers tried to avoid. Della Prince, a woman to be scared of, with her fierce bleached white hair which stood in hard, almost lacquered, two inch spikes all over her head. Her crimson lipstick bled into deep smoker's lines surrounding her mouth and black eyeliner circled her eyes, thick and dark, to make the ice blue of them glare out at everyone as though she was permanently pissed off with the world. Which she was.

Jenna hid a smile behind her hand as she sauntered away.

The only person capable of making Mason stutter, Della slammed her hands on her hips and pushed her chin out, tipping her head a long way back to glare up at him.

'I... I... I wouldn't dream of it.' He drew the authority sheet towards him through the hatch and patted his jacket pocket, searching for a pen.

Della stretched out an arm, her lips twisted with derision as she offered him her pen. 'Of course you would.'

Satisfied Mason could deal with the administrator on his own, Jenna turned just as Chief Crown Prosecutor Adrian Hall stepped through the glass front door of the police station.

Her heart slammed against her ribcage and then floundered around. It had only been a couple of months since she'd last seen him in the flesh. She'd almost forgotten how good-looking he was. The instant pull of attraction she had every intention of ignoring.

His bright, wide smile crinkled his cheeks into deep laughter lines and his eyes warmed to melted toffee.

'Jenna.' The mellow whisky of his voice poured over her as he reached out both hands to encompass her free one. 'It's been too long.'

Unable to escape, Jenna kept her fingers soft in his, neither returning the handshake nor withdrawing from it, as though he meant nothing to her. Which he didn't. Couldn't. She didn't play around with married men.

She swallowed hard, kept her gaze flat, determined, unwavering as she met his. Keenly aware that she needed to keep her attraction to him to herself. 'Adrian. It has been a while. I thought you were in London.'

'I am. I was, but I was needed here. If I'd known you were on duty, I would have brought coffee.' His voice dropped to intimate. 'You didn't reply to my last text.'

Heat flooded her cheeks, guilt sweeping over her. She'd not replied to it after Mason caught her red-handed.

Aware of Mason bumping up beside her, Jenna slipped her fingers from Adrian's.

The two men exchanged firm handshakes as Jenna took a moment to compose herself.

Mason leaned in. 'To what do we owe the honour?'

Adrian's dark brows dipped over a flash of confusion before he turned his attention to Mason. 'I've a meeting with your Chief Superintendent Gregg about the Frank Bartwell case. I'm surprised he hasn't mentioned it.'

Jenna jiggled her shoulders, she'd spoken with Gregg about the case recently, tied up a few loose ends and submitted all her paperwork. She hadn't quite expected the Chief Crown Prosecutor to pitch up on the doorstep of Malinsgate police station. 'I guess unless he needs us specifically to answer questions, he has all the files.' She looked past him through the door into the dense white fog, desperate to escape. Her pulse skipping over the resolve to keep him at a distance. 'Guess we better go.' She dredged up a fast smile and slipped around him to open the door and step outside. 'See you around.' She drew in a deep breath of fresh air as she strode over the short bridge and into the car park beyond.

Mason bustled into the passenger seat of the vehicle as she punched the ignition and slammed her foot on the accelerator. She whipped the seat belt around her and secured it with a positive click.

'Everything okay?' Mason asked.

Jenna checked the mirror, flung a glance over her shoulder and skewed the police vehicle out of the parking space, bouncing it over the speed ramp so Mason grunted. Which reminded her, she needed to follow up on who'd taken to parking the car in the bays the wrong way around. When she got chance.

'Yeah, sure.'

She pulled out onto the main thoroughfare around Telford town centre, jaw tight as she floored the accelerator straight up to the speed limit, flinging the car around the wide right hand bend and zipping it along the straight.

Aware of Mason's intense stare, she kept her eyes on the road. 'You were a little short with the Chief Crown Prosecutor. I know he's a wanker,' he tempted a smile from her, 'but there was definitely a cold-shoulder moment.'

Jenna's mobile beeped. She spared it a quick glance and then looked back at the road as she negotiated around the interchange and took the Queensway towards Oakengates and Ketley, putting her foot down so Mason jerked back in his seat. It had damn all to do with Mason if she met up with Adrian for a coffee. Damn all to do with anyone.

Mason shuffled around and leaned closer so she could see him in her peripheral vision while she drove. 'Did the married man make a pass at you?'

'No.' Too quick to answer, a ball of heat rushed up her neck into her face.

'So, he didn't make a pass at you?' He gave a childish nudge of her shoulder as she indicated to come off the dual carriageway. 'Did you want him to make a pass at you?'

'Certainly not.' Again, too quick to answer, Jenna's cheeks scalded as she hit the Greyhound Island and took the first sharp turn up the hill into Ketley Bank avenues where she pulled over. Leaving the car in gear, before she switched off the engine, she notched up the handbrake a little harder than normal so the car didn't roll back down the steep incline.

Jenna leaned over and plucked her handbag from the passenger footwell where she'd tucked it beside Mason's feet. With a quick glance in the rear view mirror she checked her face, smoothing the fine lines under eyes swimming with regret, then ran a swift hand through her hair.

With a low grunt, Mason grabbed the file and gave it a quick scan.

'Bob Mills.' He peered out of the window through the thin wisps of fog layering the street. 'Yeah, this is the right address.'

Jenna cruised her gaze over the three bedroom rabbit hutch of a house with its neat patch of Astroturf grass and one foot white plastic edging fence available from Home Bargains, a pound for five lengths. It must have cost at least three quid.

The chime on her phone sounded again just as she picked it up from the console. She tilted the screen away from Mason. One dark eyebrow lifted at her and her stomach lurched as she glanced at the name on the screen. She slipped her phone into her pocket and locked away her thoughts. She'd deal with Adrian later. Much later. Possibly never.

She stepped from the car, shutting the door with less ferocity than when she got in, and flicked the lock on, checking the doors just in case. They'd be lucky if the wheels were still intact when they got back if the neighbours got wind of a police car in the vicinity.

They took precisely four steps along the pathway up to the front door. Mason rapped his knuckles against the wood and stood back for Jenna to take the lead.

Silver eyes turned to ice as the man who opened the door grazed his gaze over the pair of them. Jenna took a step back as she reached for her ID, having already learned the hard way not to get her face too close to a cornered man.

She tipped her lips in a friendly smile, already alerted to his defensiveness by the way he shot his hip forward and leaned against the doorway, effectively barring their way.

'Mr Mills?'

'Yeah.' Aggression pulsed from him.

'Hi. I'm Detective Sergeant Jenna Morgan and this is Detective Constable Mason Ellis.'

'And?'

She kept her smile in place. 'Would it be okay to come inside, Mr Mills?'

'Why? I'm a busy man.'

Pushed to the point of arresting him without the required initial questions, Jenna made one last-ditch attempt at niceties. 'We've had some information regarding the Mervyn Lucas Charity that we hope you may be able to help with.'

His lips pursed.

'You are the treasurer, aren't you?'

'I am.' He nodded, his mouth turned down at the edges, but he stepped back, extending his arm in an invitation for her to enter. 'If you wouldn't mind taking your shoes off.'

Relief flooded her. Half the battle was to get in the front door. She kept her smile benign and slipped her shoes off, leaving them on the brand-new hallway carpet. It was only polite to do as he asked. Doubtful that he would strike out, her muscles tensed nonetheless in readiness as she slipped past him through the close confines of the hallway.

'Where would you like us?'

'Outside, but, failing that, the door on the left.'

Mason stepped between them, his hulking presence dominating the small space to give her the safety net she required.

Jenna walked through into a small living room with a round, extendable dining table and four chairs on the right and an 'L'-shaped floral patterned sofa on the left. All brand new. She curled her toes into the plush pile of the carpet, inhaling the scent of new wool. No synthetic polymers in this house.

'Bob?' The soft tones of a woman's voice sounded. Jenna turned as a petite blonde woman came into the living room, her face wreathed with concern.

'It's okay, Julie. The police are here to chat about something at work. It's nothing for you to concern yourself about.'

'I don't understand. What have you done, Bob?'

'Julie.' Steel edged Bob's voice. 'I've done nothing. The police are only asking for my help.' Face frozen in hard lines, he turned to Jenna. 'Isn't that right?'

With a search warrant in her file, it was difficult to agree with the man, but Jenna forced a smile and chose neutral. 'Mr Mills is helping us with our enquiries.'

Thin, plucked eyebrows raised to wrinkle the woman's forehead. Her lips pursed as she took in both Jenna and Mason. 'I'll stay, if you have no objection.'

Bob's lips quivered for a brief moment before they settled into a straight line as his wife perched on the edge of an armchair and folded her hands in her lap, gazing around at the other three expectantly while she waited for the story to unfold.

As they took their seats, Jenna glanced around at the other items of expense dotted around the room but kept her thoughts to herself. 'Mr Mills' – there was no way, it appeared, he was about to invite her to call him by his first name – 'we have been alerted to a few anomalies at the charity you work for.'

'Oh, Bob.' Mrs Mills touched her fingers to her mouth as she sighed out her husband's name.

Bob sniffed, linked his hands loosely and settled back in his chair, remaining silent, his steely eyes never flickered, and Jenna knew in that moment that the man was guilty of the crime. She just needed to prove it.

'Can you tell me how long you've worked for the organisation?'

He poked out his bottom lip and rolled it over the top one. 'Probably two and a half years.'

'Mmm-hmm.' Jenna opened the file and stared blind at the information in front of her. She didn't need to see it, it was already etched in her mind, it simply gave her control and time. 'And you are responsible for the accounts?' She glanced up, met his gaze.

'I am.'

'Good. And with regard to the money, donations and so on, can you tell me who handles this? Is it direct into the account, cash, cheque?'

He shrugged. 'All of those.'

'Right. And what do you do when you receive cash?'

He linked his fingers together. 'I write a receipt. Give it to the person who makes the donation.'

'Good. Is it possible to see these receipts? Where do you keep them?'

'I scan them onto the laptop.' As he twisted his fingers, the knuckles turned white. 'Enter them into the accounts.'

'Okay. Can I take a look?'

He ducked his head and blew out a breath as he squeezed his fingers even tighter into each other. 'I don't think so.'

'Is there any reason why you wouldn't want me to look at the receipts?' she glanced back down at her notes, the three receipts for cash which had been produced from donors. Close friends of the president of the association, they'd raised concerns that the full amounts hadn't been declared once they'd queried their tax relief in preparation of their accounts. These were only three of possibly dozens.

'It's none of your business.'

Jenna chuckled. 'Mr Mills, I think you'll find that fraud is our business.'

He jerked upright, offence written all over his face. 'There's no fraud. No one mentioned fraud.' He came to his feet while his wife stared up at him, eyes wide, mouth open. 'I think you should leave now. I want you out of my house.'

Jenna closed the file and smoothed her hand over it. 'Mr Mills, I believe we have enough evidence to arrest you and I have a warrant to search your premises and...' she pushed herself to her feet to look him in the eye, '... seize your company laptop and any other computers you have access to within the premises.' She slipped the warrant from the file and held it out to him.

He shook his head, taking a step backwards to bring the back of his knees up against the chair he'd just vacated. 'You'll find nothing on those computers, there's no evidence. I've taken nothing. Nothing at all.'

'Bob?' Mrs Mills voice cracked as she fluttered a delicate hand to her chest.

Mason rose slowly to his feet, tension pulsing from him. Jenna sent a subtle hand movement to keep calm. She had the situation under control. Things would be fine. The guy might be a major prick, but she was convinced he wasn't about to assault anyone. Fraud was one thing, assault another. She wasn't stupid enough to take her attention from him though.

'In that case, Mr Mills, you won't mind if we take a look.'

'You can't look unless I give you the password.' His tone turned belligerent.

'No, indeed.' Jenna sighed. 'But I can hand it over to our IT experts who will bypass your password and get into the accounts anyway. It would make it easier if you co-operate.'

'Nothing's going to make this easier for me and my wife. We've police officers in the front room.' He flung his arm outwards. 'A police car outside. For God's sake, what will the neighbours think?'

Willing to pacify him, Jenna stepped forward, her hand outstretched. 'It's an unmarked car. We could be anybody, Mr Mills, not necessarily the police.'

'You couldn't be anybody. It's bloody obvious who you are. In your suits. Fucking pigs.'

On high alert, Jenna jerked her chin up so Mason got the message. His cool blue eyes turned to ice as every sense in Jenna went flat and she gave Bob Mills her full attention. 'We're not here to entertain the neighbours, Mr Mills, we're here to conduct an investigation into serious allegations of fraud. Neighbourhood gossip is not my concern.' With no other alternative, Jenna looked Bob Mills in the eye. 'Robert Mills, I am arresting you on suspicion of—'

Mason took a step forward, his hand outstretched to take a hold of Bob Mill's arm. An ear-piercing shriek tore the air and a raging, screaming virago hurtled into Jenna, Julie Mill's slight weight enough to make Jenna stagger sideways. Jenna whipped her head around to meet the venom in the other woman's eyes as her clawed hands reached for Jenna's hair. Julie yanked and tore at Jenna's tender scalp. Pain screamed through her and burst from Jenna's lungs.

'You fucking bitch!'

Julie's long nails grazed barely an inch from Jenna's face. Pure instinct and reflexes kicked in and Jenna snaked her hands around the other woman's wrists. She squeezed until Julie's angry scream turned into a pained yowl.

Jenna twisted one arm behind Julie's back and put the woman on the floor, face into the new shagpile. 'Julie Mills,' she spat out, 'I'm arresting you for assaulting a police officer.'

Before she could complete her recitation of the Miranda act, Julie shrieked, 'He did it for me. He did it for me.' Eyes crazed, Julie bared her teeth, with no sign of remorse.

Not affording her any benefit of the doubt, Jenna whipped out her restraints and put them on her assailant, reciting the rest of the Miranda act without stopping.

Her breath heaved in until her lungs burnt. She hauled the slight woman to her feet. 'I don't care who the fuck controlled who. You're both under arrest.'

Bob stood defeated, eyes dull as he looked at his wife with something bordering on revulsion. 'She's right. I did it for her.' His lips rolled in on themselves. 'Nothing is ever enough for her. She wanted it all. A better house, a new kitchen, a bigger bathroom, a holiday. She was never satisfied.' He stared at his wife. 'Nothing was ever enough. I was never enough.' He shook his head in defeat before he spoke to Jenna. 'You'll find all the evidence on the computer. I'll give you the password, show you where it all is. I accepted cash donations, gave a receipt for the full amount, but changed the receipt before I uploaded it onto the computer and took the difference. It wasn't difficult. I didn't think anyone would notice. They have so much money, why would they check their tax situation?' He ended on a small sob. 'Twenty-four thousand pounds doesn't go a long way towards what she wanted. There would always have been more.'

Cold from the inside out, Jenna met his pathetic gaze. 'Twenty-four thousand pounds would have gone a long way to helping a child with leukaemia, Mr Mills. Possibly even saved lives, and that's what you've deprived someone of.' She waved her hand, encompassing the whole room. 'For this. To keep your wife happy.'

She unclipped the radio from her belt and called for assistance as she considered it may be better to separate the two of them in case Julie decided to kill her weak husband before they arrived at the station.

It didn't take long for two patrols to arrive as they'd both been in the area.

Jenna closed the car door on Bob Mills as her backup took him to Malinsgate. She glanced at her watch, relieved it was almost time to go home. She'd give Bob Mills time overnight before she questioned him again. His harridan of a wife already despatched.

She slipped into the driver's seat of her own vehicle and massaged the back of her neck. 'Tell me, Mason, why is it I'm always the one to get attacked?'

Mason's lips twitched up. 'Fuck knows. But I'm the good-looking one and you've got a face that obviously deserves to be smacked.'

He elicited a reluctant smile from her. While she waited for the car heater to warm up, Jenna scrolled through the texts on her phone. One from Fliss. Jenna grinned. As if Fliss needed to remind her they were out tonight. A date. With a Sainsbury's shared trolley and the nightmare of food shopping with her sister.

She glanced sideways at her partner. Had Mason asked Fliss out on a date? He hadn't mentioned it, but then again, she'd told him in no uncertain terms she didn't want details. He'd let her know in his own sweet time. It wasn't for her to push.

She tapped onto the messages from Adrian.

Good to see you today.

Did I do something wrong?

What about that coffee? I'd like to talk again but I'm only here until tomorrow evening, then I have to get back to London.

They'd had a moment, just a brief flicker of attraction, and if he'd not been married, that flicker could have flared into an inferno, but Jenna squelched any further thought of the very attractive Chief Crown Prosecutor. Avoidance was probably her best form of protection.

She closed the app, slid the car into gear and headed back to the station.

24

Disappointed, Ryan checked the time on his phone, saw there were no messages and sipped at his flat white while he gazed out of the coffee-shop window. He'd not been able to convince himself to try another caramel latte since he'd thrown it up in a wave of humiliation. The mere thought of all that sweetness curdled his stomach in an oily glut and the vision of the slaughtered girl flashed into his mind.

With a deliberate turn of his head to disperse the image, he watched an old lady struggle with the heavy door, a slight wince passing over her features as it knocked her shoulder. He lurched to his feet, but by the time he'd crossed the room to help, she was through and he stood for a moment, lost.

He'd almost cancelled the coffee date himself, his heart not quite in it after Marcia had been killed. But he hadn't known her. There was no connection apart from one encounter with her. Jenna was right. He needed to move on. It wasn't his fault. Pure coincidence. That was all. And if he was truthful with himself, he'd have never pursued another date with her. Visually, she may have been his type, but nothing else fit.

It didn't really matter how hard he tried, he couldn't shake the memory from his mind. Poor woman. Slaughtered. Literally like a pig. Throat slit.

The *Shropshire Star*'s freelance journalist, Kim Stafford, hadn't hesitated to throw the ex-boyfriend, Ray, to the wolves in the first instance. They had no idea where he got his information, but he appeared to be back-pedalling and hinting at something more sinister.

Ryan tipped his head back to rest it against the seat and the image of Marcia flashed in his mind.

Heat travelled up his neck and he tugged at the hoodie he wore to let some air in. A quick change of direction was what his mind needed. He glanced at his phone to check the time.

Carla wasn't coming. He'd been stood up. They were supposed to meet at 11.00 a.m. He'd even managed to change his shift to accommodate her day off, otherwise it would have been another four days before they'd be able to meet up. He'd put himself out and now he had to work Saturday night instead of going for a drink with the lads. It rankled.

If she couldn't find a second to drop him a quick text, then maybe she wasn't the right one for him anyway. It wasn't as though she was the only woman he'd arranged to date.

He'd set himself a goal. Two coffee or drink dates a week for the next three weeks. Six nurses. He was bound to click with one of them. If not, it was back to the drawing board. He was sick of the pokes and jibes the others made about him being too young to shave, too sweet to date. He wasn't sweet.

He slipped his fingers over his smooth cheeks, rubbed his whisker-free chin. He couldn't help it if he had a baby face. His dad said it had taken him until he was thirty before he needed to shave on a daily basis. Christ! Why couldn't he be like Mason? The guy always had that cool, five o'clock shadow going on. By the time a twelve hour shift was finished, you could grate cheese on his face. Not that Mason appeared to have any more success in dating than him.

At least Ryan was making an effort.

The young nurses didn't appear to have a problem with him. He'd had a pretty high success rate online. Carla was only the second one he'd asked out, and the second one to accept. Most would consider it a 100 per cent strike rate. A success.

If he could count one dead and being stood up by another any kind of success.

Ryan glanced out of the window at the virtually empty street except for the suited man who thought he could leave his car on double-yellow lines. The traffic warden would soon disillusion him of that notion. They were pretty fast in this neighbourhood.

With a reluctant smile, Ryan slipped back into his seat and picked up his coffee. The hot liquid scalded his tongue and he clipped the cup back on the saucer while he watched out of the window again. He'd give her to the end of his drink and then he'd go. He glanced at his phone, resisted the temptation to send her a quick reminder. Maybe she'd forgotten. Maybe she'd been delayed. Ryan sighed as he cast a sideways glance at the offering of cakes. If she came, he'd have another coffee and a slice of the coffee cake. If she came.

It seemed a shame. He'd been quite hopeful about Carla. They'd got on so well online. She'd seemed funny. From her profile picture, she was exactly what he wanted. Dark auburn hair, and lots of it. The pure, milky skin of a redhead with a smattering of freckles. And eyes. Big, tawny eyes. Physically fit, fitter than him. She was training to run the London Marathon. Their conversations had been... engaging.

He glanced down the street in the vain hope she might be running along it towards him.

Empty.

Perhaps he should get fit, build some muscle. He clenched his hands together, so his muscles bunched in his upper arms and flexed his chest out. He huffed out a breath and deflated, sank back into the small velour bucket seat, his arms a protective wrap around his skinny chest. Weightlifting might be a better option, lending his profile a little more honesty.

Honesty. It didn't particularly bother him. As he'd said to Jenna, everyone lies on dating apps, everyone knew they did. It was accepted, understood.

Initially, he'd been a little blasé about the whole idea and not taken much care with the profile until he saw how many matches he needed to trawl through to find someone who appealed. Then he'd narrowed his search. He liked gingers, always had. They held such appeal, he had a particular soft spot for Emma Stone. He'd fed that into the app and then thought what the hell, I'll drop in the description of my dream woman. Turned out his dream woman wasn't so easy to come by. Six in all within the area he'd defined. He either needed to widen the area or change the profile. It wouldn't necessarily be his dream woman any more, but whoever got that in life anyway?

He glanced at his phone. He could text her, ask her where she was, but he didn't want to be pushy. It was her turn to text.

He drained his cup and sat a while longer. It was clear she wasn't coming. He'd have to start again. He hadn't even factored the other girls in yet, he only wanted to chat to two at a time maximum. It would be crass to mix them up.

The messenger on his phone pinged and he tilted the screen so he could see and shot upright in his chair. It was her. Carla.

He swiped the screen, so the full message opened.

Hi Ryan, I'm really sorry. I've had a family emergency and gone home for a couple of days. I'm back on shift later in the week, but perhaps we can rearrange for another day? I understand if you don't want to.

He stood, picked up his cup and saucer and slipped it onto the counter before he left the coffee shop. A gentle flush of excitement trickled through him. He may have been stood up, but she had a reason, an excuse. An apology.

He tapped his thumb on the screen. Hesitated.

He wouldn't reply straight away. There was no rush. He'd play it cool. There may have been a family emergency, or she'd just forgotten about their date. It was hardly a date. Just a coffee.

He brushed aside his doubts and made his way to his car. He'd head back home for a while, kill a couple of hours with his mum while he waited to go back on shift. Then he'd reply. He glanced at the message still on the display of his phone. He didn't want to appear too keen.

He typed:

Let me know when you get back

He hit send.

25

Food shopping with Fliss was a damned nightmare and a Saturday evening couldn't be worse. Why the hell they didn't get it delivered, she'd never know. Perhaps it required for one of them to be organised, or just have five minutes to think the process through.

Jenna reached into the trolley and slipped the huge packet of crisps back onto the shelf.

'I saw that!'

Jenna turned cold eyes on her sister. 'We don't need them.'

'But I like crisps.' The whine in Fliss's voice just made Jenna grind her teeth. She wasn't about to win this one.

With a tut, she turned, swept up a small multi-pack of crisps and flung them into the trolley. 'There, that's all we need.'

As another pack landed swiftly on top of the first, Fliss grinned at her. 'Special offer, buy one, get one half price.'

Jenna blew out a disgusted breath and stared at the mishmash of crap in the trolley. 'There's not a single meal here, Fliss.'

Fliss leaned in to ferret in the bottom of the trolley. Triumphant, she swiped out a packet and wafted it under Jenna's nose. 'Breakfast. See.'

'Oh, God.' Jenna snatched the packet back and threw it in the trolley. 'Breakfast is not pain au chocolat every day, Fliss.' The girl was impossible. If it was left to her, they'd live on sugar and be diabetics in no time. She scooped six small boxes out of the trolley with the intention of landing them back on the shelf where Fliss had just obtained them.

'Uh, uh, no.' Fliss took them from her hands and placed them back in the trolley. 'Three for two.'

'It's still a stupid price to pay for a disposable cup of coffee.'

'The whole lot of these are less than you pay for one.'

'Rubbish.'

Fliss shot her a sly look. 'How much did you pay Ryan to get you a coffee the other day?'

Busted. 'How do you know?'

'Mason told me.'

'Mason?' Bastard. He'd not given any hint of contacting her sister. Perhaps he'd made his move after all. 'When?'

'He texted me.'

Jenna pushed the trolley around the end of the aisle and kept her voice casual. 'You're texting with Mason?'

'It was only to let me know about your coffee. He thought I'd find it funny as I was the one responsible for your hangover apparently.'

Fliss turned away to swipe a box of Lucky Charms off the shelf. Jenna pulled it from her hands and put it back as she ran an assessing gaze over her sister. Interesting, that rosy flush that crept up Fliss's neck when Mason's name was mentioned. Cautious, Jenna turned away to pick up a box of porridge oats. She dropped them in the trolley and moved on. Mason's approach was no business of hers. However he wanted to go about it, it appeared her sister may be receptive to his decided lack of charm.

Jenna swept along the next aisle, only pausing to snatch up a bottle of mineral water, frightened to linger in case Fliss filled the trolley with sugar filled drinks. She turned at the end of the aisle, leaving Fliss to study the next special offer on the shelf and pulled up sharp as she almost rammed into a man, bent at the waist, studying the special offer rack.

As he raised his head and his gaze met hers, a lazy smile curved his lips and a surprised thrill shot through her veins.

'Hello.' The warmth in Denton Harper's cobalt eyes proved irresistible and Jenna found herself smiling back. Distracted the last time they'd met, she'd not really appreciated how very attractive the man was, with his mop of blond hair in an unruly flop against his forehead. The jeans and casual grey jacket suited him as much as the smarter outfit he'd worn before.

Self-conscious of her own appearance, Jenna raised a hand and ran her fingers through her choppy brown hair she'd yet to have cut and pushed it back from her eyes. She let out a soft wince as her fingers grazed over the tender spot on her scalp where Julie Mills had yanked out her hair.

'Hi.'

Proud of her intelligent response, Jenna nodded, her fixed grin firmly in place.

Without seeming to notice, he pointed at her trolley with the packet of dried spaghetti he held in his hand. 'Big family? Looks like you're feeding the five thousand.'

Embarrassed, Jenna glanced into the crap filled trolley and grimaced. 'No, just a sugar addicted sister, I'm afraid.'

'Ah.' His lips curved upwards, and a small dimple winked into his clean shaven cheek. 'No family, then?' One eyebrow flicked up and sent a flutter through her chest. Jenna leaned her forearms on the trolley and flashed him a smile. He was asking if she was married.

'No. Just Fliss.'

'That's me.' Her sister bumped her shoulder, making Jenna snap upright again as Fliss stepped past her and held out her hand. 'And you are?'

Without a suggestion of surprise, Harper transferred the spaghetti into his left hand, reached out and grasped her sister's hand. His smile widened to show perfect white teeth. He made the contact with Fliss brief and flicked Jenna another glance before he replied. 'Denton Harper. I met your sister the other day. Through work.'

'Oh, okay.' Fliss tilted her head to one side as though she waited for him to expand his explanation.

Instead, Harper turned back to Jenna. 'Are you okay? I hope you weren't hurt.'

About to raise her hand to her hair again, Jenna dropped it to the trolley and gripped the handle to stop herself. She was no teenage girl with a crush, but she was ready to act like one.

'No. I'm fine. Thank you for asking.'

'No problem. It happened so fast, I didn't check how you were. I think we were all a bit shaken. I needed to be careful not to compromise my relationship with my patient.'

'I understand.' Aware of Fliss's close observation, Jenna dropped her voice and glanced down into the trolley, raising her gaze again to meet his. 'You were very professional.'

Harper nodded, his lips flattening out. 'It's not always that way. Anyway...' he waggled the packet of spaghetti, 'this is all I needed.'

As he turned to leave, curiosity got the better of her and Jenna halted him. 'Denton, how come you're here?'

Confusion flitted over his handsome features. 'Here?'

'Don't you live near Long Lartin, in Worcester?'

His face cleared. 'Ah. No. I live in Telford. I commute. Just down the road from here in fact. Long Lartin isn't the only prison I work in. I'm assigned to three of them altogether.'

'Ah, I see.' With nothing further to say, Jenna stood in awkward silence and waited for him to depart.

He swivelled on his heel, then back again, narrowing his eyes as he stared at her. 'Do you fancy grabbing a drink sometime?'

Jenna's heart knocked while heat raced up her neck into her face. She'd be a fool not to take him up on his offer, but still. 'I...'

Aware of Fliss's subtle move away to disappear around the corner into the next aisle and give them privacy, she still hesitated.

'I'm sorry,' he angled his head. 'Are you seeing someone?'

Words fell over themselves as her tongue refused to co-operate with her brain. 'Well, I kind of... sort of...' A vision of Adrian flashed through her mind as she admitted to herself that he was the sole reason she hadn't dated. She needed to move on. Tell Denton Harper she wasn't seeing anyone. She'd love a cup of coffee. Instead, what came out of her mouth was unplanned. 'It's complicated.' She stumbled to a halt.

Regret shadowed Harper's eyes before he jiggled his shoulders as he dug into his pocket and pulled out his phone. 'I'll tell you what. I'll give you my telephone number and if you manage to uncomplicate matters, give me a ring...'

The charm of him coaxed a smile from her and she found herself reaching into her handbag to dig out her phone, watching as the fine flop of his hair fell over his forehead when he dipped his head to read out his number. She'd be an idiot not to ring him.

He raised his head and met her gaze. 'Are you going to let me have your number too? So, I can check if you've sorted out your... complication?' He tilted his head to one side and his eyes crinkled at the edges.

Without another thought, Jenna tapped the dial on her phone and let it ring out to his.

With a flash of a smile, Harper jiggled his phone. 'I've got you now.'

A tremor of excitement rushed her veins and set the heat in her cheeks to burn as he moved off.

As Jenna rounded the end of the aisle, Fliss melted against the special offers shelving unit, her hand held to her chest. 'Where the hell did you meet him? He's fricking hot.'

As blood rushed in her ears, Jenna blew out a breath. 'He is rather.' She lowered her voice. 'I met him at Long Lartin prison the other day.'

Fliss's jaw dropped open and she gave a quick glance up and down the virtually empty aisle before she lowered her own voice. 'Is he a criminal?'

'No. He's a prison counsellor.' She pushed her hair back from her face.

'What did you say when he asked you out?'

'I didn't commit.'

'Are you mad?' Fliss's harsh whisper battered her. 'Why the hell not?'

'Because...'

With a disgusted snort, Fliss pushed away from the shelves and grabbed the trolley from Jenna, driving it down the aisle so Jenna had to trot to keep up. 'So, you're still holding out for the gorgeous Chief Prosecutor.'

They'd had the conversation before.

'It's...'

'Complicated.'

'Yes.'

'I don't understand. How can it be complicated? He likes you, you like him. Date him. Jump his bones, see if he's any good in bed. If he's not, dump him and move on.'

Her sister made it sound so straightforward, uncomplicated. Unemotional.

'It's not that easy, Fliss. He's married'.

'Obviously not happily.'

Frustrated, she put on a spurt to keep up and snatched the trolley from Fliss before she managed to mow some poor pensioner down.

'I wouldn't know. He's not made a pass, asked me out, indicated that he wanted anything more than the professional relationship we shared. But I really like him. His looks, his intelligence, his whole demeanour and, quite frankly, if I hadn't been worried sick over you, I would have paid far more attention. As it was, I simply overheard him tell Donna that he was married. End of story. He probably hasn't a clue that there was even a smidge of attraction.' The little white lie didn't make her feel any better. Of course he was aware. Why else would he have texted her? Why the confused expression when she'd been cold towards him? 'It's probably all in my head.'

Fliss grinned and waggled her perfectly arched eyebrows. 'In the meantime, you have the hot guy's telephone number.'

Jenna checked her phone with Denton Harper's name. He may be just the right distraction from Adrian, but she didn't necessarily have to confide in her sister at this stage. She needed thinking time and Fliss was more likely to force her down a path she wasn't necessarily ready to follow. 'It doesn't make any difference, I'm not going to ring him.'

'Well, you're an idiot. I would, if I were you.'

Without a thought of Mason, Jenna looked at her sister. 'You ring him, then.'

'You've got to be kidding me. The way he looked at you? He's not going to settle for second-best sister.'

Offended on her own sister's behalf, Jenna protested, 'You're not second best.'

'In his eyes I would be.' Fliss flicked her long blonde hair over her shoulder and reached for a dual pack of Danishes, sweeping it into the trolley alongside all the other unhealthy meal choices. How she'd managed to conjure up beef stew was beyond Jenna, but it appeared to have been a one-off if the current trolley status was anything to judge. 'Besides, I have more pride than to take on your leftovers.' She smiled and threw a loaf of thick-cut white bread into the trolley. 'But if you start to date him, I can't guarantee I'll be able to keep my eyes off him.'

Jenna whipped the loaf of white bread out and replaced it with wholemeal.

'As long as it's only your eyes.'

Fliss chortled and slammed in a packet of pancakes, followed by a jar of maple syrup. 'Not that I complain about the look of the handsome Adrian. He does have his appeal too. Especially those shoulders. The width of them.' She gave a delicate shudder so Jenna could only shake her head. 'I can understand why you're hard-pushed. The choice you have. The good-looking and highly respectable Adrian, or the sexy, hot as hell, down and dirty – because I do believe he's fully capable of down and dirty, the way he looked at you, I'm surprised he didn't singe your skin – counsellor.'

Reluctant to admit he had, Jenna turned away and selected a bottle of Nero d'Avolo from the shelf and placed it in the trolley and simply sighed as Fliss reached for another. She cast her gaze around and tried to ignore the two elderly ladies who made no bones about listening into their conversation. She needed something healthy, or she'd shrivel away trying to avoid all the carbs and sugars Fliss had selected. They needed to return to the fruit and veg aisles.

As she pushed her phone into her back pocket, it buzzed to signal the arrival of a text.

She hauled it back out and glanced at the screen.

Jenna, give me a ring when you've sorted out your… complication. No strings. Coffee would be good.

Before Fliss noticed, Jenna flicked the screen off and shoved the phone into her pocket again. Perhaps she'd made a mistake allowing him to have her number. It wasn't fair to let him think she was available, even if she was. She needed to redirect her thoughts away from Adrian and free up her hormones so they could trot after someone else.

26

Where the fuck was she? Just where the fuck?

Shrouded in dark, he slipped in through the back window of Carla's house, the old, loose frame not so difficult to prise open. Each time he entered, it was a risk, but he needed to check what he already assumed was true.

She'd gone.

Bolted.

Anger seethed beneath the surface as he peered into each empty room, clinging onto the wild explosion of anger which threatened to destroy his iron control.

On silent feet, he sneaked upstairs to check, panning the light from his torch around the darkened hall and into the bedroom.

She'd taken the fucking cat. If she hadn't, he'd have slit its fucking neck, skinned it and left it hanging from the false oak beam in her living room to teach her a lesson, a small one before the ultimate one.

He clenched his teeth so hard, his jaw popped.

She'd gone.

Fury leapt out to put a stranglehold on his throat. Desperate to release the wild howl, he flung back his head and let it burst out in a torrent of frustration.

'Carla,' he yowled.

Louder.

Veins, muscles, sinew all stretched to snapping point.

'Carla!'

He bolted down the stairs and burst into the kitchen. No longer in control, he slammed on the light, oblivious to whether anyone could see the glimmer of it through the blind he quickly yanked down. He didn't care. She'd ruined the plans he had for her.

His wild gaze skimmed around for something to break, anything to throw, smash, destroy. He snatched the small bone-china coffee mug she'd used that morning and placed upside down on the drainer. The one she used for her precious fucking espresso coffee.

He flung it with all his might, satisfaction warming his chest as it exploded up the wall, tiny golden fragments of china shattering over the floor.

A small sense of gratification curled in his belly, but it wasn't enough.

He pulled his lips back in a snarl and whipped his head around in search of something else. Something to rip apart.

Carla had OCD and never left anything out on the surfaces, except the espresso machine. He snatched it up and yanked the plug from the socket, lifted it to shoulder height and then froze.

His breath soughed in and out to burn his lungs. His flesh tingled. The pain in his right eye stabbed through from his brain and his arms went numb as the migraine hit.

He crumpled to the floor, electrical circuits frying in his brain, and every thought process melted away. He loosened his grip on the espresso machine and pushed it away as he sank his head onto his knees and waited. There was nothing else he could do but wait. His speech, if he tried it, would be slurred.

Lights flashed behind his eyelids and pins and needles stabbed at his hands. He'd make her pay. It was all her fault. She'd put him under too much pressure. He'd failed.

He kept his eyes closed, let out a hum to comfort himself as the gentle vibration rolled through his throat. A few more minutes, that's all it would take and the ocular migraine would lift.

With a pained groan, he slid over onto his side and tucked himself into a tight foetal position, oblivious to the passage of time.

The iciness of the tiles soaked through his clothes and skin, seeping through to stiffen his joints and make it impossible for him to slip into a recuperating sleep.

He drew in a breath and raised his head. The bright sparks of light had moved to his peripheral vision and he squinted through the darkened tunnel.

The need to move, leave the house, sneaked past the fog into his brain. It was obvious she wasn't coming back anytime soon, and he had a schedule to keep. He blinked his vision clear and stared at his knees, so close to his face.

Nausea rose in his throat as he unfurled, muscles cricking in protest at each slow movement. Pain wracked his head, so he had no option but to hold it in his hands while he gathered himself for the next move.

Exhaustion nipped at him, but he pushed against the wall and staggered to his feet, picking up the espresso machine from the floor. Through his brightened vision, he stared at his hands. DNA. What had he learned? Don't leave your fucking DNA all over the place.

He fished in his back pocket to pull out a pair of medical gloves. The pair he'd meant to snap on just before he murdered her. He wriggled his fingers into them and opened the cupboard under the sink to pull out her bleach and a cloth.

The shards of her favourite mug scattered over the kitchen floor made his face ache while he swept them up, trying not to dip his head as each movement thunked his brain against the inside of his skull. He poured them into the sink and washed each piece with the bleach, then dumped them in her virtually empty bin, except for two used sachets of cat food.

She must have taken off straight after she got home from her run. He'd pushed her too hard.

Anger boiled just below the surface, but he had a grip on it this time. His thought process wasn't fully up and running, but it was clear enough for him to step his way through the treacly mess he'd created.

He wiped the tiny particles of glittering gold from the wall, stepped back to check his work, then sterilised every surface in the kitchen, whether he thought he'd touched them or not.

By the time he'd cleaned the entire room, control slipped back into place. He'd made a mistake. He should have withdrawn instead of being cocky. He thought he'd pushed her to the edge, but he hadn't, he'd pushed her over it.

He flicked on his small torch and made his way up the stairs, cleansing every surface he'd touched – the bannister, doorknobs, doors.

It wouldn't happen again. Control was the key. He knew that now. Control of her, control of him.

He made his way back downstairs to the kitchen, placed his hands on his hips and ducked his head as his mind, still sparking, focused.

If he was to stick to his schedule, he needed to move on. It grated on his nerves to leave her behind when his heart had been set on her, but he had no choice. She'd return at some point, but it was time to look further afield. That's why he had developed back-up plans with additional women scheduled in.

He dragged his thoughts back into line and scanned the room with a keen gaze. It was done. He dumped the cloth in the bin, lifted out the liner, replaced it with a clean one and let himself out the back door, turning the key before he pocketed it and slipped down the darkened alley next to Carla's house.

Six houses down, he opened their red-topped bin, threw in the rubbish bag he'd brought and kept his gloves on until he reached the car he'd parked further down the street where it wouldn't be noticed amongst all the others.

27

They made it so easy.

He wriggled his fingers into his gloves and lifted the key he'd found suspended from a nail in her garden shed and let himself into the little semi-detached house at the end of the cul-de-sac. Covered by a waterproof coat, she'd thought it was safe to leave the key there, but when your trade was breaking and entering, it didn't take rocket science to figure out where to look for the emergency key. The one you left for your neighbour to call to water your plants, feed your cat, check your mail.

Have an extra key cut. Give it to the fucking neighbour. If you can trust them to come into your house while you're away, you can trust them all the time.

He dropped his backpack with all the kit he needed on the floor and scanned the small kitchen, curled his lip as he checked out the sink filled with greasy, cold water and dishes. Dirty bitch. It didn't matter how long their hours were, they could make time just to rinse a few fucking bowls.

He yanked the chain attached to the plug and watched the water drain away. It would be good to study her face when she realised someone had been in and cleaned up after her. He'd install the small camera he'd brought in his backpack above the kitchen window blind, like he had with the one in her bedroom before he got disturbed. He'd link it to his phone so he could take his time and observe her.

His blood heated at the thought of her long, naked legs as she padded around her house with next to nothing on.

He stared up at the window blind above the small, square window at the front of the house. It overlooked nothing but the pathway up to the attached house next door providing the privacy he needed to complete his task. Middle of the day was often the best time in a modern, secluded neighbourhood where the neighbours were all professionals who would be at work. From mid-afternoon onwards, when they all arrived home with their kids, there wasn't a chance in hell he'd be there. The risk was too high.

Satisfied with his plan, he pulled out the small white camera and checked the setting. It was good to go. At full stretch, he reached out, but without positioning the camera slightly behind the blind, it would be on full display. It had to be inconspicuous. Espionage. He'd have made a good spy.

He grunted as he leaned further across the sink, overextending to place the camera too far forward. His lungs burned as he held his breath and poked it with the tip of his fingers. It gave a precarious wobble and toppled over the edge of the blind, held on only by its flimsy base.

Frustration roiled in his stomach. He drew the camera back down and stamped on his rising temper. It was fine. Everything would be fine. Control was all he needed. Control and a longer reach.

He raised his leg and hoisted himself onto the bench, made a quick job of fixing the camera so it peeped out from above the blind. Unless she was tall, very tall, she'd never see it from below.

As he lowered himself back on his haunches, his gaze clashed with the young woman's directly outside the kitchen window. His pulse spiked, the shock of it stole his breath, so he froze, unable to take his eyes from hers. Surprise lit her features as she stood, one hand halted halfway in greeting. She tilted her head to one side and her brows drew down.

Shit. Who the hell was she? It wasn't Julia.

She could see him. Identify him.

He scrambled off the bench and made for the front door, slipping his gloves from his hands so he wouldn't raise her suspicions before she could take off down the street or wherever the hell she'd come from.

Fuck it. And fuck nosey neighbours.

He threw open the front door, plastered a wide smile on his face as he tucked the gloves in his back pocket.

Fucking woman.

'Hi, I'm Derek.'

Her long blonde hair, flicked over one shoulder, shimmered in the afternoon sunlight. Petite and slender, she hesitated, her weight balanced forward ready to take flight.

Fuck it.

He stepped forward, holding his hands wide in a friendly gesture. 'Julia asked me to fix her blind.'

'Julia?'

Fucking hell. He cast his mind back. Had he got the wrong name? He couldn't have. If he did, he needed to brazen it out.

'Yeah, Julia. I'm Derek, her friend. Didn't she mention me?'

Her expression darkened. 'No.' The woman's jaw settled into a solid line. He took a step towards her and she took one back, wariness streaking across her face. 'Why would Julia mention you to me?'

Confusion rolled over him at the gritty challenge. 'I dunno...'

'I don't even like her. Why would she tell me anything? All she does is bitch about the volume of my TV and threaten to call the police if she finds dog shit on her lawn. She always blames my Alfie, poor little thing.' She never confirmed or denied whether Alfie was the culprit.

The tension drained from him and he bestowed her with another grin, this time more natural.

'I'm sorry you don't get on. I assumed when you saw me, you'd think I'd broken in. I've got a key.' He dipped his fingers into his pocket and jangled it in the air, taking the risk that she'd never been asked to call around to Julia's and recognised the spare key from the tiny shed at the side of the semi-detached house. 'I didn't want you calling the police.'

Visibly relaxed, she threw back her head and laughed, her throat a slender, white column. She wasn't the right copycat profile, but his hunger stirred. He preferred a blonde.

With sly delight, he moved closer to her. This time, she never moved back.

'I'm not too keen on Julia myself.' He shot her an engaging smile, he knew it worked on the ladies, he'd practised it in the mirror. 'She's a bit of a user.' He shrugged. 'But she's my sister's friend and she asked me for a favour. I was a bit stuck. I didn't want to upset my sister. She thinks Julia and I would make a good item.'

She shifted her weight from foot to foot before taking a step closer, a hesitant smile curving fine lips. 'I can imagine.'

He reached a hand towards her, palm up. 'I didn't catch your name.'

She laughed and stroked a stray lock of hair back from her cheek, her lively blue eyes flirting back at him. 'I didn't give it.' As though she'd made up her mind he was safe, she stepped forward and held out her hand. 'Karen, hi.'

'Hi.' He enclosed the coolness of her fingers in his hand and held on while he gazed down at her, treating her to his most engaging smile. 'I don't suppose you'd...?'

Her eyes lit with curiosity and a dark thrill warmed his veins.

Almost.

He'd almost got her.

Softly, softly, catchy monkey.

He made himself tuck his hands in his back pocket, shoving the key in deep. He took a step away from her, shooting a self-conscious glance over his shoulder. 'I don't suppose you have time to give me a hand for a minute?'

'Doing?' Sharp, the woman bore no naïveté. She'd evidently been around the block and lost a great deal of faith in human nature. They'd probably get along very well. If he allowed her to live. Which he couldn't afford to do now she'd seen him.

To keep her onside, he gestured to the front door he'd left wide open, controlling the excited tremor in his fingers. She needed to hurry. It was a quiet neighbourhood, but every second he stood outside with her, he ran the risk of someone else seeing him.

Without making it obvious, he cast his gaze around and shrugged. 'I dropped a screw down the back of the blind and I can't find any spares.' He wiggled his fingers at her, nudging aside the quick escalation in his heart rate as he sensed her compliance. 'My hands are too big to fish it out. Would you mind?'

Suspicion lurked in her eyes. 'Don't you have another screw?'

He snorted, injecting derision in his voice. 'They're Julia's screws. It's the last one.' He lowered his head in defeat. 'It doesn't really matter, it means I'll have to come back.' He peered at her from under his eyelashes and shot her a regretful smile.

She skimmed a hand over her curvy hip and then crossed her arms under her pert little bosom to draw the soft swell of them to his attention. 'What's it worth?'

Taken aback, his smile dropped from his face and he frowned at her. 'I'm sorry?'

Now she had the upper hand and stepped into his space. 'If I help you, because this is not for Julia, what's it worth?'

'Umm.' His mind blanked out. Dear God, did the crazy cow want him to pay her?

'Oh, come on, Derek.' Her lips curved up at the edges as she gave a flirtatious flick of her hair. 'Coffee, lunch... dinner? Get your act together.'

'Ah.' Back on track, he laughed. Greedy little bitch. Manipulative. She thought she had it all her own way. 'We can start with coffee.' He ran his tongue over his front teeth, leaned his head closer to hers. 'If that goes well, we could progress to dinner.'

She tilted her head and blinked up at him. 'Sounds like a plan.'

Even if it was a plan to get herself laid with someone who was a potential boyfriend of Julia's. Evidently, the woman was an even bigger bitch than he'd first suspected. Perhaps he'd do Julia a favour.

Anticipation rode high as he turned away, confident he'd tempted her enough. His chest squeezed tight and his breath came in short pants as he curled his hands into fists.

Karen followed him through the narrow hallway into the kitchen and never saw it coming. The backhander he dealt her exploded her nose. The blood sprayed further than he could have imagined over the grubby little kitchen to leave a speckled pattern over the cabinets, lacing up the greasy tiles.

Her round arse hit the floor with a neat little slap, and he yanked her lightweight body up again so he could administer another blow, splitting her lip this time. Her head lolled to one side and her eyes rolled backwards in a dead faint as he hit her harder than he'd intended.

Irritated with the ease with which he'd managed to knock her out, he towered over her, feet either side of her body. His blood pumped fast and furious through his veins as he glanced out of the window at the empty street. Shit, if anyone came by, they would see.

He yanked down the blind, spun around and raced out of the kitchen to slam the front door before any other nosey bitches came to see what was happening.

He strode back into the kitchen, his skin buzzing with excitement.

He stared at the inert body.

More. He wanted more than the mere satisfaction of an easy kill. The bitch had spoiled all his plans for Julia, but right now he had someone he could take his frustration out on. If only she'd have the decency to wake up.

He hauled her up again by the ugly green designer hoody and whipped the zipper down. Her head cracked on the floor with a satisfying thunk as he wrenched off her thin T-shirt and let her flop back, determined to see those breasts she'd deliberately flaunted at him.

Breasts he revealed as he stripped the tarty pink lace bra from her and flung it on top of her hoody and T-shirt.

The desire to see fear in her eyes had him slapping her across the cheek. 'Wake up, you bitch. Wake up.' He slapped her again, the sharp sound filling the little kitchen but not satisfying his bloodlust while she remained motionless. He needed her awareness, longed to watch fear fill her eyes.

With plenty of time before Julia was due home at 6.00 p.m., he knelt by Karen's side as the red curtain of hate closed around him. His pulse pounded like a runaway train, until no other thought could squeeze through. He wrenched her Lycra leggings and knickers from short, shapely legs and sat back on his haunches to wait, his breath soughing through burning lungs as desire buzzed through his veins to set his skin on fire.

28

He clawed trembling hands over his face. Stupid, stupid fucker. He dragged tear drenched fingers from his eyes. He'd fucked up. A fist clenched in the pit of his stomach as he rocked in the corner of the room.

He'd not followed the rules. All he'd needed to do was follow the stupid fucking rules. Instead, in his blind fury, he'd lost sight and ignored them.

He stared over at the crumpled, broken body with bloodied, purple face where he'd beaten her senseless twice, a red mist of fury at his earlier failure rising to swallow him up. He trailed his gaze over her nakedness and retched. Blood and semen stuck her thighs together. There was nothing he could do about that except douse her in a good amount of bleach and hope it washed away all traces of him.

He swallowed hard. He knew that would never happen, but if he was to get through this, he needed to believe it was feasible.

The sight of her wasn't what made him sick. There was a certain dark pleasure in what he'd achieved. He'd done it before, knew the pleasure was a sickness that had taken him so much further. Rape. That's why he'd been in prison.

All that DNA, though, *his* fingerprints, *his* semen, *his* vomit.

He pushed through the fogginess in his brain as whirling sensations overwhelmed him. He centred his attention on his own flaccid dick, covered in her blood from ramming so hard into her. That's what sickened him. Not the act. From what he remembered through the red haze of desperate, ferocious lust. No. He was sickened because this was what would get him caught.

He touched shaky fingers to his swollen lip, where she'd head-butted him in the brief moments she'd revived. Bitch knew how to scrap. Dark pleasure had torn through him as he'd put her down again. Just where she belonged. He had no regret about that. His regret was the loss of control, the mess he'd made. The crime scene. His crime scene.

He should have watched out for the deposit of pubic hairs. Used a fucking condom. But not a single thought had entered his head as he'd poured his rage down on her.

Panic sliced into his heart.

He circled his gaze around the room, crazed by the sheer destruction. He needed to make good. He gasped in another lungful of air, nodding to himself as he assimilated the situation.

He scrambled to his feet, using the wall to brace against. He flicked a glance up at the kitsch wall clock and huffed out a stressed breath.

He could do it. Bleach. Wash everything down. Clean the fingerprints off. Panic skittered through him. He needed the kitchen chair, rope, he'd forgotten a fucking basic rope. His mind sparked into action. A dressing gown tie would do.

It wasn't too late. He could rectify the situation. He scrubbed his hands along his thighs, less to remove the blood, than to get his circulation going.

Fuck! Fuck, what had he done?

He wrenched on rubber gloves, all too late for the fingerprints he'd already smeared all over the place. He swiped the back of his wrist across his sweat-beaded upper lip and lifted the blind a mere inch to scan the front garden and check for movement from the neighbours before he started on the task. Still quiet outside with no cars around. Everyone at work.

He dropped the blind back into place and stepped back.

The mournful howl of a dog seeped through from next door and sent a shudder through him. Little fucker probably knew his owner was dead. They sensed these things, that's why he never went near them. He'd never break into a house with a dog, no matter what size or breed it was. Too fucking dangerous.

The hard tremor of his fingers refused to still as he hauled on the white PPE suit over the top of his clothes. The ones soaked with her blood and DNA, traces of her bodily fluids soaked into his jeans and possibly strands of her hair where he'd wrenched it from her head to stop her vicious attack. He grabbed a cloth and sluiced away evidence he should never have left in the first place. All too late, he knew. Surprise caught him at the dead weight of her for such a slight person.

He scrambled over the body to haul her upright into one of the two straight-backed, wooden kitchen chairs. Her cheek stroked against his and he reared back, revulsion adding to the tremble, while he shook all over until it almost broke him apart.

The smear of wet blood on his skin sent panic skittering into the heart of him. He swiped the cloth doused with bleach over his face, hissing at the burn of it.

He glanced over at the sink, considered flushing water over his cheek and then reconsidered. They'd check the sink, the plughole, the drains, for evidence of DNA. And his DNA was on the system. He had no idea what skin cells he would wash down there. He settled for scrubbing the sleeve of his PPE suit over his skin until the burn subsided to a gentle glow.

Blinded by panic, his belly contracted, and the foul stench of his own fart stuck in his throat. He raced for the downstairs toilet, wrenching the PPE from his body in a desperate effort to get it off before he shit all over it.

His bowels purged themselves in the porcelain toilet as pain clawed at his stomach, so he curled forward with his head touching his knees.

The putrid stench of it had him raising his head and breathing in through his mouth in an effort to avoid fainting.

He grabbed the roll of toilet paper from the shelf beside him and wiped himself as he stood long enough to reach behind and flush the toilet. He was fucked if they decided to test for DNA down the toilet. He was fucked anyway.

He cleaned himself up, flushed again, then sat for a moment while the fast pace of his heart slowed down and the stabs of pain subsided.

When he was sure he'd expelled everything he could, he came to his feet, pulling his underpants and trousers up, yanking the PPE up over them once again. Sharp pains griped again, but he gritted his teeth and looked around for the toilet brush and disinfectant, pouring a small amount on the gloves he still wore to wash them clean. One pair wasn't enough. Next time he'd make sure he brought several so he could strip them off at each stage of the clean-up.

He staggered from the toilet and stared around. It was too much, all too much. He didn't have a problem with the job, rape brought a dark enjoyment, the addition of killing her hadn't disturbed him one iota, but the fallout was too hard. He needed to consider whether it was worth it. Would he do it again? Would he be given the opportunity?

Panic pressed down on him as he raced upstairs, the chocolate brown of the carpet concealing any traces of bodily fluid his shoes deposited on it. He'd have to take the risk that none of the DNA was traceable to him, if they were going to catch him, it was unlikely it would be from any tiny piece of shit on the stairs.

He wrenched the tie off her dressing gown and while he thought about it, he snatched the tiny camera he'd installed in her wardrobe and raced, breathless, back down the stairs.

The corpse, in the absence of support, had flopped back onto the floor, but a thrill of pride shot through him. He hauled her up again into the pose as far as he could remember. Without referring to the photograph in his bag, he positioned her, yanked the tie hard around her waist to keep her in position. He'd done it with no outside help. It was his job, his pride.

He stared at the kitchen and let out a dark chuckle. It was cleaner than when he'd arrived. He hoped Julia appreciated the free house clean.

Before he forgot, he reached up and snatched the other camera down from behind the blind. There was no further use for it in this house and he wasn't made of money. Besides, they may be traceable. He may have bought them down the pub for a fiver, but you just never knew.

While he wrapped the wire into a small roll, he tilted his head to one side to study the limp body. Stupid bitch. Hadn't the intelligence to realise when a predator was in the room. Served her fucking right.

He slid open a kitchen drawer, the bright glint of light from sharp knives stilled his hand for a moment as he studied them. He selected a short handled thin blade and placed it on the counter beside him.

He wrapped his gloved hand in her hair and yanked her head up. She didn't deserve the makeover. His lips twisted as he took in the mess she'd made of herself. Blood, snot and tears. He swiped her face with a bleach drenched tea towel, scrubbed at it, but couldn't remove the deep imprint of his fists. He dipped into his backpack and retrieved the make-up. Using a cheap sponge applicator, he swiped the blue across her purpled eyelids with careless disinterest and then smeared crimson lipstick over her swollen mouth.

With his fist still in her hair, he tilted his head to one side and slashed the knife across her throat, not so deep as to make a mess but deep enough that it was an acceptable copy of the original.

She'd have to do. She wasn't the one he wanted in any case. She'd ruined that for him. He'd have to look at his list again, find a match. She'd certainly fucked up any chance he had of coming back for Julia.

Dark amusement shifted his mood.

Julia.

His chest rumbled with laughter. He'd wanted to spook her then kill her. The cameras were just for his own satisfaction. To watch her move around the house, observe the awareness dawning that she was being watched.

Her death was no longer on the cards, but he could never have anticipated the terror this one act would invoke in Julia. It was just a shame he couldn't risk leaving one of the cameras, but the police would go through the place with a fine-tooth comb.

Perhaps, when the initial furore was over, he'd contact her again. Ask her out on a coffee date. See how she was holding up.

All provided they didn't track him down.

He rubbed his aching chest as he settled on the idea, imagined the emotional mess she'd be in and grinned before he set to work on Karen again.

Instead of cleaning up the wash of blood over the messy heap of her clothes, he dropped the hold he had on her and listened to the muffled thunk as her chin hit her chest. There was no point dressing her in the nice, neat scrubs Julia had in her drawers – the only neat thing about her. Karen wasn't a nurse. It would look like he'd made a mistake. Fucked up.

It was her who'd fucked up. And she'd paid the price. She could stay naked.

His stomach contracted again as he raked his gaze over the small kitchen and took up another cloth, dousing it in bleach and water and then wringing it out over the sink. With broad strokes, he swiped the surfaces clean, conscious of time slipping away.

He rolled up Karen's clothes and the tea towels he'd used, rammed them into his backpack, then grabbed Julia's mop, plunging it into the scalding water he'd run into the bucket, and added a few glugs of disinfectant. He swiped it over the tiled floors, side to side, as he walked back towards the door like he'd been taught in prison so they left no footprints in the wet, something that could identify them. Not that he could be identified from his generic, supermarket trainers. He wasn't that stupid. His mind flicked back to the stair carpet. He no longer had the time to get a vacuum out. He'd have to risk leaving it.

Satisfied, he snatched up the backpack and flung it into the hallway and then finished cleaning the kitchen floor, then took the bucket to dispose of the water down the toilet. He skimmed around the rim and seat with another bleach-infused tea towel and then glugged the entire bottle of bleach down the toilet.

When it was done, he surveyed the room. Everything in order, each surface clean. He curled his lip with disgust. Not his finest hour.

He'd do better next time. Not make such a mess.

He backed out of the room and, with a quick survey of the street, he let himself out of the house, leaving the key in the lock as he stripped off his PPE and rammed it on top of the other items in his backpack.

The haunted keening of a dog in pain chased him down the street as little Alfie poured out his distress. He hated fucking dogs, he'd have killed Alfie as well if he'd had the chance.

29

Jim Downey stared up at Jenna from where he squatted in front of the young woman's naked body, tethered to the kitchen chair. His face wreathed with confusion, he rolled his lips inward, then blew them out again with small puffs of air.

She came down on her haunches, eye level with him, to see what he could see. Her heart sank while she ran a critical eye over the scene. Another one. Not the same, but similarities. Copycat or not, they had a serial killer on their hands. Every detective's nightmare and it happened to be on her watch. At least DI Taylor would be back in charge once he'd recovered from his jet lag.

She wandered her gaze over the familiar set-up.

'Tell me what you know.'

'I know the woman is dead.' There was no sarcasm, just factual disappointment in Jim's tone.

'Sadly, she is.'

'I also know this wasn't the same standard of work as previous.'

Jenna squinted at the body. Similar pose. Victim tied to the chair. Head flopped forward. Naked though.

Jim came to his feet, pointed with a pencil. 'He hasn't taken the same time and care with her.' He circled the pencil in the air above the young woman's head. 'The make-up is sloppier. Rushed, maybe.'

'It was sloppy before. A bloody disgrace no woman would be seen wearing.' He was a man, what did he know about make-up?

'Not really. It was a parody, meant as an insult. If not to his victim specifically, then to all women. As though he had no respect, he wanted to show what in his mind women wearing make-up look like. Sluts, whores...' His voice trailed off.

Jim tucked the pencil behind his ear and leaned forward, using both gloved hands to raise the victim's head with gentle reverence, in direct contrast to the suggestions he'd made about the attacker.

The woman's battered and bruised face had Jenna sucking in her breath through her teeth.

'Dear God. He must have fists like hammers. It looks as though he's broken every bone in her face.' The soft bloatedness of it tugged at Jenna's heart.

With a sharp intake of breath, Mason reflected her own shock as he reared back from where he'd leaned over to get a closer look.

Jim's mouth pulled down at the edges as he inclined his head, eyes filled with a deep sadness.

'He quite possibly has. Perhaps the previous victim, Marcia, didn't put up a fight and maybe this one did, but it seems like a compete loss of all control.'

Jenna nodded her agreement while she tried to see beyond the discolouration of the woman's skin at what Jim drew her attention to. 'Could he have been in a rush? More flustered? If she'd fought back, maybe she took more time than he expected and got frightened, became panicked.' Jenna squinted at the victim. Slashed across the woman's face, she could see now that the make-up lacked the deliber-ateness of the previous victim's.

'Could have been.' But Jim's face reflected shadows of doubt. 'When we checked the make-up on Marcia's face, it didn't match any of the make-up she had in her house.'

Jenna nodded, recalling that snippet of information. 'Mmm, so we assume it was a deliberate choice of colour which the perpetrator provided. Brought along with him. Came prepared for the job.'

'Yes. We're tracing the brand, the colour. It takes a while. There are so many out there.' Jim lowered the dead woman's chin onto her chest and stepped back to rest his fists against his hips while he chewed on his top lip. 'If you want my opinion, I don't think it's the same make-up.'

Jenna screwed her face up. She always wanted his opinion. She'd never known him to be wrong on any matter. Jim Downey only offered his expertise in areas he was confident he'd not be challenged on. If it wasn't his area, he was old enough and wise enough to recommend where to get the information.

'Why?' She reached forward, kept her hands light as she raised the girl's head and cruised her gaze over the face, closing out the damage to focus in on the eye make-up. The style, the colour. Darker blue than before, she guessed, not as garish. 'Could just be the darker skin tone, the bloodied, burst vessels.' She traced the puffy, misshapen line of lips with her gaze to zero in on the texture of the scarlet lipstick and cast her mind over the previous victim's. 'It's glossy.'

Again, Jim nodded while Jenna continued to peruse.

'Was the previous one a dull lipstick? Red, but you know, what do you call it?'

'Matte.'

At the sound of another voice, Jenna glanced over her shoulder, reminded that Ryan was there. He stood further back from the scene, close to the door, possibly in case he puked again. She couldn't blame him. There had been times in the beginning at crime scenes when she'd wanted to barf. With a little flick of pride at the fact that she hadn't, she shuffled to ease the ache in her thighs as she'd squatted for longer than was comfortable.

Aware Mason had stepped in over her shoulder again, she had no choice but to remain where she was. 'Bastard.' The low-whispered retort only reflected her own thoughts. About to lower the girl's chin,

Jenna halted. She had to give the lad a chance. His pride was also at stake. 'What else can you see, Ryan?'

She sensed Mason moving back to allow the younger man access.

Solid this time, Ryan stepped in close, hunkering down until he was shoulder to shoulder with her, at ease moving into her personal space. The burn of pride warmed her stomach at his competent, respectful demeanour.

He studied the form with intensity, eyebrows dipped low as his gaze skimmed over the victim's face, down to her chest, where he halted his perusal.

'Blood.'

Surprised at the speed with which he called it; Jenna questioned. 'What about the blood?'

'There isn't as much.'

'Okay. Why do you think?' Testing him, Jenna raised the young woman's head higher to expose the gaping slash to her neck.

He leaned in closer, blew out a jagged breath, but held. 'It's nowhere near as deep, more superficial, as though it was just done for effect. He slashed her throat post-mortem?'

She nodded and glanced at Jim for his approval. 'Possibly. What can you smell?'

Ryan had no need to draw air in through his nose, the acrid reek of bleach and blood already coated the insides of their nostrils, so Jenna knew it would be days before the remembered stench of it cleared.

'Bleach.' Ryan's eyes widened as he turned to her, almost nose to nose. 'He's cleaned her down.'

'Yes. It appears that way.'

With the same propriety she'd witnessed from Jim, she let the woman's chin sink back and slid her fingers from underneath.

'I think that's something else we need to compare with the first victim. I can't recall any mention of bleach used on the actual victim.'

Jim Downey shook his head in disagreement. 'No, there's definitely a similarity there, the first victim, Marcia Davies, was thoroughly washed down with bleach. Maybe a different brand because he's used what they have under their own kitchen sinks, but he's definitely used the same technique.'

Jenna straightened, her thigh muscles screamed their protest and a groan escaped her lips before she could stop it. All she could do was attempt to talk through it. 'Why would he have used bleach, Ryan?'

Ryan bounced upright, showing no sign of any such aches and pains. He frowned, tugging at his top lip with his teeth as he studied the victim, a move so like his father's, Jenna swivelled her head to check out both Downeys.

Ryan scratched the side of his nose. 'To clean away his mistake.' He took a step back, his eyes gave a slow sweep of the surrounding area. 'He made a mistake and he wanted to cover it up. Or wash it away.' Before Jenna could agree with him, he rushed on. 'Of course, his success in that area all depends on the type of bleach he got hold of. He's taking a big risk if he depends on using whatever they have in their houses.'

Wide eyed, Jenna stared at Ryan as he continued the lesson he'd evidently learned from his dad.

'There are two types of bleach. Chlorine based or oxygen based. If he's used chlorine based, there's no amount of scrubbing is going to wash away evidence of blood because once CSI,' he glanced at his father, 'spray luminol, it'll glow blue wherever there's blood contamination. If it's oxygen based, if the perp has done a good job, there's no guarantee CSI will be able to find any traces.'

Jim's solemn gaze met hers with approval. The lessons never stopped, no matter how long you were in the job. Teaching and learning. 'Good work, son.' He gave Jenna a respectful nod. 'We'll get the report back from the coroner before we use this kind of information. Right now, it's supposition, but it gives you a ballpark picture while we wait.'

Jenna moved towards the door, stripping off her gloves as she went, tossing Jim a grateful smile as he held out his hand to take them from her. She'd wait until she left the house before she took the entire PPE off. 'Do we know who the victim is?'

'No.' Jim shook his head. 'I've not heard anything, but you'll find out more in there.' He gestured to the living room.

'We'll need to get back to the station, hand over what information we have to PC Wallis so she can data compare. Personally, I can't see any physical similarities with the last victim straight off, so it's not a look he's going for, but let's go and speak with the young lady who found her.'

She skimmed through the hallway into the messy lounge, assumed as CSI hadn't taped it off, it wasn't the subject of a burglary, although it could at first inspection be mistaken for one.

White faced, shocked, the young woman stared glassy eyed as Jenna stepped to one side to allow Ryan and Mason to squeeze through behind her.

Jenna kept her voice soft. 'Hi, and you are?'

'Julia Clements.' Voice barely above a whisper, Julia's russet coloured eyes flooded with tears. The smother of freckles stood stark against her pale, waxy skin. Her auburn streak of hair glowed like an ember around her head as the pale blue of her medical scrubs complemented her skin tone.

Jenna's stomach gave a sharp contraction as she stared at the woman in front of her. Oh, dear God.

From the corner of her eyes, Jenna caught Ryan's shoulder slump and made a slow, cautious head turn in his direction to shoot him a silent question.

Face in frozen impassiveness, Ryan's eyes danced with desperate communication, intense enough to send Jenna's heart spiralling in a downward rush.

With a barely distinct inclination of her head and slow blink to acknowledge him, Jenna turned away and lowered herself into the sagging seat cushion next to Julia on the sofa.

'Julia. I'm DS Jenna Morgan.' She skimmed one hand, palm up towards her officers as she held her badge in the fingers of her other hand. 'This is DC Mason Ellis,' She kept a close watch on the young woman next to her on the sofa. 'And DC Ryan Downey.'

A flicker, nothing more. It would keep for now. She touched a hand to Julia's where it rested on her leg. Kept her voice soft.

'Can you tell me what happened, Julia?'

'I don't know, I don't understand.' Tears rolled down her face and Mason passed a box of tissues over from the small, occasional table stacked high with magazines and used coffee cups.

Julia accepted a tissue, made a pathetic dab at her nose with fingers that trembled so hard, Jenna was surprised she managed to locate her face.

'I came home from work. I was on days. I finished at 6.30 p.m. She was there.' She flicked the tissue at the kitchen. 'Just there.' She swiped the tissue over her eyes and smudged mascara in a thick streak along her cheekbones. 'I have no idea what she was doing in my house.'

'Do you know her?' Jenna steered clear of calling the woman a victim as she needed to keep Julia's mind away from the death and focused on the actual person.

'Karen Prestwich. She's my neighbour.' A pained sob escaped Julia, sticking in her throat before she hiccupped it away.

Jenna pulled on the thin thread of connection. 'Did she have a key?' It wouldn't be unusual. Neighbours often did.

'No, she didn't.' Confusion flitted over Julia's face. 'There was a key in the door when I arrived. She raised her fingers to press them against her wrinkled forehead. 'I assumed my mum had been around and accidentally left it in the lock. I'm sorry. I never mentioned. I never thought, in all the...' She fluttered her fingers. 'confusion.'

Jenna glanced at Mason. They'd circle around to the key again, but right now, Jenna needed to get the big picture.

Julia lowered her hands to her lap, balled up the tissue in her fingers, then started to shred it, guilt hovered in the depth of her tear drenched eyes. 'Karen didn't have a key though. We didn't get on.' She threw the shredded tissue with the rest of the mess onto the table. 'I don't know why, but we never hit it off from the start.' She reached over, took another tissue and blew her nose, this time with less finesse and more desperation. 'I work shifts. She always played her music so loud. Her dog barks. I threatened to call the police.' She shrugged. 'I never did, of course.'

This time, when she balled the tissue, her hands stilled, and she stared at the far wall as though she could see through into the other woman's house.

'I complained to her when her dog pooped on my front lawn. We fell out. She didn't see the harm in her dog using my lawn as his toilet. She never picked it up. After that, she'd park her car just enough across my parking space, so I struggled to get in. Never enough to block it completely, but just enough to irritate. We're the last two houses in the street, so our parking spaces are next to each other, here.' She gave a vague wave at the right side of her house where Jenna had parked the unmarked police vehicle, leaving the blue lights flashing. 'It was as though she gained pleasure in pushing the limits to see how much she could get away with before I broke.'

Knuckles white as she squeezed her tissue, she dropped her gaze to the floor and Jenna let her run with the guilt explosion. They'd get more from her if Jenna allowed her to purge herself and it may help Julia to talk it through.

'She had to walk down the path from her parking space, past my kitchen window to get to her house.' She raised her clenched fist to her mouth, pressed it against trembling lips. 'She'd look straight in the window, every time, and stick her middle finger up at me.' Her breath hitched as she drew it in. 'We really hated each other.' She gazed around at each of them in turn. 'Not enough to murder her though. I couldn't have murdered her.'

Jenna already knew that.

As though she'd suddenly dried up, Julia fell silent.

Jenna touched the back of the other woman's hand. 'You're not a suspect, Julia. You're a victim too. The crime has happened in your house. Your home. Believe me, we're not looking at you for this.'

Mason moved a pile of magazines and settled himself on the battered armchair opposite. He kept his voice low and smooth as he leaned forward to direct her attention to him. 'Julia, can you tell me of any reason you can think of why Karen would be in your house?'

She raised confused eyes to him. 'None whatsoever. I have absolutely no idea why she would be here.' As much at a loss as them, Julia spread her hands and let the tissue drop on the floor. 'Why was she here? She had no reason to come in.' Her brow rippled in deep furrows. 'Did she break in? Why would she do that?'

As Jenna hadn't yet checked with CSI whether or not there had been a forced entry, she shrugged her shoulders. 'We don't have that information yet, Julia.'

Ryan leaned against the wall, his gaze stuck on Julia as he gave a soft cough. Jenna raised her eyebrows at him, gave a slight inclination of her head to give him permission to speak.

'Julia.'

She whipped her head up, narrowed her eyes at him. 'Do I know you? I feel I should.' Slow, dawning recognition slid over her face and her pale, freckled skin flushed florid. 'Oh, dear God.' She ducked her head and her ears pulsed a deep crimson.

Jenna touched Julia's knee to pull her attention back in. 'How do you know DC Downey, Julia?' Aware of Mason frantically scribbling in his notebook, Jenna made a conscious decision to keep her attention on Julia. Rather than allow herself to be distracted by taking notes, she kept her notepad in her pocket. Mason was more than reliable.

Julia raised her head and cupped her glowing cheeks with white fingers. 'I'm on a dating app. Y'ello.' She shot Ryan a quick glance. 'We've been talking.' She glanced at Jenna. 'Does this complicate matters?'

Aware of Ryan's discomfort, Jenna shot him a quick glance. They'd discuss the dating app further when they got back to the station, but Jenna needed to keep Julia focused at this point.

'I can't see why it should. Do you speak with anyone else on this app, Julia?'

Almost choking with embarrassment, Julia nodded her head.

'Who else do you speak with?'

Julia covered her mouth and shook her head, tears forming in her eyes again.

Jenna brought her face level with Julia's, her gaze intense, urgent. 'Many?'

'Around forty. Maybe more?'

Jenna caught the flash of shock on Ryan's face before he disguised it. Mason's head remained lowered, but his pen hand stalled before continuing in a move no one else was likely to have noticed.

Judgement was not her entitlement, but how the hell did anyone manage to talk to forty plus people on a dating app and keep them all straight? Curious to know how many women Ryan spoke with through this app, Jenna parked that question for later. It may be relevant. It may not.

She made a mental note never to use a dating app, no matter how tempting the idea seemed. She'd never been enamoured with the thought, now she was downright scared by it. She pushed the thought aside. They'd come back to Y'ello at another time, although it seemed there may be a recurring theme.

Right now, she needed to bring Julia back on track.

'Okay, Julia, can you walk me through what happened when you discovered Karen in your kitchen?'

Julia drew her hands away from her face and sucked in a long, slow breath, her eyes losing focus as she took herself back in her mind's eye.

'I came home from work. I was late. Again. My shift had run over, and I just wanted to come home, eat, crawl into bed.' Her eyes reddened again, and she blinked. 'I cursed her for leaving her bin across my pathway again. Inconsiderate cow bag I called her.' A short sob escaped her, and Julia swiped the smear of liquid snot from under her nose with the back of her hand.

Mason reached out the box of tissues and let her take another one. She blew her nose, a lost look in the depths of her eyes.

'My hands were full, I'd just been to the supermarket. I lugged three carrier bags and I had to move her bloody bin again.' She shook her head. 'I walked into the kitchen and she was there, naked.

Slumped, asleep I thought, in one of my chairs, like she was waiting for me.' She raised her hand to tuck a stray lock of auburn hair behind her ear. 'But she wasn't waiting. She was dead. I knew it straight off. The way her body collapsed, broken. Lifeless. But I had to check.'

A little sharper than she intended, Jenna interrupted. 'You touched her?'

With a visible jerk, Julia sat upright. 'I did. She was flopped in my chair, she wasn't wearing any clothes. I wondered what she was doing. "What the hell?" I said. "Are you fucking drunk?" But something inside me told me she wasn't. I'm a trained nurse for fuck's sake.'

'A nurse?' Another piece of the puzzle slipped into place.

Oblivious of Jenna's line of thought, Julia continued, 'Yeah. I know a dead body when I see one.' Raging, she turned to each of them in turn, finally settling her desperate gaze on Jenna. 'Only I didn't. I just thought there was something wrong; she'd taken drink, drugs. She seemed to party a lot. I had no idea she was dead until I touched her shoulder and she fell further forward.'

The sound of a pained animal strained from her throat as she covered her face with her hands, soft sobs escaping from between her fingers.

Jenna kept her voice gentle, so Julia didn't turn defensive, but she needed to know every aspect, straight away while the detail was fresh. 'Did you move her?'

Julia dropped her hands to her lap, shook her head and blew out an anxious breath. 'No. But when I touched her, her shoulders slumped forward in the chair.' She demonstrated, rolling over from the waist. 'Her head dropped lower on her chest. That's when I knew for sure. I pressed my fingers to her neck to find a pulse. Her skin was already waxy, no sign of life. Minimal rigor mortis at that stage. Her neck was still a little loose, but not entirely floppy.' She closed her eyes and her nostrils flared, turning white at the edges. 'My fingers slipped into the laceration there.' Julia blinked away another wash of tears and stared out of the window. 'Someone killed her. In my house. They tied her body to my chair, and used my dressing gown tie, I think it's mine.

Navy blue.' Her voice escalated to a pained wail. 'Why did they kill her in my house?' Almost begging for an answer, she turned her confused expression around the room.

If Jenna had the answer, she'd have already made the arrest. The sinister connection already made, but she wasn't ready to discuss it with Julia. What she did need to do was make sure the woman was safe.

'Julia, do you have someone you can stay with for a few days? A friend, family?'

Julia's eyes shot wide, as though the prospect of her being the intended victim only just occurred to her. 'It could have been me. He might have killed me instead of her.' She shot to her feet and stood poised, as though she was ready to run.

As casual as she could, Jenna stood, reached out a hand and touched Julia's arm.

The woman whipped her head around and stared at Jenna. 'Oh God, I can't stay here. I don't want to stay here.' A fine line of sweat broke out on her forehead and upper lip as she pulled in rapid breath after breath. 'Oh God, how am I to live here now, knowing that poor woman was murdered in my house?' A fresh wave of sobs wracked her body. 'And it could have been me. It's possible he could have been after me.' She wrapped her arms around her own slender waist and bent almost double as she sobbed. 'I didn't like her, but I'd never have wished this on her. Not this.'

30

Jenna cradled her head on one hand while she scanned through the file before she tapped the keyboard and sent a 360 degree image of the crime scene to the large white screen behind her. Her mind buzzing with the sheer volume of information, she stepped through each piece of evidence, carving out the picture while she waited for the assembled team in the incident room to settle. She had so many balls in the air, she needed to get the team briefed, so each of them could make a start on their allocated tasks.

'He wasn't after her. Not Karen.'

She peered at Ryan through her fingers and could do nothing but agree. At this stage, purely an assumption, an instinct, one she knew Ryan had already developed.

Without disillusioning him, she needed to ensure he didn't run off at a tangent. He needed to stick to the physical evidence they had without jumping down a rabbit hole on a whim. That entailed waiting for forensic evidence.

Did they have a copycat on their hands? There were so many similarities to Marcia Davies' murder and yet so many differences, they couldn't jump to the conclusion that the perpetrator was the same person. They needed facts. Forensics.

'That's a possibility.'

Ryan opened his mouth, but all it took was a raised eyebrow from her and he closed it again. He knew the value of hard evidence against circumstantial.

She drew in a breath as she straightened to address the assembled team.

'The victim, Karen Prestwich, was a social worker. It was her day off. Her boyfriend, a teacher at the local secondary school was at work, all day. Solid alibi. Two thousand kids, dozens of teachers and assistants his witnesses.' She whipped up a dry smile and continued. 'We have absolutely no clue as to why the victim was in this particular house. The house which belongs to Julia Clements.'

Jenna patrolled her gaze around the officers in the room to make sure they were all onboard so far. 'Julia and Karen couldn't stand each other. Karen did not, according to Julia, have a key to her house. However, Julia informed us earlier that there was a key in her small shed in the back garden.' She gave them a moment for the groans and eyerolling to ensue and then reeled them back in. 'Yeah. DC Ellis checked and there was no sign of the key in the shed.'

Jenna dropped her gaze down to her notes. 'CSI inform me that the initial findings are that there was no sign of a break-in. In fact, there was a key in the lock on the outside of the door when Julia arrived home. She initially thought her mum might have called around. It wasn't unusual for her to drop something off on her way past, but she'd never left the key in the lock before. This needs to be followed up with Julia's mum before we can confirm that the key in the shed was used to open the front door.' Jenna raised her head. 'PC Wallis, can I ask you to do that?' As PC Sabrina Wallis inclined her head, Jenna continued. 'We can only assume that either Karen Prestwich let herself in.' She surveyed the room. 'Or the perpetrator did.'

She searched the roomful of people to check they were all keeping up to speed before she delivered the next part.

'Julia returned from work to find Karen Prestwich in her kitchen. Naked and already dead.' Her gaze skimmed over her team to watch their reactions with a close eye. 'Although in shock at the time, Julia said she checked Karen Prestwich for signs of life and could confirm she'd probably been dead for some time. Julia is a nurse at The Princess Royal Hospital.'

She listened for the connection to hit, scanned the room as it did, conscious of the rabbit hole she'd happily jump down with the majority of them, if not for the evidence.

She held up a hand before the commotion could take off. 'We'll stick to the facts before we move on to the instincts and assumptions.' As they fell silent, she continued. 'Fact.' She counted them off on her fingers. 'At approximately 1830 hours, another young woman was discovered murdered today. Fact. There is a similarity to the modus operandi of the first victim. Fact. Unlike the first victim, Marcia Davies, this woman, Karen Prestwich, appears, on initial findings, to show she was subjected to a violent *rape* prior to her murder.' She ignored the sucked-in breaths, the pained groans and raised her voice over the noise. 'Fact. If this is the same murderer, he was not as neat and precise on this occasion. Indeed, according to Jim Downey, our Chief Forensics Officer, compared to last time, he was downright sloppy.' She blew out a breath. 'Fact. The perpetrator cleaned up anything pertaining to DNA evidence with bleach, so he had some idea of what he was doing. That having been said,' she gave a crooked smile, 'Jim Downey is confident that the clean-up was nowhere near good enough and, although it's early yet, Jim and his team will be there for several days working on the principles of exchange because this man will have left something of himself behind, no matter how miniscule. Fingerprints, fibres, footprints, bodily fluids, DNA. The deceased in particular should show a considerable amount, because although she's been cleaned down with bleach,' which she didn't need to explain to her team that used properly, bleach would destroy DNA, 'one of the main factors is, *did he wear a condom*? Again, we have to wait for confirmation from forensics at this point. This all takes time, they'll rush things as much as possible.' Seventy-two hours was the average time and the clock was ticking.

Jenna crossed her arms and leaned her backside on the desk as she scanned the room.

'Questions?'

Ryan's arm shot skyward, his skinny neck jerking in his oversized collar. Jenna resisted the urge to sigh out loud.

'DC Downey?'

'Is he targeting nurses, Sarg?'

Maturity and experience would bring him a little diplomacy and tact. In the meanwhile, she'd take his line of questioning and run with it.

'It could be coincidence. Certainly, at this early stage, we don't want to release that possibility to the press, and I'd appreciate it...' she emphasised, holding her hand aloft. '... if everyone here respects that. If word gets out on what is only an assumption at this point, we'll have every nurse in the county demanding police protection.' Just as they had years ago when Paul McCambridge murdered four nurses in quick succession. She stabbed her finger on the file in front of her. 'This information is to stay in the room, I do not want any leaks to the press. Is that understood?'

Jenna narrowed her eyes as she met the gazes of the officers in the room. If any one of them leaked it, there was the possibility of a murder happening right there in the station.

She gave them a moment to digest the information. 'Anything else? Yes, DC Wainwright?'

'Is he targeting a particular look?'

She sighed. 'There is a distinct possibility that if the perpetrator is the same, then he may be following the MO of Paul McCambridge who targeted women – nurses – with red hair, or as PC Downey calls them, gingers.'

Ryan squirmed as the blood rushed to his face. 'It's not meant as an insult, Sarg, that's what we call them, it's what they call themselves. Ask any of them. They're more insulted with the term redhead these days.'

Jenna bowed her head in acknowledgement of his reasoning and contemplated the thought that she was half a generation ahead of him and things changed.

'Although Karen was not a "ginger", Julia is, and it may just be that the neighbour was in the wrong place at the wrong time. We may never know. There are only two people who do – one of them is dead and the other is currently at large.'

'One other connection,' Jenna cast her glance around the room to gauge the reaction. 'As we all know, DC Downey met Marcia Davies, the first victim, the night before she was murdered. DC Downey was also in contact with Julia Clements, the woman whose house the second victim was found in, through the same dating app, Y'ello.' She paused to give her team a chance to absorb the connection. He'd not yet met up with her.

She caught Ryan's gaze across the room. 'So, DC Downey, just to clarify the nature of this app, how many women do you talk to at any one time?'

Skin flushed a healthy pink, Ryan stumbled over his words as he tried to get them out. 'Well, errrm, around eight maybe. Perhaps less. Never more. I just couldn't. I wouldn't be able to keep track.'

Her intention was never to humiliate him, but to gain as much information as possible.

'Julia appeared to be able to.' She glanced around. 'Julia managed forty.'

'Jesus.'

'Wow.'

'Hell.'

'For fuck's sake, how did she keep track?'

Judgement. There was no point trying to avoid it.

Jenna nodded. 'Forty, I would say, is quite considerable.'

'Forty is a fucking shitload.'

Jenna's lips twitched up at the corners at the decidedly unsubtle tones of Mason. He called it as he saw it.

'Shitload or not, that's where we're going to start. Forty, and these are only the people she is currently talking to, not the one's she's already been in contact with, perhaps dated and discarded, not the ones she has on hold for the next round. It's a massive job and it won't be a quick one.' She held up a hand to contain the grumblings. 'Digital forensics currently have Marcia's phone, Karen's and also Julia's. They're going to extract the information, check if there are any crossovers. As you all know, digitally, this is a real challenge with "cloud" applications. Evidence needs to be captured in real time, so the team may have difficulties if the perpetrator knows digitally what he's doing. He may well have covered his tracks. We haven't ascertained any of that yet. It's way too soon.'

Salter looked up from the notes he'd been scribbling and waggled his pen in the air to catch Jenna's attention.

'DC Salter?'

Never one to be rushed, Salter ran his tongue over his teeth before he spoke, his long, slow Yorkshire drawl his cover for a bright, intelligent mind. 'Let me get this right, Sarg. We've got a serial killer on our hands.' He placed his pen on the desk in front of him, leaned back and crossed his arms over his broad chest. 'And DC Downey has both women on his dating app.'

'No. DC Downey has one of these women on his dating app.' She corrected.

'And the owner of the house the second woman was killed in is also on his dating app.'

Jenna cast Ryan a quick glance to communicate her support before she gave one, slow nod. 'Correct.'

'And both women were nurses?' As Jenna opened her mouth to reply, Salter unfolded his arms, picked up his pen and gave a sharp rap on the desk. 'The woman who owns the house, not the murdered woman.'

'Yes.'

He placed his pen on the table and his sharp gaze met hers. 'I'd like DC Downey to let me take a look at that app, explain it to me further and see what's what, like.'

Grateful for his show of support, Jenna shrugged, 'Digital forensics have possession of DC Downey's phone.'

Ryan's hand went up in the air.

Without noticing, Salter crossed his arms over his chest. 'That's a bugger. We could do with knowing what other women Ryan has on his app.'

Ryan waggled his hand and Jenna raised a finger to halt him. 'That's one of their priorities.'

'We need it now,' Salter grumbled.

Ryan let out a small cough, which Jenna could no longer ignore.

'Yes, DC Downey?'

'Digital forensics took my phone but supplied me with a new one, everything is mirrored. I can show Salter the app, Sarg.'

Jenna glanced up just as the incident room door swung open and DI Taylor stepped through, a thick file tucked under his arm. Her gaze bounced off his as he scratched his ear, his eyes still glazed from his long flight.

'Carry on, DS Morgan.' He wandered over to the side of the room and perched on the desk Donna sat behind.

Jenna directed her attention back to Ryan. 'I'm sorry, DC Downey, but we have to be very careful we don't tread on forensics' toes. We need clear continuity of evidence and if you interfere or take action when you shouldn't, any court case dependent on the evidence on your phone will be right...' she paused to draw in a breath.

'... royally fucked,' Mason finished her sentence for her. Not quite how she would have put it, but the sentiment worked.

She shot a glance around the room and waited for the laughter to subside. 'Any questions?'

'Door-to-door?' DC Trevor Simms asked from the back of the room, where he always took up residence in case someone mistook him for a police officer and gave him some work. Solid he might be, but the avoidance of anything taxing seemed to be his sole aim in life. Surprised he'd even raised his head above the parapet, Jenna took a stunned minute before she answered him.

'Door-to-door is being conducted as we speak. Any information will be relayed back to us, but it appears that they're not exactly the most neighbourly community. Mostly, they get up, go to work, come home, watch TV and go to bed.' She reeled off the sad routine of these people's lives, realising how closely it resembled her own. Or lack of one. She needed to get one and stop moping around. 'Anything further?'

At the vague mumble, Jenna took it that they'd finished and stepped to the desk nearest her. 'Pick up an information pack or access it from a computer. If anyone needs to discuss anything, you know where I am.'

As the group dispersed, DI Taylor waved her over to where he sat with Donna and Mason with Ryan hovering by the door.

'Sir, I thought you were on holiday until tomorrow.'

'Not any longer.'

'What time did your plane get in?'

He rasped his fingers over his rough cheeks. 'Ten this morning.' He glanced at his watch, winced. 'I got five hours' sleep in. Good enough.' Not on jet lag, but it was up to him. 'Chief Superintendent Gregg has apprised me of the situation and DI Evans has handed over to me as he also has holiday booked and wanted to get away before he gets it cancelled.' He rubbed his bloodshot eyes. 'I've spoken with the prison governor; she confirms that they've checked the room where you interviewed Paul McCambridge and the photo isn't there. They've searched his cell, confiscated a mobile phone, no SIM card found.'

'He probably swallowed it,' Ryan interrupted.

'That's not got to be healthy.' Mason scratched his fingers across the black stubble forming on his cheeks so they rasped.

Ryan shrugged. 'Nah, doesn't harm. It's mainly silicone, with a very small deposit of copper, possibly a touch of gold. Very little metal. Mostly they can't even detect them with X-rays, depending where it is in the system. If he's chewed it...'

At the glazing over of Mason's eyes, Ryan stumbled to a halt.

'Thank you, PC Downey.' DI Taylor scrubbed his hand over his short, grey hair before he continued. 'They also confiscated all privileges – TV, radio, books – and the governor's confirmed that McCambridge has been given maximum lock-down for twenty-one days. That means no privileges, no gym, no outdoor time and no contact with anyone other than his assigned guards.'

'Shit. And they thought me hitting him was tough. That's got to be wrong. It's not a punishment, it's a direct route to insanity. Twenty-one days in complete solitary.' Mason shook his head.

'It didn't take twenty-one days, only twenty minutes. Apparently, he kicked off again the moment they took his TV, and broke a prison officer's wrist, despite being tranquilised. They claim we've set his treatment back years.'

'God forbid we upset the serial killer,' Mason grumbled.

Irritation cranked up and Jenna snorted. 'It's not a case of us setting him back by visiting him. I think he's overwrought with the idea that someone else is doing his killing for him. He's excited, inflamed. We never even raised his awareness of the killing, he already knew. If we hadn't gone there to question him, who else would they be able to blame?'

Jenna paced across the room, picked up a file and strode back. She handed the file to Donna, mouthed a thank you to her and faced the others.

'I place the blame firmly on the prison. They should never have informed him of the murders.'

Taylor glanced up from the notes he studied. 'I don't think they actually informed him themselves.'

'No, possibly not, but they certainly gave him access to the information, let him see the newspaper, hear the press release, see it on his illegal mobile phone.' She swiped up a pen and tapped it against the palm of her hand. 'He kicked off nicely just in time for our arrival.'

'I can't disagree, Jenna.' Taylor nodded. 'The governor offered to interview the members of staff who were present, but Chief Superintendent Gregg told her we'd prefer it if we could do that. We need more information in the light of this latest murder anyhow. We need to know if McCambridge has anything to do with them. Who is pulling his strings, or whose strings is he pulling?'

'Absolutely. At the least, I believe he's in contact with the copycat. It's his MO, sir. There are things never released from the original murders only we and McCambridge know that the copycat has emulated. It's as though the perpetrator has been coached by McCambridge. He may have mucked up with this latest one though. Julia was the target. Somehow it all went wrong and Karen ended up dead.'

'Agreed. Right then.' DI Taylor gave a low grunt as he rose from the chair and placed one hand on his hip, pain wriggling over his forehead. 'Take DC Ellis, Downey and McGuire, get back to the prison, stay in pairs, and I want you to question everyone who was there, including Paul McCambridge.'

Her heart dropped like a stone. 'Yes, sir.'

31

Awkward was the only word to describe what she needed to do.

Professional was the only way forward.

Damned if it wasn't still awkward though.

Jenna gave an impatient tap of her pen on the pad in front of her while she waited in the interview room of Long Lartin, her heart skipping a beat every time footsteps echoed along the hallway.

'You okay, boss?' In an unusual display of concern, Mason leaned back in his chair, stretched and yawned until his jaw cracked. Yeah, he'd probably scratch his arse in a minute just to wrap everything up.

Unwilling to allow her irritation with the situation to transpose into annoyance with her partner, Jenna ducked her head and studied the notes she'd written earlier. 'Yep. Everything is fine.'

'If you want—'

The door opened with a silent whisper and Denton Harper slipped inside, a half-smile of greeting on his face so a dimple winked in and then out again. 'DS Morgan.' He held out his hand. 'I didn't think we'd see you again so soon.' She touched her palm to his and frissons of awareness heated her at his cool attractive looks.

She sent him a quick smile. 'Unfortunately, it's a necessity.'

Deep aquamarine eyes turned serious and held her gaze.

Mason shouldered through. 'Good of you to agree to see us.'

Harper turned his attention on Mason, the concern in his eyes undiluted. 'DC Ellis. Good to see you again too. I hope your fist never suffered too much from the punch you threw when we last met.'

Mason leaned in, grasped Harper's hand and grinned. 'When duty calls, there is no pain.'

Harper's smile wavered, then kicked up again as he withdrew his hand from Mason's. 'Please,' he invited. 'Take a seat.

As Jenna sat, she narrowed her eyes at the good-looking man opposite. Almost a distraction, but she had a job to carry out and she'd do it with the utmost professionalism because that was the way she'd learned to do it.

She swiped up the disposable cup of coffee she'd been offered and took a decent gulp, almost spewing it back out as the sour taste hit the back of her throat and threatened to punch a hole in it with the strength of its acidity. Tears rushed to her eyes as she gulped the foul stuff past the blockage of throat muscles making their protest known. She covered her mouth with her hand as she gave a delicate cough to disguise the choking sound that wanted to burst out.

Sympathy swirled through Harper's eyes as he picked up his unopened plastic bottle of mineral water and waggled it at her. 'You may find this is safer.' He pushed it towards her over the desk in a clear invitation for her to take it.

She accepted it and twisted the lid off. She took a swig, the sweetness of the water washing away the bitter taste of the coffee.

'Thanks. I've had some bad coffee in my time, but I didn't realise they'd replaced it with sulphuric acid.'

Harper raised a smile as she screwed the lid back on and placed the bottle to one side.

'And thank you for agreeing to see us again. The last time was particularly unpleasant, so we do appreciate your co-operation.'

'No problem.'

She needed to toe the party line, keep the interview formal, there was no space for personal likes or dislikes. 'We realise that you are privy to certain information, which is confidential between yourself and your client, but I'm sure you appreciate also that we are investigating at this stage a second murder.'

A flash of surprise crossed his features before his mouth tightened and he nodded. 'McCambridge is fully aware of my obligation to report any criminal activity or concern to the police. Inmates are informed of this before any counselling is started.' Harper linked his fingers together and rested them on the table between them. 'What happened?'

'Yesterday evening we were called to attend another murder, which we believe, like the first, has a direct link to Paul McCambridge.'

Harper did nothing but nod his understanding, the tension in his jaw demonstrated the man's own horror.

Jenna tapped the closed file she had on her desk. 'If we can come back to that in a minute, I need to clear a couple of other matters up.' It would give him a moment to settle. 'When we attended the prison last, you saw the photograph we presented to McCambridge?'

'Yes.' His eyes met hers, direct, concerned.

'Had you seen it before?'

'Yes.'

'Do you know the identity of the victim in the photograph?' She continued to hold his gaze with her own.

'I do.' He nodded. 'A Shirley Boswell, I believe. A young nurse aged twenty-three. It's all in his file.'

'Did you know that another photograph, one we never presented that day, but was in the file, one of the previous night's victim, subsequently went missing?'

A quick flash of surprise lightened Harper's eyes. 'I had no idea. When did it go astray?'

'During the time between us showing McCambridge the image of his fourth victim and us leaving the room. Effectively when he kicked off.'

Confusion flitted through Harper's eyes as his brow dipped low.

'I'm sorry. It was me who picked up all the paperwork, as far as I know. I handed it to you. I don't think there was anything more.'

She regretted the guilt she inflicted on him, and the concern swirling in his expression, but she needed to know if he'd noticed anything. 'You never saw anyone else pick up the photograph?'

'No. It was all a bit manic. The guards...' He put his fingers to his forehead and massaged there. 'I can't remember clearly, it went crazy, and when they left, all I could think of was to pick up the papers that were lying all around, stop people from skidding on them. It's been a while since one of our residents kicked off like that. I like to stay neutral, so they don't see me as an aggressor.'

'Okay. Thank you.'

Jenna opened her file and stared down at the stack of notes in front of her. She flicked over the pages she'd marked with little vibrant orange sticky arrows until she came across the information she needed.

'Mr Harper.' She raised her head and smiled at him, her heart kicking up as he responded with a widening smile of his own and a friendly glint in his eye. 'How long have you been counselling?'

'Eight years.'

'And of that eight years, how long have you counselled Paul McCambridge?'

Relaxed, he leaned back in his plastic chair and thought for a long moment before replying. 'Approximately four years.'

'Four?'

'Yes. Possibly a little longer. Maybe five. Certainly, quite a time after I qualified.'

Jenna nodded and jotted down the information on the pad in front of her before she glanced back up. 'How often do you see him?'

Comfortable and open, he spread his hands. 'Approximately once a week.'

'Approximately?'

'Yeah. We get given a list. Sometimes it's very long and we run out of time. Now that Mac is pretty well... *was* pretty well balanced, we don't mind if he misses the occasional session.'

'Because...?'

'Because up until the other day...' Harper made a soft clucking noise as he shook his head, '... he was what we considered stable.'

'Mmm.' She'd never seen anyone less stable in all her life, the manic light in McCambridge's eyes had struck her the moment she met him. There'd been no room for misinterpretation. Concerned that Harper had misread the man for considerably longer than he should have, she leaned closer across the table, inviting him into her confidence. 'Why do you believe he reacted in the way he did?'

'He was disturbed.'

'Disturbed?'

'Yes.' His smile tightened. 'You gave him information that disturbed him. Provoked him.'

'Okay. I made him uncomfortable, but actually I'd say he was already on the manic scale before we arrived. He'd obviously already been passed information.'

A flash of irritation sparked in Harper's eyes, the first she'd witnessed, and she pushed a little harder.

'Were you privy to that information?'

'No.' His gaze slid away from hers and then skittered back. 'I knew he'd heard something. I had no idea what. I didn't know the reason for your visit. They just asked if I'd sit in on the interview, that the police wanted some information from a past case. I'd only just arrived at Long Lartin. They should have called me beforehand, given me some warning.' He leaned back and scraped his fingers through his thick, blond hair. 'I had no chance to speak with Mac before you arrived, so I only just met up with him outside the interview room.' Harper scrubbed his hands over his face. 'I knew. The moment I saw him, I knew there was something wrong. I should have stopped it, not allowed the interview to take place. It's not normally my decision to make. I'm only his counsellor, but...' He lowered his hands, placed them palm down on the table. 'I definitely should have made representation when I saw you.'

'Me?'

'A female. A cop.'

Jenna nodded to acknowledge the regret in his eyes. 'Is that the way he shows his anger, his annoyance at something? Does he normally throw a tantrum?'

'He's been known to. Over the years, though, there have only been a handful of times he's reacted in a similar fashion.'

'Like when he attacked the governor?'

He hummed in the back of his throat. 'Female.'

'A figure of authority.'

'A *female* figure of authority. He's fine with the rest of the management here. It purely is women who pull his trigger. Each time, we need to desensitise him again and bring him back into the real world.'

'Why females in particular?'

Harper leaned back in his chair, raised his hand to his mouth and chewed at the skin at the side of his fingernail while he took a moment to consider what he wanted to say. 'There were two major influences in his life. The first, his mother. A nurse. She dyed her hair red and wore pretty garish make-up from a child's viewpoint. Bright blue eye make-up, brilliant red lipstick. Consistent with the early 1980s. From his account, there were only the two of them. She was a huge disciplinarian. Kept him in order with the back of her hand. When he was just seven, she committed suicide.' Jenna had read it in McCambridge's file, but she let Harper continue. 'He considers her suicide the most self-centred, unforgiveable, inhumane act. Effectively, her death put him in the "system" and exposed him to the vilest abuse.'

Harper took a long pull of breath in through his nose as he dropped his hands back to the table. 'This is where the second influence came in. Justine Elder. One of the foster parents. She put him through torture. Treated him like a little slave. Slapped him, punched him, bit him. Subjected him to untold abuse. Until the day he slashed her with her own kitchen knife.' That too was in the file, but it was interesting to get it from a different perspective, not so clinical.

'As an adult, McCambridge appeared to maintain control.' Harper's grin was sharp, full of sorrow. 'He's a psychopath. One day his fuse was ignited, the woman he'd dated for some time, a redhead, a nurse, suddenly exerted authority and he simply flipped.' Harper raised both hands and scrubbed them through his blond flop of hair. 'That was it. The start of his killing spree.'

Jenna nodded and closed her file. There was no need for it. It was all in her head. 'Have you seen him since we last visited?'

Regret shimmered in his eyes. 'Twice. I had very little response. He's still heavily sedated.'

'Solitary confinement, I believe.'

'The inmates have single cells. It's too much of a risk. They're allowed to integrate during certain times of the day, but McCambridge has been confined since your last visit.' There was no accusation, just a simple statement of fact. She already knew it, but she let him speak, it fell in line with everything she'd heard.

'Is he particularly close to anyone?'

Harper shook his head. 'Not to my knowledge, but then I only visit two or three times a week. Unless he mentions someone, I wouldn't necessarily know.'

Jenna nodded her understanding. There wasn't much more she needed from Denton Harper. 'Thank you. I think that's all for now, but I may have to come back if that's okay with you.'

Harper reached across the table and placed his hand on hers. 'That's fine. He'll never be released. You do understand.' Concern filled his eyes. 'We could never allow such a dangerous man back into the public domain. I would never put forward a recommendation to allow it.'

Aware of Mason's keen attention, Jenna slipped her fingers from under Harper's. 'That's good to know.' McCambridge was a psychopath and true psychopaths could never be rehabilitated. Just managed.

She scraped the chair back as she stood. 'Thank you for your help, Mr Harper. We really appreciate the time you've spent with us today.' She extended her hand and shook his, acknowledging the gentle squeeze he gave to her fingers with a small smile.

32

'Well, if he doesn't want to jump your bones, tie my hair back and call me Shirley.'

Jenna sighed. 'You're weird, Mason.'

'So are you, if you missed an opportunity there. Even I think he's hot.'

Jenna laughed. 'Who says I missed an opportunity?'

Mason whipped his head around to stare at her and made her laugh again. 'When did that happen?' His eyes narrowed with suspicion. 'Did he pass you his number when he did all that hand holding?'

A chuckle rolled out, Mason was good for her. He'd be even better for her sister. 'No, he did when I met him in Sainsbury's.'

'You went to Sainsbury's on a date, and you call me weird?'

With a full belly laugh, Jenna reached for the bottle of water and unscrewed the lid. 'No, Fliss and I were shopping, and we just happened to bump into him.'

'Happened to?'

'Yeah, he was buying spaghetti, Fliss and I were feeding the five thousand.' She shrugged in an attempt to hide the little shaft of pleasure. 'He asked for my number. I gave it to him.'

Before Mason could reply, the door burst open and the slack

bellied guard who'd been tethered to Paul McCambridge on their previous visit came into the room, all rolling shoulders and attitude.

Instead of standing and offering her hand, Jenna stayed where she was and flicked open her file containing the man's details. 'Good morning. Dennis Elks, isn't it?'

In direct contrast to Denton Harper, the man grunted as he pulled out a chair and slouched into it, annoyance buzzing in every muscle.

Jenna leaned back and cast a glance up at the high window. Weak sunshine filtered through and she sighed. She could be out there. Instead of inside a prison with a dickhead of a prison officer determined to try her patience. Was it too much to ask for a little co-operation? They were supposed to be on the same side. Attitude a world apart from Harper's, Jenna knew she was about to have a difficult time with the prison officer.

She turned her attention back to him. 'We've met before. I'm DS Jenna Morgan and this is DC Mason Ellis.'

He let out another grunt and crossed his arms over his chest as he jutted his chin out.

Mason fidgeted in the seat next to her.

'Dennis. Can I call you Dennis?'

'Yeah.'

'We're here to talk to you about the incident last time we were here. When you accompanied Paul McCambridge into this room for questioning about a prior case.'

Elks snorted and shuffled further down in the chair.

Jenna sniffed and stared at the open file. 'Dennis. Would you say McCambridge was already tense before we arrived the other day?'

The guard shrugged. 'I hadn't noticed.'

'You hadn't noticed. And yet you were tied to him.'

'Yeah.'

'It's been pointed out that McCambridge was actually vibrating with aggression before he stepped into this room.'

Anger roiled in the guard's eyes as he flashed her a glance.

'What information had McCambridge received before we met with him?' Jenna pressed.

Dennis shrugged again, unco-operative. 'No idea.'

'How long were you with him before we arrived?'

Sullen, his eyes went deadpan. 'I don't know.'

Jenna stretched a wide smile and leaned forward into his space as she tapped her finger on the table in front of him. 'Have an educated guess, Dennis. Did you escort him through the hallways, or did you simply meet just before you came through the door?'

Dennis's chin came up. 'I escorted him from his cell.'

'Right. How long did that take?'

'Fifteen minutes.'

'Fifteen minutes and you have no idea what McCambridge had heard? That's hard to believe.' She flipped over a sheet of paper and took out the photograph she'd shown McCambridge. 'Have you seen this before?'

Elks shot her another derision filled look. 'Yeah.'

'The other one I brought with us when we last visited went missing. The one of the murder a few nights ago. Not McCambridge's victim, but what we believe to be a copycat. That image went missing when McCambridge kicked off.'

The man bristled with indignation. 'When you taunted him until he smashed me around the room like a fucking ragdoll.'

Bingo, the man had engaged. Ego, pride, insult. That's what it was about.

'I'm sorry about that. I'm sorry you got hurt. We had no idea he'd already been primed and what I saw as questioning, he clearly saw as incitement.'

'It was incitement. You knew exactly what you were doing.'

She couldn't deny it. 'I wasn't aware of his mental and emotional state. Surely you were?'

'I knew he was excited about something. I had no idea what he'd heard, though.'

Elks's shoulders came down as he started to relax, and Jenna slid her hand back across the table. 'Did you see where the photograph went?'

'No, I was too busy trying to get my breath back. The stupid fuckers.'

'McCambridge?'

'No. The other guards. They should have been there. The instructions are clear. McCambridge should never have been left on his own with just one guard. Never. He's a fucking psycho. I don't know how he swung it, but he managed to have security downgraded on your visit.'

News to her, Jenna scribbled a few notes. Interesting. She never bothered to take a sideways glance at Mason, she knew he would have got the significance. McCambridge had too much power. He should never have had access to the information he did, and he'd managed to downgrade his own guard duty.

Vibrating with anger, Elks hauled himself upright in the chair. 'I've told them I won't escort him again. He's damaged my shoulder. I'm on the sick now. I only came in to see you.'

With sympathy in her voice now Jenna had him talking, she shot him a soft smile. 'We could have come to your house.'

He jerked his head back. 'What, and have the neighbours think the pigs have come to arrest me?'

Careful not to rise to his bait, Jenna backed off. They needed his co-operation as much as possible. 'Of course.' She took in a long breath and reached for her water before she backtracked. 'Other than you, can you tell me if Paul McCambridge had contact with anyone else that morning?'

He shook his head. 'Only his counsellor, but you know about him. Soft git.'

'Denton Harper?'

'Yeah, gives all the men the same nicey, nicey act. Easy enough for him, when they're not fucking bolted to him.'

Surprised at his obvious dislike of the counsellor, Jenna made a mental note. It wasn't unusual for counsellors to be disliked, but it was worth a deeper look into why Harper hadn't been with McCambridge before their visit. If he'd had the opportunity to assess him, perhaps none of the events would have happened. He had said there hadn't been enough time, but still...

She looked up from her notes and caught Elks's sullen stare. There was a possibility he didn't like anybody.

'Did McCambridge receive any phone calls before we arrived?'

Elks shook his head. 'Not to my knowledge. They're not allowed mobile phones and any private calls have to be logged. Check, but I think you'll find there's nothing.'

Jenna took a slug of her water and placed the bottle back down on the table. 'Dennis, thank you for your co-operation today, we really appreciate it.' At his soft snort, she met his eyes. 'I'm sorry you were injured. I hope you have a swift recovery.'

He pushed back his chair to loom over her. This time she felt no need to defend herself, his seething aggression wasn't directed at her but at the system. 'It's not going to be a swift recovery. I'll probably be off the whole summer – on full pay. Injured on duty. I might even have to take medical retirement.' He shot her a quick smile, about-turned and marched to the door.

As he left them alone, Jenna rubbed her fingers through her hair as she turned to Mason. 'Well, that was a bloody waste of time.'

'Agreed.' Mason stretched a wide yawn as he looked at his watch. 'How do you think Donna and Ryan are getting along with questioning the four prison officers from the other day?'

'They'll be fine.' She chewed on her bottom lip as a quiver of fear pierced her stomach. 'Let's see what McCambridge has to say.'

She came to her feet and made her way to the exit, pausing just long enough to blow out a controlled breath before she swung the iron door open and stepped into the hallway.

Dark depravity spewed from the evilness within despite the heavy sedation. McCambridge's eyes spat hate the moment they walked into his single-occupancy cell. The four guards never met her gaze but directed their stares straight at the door where they'd probably been instructed to do so.

The veins on McCambridge's neck bulged as he strained against his restraints. 'Fucking DS Jenna Morgan. What a fucking pleasure.' The slight slur in his voice gave her little reassurance that the sedatives were enough.

Jenna narrowed her eyes as she assessed whether or not the man could break free. Fear still vibrated through her system at his close proximity, not from the physical harm he could inflict if he escaped but the mere malevolence of the hatred that pulsed from him.

Aware of Mason towering over the back of her, she perched on the edge of the single plastic chair in the room, every muscle wired in case he moved.

'Mac.' Despite the threat, she met his stare straight on. 'I'm glad you remember me.'

Spittle flew from his snarling mouth. 'I remember you. I'll fucking rip your head off the first chance I get.'

Her knees turned to jelly, but she raised her chin in a challenge. 'You'll never get that chance, Mr McCambridge.' She leaned forward, not close enough for him to reach, but near enough for her harsh whisper to reach his ears. 'You'll live out your life here in this pitiful cage with all your privileges withdrawn for the foreseeable future. Possibly forever.' She drew back her lips and allowed the bitterness of her own helplessness to spew forth. 'I've seen to that. No more mixing with the other inmates.' The deadness in his eyes made her realise he didn't care if he had company or not. 'No more television, library, books. You've lost all your enhanced prisoner rights.' His dull gaze barely wavered. 'There'll be no more gym. Never again.'

The dull flicker blazed and McCambridge lurched forward, pulling up short against the restraints. 'Bitch! You fucking bitch!' Saliva flew from his slack lips.

Jenna surged to her feet, almost backing into Mason as he remained a silent sentinel behind her. She'd known the moment she walked in the cell that there was nothing McCambridge could give her. With slow deliberation she cruised her gaze around his spartan cell. 'No privileges.' Her smile stretched wide. 'Nothing.' As her gaze came to rest on him, she wrinkled her nose. 'No drugs. No phones. No nothing.'

'Fucking bitch!'

His howl vibrated down the hallways behind her, echoed by every other inmate, the sharp rapping of instruments against the metal cell doors creating a cacophony of sound to block out anything, including her own thoughts.

As the inner door clanged shut behind them and Ryan and Donna stepped forward to meet them, Mason gave her arm a brief touch. 'Let's get off. By the time we get back to the station, do the round-up, I'll need food and a can of beer.'

She remembered Fliss's earlier text.

Reminder: I've walked Domino to a state of exhaustion. Out to dinner with the other teachers until 11 p.m. (ish)

There'd be no food for Jenna. She'd have to make her own from the pile of crap they'd bought in the supermarket. She'd probably end up with salad and boil-in-the-bag rice. It would be better than the luke-warm sausage roll Mason had lobbed at her on the way to the prison, in lieu of lunch.

Exhausted from the sixteen hour shift she'd put in the day before, she could think of nothing better than her bed. With only eight hours' downtime between shifts before they raced back to the station, aware of the critical twenty-four hours, it had been non-stop. It would be dark by the time they got back.

At least the house wouldn't be empty. Domino would be there.

Mason swung the outer door open and the two guards who'd stepped close to escort them fell back without a word.

Jenna ground her teeth. 'Coffee. I need coffee.'

33

Keys in hand, Jenna poked them at the lock in the door of the darkened porch. Surprised Fliss had forgotten to leave the light on, Jenna blew out an exhausted sigh.

The footstep behind her had her swinging around, arm raised, keys poised ready to jab, only to have her hand caught in the hard fist of a black shadow. As she stepped in close, ready to knee the offender in the balls, his quiet voice halted her. 'Jenna, it's me. It's Adrian.'

The hammering of her heart almost exploded her ears. 'Jesus Christ, Adrian, what do you think you're playing at? I could have seriously hurt you.'

Amusement laced his deep voice. 'Really, you think so?'

In a swift move, she used his grip on her hand as balance and brought her knee up, stopping just short of connecting with him, but it let him know she could have if she'd wanted to.

His hand tightened on hers in a gentle squeeze as he let out a gust of laughter. 'If you didn't want to eat, you just needed to say.'

Confusion rolled through her. What the hell was he doing there? He'd never visited her home before, never had reason to. Apart from when Fliss had been attacked by Frank Bartwell.

Jenna's heart gave an uneasy hitch. He was offering her food, looking after her just the way he had when Fliss had been kidnapped. Was it something to do with Fliss and her case?

'Eat?'

'Yeah.' Without releasing her hand, he raised a bag up and gave it a little jiggle. 'I picked up a few things in case you hadn't had the chance.'

She stared at his silhouette. 'Who the hell are you?'

His deep chuckle reverberated in the dark. 'Do you want to open the door, or should we stand here all evening discussing it? The roast chicken's getting cold.'

With the temptation of food too much, Jenna slipped her hand out of his and swung around, poked her key in the lock, getting it in first time, and pushed open the door. She stepped inside, relieved Fliss had left the heating on as the warm comfort of her house greeted her a split second before Domino did. If ever they had an intruder, Domino would have them pinned to the floor in no time as he gave no warning bark, no excited yip. He waited in the darkened hallway in silence, ready to pounce.

Pounce, he did, but Jenna was ready for him and scrubbed his fur as, animated, he twirled in tight delighted circles, stabbing her toes with his sharp claws and walloping her legs with his hard, whippy tail.

When he turned his attention to Adrian, she flipped on the hallway light before she removed her coat and tossed it over the stair newel.

Adrian swept his hand over the dog's side and then scrubbed his head, holding the carrier bag behind his back to stop Domino from devouring the chicken.

'Where did you get hot chicken?'

'The supermarket.' He followed her along the hallway, into the kitchen and placed the bag on her small table. 'You want to grab plates?'

Confusion rolled through her. The last she'd heard, he'd wanted to meet up, take her out for coffee. She spun on her heel, squinted at him. 'Adrian, what are you doing here?'

He waved his hand over the carrier bag. 'Feeding you, as you don't even seem to have enough time to reply to my texts.'

She had no idea whether Adrian was flirting with her, or whether he just believed she needed looking after. She wasn't sure she could cope with his flirting, and even less sure if she was able to handle him walking away.

She turned away from him and grabbed two plates out of the cupboard, together with wine glasses to accommodate the bottle of Chateauneuf-du-Pape he dumped on the table along with the rest of the food. Her stomach howled with hunger. She might as well eat before he took it away, but he had a wife to get back to. She needed to make it clear to him that she wasn't interested in married men.

As he pulled a whole chicken out of an insulated bag, Jenna grabbed her chopping board and laid it on the table in front of him so he could put the chicken straight on it. He followed it with a container of salad, coleslaw and a box of potato wedges. Instead of waiting to be invited, he washed his hands in the kitchen sink, rooted through a couple of drawers before he turned, her carving knife in his hand.

She swallowed several times to stop the watering of her mouth. Baked beans may have been on her menu as the idea of a plain salad had palled. She gathered serving spoons and cutlery for them both and slipped into one of her kitchen chairs, more aware of him with every passing moment. His knee touched hers as he slipped into the chair opposite and she would have shot back to her feet if it wasn't for the huge dog who'd invaded her space and dumped his chin on her lap, pressing down a ton of weight to prevent her from moving.

'Domino's a thief.'

Adrian grinned as he stabbed a piece of chicken with his fork and held it in front of his lips. 'I think you've mentioned that before.'

Jenna lowered her head and started to eat, aware with every bite she took of his observation of her. She tilted her head to gaze at him. She was tall, but he was taller still. Upright in her kitchen chair, she had to raise her chin to meet his eyes.

'What are you really doing here?'

He pushed a piece of chicken into his mouth, chewed, the muscles in his jaw flexing, so she distracted herself by letting her gaze wander down his neck to watch his Adam's apple bob as he swallowed. He had a nice neck, tanned and smooth. He swallowed again, then stopped chewing, his eyes serious as she cruised her gaze back up to his. He placed his cutlery down on either side of his plate.

'I needed to speak with you, and damned if you aren't the most difficult person to pin down, so I figured I'd stalk you, feed you and see what the hell is going on.' He shrugged his wide shoulders. 'I'm confused, Jenna. When we met, I got the distinct impression that we shared... something and that if the circumstances were different and Fliss wasn't missing we'd probably have moved on that. After Fliss turned up, I gave you space. You needed it, but now I feel like the whole situation is sliding away. I don't like that feeling.' He puffed out his lips with a husky laugh that had her heart skittering in her chest. 'Fact is, I like you.'

Heat slid up her neck to warm her cheeks. She couldn't remember the last time she'd had a relationship. It wasn't easy being a sergeant, working shifts. She wouldn't date anyone at work, she'd witnessed too many disastrous break-ups to even bother, and there weren't too many civilians interested in dating a female police officer. Possibly Denton Harper, but that would never be a match made in heaven, despite his attractiveness. She'd realised today he was designed to sympathise and understand the criminal mind. She was too tough, too devoted to her job, black and white. Innocent until proven guilty and then avoided once that guilt was proven.

'Thank you.' She cut a tiny morsel of chicken, held it on the end of her fork. It appeared the Chief Crown Prosecutor really did believe in the truth, the whole truth and nothing but the truth. It was time to be as honest with him, even if she did lose her dinner. She scanned the table. Nope, he'd never be able to scoop it up now and take it with him. She'd be on him like a pack of Dominoes.

She took a hard swallow to rid herself of the food in her mouth. 'You're married. I don't date married men.'

Surprise lit his eyes, and then his lips quirked up at the edges. 'I'm separated.'

'You *said* you were married.' She dashed her gaze down to his left hand, sans wedding ring, and then narrowed her eyes at him while she studied his face.

There was no guilt as he gave an easy shrug. 'Technically, I am.'

'You're going through a divorce?'

'Yes. But I am still married. In the eyes of the law.' If nothing else, he evidently believed in the law.

'Why didn't you tell Donna that when she asked?'

'Ah, Donna.' His eyes lit with understanding. 'Because I didn't consider it any of her business at the time and I had no idea you were eavesdropping. Don't you know nothing good ever comes of that?'

Offended, she snapped her fork down on the table, oblivious of waking Domino as he jerked his head from her lap, her jaw flexed while she glared at Adrian. 'It's none of my business either and I wasn't eavesdropping, I just happened to hear. I was in the same room as you. You must have known I could hear. You never said anything directly to me. I thought you were trying to distance yourself from me after I'd...' She stuttered to a halt. 'After I virtually threw myself at you when I couldn't find Fliss.'

His lips kicked up at the edges. 'I can't imagine you throwing yourself at anyone, Jenna. You have far too much self-control.'

'What did you imagine, then?'

'Nothing at the time. Quite honestly, I had nothing on my mind except a God's honest fear that Donna was making a pass at me. I never gave it a thought that you could hear, but even if you did, you didn't need any complications in your life at that point.'

'I never considered you a complication.' He certainly was. She'd told Harper he was a complication.

'No? You had so much on your plate. I couldn't expect anything from you. At first, your mind was on your sister. Even when she was found, you were still knee deep in the case. And when you discovered it was Frank Bartwell, you didn't need the complications of a relationship and certainly not with the circumstances we found ourselves in. I was there to ensure nothing detrimental happened regarding conflict of interest and it couldn't have been more conflicted if we'd started anything. When we... hugged, you needed... support.' Hugged could be construed as an understatement, unless that was all he'd seen it as.

'You think I was looking for a shoulder to cry on?' She reached across the small table, poked him dead centre of his broad chest. 'I'm stronger than that.'

Without a flinch, he took her hand in his smooth, warm one. 'You are strong, Jenna, I have no doubt, but everybody needs a shoulder to cry on at least once in their life.'

Tiredness overwhelmed her. The pressure of the job, the tragedy of murdered women. If there was one thing she needed there and then, it was a strong shoulder to cry on.

'Everyone?' Resisting the temptation, she tugged her hand from his. 'Even you?'

He inclined his head. 'Even me.'

A sob caught in her throat. 'Who do you go to?'

He raised a hand and scratched at the dark bristles forming on his chin and gave a rueful shrug. 'These days? There's no one around. It used to be my wife.'

'Your wife?' Deflated, she leaned back as adrenaline seeped out of her. Perhaps he needed a sympathetic ear too. 'What happened?'

'Work.'

'Work? She surely knew what you did when she married you?'

'She did. But she never realised how many hours she'd spend alone. And when the revelation eventually hit her, she found someone she could spend more time with.'

'A younger man?'

'That's the beast of it. Not a younger man. An older one. Older than me by probably five years. Older than her by eight.'

Surprised, Jenna couldn't disguise her interest. 'Where did she meet him?'

'He was our builder.'

'Oh.' Uncomfortable, Jenna picked up her knife and fork and stabbed at more food to push into her mouth. 'What was he building?'

'The extension to our house.' He ran his tongue over his teeth and squinted into the distance. 'So we could start our family.'

'Oh, fuck.'

His snorted laughter was anything but amused. 'And that they did. In our extension, in our living room, our bathroom and, I believe, our bedroom.'

His pain filled her chest with the memory of her father doing the same to her mother. She placed her hand on the arm he rested on the table. 'I'm sorry. How long were you married?'

'Ten years.'

Surprised, she raised her eyebrows at him. 'You must have been very young.' Or she'd misjudged his age.

'Twenty-two. She was nineteen.'

'Wow.'

'Yeah. It was good to start with, we met at university. I'd taken a year out before I went. I was in my third year; she was in her first when we met. We did a lot of growing up together, a lot of partying, but when the partying faded, we found we had very little in common, so we decided kids would be the way to go.' He took another piece of chicken from the board, speared a couple of potatoes from the plastic pot and placed them on his plate. 'So, now I'm further down the divorce route than I was back in November.'

Tiny little hitches of breath stuck in her throat. She wasn't sure she was ready for him. On a good day, he was too much, but while she was weak, and he was kind, it would be a disaster. He wouldn't see the real her. She wasn't gentle and tearful and quiet. She was strong and precocious and loud.

A regretful smile kicked up the edges of his lips. 'So, what about you, Jenna? Where are you at?'

Instead of answering, she hit him with her own question. 'How did you know I'd be alone? I could have had someone waiting for me.' She waved her hand around the room. 'Someone at home.' Other than Fliss. She could have had a date with Denton, brought him home with her.

His smile widened. 'You could have, in which case the place wouldn't have been in darkness and you wouldn't have hauled me through the front door to devour my food.'

She stared down at the plate she'd managed to clear without realising, then stretched her fingers out for a leg of chicken.

'They could be here later.'

'They could, but I checked with Mason.'

'Shit.'

'What's wrong with that?'

'Mason knows you were coming here tonight?'

'No. Mason knows I asked him if you were involved with anyone.'

'Great.' She ripped off a piece of chicken with her teeth, chewed it with gusto. 'I'll never hear the end of it.' She slapped the bone down on her plate and wiped her fingers on a piece of paper towel, irritation skimming through her.

'He also mentioned there's some counsellor who's been showing an interest. That you exchanged numbers.'

The bloody big mouth. She'd kill him when she got hold of him.

'Mason said he was pretty good-looking. For a dweeb.'

Jenna kneaded her forehead. 'He thinks you're a prick, but it seems he was quite happy to spill his guts to you.'

Adrian smiled as he laid his knife and fork side by side on his empty plate. He pushed back his chair and came to his feet. 'I'll tell you what. You've got my number too. Have a think about it, see if you want to pursue something with the other guy, in which case just let me know and I won't bother you again.'

He scrubbed his fingers over Domino's head and then turned for the door.

The temptation to call out his name rose, so she pushed back her own chair, but couldn't quite persuade her legs to obey the command to stand. 'Adrian.'

He paused, his back to her. 'I'll see you another time, Jenna. Sleep well.'

She knew for certain she wouldn't.

34

Eyes still gritty from long hours of work and poor sleep, Jenna gave a weary blink at the assembled crew as DI Taylor nudged up to rest his backside next to hers on the edge of the desk. With a sideways glance, she could tell he hadn't fared much better and the effects of the jet lag had very definitely caught him up.

Pain tightened his features as he shuffled further onto the desk.

In the hubbub of the incident room, Jenna kept her voice low. 'Are you all right?'

DI Taylor squinted at her. 'Too long sitting on the plane. Sciatic nerve. Bloody painful. Right in my arse.'

'Have you taken anything for it?'

'No.'

'You should.'

'Vicky told me to. I haven't had a chance yet.'

Not one to baby him with two daughters, a son and an executive job on the council, Taylor's wife Vicky would have made the suggestion and let him get on with it. If he didn't take painkillers, he'd gain no sympathy.

Jenna's lips twitched as she slipped to her feet and rounded the desk to swipe the two new packets of analgesics from her desk and then grabbed a small white plastic cup and filled it from the water cooler in the corner of the room.

DI Taylor sent her a grateful look as he popped the tablets onto his hand. Two high strength ibuprofen with paracetamol and caffeine, designed to get into the system quickly. 'Thanks, mum.' He gave her a quick wink, raised the cup to his mouth and washed the tablets down with the water before placing the cup on the desk.

As he came to his feet, DI Taylor clapped his hands and instant silence greeted the urgency of his command.

'Right. We'll make this quick. We have a lot to get through.' He cast his gaze around at the assembled officers and gave them a grim nod. 'A quick update on current cases.' He held out his hand to indicate Jenna. 'DS Morgan arrested Robert Mills in connection with the Mervyn Lucas Charity fraud. She is currently compiling statements and evidence to put forward to CPS in order for him to be charged. As he has made a full confession, this will need to be corroborated, but hopefully it will go smoothly. I believe DC Downey and DC Ellis are assisting with this,' he raised his head to check the acknowledging nods from Ryan and Mason, 'together with the charges against Mr Mills' wife, Julie Mills, for assaulting a police officer and obstruction of a police officer. Again, DS Morgan will submit the files on this...'

As DI Taylor ran through the list of updates, Jenna zoned out, her gaze skipping over the officers who weren't there to listen to updates on administration but wanted to get to the point. Just as she did.

'And finally...' Jenna's attention zapped back in, '... a quick update in connection with our two murders, as I know you're all keen to get back out there and find something. At this stage, any lead will help. This person has murdered, twice, and it is our belief they will murder again.' Taylor's stony gaze cruised across the room. 'DS Morgan and her team visited Long Lartin yesterday to interview Paul McCambridge, his counsellor and the five prison guards who were present when she last visited. Unfortunately, this proved relatively fruitless.' At the united groan, Taylor continued. 'It's back to the legwork. Follow up on those door-to-doors, anyone who is free, grab the database and let's get all these neighbours visited.' DI Taylor stopped; his head raised to locate the continued moaning. 'PC Gardner, you have something to say?'

PC Gardner leaned against the back wall of the incident room, arms crossed over his chest. Young, arrogant and dangerous. 'It all seems pretty pointless cruising around neighbours who weren't even in. Can't we chivvy up forensics, so we have something to go on?'

His sentiments were probably reflected by a few other officers, but Gardner's whole demeanour exhibited an absence of respect. Jenna had nothing but admiration for DI Taylor's controlled response.

'Chivvying up forensics won't get us the right result, PC Gardner, but it may well put an entire investigation at risk if we don't get it right. In this aspect, we have to exercise patience.' Something the young PC seemed to lack.

Gardner held DI Taylor's direct stare for a moment before his gaze skittered away to allow Taylor to continue.

'PC Wallis has ascertained from Julia Clements that the key in the front door of her house was the one from the shed. We have no idea who gained entry first, Karen Prestwich or the murderer.' Taylor drew in a long breath and blew it out again. 'Forensics are working on the information on DC Downey's phone.' Ryan crossed his arms over his chest and leaned back against the wall as he nodded, stress lines deepening around his mouth as DI Taylor continued. 'Although this isn't fool proof, we want to know who the women are who fall into the same profile as the copycat.' DI Taylor stopped, his jaw flexing. 'DC Gardner?'

'Can't Ryan just message all the women? Warn them.'

Jenna's jaw dropped and Ryan closed weary looking eyes and thudded his head against the back wall. Even younger than PC Gardner, Ryan got it, he didn't need the constant reminders of how to uphold the law. Perhaps not a seasoned police officer, he wasn't a hot headed vigilante.

DI Taylor ran his tongue over his teeth, Jenna suspected to give himself a moment to control his annoyance. 'No, PC Gardner. PC

Downey cannot do that. First, they'd all think he was stalking them. Second, those that didn't would run to the press and we'd have a riot on our hands. Third, every bit of evidence that needs to be painstakingly recorded for, hopefully, a prosecution would be wiped out.'

PC Gardner pushed himself away from the wall. 'But—'

DI Taylor raised his hand to stop Gardner going any further. 'PC Gardner. We will stick to the tried-and-tested methods of policing and not run off in a wild abandonment of the law. When forensics come back to us with the information we require, which they are in the process of obtaining from Y'ello, with the appropriate legal documentation in place, we will compile an Osman list. We are expecting this any time soon, but it is a process. We will then send officers out to the addresses we will have obtained through the right channels to give these women information pertaining to a high risk of death or threat of murder. That is what the Osman list exists for. We can then offer these women protection, should they wish it.'

'If we could just—'

'Fucking wassock.' Mason muttered in Jenna's ear to draw a reluctant smile from her.

'No, we cannot just.' DI Taylor's voice hardened. 'There is no rushing the law. There is no point making a successful arrest only to have the case thrown out of court, with a flea in our ears from the judge because we have not adhered to the correct procedures.'

PC Gardner flopped back against the wall, his mouth turned down at the edges in a sullen droop.

DI Taylor scanned the room, eyebrows heavy over steely eyes. 'Any questions?' Taylor gave the room a moment in the heavy silence before he spoke. 'Let's get to work. You know where I am if you need me.'

As the team filed out, Taylor's gaze slid to over to meet Jenna's, his mouth a hard line of dissatisfaction. 'There's another pain in my arse. This one you can't get rid of with painkillers.'

35

Who'd have thought a slight woman could put up such a ferocious fight? He raised a shaky hand to the burn in his neck and brought away fingers smeared in blood. She'd clawed him, raking his skin with her long fingernails.

There was no getting away from it this time, he truly had fucked up. Right royally, without a shadow of a doubt, fucked the fuck up.

The sting in his scalp had him raising his hand to check for damage. She'd wrenched the roots from his head, leaving tender spots all over.

Legs still wobbly, he didn't have the strength to rise from where he'd slid down the wall to collapse in the corner of the kitchen.

A trickle of blood ran down his sleeve to pool in the palm of his upturned hand where he rested it on the cool tiled floor. The bitch had got him. She hadn't quite killed him, but his life might just as well be over.

He stared at the broken body, six paces in front of him, the knife he'd shoved up to the hilt into her protruded from her ribs. The knife with his DNA, his blood all over it. He'd never given it a thought as he rammed it into her with such desperation.

He closed his eyes and let his head thunk back on the wall. It wouldn't make any difference if he left more DNA smeared over the paintwork. He had no idea how to clean up this shit this time, there was no amount of bleach could wash away his DNA. He might as well hand himself over to the police now.

Exhaustion set in and his body started to relax, a soft floating feeling took him away, up, up into the dark skies with the stars beyond as his blood leached in rhythmic pumps from his body.

He jerked awake, glanced at the mess that surrounded him. He needed to clean up. If only he had help. But there was no one he could call on. He was on his own.

He drew his knees up to get his feet under him, his heels gaining no traction on the floor until he gave up and rested.

The woman had taken him by surprise.

He took in a deep lungful of air and breathed it out again, past the pain in the soft tissue of his armpit where she'd got him. Stuck him like a pig. But he'd stuck her back. Not without some considerable skill and strength. He could take pride in that. His lips curled in self-derision. Pride in the fact that he'd bested a woman – no, a girl, only half his size in a fight which should have been totally one sided. He snorted out his disgust.

Instead of shock swimming through her eyes the moment they'd met his across the kitchen, they'd flared with indignation and anger. She'd come at him, fists raised like a fucking prize boxer, pelted him once, twice, three times, before he'd managed to duck under the next flying fist. He'd closed his eyes and grabbed her around the waist. Wrapping both arms about her, he'd ignored the tear of his scalp as she'd wrenched his hair out by the roots. Her shrieks and howls had pierced his eardrums as he ploughed her across the room while she dug her heels down, the rubber soles of her shoes squeaking on the granite tiles. He'd jerked her upright, picking her off the floor and flung her at the ceramic sink, pleasure skimming through him as he'd palmed one of the knives from the knife block on her counter. Short handled, twelve inch blade, perfect balance.

But he'd misjudged his opponent a second time.

With a wild scream, she'd flung herself at him, taking him off balance, so he staggered backwards. She'd reared back her head and then slammed her forehead into his. Before he could counteract her next movement, she'd landed a hard punch to his throat. As he'd gasped for breath, she'd grabbed his knife hand and twisted, ramming it into his shoulder so he'd staggered back against the wall.

Pain more excruciating than he'd ever known had howled through him in white-hot agony. Hauling in soft pants of breath through his damaged throat, he'd blinked through the sweat dripping into his eyes and watched her make her first mistake as she turned to run.

Without a thought in his head, he'd acted on pure instinct. With a feral yell, he'd yanked the knife from the soft flesh of his underarm and launched himself away from the wall full pelt into the back of her.

As she'd hit the floor, he'd slammed on top of her. Breath rushed from her in a loud grunt and he'd grabbed her hair, wrenched her head back and took the opportunity to ram the knife home just as she twisted beneath him. The brief flicker of acknowledgement that she was about to die had guttered out as quickly as it had lit her pretty caramel eyes. Pink bubbles had dribbled from her open lips.

He'd scrambled back from her, his boots skimming through the blood oozing across the floor. Hers and his in a wallowing mix, the warmth of it had soaked through his jeans to his skin.

Panic now heated his cooling skin and he turned his head to assess the damage. She'd virtually killed him. She might have yet if he didn't staunch the flow of blood. If she'd hit an artery, he suspected he'd already be dead.

He braced himself against the wall and pushed up until he gained his feet. In a drunken stagger, he managed to get to the other side of the room and grabbed a fistful of clean tea towels she'd stacked on the bench. He bunched two of them up and shoved them inside his T-shirt against the hole in his armpit. Numb all the way down his arm, he barely felt the press of the towels against his injury.

He grabbed another towel and scrubbed at his face and over his burning scalp. Drawing it away, he stared at the blood stains soaking it.

He tried to catch his breath, but it came in short, shallow snatches as his eyesight faded to black. If he fainted, he'd never stand a chance of getting out of there. He'd probably die if he didn't get help. He desperately needed help, but he could hardly go to a hospital. They'd recognise the knife wound for what it was and call the filth.

He drew in a deeper breath. He needed to move. It didn't matter about the rules, they no longer held any importance. The main focus was to clean up and get out.

One handed, he retrieved the bleach from under the sink where everyone kept it. He held the bottle against his chest while he squeezed the lid together to unlock it with his uninjured hand, the other one too numb to feel.

He squirted the fluid around and then stared as the floor came up to meet him and then receded again. His thoughts wallowed and staggered through thickening sludge. With a stumbling gait, he managed to open a tall cupboard and take out her mop and bucket, barely able to lift the bucket from the sink once he'd filled it with scalding water.

All the research, all the information gathering still paid off as he reached for the bottle of disinfectant and glugged it into the bucket.

Without wringing out the mop, he plunged it into the water and then sloshed it across the floor, spreading the blood in an ever widening circle until it covered the entire kitchen floor. He thrust the mop back into the bucket, this time giving it a quick squeeze before he threw it over the floor again. He bumped it against her body, working his way up to her head.

One handed, he wrenched the mop away, fury getting the better of him as it caught in the long carrot coloured tresses of her hair and her head gave wet, hollow thumps against the tiles. He hammered the mop up and down, up and down, and still the stupid fucking woman's hair wouldn't break free of the mop and her head slammed harder against the floor.

For a moment, the black fury glazed his eyes over. He couldn't think where he was, couldn't see. His head spun in sickening circles as he stared at the twisted body and then sunk to his knees beside her. Every ounce of energy drained from him, he curled his body downwards until his forehead touched the smooth tiles and he tucked his numb arm into his stomach, wrapping the other one around it.

He puffed out short spurts of air as his blood pooled around him and his muscles weakened. She had killed him. He was about to die in the same puddle of blood and bleach and piss as her.

He didn't deserve it. It should have been so much simpler than this.

He was supposed to be a god. Strong, powerful, brilliant.

He'd never been any of those in his entire pitiful life. It was unlikely he'd ever be more than he was. The son of a gambling, alcoholic whore.

He toppled onto his side and lay still, the burn of the bleach soaking through his thin black T-shirt and heavy denim jeans instead of the PPE suit he'd been instructed to wear at all times.

He'd failed.

His eyelids, too heavy to keep open, closed and the soft comfort of darkness blanketed him.

36

Jenna waited up for Fliss with the weight of a thirty-two kilo Dalmatian sprawled across her lap until her legs went numb and her shoulder ached from where he rested his chin on it.

All for the comfort of knowing her sister was home. She was safe.

Jenna smoothed her hand over Domino's velvet coat, tracing the long line of scar tissue along from his shoulder to his hip while she smothered the worry that surfaced each time Fliss went out.

The soft tones of the TV brought her a little comfort, with its benign western repeat from the 1970s as her eyelids drooped and she shuffled Domino into a more comfortable position.

Muscles lax, Jenna closed her eyes and slipped into a slight snooze.

The ping of her phone jerked her awake and she blinked away the haziness of sleep as she retrieved the phone from the arm of the chair. Denton Harper's text glowed from the screen.

It was really good to see you today. I appreciate you have a job to do and you did it very professionally. Have your sorted out your complication yet? How about dinner?

Flattered, Jenna pushed upright so she could read the message once more, adjusting Domino as he grunted and groaned, a dead weight reluctant to move from the comfort of her body. She jiggled him; his head lolled as it bumped its way down her shoulder onto her stomach so she could slip her frozen feet from the footrest onto the floor. Pins and needles shot through her numbed feet as she wiggled her toes to get the circulation going once more.

She read the message again and then tapped the screen to return to Adrian's earlier message.

Coffee, cake, chat?

It was a no-brainer. She wriggled to free her trapped hand from underneath Domino's shoulder so she could type her reply.

I'm free tomorrow after 1800 hours.

Dinner, then?

Surprised at the speedy reply, Jenna grinned. Right decision.
She tapped the screen to return to Denton.

Thanks for the offer, but I think I'd like to give my complication a fair chance. You're a really nice man and also very professional, but it would be unkind of me to keep you hanging on while I sort out my life.

She stared at the screen as she waited for a reply. When it went blank, she placed her phone back on the arm of the chair and bumped her heels on the floor to rid herself of the last of the pins and needles.

Domino raised his head, tilted it as he listened and then rammed his bony elbow into her groin as he wriggled himself free from her lap to tip-tap over to the open lounge door. Alert, he waited, his connection to Fliss so strong, Jenna wondered if he merely sensed her approach, or if it was something more tangible, such as the sound of her car engine as it approached home. Whatever the reason, the dog knew instinctively she was on her way.

A full fifteen minutes it took before Fliss turned the key in the front door.

The icy blast of a February night whipped through the door as Fliss barged in, her gentle laughter at Domino's greeting soothed Jenna's heart as she realised she'd held her breath for almost the whole time Fliss had been gone.

She needed to stop. She needed to let her sister go and stop overprotecting her.

Fliss bustled through the door and flung herself on top of Jenna, giving her a swift kiss on the top of her head and making her realise she'd never let her go fully. Fliss was her baby sister and Jenna loved her.

As Fliss slipped into the seat beside her, nudging her over so she could yank Domino up onto their laps, Jenna huffed at her to make her understand she was being a damned nuisance.

Oblivious, Fliss snuggled in. 'It's bloody freezing out there.' Wide awake, unlike Jenna, she tickled her icy fingers under Jenna's jumper and screeched with laughter as Jenna scrabbled to get away from her.

'Get off, you cow.' It was good to see her happy. Jenna grinned at her. 'You had a good time?'

'Yeah. It was okay.'

'Only okay? You seem pretty stoked for someone who had an okay time.'

Fliss planted a light punch on Jenna's shoulder. 'Guess who asked me out?'

Boom! Just like that, Jenna's mouth clamped down on any reply she could imagine. She kept her eyes flat as she deliberately turned her attention to Domino, smoothing her hand over his broad head. Voice steady, she gave her head a slow shake. 'I don't know. Who asked you out?'

Fliss's next punch carried a little more weight and Jenna jerked her head upright. 'Mason.'

'Mason?' She tried, really tried, but the injection of surprise in her voice evidently didn't cut it with her sister. If Fliss was ever on jury duty with Jenna on the stand, she'd know immediately if she was lying.

Fliss pursed her lips, fine wrinkles appeared at the side of her eyes as she squinted at Jenna. 'You knew.'

'I didn't know he'd asked you.'

'You knew he was going to?'

There was no point denying it. 'Yes.'

Fliss leaned in until her nose almost touched Jenna's. 'Please don't tell me he asked your permission.'

'No, he...'

Fliss jerked back so Domino jiggled about, jamming his back foot into Jenna's stomach as he struggled to get comfortable. 'Bloody hell.'

'Does it matter?'

'Not really.' Fliss slumped back against the sofa cushions and curled her fingers around Domino's ear to give it a light scratch. 'Before I say yes to him, have you and Mason ever... you know, done the dirty?'

'No! God no!'

'Well, that's hardly a good recommendation for him.'

'Possibly not. But it's different. Mason and I are work colleagues. When we first met, he had that strange girlfriend.'

'The psycho?'

Jenna chuckled. 'Yeah, slept with him on the third date, then thought they were engaged or some shit. It took him eight months to realise what had happened and move her out. Him and I, we never had that attraction. From the word go, I've treated him like a younger brother. He's really nice. A pain in the arse, but I trust him with you, Fliss, or I would have told him straight when he asked me.'

'But he shouldn't have asked you first.'

'I don't see a problem. Mason's got backbone. It wasn't about being cowardly but being honourable. He wanted to make sure I wouldn't object to him dating my sister and that I was comfortable with it.' She slid a sideways glance over at her sister. 'He also wanted to give you enough time to get over Ed.' She sucked air in through her teeth. 'And you know... the abduction.' She touched her hand to Fliss's thigh. 'If it's what you want, then I say go ahead and give it a go.' She eyed her sister. 'If it's not right, though, dump him quickly and get it over and done with, will you?'

Momentary surprise flickered through Fliss's eyes and then she grinned as she understood. 'Of course.' She pulled her phone from her pocket and tapped out a quick message. Within seconds, a reply sounded, and she stared at the screen. 'Looks like I have a date tomorrow night.' Her smile widened as she waggled the phone at Jenna.

Jenna picked up her own phone and waggled it back at Fliss. 'Me too.'

37

WEDNESDAY 12 FEBRUARY, 08:00 HRS

At bang on 0800 hours, the last thing Jenna needed was to be greeted by a bloodbath. She'd not even got in through the station doors at 0740 hours when Mason, face grim, strode towards her with Ryan in tow. Despite the early shift and lack of sunrise, they hadn't even the decency to bring her a coffee, even though each of them protectively cradled one themselves. She'd considered confiscating one of them, but it would only be sweet, slushy shit, not the pure black, heavily caffeinated saviour of the universe she needed.

In truth, she hadn't needed to go. It was their shout, the boys could have dealt with it just as effectively as she could, but curiosity and a desire to get away from the looming paperwork pile got the better of her.

'A domestic.'

She eyed the car keys in Mason's hand as he made his way around the car to the driver's door and considered commandeering them.

He jiggled them in his hand and grinned at her over the roof of the silver Vauxhall Insignia. 'Possession, Sarg. Nine-tenths of the law.'

Unconcerned, she shrugged her shoulders and reached for the passenger door at the same time as Ryan. His eyes widened as their hands met.

'Shotgun!' he burst out.

She slapped his hand away and grabbed the door handle, pulling it upwards. 'Outranked. Better luck next time, Detective.' She slipped into the passenger seat and exchanged an elbow nudge with Mason as he sputtered with laughter.

'Nice one, boss.'

Jim Downey was already well ensconced as Jenna, Mason and Ryan walked into the bloodbath. In her entire career, with many domestics under her belt, Jenna had never witnessed a massacre of such epic proportions.

'Don't even enter this room.' Jim barely looked up from where he crouched next to the victim.

'Fuck,' Mason whispered in her ear as he leaned into her. 'There's too much blood for only one victim.'

'Two victims.' Jim took a photograph, changed position and set up for another one before he peered over the camera at them. 'The other one, white male, taken to hospital.'

'Still alive?'

'Barely.'

Jenna almost leaned against the door frame, then stepped back to inspect it. Fine blood splatter peppered it at head-height. 'Was it a domestic?'

PC Lee Gardner, assigned to the first-response team, swaggered along the hallway towards them as Jenna resisted the temptation to groan. Gardner bared his teeth in a cocky grin as he spotted Jenna. He whipped a pen from where he'd had it balanced behind his ear and tapped the small notebook he slid from his uniform pocket. 'Looks like a domestic. He slapped her around, she stabbed him, he stabbed her.'

Jim Downey straightened from where he crouched in front of the victim, impatience mixing with weary derision as he considered the PC. 'I'm flattered that you've deigned to express your two year experience, secondary-education opinion on the situation, PC Gardner. I'm sure it holds a lot more weight than my double degree, masters and doctorate.' He puffed out a sigh. 'Would you care to expand on your theory?'

A dark burgundy flush stole up Gardner's face and his eyes turned stony as his mouth tightened. 'I just gave my opinion, that's all.'

'And a very misleading opinion, if I could be so bold as to point out.'

'I can't see why, it's quite clear what happened.' Gardner's jaw squared up and Jenna heard the grind of his teeth. More than content to allow Jim to figuratively wipe the floor with him, she resisted the temptation to lean against Jim's crime scene wall and attract any attention to herself.

Jim let out a soft cough, placing the back of his hand in front of his mouth as he did. As he removed it, he took a step closer, camera still in his other hand, his eyes turned wintery. 'It's not clear, not to you, not to me. We can all assume what happened, but we know the old adage that goes along with that.' He spread his arms wide. 'There is nothing in this room that is clear. Not from my very first glance. It's one of the most confusing crime scenes I've come across, so how do you propose to solve the case, PC Gardner?' His voice still soft, Jim peered over the top of his frameless glasses to skewer the constable with a look. 'Sit on your arse at your desk, raise the paperwork, attribute it to a domestic and close the case down?'

Gardner's chest puffed out. 'Well, if no one else was involved—'

Jim cut him short, his thick white eyebrows slammed down. 'This is a crime scene!' He circled his hand over the room. 'At no point so far have we established any facts beyond,' he pointed, 'there being a dead body there.'

'A female.'

'No!' He slammed the single word out to stop PC Gardner. '*You* don't even know that for sure. We have a dead body. As yet unidentified. Ah, ah!' As Gardner opened his mouth to interrupt yet again, Jim wagged a finger at him. 'You do not know for a certainty that this is a female. *You* have not examined the victim.' His skinny chest expanded as he breathed in. On a soft breath out, he smiled. 'We can assume that the deceased is a female, but until we have confirmed identification, who's to say?'

'What about the other... umm... victim?'

'Ah, well. Once again, we cannot assume that the person removed from the scene ten minutes ago was a victim.'

Jenna scrubbed a hand through her short hair as she tried not to jump down the PC's throat. His lack of respect still lurked in belligerent eyes.

She twisted her head around, pinning PC Gardner with her coldest stare. 'PC Gardner, considering you were first on the scene and you have a notebook in your hand, so far I've heard very little of consequence from you. Facts, PC Gardner. We're police officers.' She flicked her hand around to include Mason and Ryan. 'All of us, police officers.' She lowered her voice. 'Grow up, stop showing off and do your job.'

His pale blue eyes shot wide at her attack and she drew in a long breath.

'Give me a report of the facts, PC Gardner. Make it succinct and make no assumptions.'

He pulled back his shoulders, his gaze scooting around the others before he started. 'We had a shout at 0650 hours, Sarg.' She nodded for him to continue. 'Sudden death. The mother called it in. She'd come to check on her daughter. She hadn't heard anything from her and was apparently worried. She's been taken back to her own house by PC Donna McGuire. She only lives around the corner. She's shaken.'

Jenna raised her eyebrows, that had to be the understatement of the year. It was a godsend though, that Donna was with the mother instead of the...

'Twat,' Mason muttered from behind her and had her lips twitching up.

She met PC Gardner's pale gaze. 'Did you touch anything?'

He nodded, his eyes shifting from her to Jim, less confident than he had been. It would do him good to bring him down a peg or two. He'd possibly make a good police officer if he learned a lesson. She skimmed her gaze over him, the neck of his black wicking T-shirt open wide, presumably to show off the chest he appeared so proud of when he puffed it out. She'd reserve opinion of him.

'We had to; we didn't have a choice.'

'What do you mean?'

Jim let out a heartfelt sigh and Lee's eyes flickered with doubt. 'We stepped in—'

'Rushed in like a bull in a china shop, stepping through blood, guts and gore.' Jim turned away and set up his camera for another shot.

'Stepped in, checked the bodies. The male... the second person was still alive, so we had no choice.'

'What injury had he sustained?'

'He was bleeding profusely from a wound to his left armpit.'

'What kind of wound?'

Lee flashed a quick look at Jim and lowered his voice. 'I'd guess at a knife wound. It looked pretty deep to me. I had to hold a tea towel on it until the paramedics arrived. He'd bled out a lot. It was all down his front. He was propped up against the wall.' He glanced at Jim again, his lips twisting. 'I took photographs once the paramedics were here to give the position of the body.'

She gave him an encouraging nod. He'd done his job, maybe he wasn't as bad as all that. Perhaps all that was required was training, a lesser sense of his own importance and a step towards maturity. It didn't always go together.

'They told me he'd been stabbed in the axillary artery and lost a lot of blood. He appeared to be unconscious, they said his pulse was very weak. Then they whipped him off to A&E.'

'Okay. Who accompanied him?'

'PC Massey.'

At least they'd got that right. 'Good.' She took pity on him. It wasn't every day you came across dead bodies. 'How long have you been here?'

'About an hour and a half, Sarg.'

'Okay. Get yourself back to the station, get cleaned up, have a cup of tea and write up your notes. With facts. I'll be back later.' She reached out and patted him on the shoulder. 'You'll be okay.'

As he walked away, his shoulders rolled down, his spine wasn't as stiff, and a pearl of pity stirred in her. They'd all been cocky at one time.

'Fucking twat.'

Still, Mason's pithy description wasn't far from the truth.

She turned her attention back to Jim Downey as he leaned over the body, pen in hand, as he lifted a lock of amber hair from her shoulder.

'What have we got, Jim?'

'Female, age twenty-five, five foot six, identified by her mother as Eleanor Mooney. That's all the information the poor woman gave before she collapsed.'

Jenna sensed rather than saw the tension run through Ryan. She stared at the redhead on the floor and then did a slow head turn to meet Ryan's agonised expression. 'Not another one.'

He rolled his head forward in a single nod, his gaze never leaving hers. 'She's on my list.'

'Christ. Another nurse?'

Ryan nodded again and Jenna turned her attention back to her chief forensics officer. 'Who was the other person?'

'I don't know.'

'Did the mother recognise him?'

Jim clucked his tongue. 'They didn't ask. Mrs Mooney was hysterical. One of the paramedics went with her and Donna. They've probably had to sedate her.'

Surprised, Jenna unhooked Airwaves from her belt and raised the radio to her mouth. 'Juliette Alpha 27, can you patch me through to PC Donna McGuire?'

When the static cleared, she spoke again. 'Donna, it's DS Morgan here.'

'Sarg.'

'Are you with Mrs Mooney right now?'

A low whispered response came. 'No, I'm in the kitchen making a cup of tea for her. The paramedics are with her.'

'Donna, I need you to do something for me. It's not going to be easy, but it is urgent.'

A quick draw of breath preceded her answer. 'Okay.'

'Would you ask Mrs Mooney if she knew who the man on the kitchen floor was?'

The soft sound of Donna sucking in her breath came over Airwaves, followed by a moment of silence. Jenna glanced at Mason and Ryan, deciding which one of the three of them would be better placed to do the job when the radio crackled back to life. 'Give me a minute, boss.'

Jenna plucked her bottom lip between her thumb and forefinger as she waited in the silence, the only sound the soft shuffle of the plastic bags covering Jim's shoes and the gentle suction of blood and bleach as he stepped around the victim, gathering miniscule swabs of evidence.

'Jim.'

He looked up from his position on the floor. 'DS Morgan.'

'I can't see we can be of any use now.' She looked towards the front door where reinforcements were suiting up in their PPE. 'Looks like your team are all arriving and we're only going to be underfoot.'

His lined face looked wearier than she'd noticed before. The rising death toll had to have an impact on his soul as he took ownership of each victim and saw the whole process through. Respect and tenderness always emanated from Jim.

Jenna jumped as Airwaves came back to life. 'Sarg?'

Jenna depressed the button. 'Donna, go ahead.'

Donna dropped her voice to a mere whisper. 'Mrs Mooney says she doesn't have a clue who the man on the floor was, but she wished he was dead rather than her daughter. She confirmed that Ellie was on a dating app and that she'd been arranging to meet up with someone, but Mrs Mooney couldn't remember who. She said she was sure she hadn't made any arrangements yet. She'd normally tell her mum, so she knew she was safe.'

'Okay, thanks, Donna.'

'One more thing...'

'Yes.'

'Mrs Mooney said Ellie was convinced someone had been inside her house. That she had a stalker.'

38

Adrenaline shot through her veins as she strode through the doors of the Princess Royal Hospital A&E, the fast clack of her boots smacking against the shiny, tiled floor as she headed straight for the triage office. If she broke into a run, she'd be stopped and she didn't want that, nor did she want to draw attention to herself.

Mason and Ryan matched her pace, each side of her shoulders. When she'd radioed ahead to speak with PC Massey, she'd had no reply. With the triage office empty, Jenna turned a sharp left and headed for the check-in desk. She whipped her ID from her belt and held it at the window.

'DS Jenna Morgan.' She didn't bother to introduce the others; she didn't have time. 'A man was just brought in by the paramedics, accompanied by a police officer. I don't know the man's name.'

'I'm sorry, but without the man's name...' The receptionist flushed, her plump cheeks wobbled as Jenna waited for a reply. 'I'm sorry. I can't help you.'

Jenna ground her teeth, on the point of snapping. 'Could you please point me in the direction of someone who can?'

Mason leaned over her shoulder and grinned. 'It's important, a matter of life or death.'

The woman almost fell off her chair as she pushed it back from the desk and came to her feet all in one clumsy motion. 'I'll get someone. I'll get...'

Rather than wait for the woman to return, Jenna spun on her heel and followed her as she came out of the office and took off on a fast trot through the doors into the inner sanctum of A&E.

Jenna held her badge high so it could be seen by any interested parties.

Quiet at that time of the morning, Jenna managed to keep sight of the woman who looked as though she was about to disappear down a rabbit hole at any moment.

As she pulled up to the nurses' station, Jenna leaned in. 'Hi, I'm DS Jenna Morgan. I'm looking for a man who has just been brought in in the last half hour, possible knife wound, accompanied by a PC. Do you have any idea where he might be?' Prepared to walk through cubicles, stripping back curtains, Jenna gave them a millisecond of a chance.

The young male nurse on the other side of the desk smiled up at her, his brilliant whitened teeth glowed in the bright, electric lights. 'Absolutely. Come this way.'

Aware of her shadows, Mason and Ryan, Jenna followed the nurse as he reached out for a green curtain surrounding one of the cubicles and whipped it back.

All four of them stared at the empty area.

Jenna lowered her head to her hands to scrape them down her face. 'Where the hell is he?'

Surprise flitted through the nurse's eyes as he turned to meet her gaze. 'He was here less than five minutes ago. I was taking his blood pressure and temperature.'

'Where was my officer?'

Flustered, the nurse held onto the hem of his scrubs tabard and jerked it down, then smoothed his hands over his stomach. 'He went for a coffee while I conducted the tests.'

Jenna pushed her tongue into the side of her cheek while she tried not to raise her voice. 'Did you see him return?'

The nurse shook his head. 'No.'

Irritation sparked as Jenna stared at the nurse. 'Have you lost your patient?'

The nurse whipped his head up and met Jenna's hard eyed stare with one of his own. 'Have you lost your suspect, love?'

Mouth twitching upwards, a secret admiration stirred at the nurse's comeback. He'd take no shit. Not from anyone.

Jenna rubbed her fingers over her mouth, just about to reply, when a bed trolley pushed by a porter swept around the corner, a police officer on one side, a man in full blue scrubs on the other.

The nurse raised a hand and patted his own chest, his relief palpable.

Jenna almost sagged against the wall herself as she puffed out a breath and smiled at PC Massey. 'Hey, Phil, how's it going?'

'Good.' Oblivious of the momentary panic, PC Massey glanced around at the small crowd waiting for him. A flash of surprise raced across his face. 'We needed a quick X-ray to make sure the knife hadn't gone into the bone.'

Jenna sucked in her breath as she cruised her gaze over the bruised and battered comatose figure on the trolley. Whatever had happened, someone had made a good job of beating the crap out of him.

She glanced away and forced a reassuring smile for PC Massey, then turned her attention to the doctor as the porter wheeled the patient into the empty cubicle, flicked on the brake with his foot and left them.

'Doctor...' she squinted at his name badge, 'Jones. Hi, I'm DS Jenna Morgan, this is DC Ellis and DC Downey. Could you give me an update on this patient?'

His patient his first priority, the doctor spoke over his shoulder as he checked the IV line. 'Stab wound victim, arrived approximately,' he glanced at his watch, 'fifty minutes ago. Main priority was to stabilise the patient, get a line in for the IV, which is set up, and a blood transfusion, we're just waiting on bloods for him now. He's lost a lot.'

Not as much as his victim, Jenna was almost tempted to inform him. But it was none of the doctor's business. He was there to do his job. To preserve life, which he was doing. The police had passed that responsibility over to him, it was now Jenna's job to protect and serve.

She stepped closer to the bed as the doctor finished and turned to pick up his notes. 'What else?' She squinted down at the inert patient.

'I've irrigated the wound. As there was no weapon to check, we've X-rayed his shoulder to ensure there's no foreign object inside, broken blade, et cetera. I've had a good ferret around in there to make sure there isn't any broken glass either.' He scribbled on the paperwork attached to the clipboard. 'I'll just go and check the X-ray now, and then I can stitch him up. After that, we'll see to the less urgent injuries.' He ran his gaze over his lifeless patient, sympathy lacing his voice. 'Looks as though he's taken a hard beating.'

Jenna nodded and left the doctor to wander off, with Mason trailing behind him. Pleased she never had to instruct Mason, she left him to get on with it as she took in the state of the man on the hospital trolley.

She cruised her gaze over him. Less than optimistic about the reason he was there, she found no pity in her soul, just a deep desire to know that this was the man they were after. That the killings were over. The first had been one too many. The third had scraped her nerves raw.

DI Taylor's voice over Airwaves whipped her out of her reverie. 'DS Morgan?'

'Sir?'

'We've had a match on the DNA results back from the lab for our second victim, Karen Prestwich.'

'That was quick.'

'It is. Jim Downey put a rush on the swabs he obtained from the victim. Despite his herculean attempt to clean up, the perpetrator managed to leave his semen inside the victim. Forensics ran the results through the system and found a match.'

Jenna never took her eyes from the comatose man on the bed. His thin face beaten and disfigured, the purple bruises livid under his eyes, his nose crooked. From the blood still coating his cracked, swollen lips, there was a possibility he had a missing tooth or two. Sickening though it looked, any sympathy she had remained on hold at the memory of the dead woman.

'His name's Mark Pearson. Previously convicted of three indecent assaults and rape. Salter and Wainwright are on their way around to his address with a warrant to enter. PC Wallis has been despatched to talk to his parole officer.'

At last, things were moving. If the name fit the man in front of her, it would be a relief. If he lived, they'd know more.

The urgency of the voices caught her attention as the nurse and porter bustled back.

'What's happening?'

The nurse gave Jenna a brief glance as he lowered the bed and the porter stepped to the other side. 'We need to get him into theatre now, the bleeding hasn't stopped, it's internal.' He grabbed the IV bag off the trolley to hang it on the side of the bed and trotted alongside as the porter rushed down the corridor.

'PC Massey, follow that trolley, don't let him out of your sight until he's in theatre. Set up a post outside and don't leave it until I send someone to relieve you. I'll get PC Gardner out as soon as possible.'

PC Massey snorted, 'He's a waste of space, can't you send me someone who won't try to date all the nurses. Cocky little prick.'

Before she could reply, he dashed off after the trolley.

She turned as Mason arrived back. 'Mason, Ryan, let's get back to the station and find out if we have our killer or not. We have work to do.'

39

Jenna chewed her bottom lip as she waited for the rest of the team to settle down. She'd taken twenty-five minutes in the rush hour traffic to return from the Princess Royal. Couldn't they have had the team assembled, ready for when she got back? She'd not even stopped to pick up a coffee.

DI Taylor harrumphed to attract everyone's attention and silence fell in the small room. 'Okay, here we go folks.' He opened the buff file he held in his hand and took a moment to adjust his small reading glasses, wiping at the corner of his eye with his white handkerchief before he tucked it in his pocket and looked around at the team. 'This morning at 0710 hours, Mrs Mooney called around at her daughter's house as she was concerned that Eleanor Mooney had not contacted her since the start of her shift the previous day. This, apparently, is out of character for Eleanor. They have a close relationship and they're always in contact. Eleanor wasn't due into work that day, but Mrs Mooney thought she would check in on her way into work. Her shift begins at 0800 hours.'

DI Taylor removed a photograph from the folder and passed it to the first of the team to circulate. 'Mrs Mooney currently has her GP with her and has been given a high dose of sedatives to keep her calm.'

He scanned the room, his lips twisting as he sucked air in through his teeth. 'Unfortunately, that's the end of any information that we can obtain from her for the time being, but in the meantime PC Donna McGuire persuaded a huge amount of information from her. It appears Mrs Mooney dealt with the shock by talking.'

'Did Donna get anything decent from her?' Jenna enquired, chewing a broken thumbnail.

DI Taylor threw her a glance of approval over the top of his half-moon glasses. 'Fortunately, yes.' He referred to his notes. 'Mrs Mooney, Claire, entered her daughter's house using her own key. She said she smelt the blood immediately. She's a nurse herself so she said she recognised the unmistakeable aroma straight away.'

Jenna took a slow breath in through her nose. Once you smelt blood and death you could never get it out of your nostrils. She'd recognised the stomach-lurching scent the moment she'd walked in the front door. She screwed her eyes shut and swallowed, but the image materialised in her head and she popped them open again.

Concern flickered through DI Taylor's eyes as he met her gaze across the room, but he said nothing as she sent him a reassuring smile.

'She says she stepped into the kitchen before it even registered. She dashed to her daughter, checked for signs of life, called the police and paramedics.' With a quiet snort, DI Taylor surveyed the room. 'They arrived before we did, by which time, she'd checked the other body. Male, aged thirty to thirty-eight, we believe. No identification on his person, although there was a rucksack on the floor nearby which will be checked by Jim Downey as soon as he has first priorities in place. The male had a pulse, weak and thready, but a pulse all the same. The paramedics whipped him out of there as quickly as they could. Beaten half to death, deep knife wound to the left armpit.' Taylor paused. 'Any questions so far?'

Salter looked up from the photograph he'd been handed. 'What's the relationship between the two victims? Is it a domestic?'

'At this stage, we have no idea. Claire Mooney claims her daughter wasn't seeing anyone, that she was actually using a dating app...' Taylor's gaze drifted over to Ryan.

Stress lines dug in deep around Ryan's mouth as he rolled his lips inwards and muttered, 'She's on my list.'

Taylor squinted at him. 'Say that again, DC Downey.'

Louder, 'She's on my dating app list, sir.'

Taylor blew out a breath. 'That's what I thought you said.' He covered his face with his hands and rubbed, dragging them back through his hair before he stared at Ryan. 'What a mess, what a mess, what a mess.'

Jenna held her tongue as she waited for DI Taylor to continue.

He delved into the file and withdrew a second photograph and sent it around the room in the opposite direction. 'PC McGuire managed to persuade a photograph of Eleanor from Claire. It was framed on the mantelpiece of her fire.'

Good for Donna. Experienced, she shaped up to be an excellent police officer.

Jenna held her hand out for the second photograph as it arrived with the first and stared at the image of a beautiful woman, golden eyes laughing into the camera, lush curls of amber hair waterfalled over one shoulder. A young woman, full of life. Now dead. Jenna's gaze took in the murder scene as she was passed the first photograph.

The pang of loss struck Jenna in a way it never had before the disappearance of her own sister. She controlled her breathing, slowed her heart rate down, but heat rushed up her neck. With the central heating on in the station, it wasn't overly hot, but it was stuffy, and Jenna struggled to draw fresh air in through her lungs.

She glanced at the window. Would anyone protest if she pushed it open? It could hardly be opened wide with the window restrictors in place, but any hint of a draught would do to take away the light-headedness.

Mason took a couple of steps back and swung the window open the six inches the restrictors allowed and then moved forward to take the photographs from her as though he'd read her mind. She glanced back

at him with a grateful smile and knew for certain he had as he passed
the photographs down the line.

The cool rush of winter air washed over her, reviving her flagging
senses and she tuned back in as Taylor continued.

'Eleanor Mooney was a twenty-four year old nurse. She'd recently
broken up with her boyfriend. According to her mother, she'd started
to use a dating app but hadn't got so far as meeting up with anyone.' He
glanced at Ryan for confirmation.

Relief swarmed through Jenna's system as Ryan shook his head.
'We'd had a couple of conversations. That's all. She seemed nice, but
I've been in contact with someone else, so I'd kind of put Ellie on the
back-burner for another day.' His shoulders rolled in as he shuddered,
shooting them an apologetic look as he crossed his arms over to rub
warmth back into them.

Guilt that it may be from the icy blast of air coming into the room
did not persuade Jenna to close the window, instead she moved closer
to Ryan to perch on the edge of the desk next to him. She gave his arm
a brief touch to let him know she understood, just as Mason did for
her. She dropped her hand before anyone else paid attention.

Three deaths, each one of them connected to Ryan, no matter how
intangible it was, to him it was real, and his feelings of guilt were
palpable.

Taylor flipped over a page and absently scratched the top of his
head. 'According to Donna, one of the things Mrs Mooney stressed was
that Eleanor had been convinced someone had been inside her house
for the past few days.'

Jenna's spine cracked as she straightened, casting a quick glance at
Ryan as Taylor continued.

'Mrs Mooney had wanted her to inform the police, but Eleanor
apparently didn't want the attention in case she was mistaken. She was
very independent, strong, athletic. She went to keep fit and kick-
boxing. But something spooked her. It was little things – an ornament
moved, a coffee mug in the wrong cupboard. Missing underwear.'

Jenna touched Ryan's arm again, this time giving it a gentle squeeze to gain his attention. 'Didn't you tell us that the first victim, Marcia Davies, had said she thought there was someone watching her?'

Ryan nodded, his eyes swirled with doubt and worry. 'She told me she thought there'd been someone in her house. Little things that she couldn't explain. A coffee cup moved. She never mentioned underwear.' His neck flushed and he dipped his head to stare down at his feet. 'Why would she? I'd just met her.' He brought his head back up, his cheeks flaming. 'The main point she made was that she could feel someone's stare on her all the time. She thought it was her ex. Turned out it wasn't.'

Taylor picked up another file. 'Victim number two. Karen Prestwich.'

'She wasn't a nurse,' Wainwright interrupted.

'No.' Taylor held up a finger. 'But, as we've established, Julia Clements was, and Karen was murdered in her house.' He glanced around the room. 'Who interviewed Julia after DS Morgan's initial interview?'

Salter raised a finger. 'Me.'

'I don't suppose you asked her if she thought someone was watching her?'

'No.' Salter straightened up from where he slouched in an operator's chair. 'At the time I questioned her, there was no reason I should ask. We didn't know there was a connection, we didn't suspect he spied on them first.'

'Okay.' Taylor jotted down a note. 'Revisit Julia, DC Salter.'

'She's living with her parents, the other side of Shrewsbury for the time being. Said she couldn't bear the thought of going back to a house where someone has been murdered. She mentioned selling it.'

'I don't blame her.' Mason muttered.

'So, revisit,' Taylor reiterated, 'ask if she had any feelings of being watched. Anything moved, touched, taken.'

Salter nodded and bent his head to write notes of his own.

'Is there anything further?'

Ryan raised his hand.

'Yes, DC Downey?'

'Sir, have we identified the man from this morning? Does his DNA match that found at the first scene? Is he the killer?'

'Get to the point, boy, don't beat about the bush,' Mason mumbled.

A rumble of laughter ran around the room to lighten the mood.

'First.' DI Taylor held up one finger. 'The DNA from our second victim's house matches that of Mark Pearson. Ex-con, released nine weeks ago from...?' Taylor pointed at Ryan.

Ryan's eyes shot wide and his full bottom lip dropped. Like a light going on, his head came up, his eyes gleamed. 'Long Lartin, Sir.'

Taylor smiled. 'Long Lartin. And who do we know is resident at Long Lartin?'

'Paul McCambridge, Sir.'

'Bingo. Paul McCambridge. DC Ellis, could you follow up on that? Liaise with Intelligence, get them to contact Admin at Long Lartin to gather all the information they have regarding the relationship between these two. We know Long Lartin is mainly single cell, so how have McCambridge and Pearson communicated? When did they meet? How long did they know each other before Pearson was released? You know the form, DC Ellis. Push, man, push. We need this information yesterday. God, we want an end to this killing spree. It's already escalated faster than we can keep up with.'

Anticipation rippled around the room.

Jenna's shoulders relaxed as DI Taylor continued. 'Second.' He pulled a photograph from his folder, with his smile stretching wide to send deep brackets out across his cheeks. 'This is an image of Mark Pearson.'

The desire to snatch it from Ryan's hands as Taylor passed it to him was almost too hard to resist. Instead Jenna reached out and held the corner between her forefinger and thumb. Stark eyes stared from a thin face.

'That's him,' Ryan whispered. 'That's our man in hospital.'

Not as convinced as her young DC, Jenna squinted at the image. It was difficult to compare the picture with the man she'd seen in hospital whose face had been battered beyond recognition and whose bruised eyelids were closed. 'I don't know.'

'Definitely.' The strength of Ryan's conviction almost carried her along, but she really couldn't confirm either way.

She shook her head, doubt skimming through her mind. 'I'm not sure.'

'Look.' Ryan's enthusiasm was contagious. He jostled closer, almost bumping her off the edge of the desk. 'Here, the shape of his head. The spacing between the eyes, the gap between his nose and mouth. Look at the ear, the left one, it has a strange fold over at the very top. I noticed it when we were at the Princess Royal when the doctor was checking his stats.'

Jenna squinted at him, as she let him run with it. Perhaps he had a talent for facial recognition. She'd look closer into that when they had more time.

'Also,' Ryan dug a sharp elbow into her ribs to get her attention and she shot bolt upright, not from the jab hurting but more a sense of surprise at his marked increase in confidence and familiarity. She tried not to react as Mason smirked at her. 'See here?' Ryan jiggled the photograph they both held on to. 'His hairline sweeps here, it's irregular.' He traced the line around Mark Pearson's forehead, tapping the mid-centre with his fingernail. 'A widow's peak.'

She couldn't deny what he said, but her image of the man on the trolley evidently wasn't as clear as Ryan's.

DI Taylor plucked at his bottom lip as he studied Ryan. 'We'll have confirmation through from CSI once they process the DNA samples from the blood in the kitchen. There's a hell of a mess in there as there seemed to be an entire bucket of water and bleach swimming all over the floor, which would mix both blood types together. Jim Downey thinks he has a clear sample from the wall behind where the male, possibly Mark Pearson, was propped.'

'Shame no-one thought to take a buccal swab, we could have had the results back by now.' Ryan shrugged.

Taylor looked at Ryan, one side of his mouth kicked up. 'I think there may have been a human rights issue if we'd opened the man's mouth and taken a scraping from his cheek without his permission or indeed knowledge, as I believe he was unconscious when the paramedics removed him from the scene.'

'The day will come,' Mason replied, giving Ryan a sly nudge.

DI Taylor ignored the two of them and turned to Jenna. 'Who have you got stationed at the hospital?'

'PC Massey. I've also asked DC Salter and DC Wainwright to check on the situation after the briefing.' Both DCs gave a brief nod of acknowledgement. 'They can give PC Massey a tea break. Mark Pearson's currently in surgery, so I would imagine, unless he's Lazarus, he'll be going nowhere for some considerable time. He's lost a huge amount of blood.'

'Looks like she'd kicked the shit out of him.' Filled with admiration, Mason turned to the rest of them. 'She must have put up one hell of a fight, poor woman. She deserved to have lived.'

Jenna chewed her lip as she gave them a moment of murmured comments before she continued. 'They were about to give Pearson a blood transfusion as well as patching him up. I suspect he'll be in surgery a considerable time, recovery and then I'll arrange with the hospital to have him in a private room so we can keep a close watch on him. If we consider it necessary, we'll cuff him to the bed once he becomes active. Otherwise, I suspect just an officer posted inside the room would be appropriate at this stage.' She caught DI Taylor's gaze. 'I've arranged for PC Scanlan to relieve PC Massey later.'

'Excellent.' DI Taylor shuffled the paperwork back into the folder as it was returned to him and slapped it on the desk at his side. 'Are we done here? Does everyone know what they're doing? Good. Let's get to it.'

40

Jenna rubbed at the deep lines across her forehead in an attempt to smooth them before they became permanent wrinkles. Fat chance. Not even over the hill of thirty for another eighteen months, age was hardly an excuse.

Since her mother's death and Fliss's kidnap though, the fine lines seemed to have cut deep and where they used to smooth out by mid-morning, they stayed up late to party all night.

Another bloody long day. A whole week full of them, and she was on her knees ready for a rest day, but it wasn't practical.

She plopped into the straight backed green plastic covered hospital chair and the air whispered out of it in a gentle whoosh in the quiet room with barely a sound from the sleeping patient, the hushed bleep of the monitors a rhythmic pulse beat in the background.

Convinced the man in the bed was their culprit, Jenna waited.

The view of the car park from the window virtually the same one as a few months earlier when she'd sat beside her sister's bed waiting for her to recover – twice. Once from her kidnapping and fall down the Ironbridge Gorge, and the second when her kidnapper had come after her again.

With idle curiosity, she watched the cars cruising up and down the aisles of the brightly lit car park, drivers looking out for the one precious space to become free. At the hoot of a horn, Jenna turned her head. A gorgeous apple green Scirocco nudged its way into a space already being reversed into by a gold Ford Escort. At the possibility of witnessing a minor road rage, Jenna tore her gaze away, exhausted, closed her eyes and tipped her head back against the high back of the chair so she didn't have to observe the argument that was about to ensue in the car park. She didn't have the capacity to deal with it.

Soft black clouds plumed across her consciousness as she drifted, her muscles going lax. Blood, dark crimson washes of it, stole into her mind. A woman's body sprawled, throat slashed. The fresh face of a young woman whorled in front of her and then, with a vicious stab, flashed into the image of Fliss.

Her eyes shot open and Jenna jerked upright, heart firmly lodged in the back of her throat. She sucked in long, slow breaths and blew them out again, conscious of controlling the wild hammering of it. Desperate to choke back the rush of nausea, she closed her mind and forced herself to the present, aware that if she dwelled on the past, it had the power to destroy her.

She chewed on her bottom lip and eyed the man in the hospital bed. The bruising, already darkening to purple, covered the whole of his face, distorting the shape of it enough to make Jenna wonder how Ryan could possibly have recognised the man from his photograph. Even his jawline was swollen. She could barely see beyond the damage to the man underneath.

He wasn't going to wake any time soon. It could be a long wait. She tipped her head back to lean it on the chair and broke into a yawn so wide her jaw cracked. She'd dropped in for half an hour, not exactly on her way home, she'd gone out of her way to get there, but she needed to know. Needed to see him for herself and judge what his condition was.

The boredom simmering in PC Scanlan's eyes had persuaded her to offer him a half hour comfort break. Toilet, tea, food, walk, buy a book from the Friends of the Hospital. The guy had been there for hours with nothing to do but watch someone breathe. It wasn't as though Mark Pearson could make a break for it.

The cheap plastic of the chair squeaked as Jenna shuffled herself into a better position, crossed one leg over the other and wrapped her arms around her to keep the warmth in as tiredness washed black waves over her, and her eyes drifted shut.

'He's a lucky man, it was touch and go in there.'

Jenna twisted around to look at the soft voiced man in pale blue-green scrubs behind her.

'He's stable now though.' He reached out to touch her shoulder, a gentle offer of comfort.

She smiled at him, pushed out of the chair, forcing her tired limbs up and stretched out her hand to him. 'Hi, I'm DS Morgan, West Mercia Police.'

His eyebrows winged up as he grasped her hand in his own. 'John McCarthy. Anaesthetist.' He grinned. 'Princess Royal.'

Jenna jerked her head in the direction of her suspect. 'I wanted to check if he's fit to question.' She stared at the comatose man in the bed, the stupidity of her statement not escaping her, but exhaustion had crippled her ability to think straight.

John tucked his hands into his scrubs' pockets. 'He's sleeping quite naturally now, out of danger, but he's going to have a long recovery time, I would imagine. We've got him on morphine, so he's out of it, I'm afraid. We had to give him blood, he'd lost one hell of a lot. Nicked an artery. He was damned lucky. If it had been a touch deeper, he would have bled out, the amount of time I'm told it took for him to get to hospital. Bloody miracle he's not dead.' He slipped the clipboard off the end of the bed and ran a cursory gaze over it. 'I heard it was a fight. How did the other fella fare?'

She shrugged, it wasn't something she was prepared to discuss before she'd asked the man in the bed some questions. 'Not brilliantly.' She lowered herself back into the chair, conscious of the gentle farting sound emitting from it, but John didn't appear to have noticed. He was probably used to all NHS hospital chairs making the same noise.

She placed a hand over her mouth as she broke into another yawn.

John glanced at his watch. 'Long day for you too? I'm done now. Thirteen hours and, provided I don't have another emergency in the next fifteen minutes, I'm off and home to my wife.' As though the yawn was contagious, he managed one himself, following through with a loud groan. 'It's supposed to be date night, but the most romantic thing I can think of is a long, deep sleep.'

Date night. Adrian. She glanced at her phone to check the time again. She'd never given him a thought. Like John, the best thing that could happen to her would be twenty-four hours of sleep.

At the movement in the doorway, she slipped her phone away, missing the opportunity to send a quick message to Adrian as she glanced beyond John at the uniformed police officer. Her heart sank as PC Gardner strutted into the room, his head doing a little chicken dance on his shoulders like he was about to peck someone.

As his gaze hit hers, surprise flickered through and was gone before he stepped inside, stretching his neck so she heard the crack and grind of it from where she sat.

Smile stiff, she remained where she was and looked up at him. 'PC Gardner. To what do we owe this pleasure?'

'Sarg.' He jerked his chin in a greeting like she was his best friend, not his senior officer. She narrowed her eyes as she considered his inherent lack of respect, not only for her but, it appeared, any authority as he nudged his way past John with no consideration for personal space. 'I thought I'd come and arrest the murdering bastard before I go off shift.'

Passion in his voice didn't inspire respect, but a bolt of true concern whipped through her. The officer had experience, training and yet his gung-ho approach and lack of regard for any rank dominated, to the detriment of the case if he followed through with his intentions. It wasn't unusual in their line of work. Police officers were, by nature, strong personalities, bred to make snap decisions and work independently. Along with these traits, they needed compassion and the ability to follow rules. It appeared PC Gardner lacked both.

Jenna lowered her head for a moment while her mind raced, her fingers gripping the chair arms. She pushed out of the chair and, the same height as him, she came eye to eye with PC Gardner.

Aware of John's keen attention, she let the ice in her voice trickle through as a clear warning. 'Thank you, PC Gardner, but that won't be required.' She opened her mouth to continue, but words burst from him.

'He's a fucking murderer. He killed her in her own kitchen. Didn't you see it, were you at a different scene to the one I witnessed?' Anger gripped him as he pushed his face close to hers. 'Are you just going to stand there with your thumb up your arse and let him get away with it? Why the hell has no one arrested him yet?'

Frustration sparked to boiling point. This time she put an edge in her voice which should brook no argument. 'PC Gardner. You will conduct yourself with absolute professionalism at all times, but specifically in the presence of a member of the public.' She flicked a glance at John, conscious that he'd become far too interested just to sidle out of the room. It wasn't her concern. He may be witness to a little verbal punch-up, but her main priority was to stop the idiot in front of her making a move that had the potential of destroying any case they may have against the patient. 'I'm in charge here and I suggest that you leave it to me to make decisions which will impact upon the case...'

Before she could get any further, Gardner interrupted again and ratcheted her own annoyance up a notch. 'He's mine. I was first on scene. I want this arrest.' Eyes flat and hard, he glared at her.

Surprise rippled through her at his possessiveness, but she had no intention of backing down. 'I think you'll find the case has been assigned to me, PC Gardner.'

'Then you should have arrested him already. The man's a murderer!'

Her gaze flickered to the door as Mason stepped inside and touched the anaesthetist on the arm.

Instead of John stepping from the room as she assumed Mason had intended, he turned, shot him a smile, crossed his arms over his chest and leaned against the wall, intent on enjoying the entertainment. Without causing more tension, Jenna understood there was nothing Mason could do further to defuse the situation. It was up to her.

'PC Gardner, would you like to step outside and discuss this further?' She reached out a hand to Gardner, but he shrugged her away with a violent jerk as though her touch was an offence.

'No.'

A coldness slicked over her. He wasn't to be moved. Neither was Jenna.

With a fixed smile, she flicked a glance at her partner. 'DC Ellis. Door.'

Mason stepped inside, closed the door and leaned against it. It didn't matter if the anaesthetist was still in the room, the job had to be done.

She stepped into Gardner's space, close enough to touch. Keeping a hair's breadth between them, she stuck her face in his. 'You will listen to me. As your senior officer, you will take notice...' His lips parted and she shot him down. 'Not another word or I'll have you up on a discipline. If you are so stupid that you need me to explain exactly why you do not arrest this man, then perhaps you should reconsider your career path, especially in view of the fact that you have no respect for your senior ranking officers.' She drew a breath, sensed him about to interject again, and held up a finger, almost up his nose. 'Quiet!'

Obvious that, without an explanation, the officer wasn't willing or happy to release the firm grip he had on his misplaced principles, Jenna put a brake on her own annoyance winging its way upwards and lowered her voice. 'There are several reasons why you cannot arrest the man in the bed. One, entirely relevant and most important,' she raised her voice a touch as she held up her thumb in his eyeline to keep his attention in place. 'He isn't in a fit condition. He's comatose. You cannot arrest someone in that state. His brief would have a field day, the Force would be made a laughing stock and any case we had would be thrown out of court.' She sucked in a long breath. 'Two...' She held up her forefinger. 'You arrest him now and the clock starts to tick. Three.' She stuck another finger in the air. 'I do not want that clock to start ticking until I know for sure he is in a fit state to answer questions.' With her raised fingers, she pointed at the man in the bed. 'He is not in a fit state to answer to anyone but his own god and may not be for several days for all we know. Four,' She raised another finger and pushed ice into her voice. 'If you arrest him, the clock ticks, it runs out, I...' she curled her fingers into a fist and punched her own chest. 'I will have to go to the magistrates and ask for an extension and justify why we need one.' Her voice dipped to gravel. 'Do you know how difficult it will be to admit to the magistrate it was because a prick of an overzealous, inattentive officer made a balls-up of the entire case because he forgot the basic rule of justice within the British system which is...' she hauled in air through her nostrils and then spat out, '... innocent until proven guilty.'

Rather than turning the puce she expected, Gardner's blood drained from his face and he blinked three times and gave one jerky nod before he sidestepped her and took the four steps to the door.

Without a flicker of his normal amusement, Mason grabbed the door handle, turned it, pulled open the door and let the other officer through. The quiet shush of it underestimated Mason's mood. A slow smile stretched his mouth. 'Well handled, Sarg.'

Admiration glowed from the eyes of the anaesthetist as he uncrossed his arms and rested his hands on his hips, a crooked grin spread over his face. 'Well played, DS Morgan.' He winked and moved towards the door, turning before he let himself out. 'Should you need a witness to any of that, you can count me in.'

Mason stepped out with him, she presumed to take his details in case they did need him. He snicked the door closed behind them while Jenna moved to the visitor's chair and melted into it, a soft tremble weakening her limbs.

A few minutes was all she needed to recuperate.

She checked her messages and zapped a short one to Adrian. She could beg off their date, but she suspected seeing Adrian was what she needed. She'd already changed the time twice, with a third attempt she could only hope he understood.

She let the rhythmic beep of the machines soothe her as she leaned her head back against the chair and closed her eyes to breathe in the air-conditioned air, knowing PC Massey would be back at any moment.

Exhaustion hit her as she released another yawn and cracked open her eyes.

Her heart stopped.

The hollow-eyed stare of the man in the bed held hers. His cracked and bruised lips parted to reveal blood caked gums where two of his front teeth had been smashed out. It didn't stop the evil gleam from between bruised eyelids or the sly grin that slithered over his face. A fist squeezed her heart to still the breath in her throat.

He raised his hand a few inches from the bed and gripped the patient-controlled analgesia pump.

His low voice grated out just above a whisper. 'You think it's over.' With a gravelly chuckle, he clicked the button on the morphine pump three times to send him into oblivion, his hoarse voice fading on his last words. 'But there's another one.'

41

Unsettled by his words, and more exhausted than her brain could comprehend, Jenna pulled her car up outside her house and turned off her engine.

There was nothing further she could do. She'd let DI Taylor know so he could brief the next shift. If there was another body out there, it would be like looking for a needle in a haystack. They needed to check on the Osman list they'd compiled and wade through the missing persons' register. She'd pick it up the following day, which at least promised a return to normal hours. They had their man, all they needed was to compile the evidence file.

For now, though, she needed to let go and enjoy the downtime.

Jenna stumbled in through her front door and held still while the huge white spotted dog pummelled her with his love. His hot tongue streaked over her face and wiped away the pain of the day.

With a low chuckle, she encouraged his huge paws off her shoulders and gave him a rib rub as she muscled her way past him into the kitchen.

Fliss turned, a wide smile curved her generous lips, light green eyes dancing with excitement. Eyes that had been emphasised with the dark

smudge of dusky eyeshadow, turning her sister from day-time infant
teacher to night-time vamp.

'It's date night.' Her gaze chased over Jenna and her beautifully
glossed lips pulled down at the edges. 'Mason's picking me up at 8.30.'
She indicated the kitchen clock with ten minutes to spare.

Jenna shot it a quick glance. 'He may be running a little late.'

At the ting of Fliss's phone indicating a text message, Jenna made
an escape out of the kitchen door. She slipped off her ankle boots and
tucked them into the boot cupboard under the stairs, out of temptation's way if Domino was to be left alone. Otherwise he'd chew them to
shreds before they returned.

She sprinted up the stairs, her long legs taking them two at a time,
the burn in them making her flag by the time she reached her room.

She'd had to delay Adrian by another half an hour herself. It would
give her enough time for a quick shower and to sling something
halfway date-like on. She'd not even looked in her wardrobe, seriously
doubted she had anything even remotely suitable for a dinner date and
considered if he'd be insulted if she threw on a pair of jeans and a
baggy jumper. He'd be on a winner if she didn't fall asleep, head down
in the soup.

She jiggled her shoulders and let the heavy woollen jacket slide off
as she walked into her bedroom. She tossed it onto her bed and raised
her fingers to unfasten the buttons on her white cotton shirt and pulled
up short.

Hanging on the outside of the wardrobe door was a simple black
shift dress overlayered by an ankle length, long sleeved leopard-print
shirt.

Speechless, Jenna stared at the outfit she would never have chosen
for herself, but nonetheless couldn't get over the sheer beauty of it. She
stretched out fingers to smooth over the soft material. Something
beyond her imagination, and possibly beyond her pocket.

'I thought you may not have much time to find something to wear.'

She glanced back at her sister in the doorway to her room. 'Oh
Fliss, it's beautiful.' She spread her hands to encompass Fliss and said

what she'd been unable to say downstairs when the phone had interrupted. 'You're beautiful.'

Dressed in knee length high heeled boots, making her top the six foot mark, she wore slimline black jeans tucked in. Fliss slipped on a crimson suede jacket over the top of a pure white silk blouse. Crystals sparkled at her ears and her smile spread wide. 'It's been so long since I dated, since I even dressed up.' She smoothed her palms over her hips. 'I feel... weird. And a little shaky. I can't believe I'm going out with Mason.' She pressed her fingers against her lips. 'I always thought he was hot, even when I was with Ed, but who would have thought he'd ask me out?' She did a little jiggle, then stepped forward, grabbed Jenna and spun her around until she faced the compact en-suite bathroom. 'Go. Shower. Hurry.'

The pat on Jenna's backside had her trotting in and slamming the door behind her. It was no use, of course, to expect privacy. As she stripped, Fliss flung open the door and stepped inside.

Still scraping her short hair away from her forehead, Jenna ignored her sister's incessant talking and stepped under the thankfully scalding water. Meant to be a quick body wash, Jenna realised she needed more than that to scrub away the tiredness of the day. As the steam rose, she closed her eyes and tipped her head back to appreciate the pound of the water that managed to drown out Fliss's voice and give her a moment's white noise so her mind could empty.

It may have been a mistake encouraging a relationship between Fliss and Mason. She really didn't need to hear how hot he was. She hoped to God Fliss didn't give her details if they had sex.

She slammed the water off, flung open the door and grabbed the towel from Fliss's waiting hands. 'I don't want to know.'

'What?' Fliss's eyes widened.

'I don't want any details of your sex life with Mason. I have to work with the man.'

Surprise flitted over her sister's face. 'Ummm, okay. But what brought that on? I was talking about the outfit I bought you.'

Tiredness had made her paranoid. Still... 'You would. Eventually.

But don't.' Already pink, she scrubbed her skin with the downy towel until it glowed, then wrapped a smaller towel around her head. She swiped a cloth over the mirror and peered at her face. Red and blotchy from the heat of the shower, she was a mess. 'Oh, God.'

'Come here.' Fliss grabbed her wrist and Jenna almost lost her towel as her sister dragged her through into the bedroom. She glanced at her watch, pushed Jenna down onto the bed and followed her, sitting sideways as she swiped up a huge make-up bag and placed it in her lap. 'We have thirteen minutes before Mason comes to pick me up.'

'Thirteen minutes before Adrian arrives too.' Jenna grumbled from under the towel as she rubbed her hair until it stood on end.

'Good grief.'

Before Jenna could move, Fliss's fingers stroked a cooling liquid along her overheated cheeks and forehead, down the length of her nose and along her jawline. Jenna closed her eyes and gave in to her sister's ministrations. She was good at this. Better than Jenna. Jenna wouldn't bother normally, but the blotchiness...

Domino ambled in to observe the sisters for a brief moment, before he hung his head and lumbered onto Jenna's bed, turning in a tight catlike circle before he grumbled his objection at being ignored and lay down.

Quick brushstrokes smoothed over her eyelids and Jenna's body melted into the soothing routine her sister employed. She opened her eyes and Fliss handed her a mascara wand. Not the closest friend of mascara, Jenna found she smudged it more often than not and finished up by the end of the day looking like a panda or having to wash it off in the police station washrooms by lunchtime. All the same, she only needed to wear it for a scant few hours.

Fliss held up a small mirror and Jenna leaned in to swipe the mascara over her lashes, impressed at the smooth blend of golds and browns over her eyelids with the shimmer of oyster under her arched eyebrows.

With no more time to admire herself, she pushed up from the bed and grabbed the underwear Fliss had laid out for her and yanked it on.

Not new, it was still smart enough, should she feel the need to get naked at some point during the evening.

She snatched up her deodorant and rollered it under her arms and then spritzed something Fliss had bought her on her neck and wrists. The sultry aroma of it rose from her warmed skin to make her wonder about the whole getting naked prospect.

She shot Fliss a quick glance as her sister handed her the shift dress. 'I'm a bit jittery too. I like Adrian. What if I make a balls-up of this?'

Fliss grinned. 'Why would you do that?'

'I have with every relationship I've had so far.' She wiggled her backside as she persuaded the dress up over her hips and pulled the wide straps over her shoulders, turning her back so Fliss could zip it up.

'I don't think so. You haven't made a mess of it. I think you've never found someone you liked enough to be bothered.'

Jenna opened her mouth to deny it, but Fliss saved her the bother by turning on the hairdryer and blasting it over Jenna's head. Her vigorous rub almost pulled Jenna's hair from her scalp as she touched the tender spot where Julia Mills had yanked it. Jenna hissed as Fliss's hand scrubbed over it again, and she jerked back, grabbing the hairdryer from her sister.

Unoffended, Fliss turned her back and slipped the straighteners out of Jenna's top dresser drawer and plugged them in to heat up. She glanced at her watch and held up six fingers. Six! Six minutes.

Jenna snatched the straighteners off the small cream dressing table and whipped them through her hair without even looking in the mirror. She'd run out of time to primp and pose.

She switched them off at the electric socket and spun around in time to catch the chiffon shirt Fliss threw at her. She slid her arms in and left it open at the front to show off the plain black shift underneath. She stared at the heels Fliss placed in front of her. At least four inches.

'Fliss, I can't.' She couldn't remember the last time she'd indulged in kick-ass heels. She'd probably break her neck.

'Just try them, they're not as steep as you think, they've got this hidden sole thing inside.'

Jenna slipped her feet in and turned at last to look at herself in the full length mirror. The same dress size as her sister, Fliss had chosen the perfect fit. The perfect shape. The perfect colour.

Although Jenna would never have picked it out for herself, the subtle flamboyance suited her, the dark bronze in the leopard print picking out the tones in her hair and the hazel flecks in her green eyes.

She turned sideways as she caught Fliss's gaze in the mirror. 'Thank you. I can't believe you managed to dress both of us tonight.'

'Ah, no problem.' Fliss pressed herself against Jenna, wrapping one arm around her, and held up her phone for a selfie. 'I left the receipt on your dressing table. You can transfer the money over to me when you get a moment.'

The doorbell chimed and Fliss swept from the room to leave Jenna, mouth agape, staring into the sad eyes of a Dalmatian who was about to be deserted for the evening.

42

Jim Downey scraped at the thick grey whiskers on his chin while he leaned shoulder to shoulder with Mason and Ryan to study the computer screen, his half-cut glasses perched on the end of his long nose. 'It went to wrack and ruin.'

Jenna wrapped her arms around her waist to keep the warmth in while she peered over their shoulders, aware of the rest of the team's attention.

'Started neat, almost perfect, with his first victim, Marcia Davies.' Mason flicked the photograph of Marcia up on the screen.

Jim Downey squinted at the screen. 'It's a DNA nightmare, there's so much of it. The blood loss from Marcia was immense, it washed over everything. That, together with his dousing of bleach, which killed off so much evidence, it's untrue. It doesn't mean to say we won't find the evidence to connect the murders, but it takes time and currently we have nothing.'

DI Taylor hummed in the back of his throat, his narrowed eyes directed to the screen. 'The pose is almost an exact copycat of McCambridge's fourth victim. McCambridge had perfected it by then.'

'Mmm.' Mason agreed. 'The copycat killer started with perfection. Then he made a mistake with victim two. Karen Prestwich.'

Mason tapped the keyboard and brought up the second victim on a second screen. 'He made a mistake somehow with his choice of victim. Messy, but still within the parameters of the copycat.'

Jim rubbed his fingers over his chin and squinted at the screen. 'DNA from the semen collected from the victim matches that of Mark Pearson.'

'Which ties him into victim three.' Mason tapped again. 'Eleanor Mooney's murder went to shit.'

'A bloodbath.' Jenna blew out a breath.

The photograph Jim had taken of the third scene took on the surrealness of a horror movie. Blood splatter coated every surface, floor, cupboards, benches, ceiling. The pattern daubed the room as though someone had exploded a blood bomb in the middle.

'So much DNA in that room, all mixed together like a cocktail. We're currently eliminating anyone else who had access to the room. It's a nightmare. Paramedics, police officers, the mother. However, the main mass of DNA we believe belongs to the two – for the sake of argument – victims.' Jim pushed his glasses higher up his nose and puffed his lips out. 'It doesn't make sense to me.'

'No,' Jenna agreed. 'There were only two people witness to what happened. One of those is dead, the other, I suspect, after his attitude during the brief moment he came around last night, isn't going to co-operate.' She cupped each of her hands on Jim and Mason's shoulders as she leaned over them to study the third scene in closer detail. 'I've asked the hospital if they can reduce his self-app of morphine so we can drag some sense out of him, but they say he needs the pain relief.' She huffed out an irritated sigh. 'He said "there's another one". We need to question him. Find out if there's another body. In the meantime, we're working through the Osman list.'

DI Taylor leaned in. 'I'm going to get Chief Superintendent Gregg to pull the authority on that. At least we don't have to use up resources on providing police protection any longer. Bloody logistical nightmare. I need to get everyone back to their normal shift patterns.' He sent them a weary smile. 'I'll catch up with you later. Good work.'

As DI Taylor swooshed the door closed behind him, Jim rubbed a weary hand over his eyes. 'We just need to find the other body.'

'I don't know if we will until we can wake him up and have a proper conversation. He had huge blood loss, he'd been under anaesthetic, he was on morphine. He could just have been hallucinating.' But the momentary connection she'd had when his gaze bored into hers had her skin itching with the jab of a thousand tiny needles.

'Time. It all takes time.' Jim reached up to pat the hand she rested on his shoulder. 'I hear you had a bit of a run in with PC Gardner.'

Jenna swung her head in Mason's direction. Genuine surprise flashed through his wide blue eyes and he shook his head in denial that he'd told Jim anything.

Jim swivelled around on the chair to face her. 'I know John. The anaesthetist.'

Jenna dipped her chin to acknowledge him. 'Interesting.'

Jim's lips twitched. 'He said you wiped the floor with him.'

'Little twat deserved it, and more. You should have had him up on a disciplinary,' Mason grumbled.

Jenna shrugged. 'He's got to learn. Disciplining him may have been the wrong route to take under the circumstances. I hope what I said to him will have some effect.'

Mason rolled his lips inwards and shook his head. 'He's too full of himself. Let's just hope he doesn't apply to join the firearms. He's too trigger happy.'

As the impact of that hit home, Jenna fell silent.

'You know the other thing about him?' Jim removed his glasses and rubbed his fingertips over the red indentations either side of his nose. 'When I had words with him the other day, someone mentioned they thought he was related to that journalist. What's his name?'

Mason's head reared up. 'Kim Stafford?'

Shockwaves rippled through her. 'You've got to be kidding me. Kim Stafford is related to PC Gardner? He can't be.'

'Yeah,' Jim nodded. 'I'm sure. Who the hell told me?' He squeezed his nose between thumb and forefinger and screwed his eyes closed.

'Bloody hell, if I think of them, I'll let you know. It was a passing comment. May well have been one of the paramedics. If I remember right, they said he was some cousin of Kim's wife.'

Thoughts whirled through her mind as Jenna paced away to the window. She scrubbed her fingers through her thick hair and stared out at the car park. Could it be that simple? Was PC Gardner giving Kim Stafford the heads-up when an interesting case rolled in? She closed her eyes. Yeah. It was definitely a possibility.

She pressed her fingertips to her closed eyes as an uncomfortable heat built in her chest, pressing down to restrict her breathing. She thought she'd dealt with the officer. Instead she'd more likely pushed the man too hard. She should have taken it further, reported him upline, at least let someone know, but her own sense of justness had made her believe she'd given him the roasting he deserved without taking it any further. He should have learned. Like she learned lessons every day of her life while her career moved on and her character evolved.

Tempted to curl up in the corner while she dealt with her own spiking ego, Jenna dropped her hands from her face and watched while three cars cruised the overfilled police station car park looking for a space.

A picture of the view from Mark Pearson's room flashed through her vision. Car park filled to capacity. Car after car crawling up one aisle, down the next, a constant source of frustration. The flash apple green Scirocco. A few years old. The same make, model and colour that Kim Stafford owned.

She crushed her hands against her face. What an idiot. A giant fluorescent pink finger lit the back of her mind as PC Gardner walked into the hospital room a millisecond after she'd spotted the Scirocco. Kim Stafford's Scirocco. More than a simple coincidence.

Damn, damn, dammit.

She dropped her hands from her face. She didn't have a choice in the matter.

She swung on her heel and headed for the door. 'I need a word with DI Taylor.' She yanked at the handle and tossed over her shoulder. 'Mason, meet me downstairs in twenty with the car keys. I think we may need to revisit the hospital, too. If PC Gardner's done what I think he has, then Kim Stafford's about to blow the lid off this case.' She glanced at the time on her phone. 'He may well have already done it.'

She strode the length of the hallway, her long legs eating up the ground between the offices while she prayed that Mark had dosed himself up enough to be of no use if Kim tried to interview him.

With barely a pause to knock, Jenna flung open the door to the boss's office. Too experienced to overreact, DI Taylor raised his head, his calm gaze skimming over her above the paperwork he held in his hand.

'Sir!'

'Jenna,' in the absence of anyone else, Taylor dropped her formal title and addressed her with a familiarity she was comfortable with. 'Take a seat.'

Too wired to sit, Jenna closed the door and stepped up to his desk. She linked her fingers to keep them still. 'Sir, I had an incident yesterday with one of the uniformed officers.'

Taylor cleared his throat. 'So I believe.'

Surprised by his knowledge, Jenna raised her hands to her face and tapped her fingertips against her lips. Did everyone know? 'Who told you?' She couldn't believe Jim Downey would have leaked that sort of information about her to a senior officer. He wasn't the type to gossip.

'The duty sergeant, Alan Lyford.'

Jenna dropped her hands to her sides. 'What did he have to say about it?' She felt no need to defend herself when she met the quiet calm in Taylor's eyes.

'Apparently, PC Gardner attempted to lodge a complaint about you.'

'Attempted?'

'Sergeant Lyford told him he should take twenty-four hours to cool off and then come back to him if he still wants to make a formal complaint. I believe he advised him otherwise. He gently reminded him that he was in the wrong and that as his senior officer you had every right to take the action you did. He suggested it might make him look unprofessional.'

Jenna backed up to the chair and let herself sink into it. 'I gave him a bollocking, sir, and a bit of a lecture. He was being arrogant, sir.'

'So says Sergeant Lyford.'

Relief relaxed her enough, so she leaned back in the chair and crossed one leg over the other. 'Apart from his arrogance, I pulled him up because he wanted to arrest our suspect. I explained protocol and process to him. He didn't seem to appreciate it.'

Taylor's lips kicked up at one side. 'I can imagine. From what I've heard, he's a... challenging character.'

She should have felt relieved, but the wriggle of anxiety still churned in her stomach. 'I also heard something else about PC Gardner.'

The smile slid from his lips. 'Is this something official?'

'Not necessarily. Not yet. But there is a possibility if what I heard is true.'

'Tell me.'

'Apparently, PC Gardner is related to Kim Stafford.'

'Kim Stafford, freelance journalist?' Taylor's lip curled with distaste.

'That's the one.'

'The journalist who seems to have a little too much insider knowledge?'

At her nod, Taylor pushed forward to lean his elbows on the desk, his bright mind already latched onto the same connection. 'Do you suspect Gardner of passing on information to Stafford?'

'I wouldn't necessarily, I would hope he would honour his badge, sir. But yesterday when I was in the suspect's hospital room, I believe I may have seen Stafford's car circling the car park. Right after that was when PC Gardner walked into the room and we had our little set to.'

'And you thought you'd hold this information until now because...?'

Heat flooded her neck and face as the implication was made. 'No. I wasn't holding it back, it never occurred to me at the time. I may be wrong about the Scirocco belonging to Stafford. I made the connection when Jim Downey mentioned their relationship. It wasn't a deliberate omission.'

Calm eyes devoid of accusation connected with hers. He was on her side. He was always on her side, but he needed the ins and outs, the fors and againsts, the finer details. 'Okay. What would you propose our next steps are?'

She tugged at her bottom lip with her thumb and forefinger. 'Quite frankly, I don't know. I need to have a think about it.' She cast her mind back to her sister's case, when Stafford had reported on it with inside information he should never have had access to. 'I need to check what Gardner had to do with Fliss's case.'

'I can do that.' DI Taylor jotted something down on the notepad in front of him.

'First, though, my main concern is that Gardner may have arranged to meet up with Stafford yesterday in the suspect's hospital room. I don't know the reason behind why they'd do that, other than Gardner grabbing the glory of arresting a serial killer and having Stafford splash it all over the papers.' She scrubbed the tender spot on her head and blew out a breath. 'If that's the case, and my conversation with Gardner never had any impact, I'm worried they'll try it again.' She pushed up from the chair. 'I need to put some precautions in place at the hospital and also to check if our suspect is in a fit state to answer questions.'

DI Taylor glanced at his watch, pushed his chair back and came to his feet. He leaned both hands on the desk and took in a long pull of air. 'I'll come with you.'

She kept the surprise to herself. It had been a while since the Inspector had accompanied her; he was always tied up in meetings or with paperwork. Some days being the teacher meant losing sight of the job.

He gave a long stretch, each bone and joint cricking and popping. 'I could do with the fresh air, less bullshit.' He grinned at her and she saw the officer beneath the rank. The enthusiastic passion of the beat bobby he used to be. A man who now drowned in paperwork on a daily basis. She felt it herself from time to time and wondered if she ever really wanted to be promoted above the rank of sergeant.

As he rounded the desk, she remembered. 'DC Ellis is meeting me downstairs with the car keys.'

'Excellent. If we need someone punched, he's our man.' Light of foot, he passed her, holding open the door for her to move in front of him. The flash of youthful exuberance rendered her speechless.

Deadpan, Mason watched them move down the staircase, DI Taylor once again in front. If she'd not been aware of the CCTV, she would have held her hands in the air and shrugged, but the contact she made with Mason through a quick raise of her eyebrows gave him all the clue he needed.

'Sir.'

'You're driving, DC Ellis.'

Mason twitched his eyebrows at Jenna as DI Taylor marched past. She sent him her brightest smile. It meant Mason couldn't ask anything about her date. The one she'd like to keep to herself for now. Just as she'd like him to keep his date with Fliss to himself. She really didn't need any details from him, she'd far rather they kept it to themselves. For now at least.

43

A low electronic buzz blanketed the virtually empty hallways, so the quick clip of their shoes echoed with staccato precision.

Wordless, they strode through the hospital, every footstep bringing them closer to their suspect.

A thread of anticipation wound its way through Jenna. If he was awake, she'd question him. If he was still asleep, she'd see if the medical staff could lower his morphine dose and bring him around.

Static crackled through the radio followed by PC Massey's voice. 'Sarg?'

'PC Massey. Is everything okay?'

Far along the corridor, PC Massey headed towards them, still speaking into the Airwaves radio. 'I have a situation here.'

Jenna put on a spurt to charge ahead of the others. She spoke into Airwaves as she approached before he even looked their way. 'We're here, I can see you.'

Relief washed over his features as he marched towards them.

The first to speak, Jenna dashed to his side. 'What's happened?'

PC Massey shook his head. 'PC Gardner just arrived. Made out that he was here to give me a break.' Phil shook his head, his jowls wobbling. 'He's a shirty little git, pardon me, Sarg, but he is. He told me to get myself a coffee. I was sure he's not assigned here, not after yesterday when he tried to strong arm you.'

They all knew, it appeared, but not through any of her sources, it was Gardner himself who couldn't keep his mouth shut.

'Sarg, I have no idea what he's up to, but I don't trust him alone in that room with our suspect.'

As DI Taylor caught up, he touched PC Massey's elbow. 'It's okay. We'll deal with it, whatever it is. You go and take a break for thirty minutes. Cup of tea, bacon butty and a brisk walk. When you come back, it'll be like nothing ever happened.'

Massey grinned. 'Sir.' He strode off in the opposite direction, shoulders back as though a weight had been lifted from them.

'What the hell is he up to?' Jenna and Mason followed DI Taylor as he flung open the ward door, his long legs eating up the distance along the hallway, every inch of him in senior ranking officer mode.

The instant change in atmosphere as they came off the main hallway into the ward struck her as the electronic buzz escalated to a blanket of beeps and rings overlayered with hushed urgency.

As DI Taylor hesitated, unfamiliar with the terrain, Jenna swept past him, making her way along to the far end of the corridor where there were two side rooms off the main wards. The first stood empty and she barely spared it a glance, but in the doorway of the second one, a figure she would recognise from twenty paces entered the room.

'Wait!' She punched the word out, gratified to see the figure freeze, fury burning her gut. She'd have the little shit, tear him apart limb from limb. If Mason didn't get to him first and simply punch him. 'What do you think you're doing here?' She kicked command into her voice and as the figure turned, a thick layer of grease coated her stomach. Her hatred of Kim Stafford had never dissipated over the years, only grown stronger the more often she came across him.

The thinly veiled sneer did nothing to intimidate her as she stepped into his space. 'On whose authority are you here?'

He jerked his neck to one side in a nervous twitch. 'Freedom of the press.'

'You have no such freedom when you step into a police cordon.' She had no desire to touch him, but he didn't appear to want to move from the spot he was in. His dark eyes glimmered with the same hatred reflected back from her. She'd never feel any different, she'd never be able to flick off the slime from her boots when he was around.

His acne scarred cheeks dimpled into deep creases. 'I heard no objection from the police officer when I stepped into the room.'

She peered past him at PC Gardner, taking in his clenched jaw and angry gaze, and never hesitated as she gave her attention back to Stafford. She'd expected Stafford to sacrifice his own cousin by marriage. Slimeball that he was. 'Nevertheless, there's an objection now and if you fail to remove yourself from inside this room within the next ten seconds, I will have you arrested and taken to Malinsgate police station for questioning.'

'Questioning? On what charge?'

'Obstruction of a police officer, perverting the course of justice.' She counted off on her fingers. 'Contamination of evidence, breach of the peace.'

Kim Stafford spread his hands wide, appealing to the room at large. 'I've done nothing wrong, just accidentally stepped inside a patient's room. I had no idea it was a crime scene.' Apart from the obvious placement of a police officer inside the room.

With no desire to correct him, Jenna squared her feet and waited.

He leaned into her, the puff of stale coffee on his breath made her gag.

'Your breath stinks, Kim. You should floss more often.'

Insult leapt into his eyes and again his head juddered.

'And the clock's ticking.'

He recovered far quicker than she'd expected, but then his skin was thick enough for the insult to only skim the surface. 'Talking of ticking clocks. How long has he got?' He nodded his head in the direction of the still sleeping suspect. Jenna never thought for a moment Stafford meant how long had the suspect left to live, but how long did they have left to question him. Which meant his cousin by marriage hadn't told him that the suspect hadn't yet been arrested.

She declined to answer the man, instead, she took a sideways step to shield any view of their suspect from him and stretched out her hand to indicate the door. 'We'd appreciate it if you left the room immediately in order to ensure this place is not contaminated by your presence.' He could take it to mean anything he wanted, but forensics had swept the room and suspect entirely, and Jenna meant for him to remove his disgusting, slimy presence before she threw up.

Fury gleamed from his narrowed eyes, but he sidled around her and disappeared down the hallway.

Jenna looked past DI Taylor at the man in uniform beside the bed.

'PC Gardner,' Taylor addressed him. 'Step away from the bed.'

'But the perpetrator—'

'The *patient* is absolutely fine. Now step away from the bed and take yourself from this room. Immediately.' DI Taylor pitched his voice to a gravelly command as he turned his body into the officer's, his chest almost touching Gardner's, leaving him with no option but to step back into the hallway. With his hand on the door, DI Taylor stared at Gardner with deadly intent. 'You make sure you report to me when I return to the station.' He glanced at his watch. '1400 hours.'

'I'm off duty at 1400 hours.' His lack of respect had Jenna sucking her breath in, he'd not even had the decency to address the rank of the man before him.

Ice whipped into Taylor's eyes. 'Then make it 1330 hours, PC Gardner. What I have to say to you won't take long. Professional standards may need more of your time, but that'll be between you and them.'

Flushed scarlet, Lee Gardner spun around and stalked away through the long hallway.

Jenna studied the man in the bed and saw the glimmer of cracked open eyelids from beneath his eyelashes as he watched her.

'Good of you to join us, Mr Pearson.'

He blinked, surprise flickering beneath the exhaustion, enough to confirm she had the right man.

Jenna pulled the chair closer to the bed and sank onto it. She leaned her elbows on her knees and dangled her hands. 'Mark. Did you speak with either of the men who just came in?'

Pearson's lips stuck together as he tried to answer her.

Jenna reached out for the glass on his overbed table, topping it up from the small water jug. The straw popped up, but she straightened it and held it close to Pearson's lips so he could angle in for a drink.

After several pulls, he flopped back onto the fat hospital pillows, weariness etched in every line on his face. His gaze stayed on her as she waited for him to talk. He opened his mouth, the dark gap where his teeth were missing drew her fascinated gaze as he mumbled. 'I faked sleep.'

Unsympathetic, she eyed him. 'You seem to have a talent for that.' She glanced at the morphine administrator dangling from the bed so he could no longer reach it. Without retrieving it, she pointed at it. 'Do you need this?'

'Yes.'

'Did they take it away from you?'

He slid his gaze over to the window without answering and she threw a glance at Taylor while he rooted in his shirt pocket for his glasses.

Jenna took hold of the morphine pump and placed it back on Pearson's bed within reach of his limp hand as a man in scrubs came into the room. 'Can I help anyone?' Short and square with thinning hair and a world weary look, he peered around at all three officers in the room and then glanced at his patient.

Taylor stepped forward, holding out his hand to the doctor. 'DI Taylor, West Mercia Police.'

The man took his hand for a perfunctory shake. 'Doctor Ian Morris.' He picked up the clipboard with Pearson's notes to study them.

DI Taylor bestowed the doctor with an indulgent smile. 'Would you say our patient is fit for questioning?'

Doctor Morris raised his head. 'I can't see why not. He's due for discharge this afternoon. All his vitals are registering within the acceptable range.' He unhooked the morphine line and disengaged it, reaching out to loop it over the metal stand at the side of the bed. He pointed at the canula in the back of his patient's hand. 'I'll get one of the nurses to come and remove this for you.'

Pearson's panicked gaze darted from the doctor to Jenna and back again. 'But I'm in pain. I need—'

"We'll get you some paracetamol and codeine. You'll be fine now.' The doctor swept over his patient's objection and looked down at the notes again. 'He doesn't have a reason to stay any longer. I can discharge him now if you like.' He plucked a pen from his top pocket, wrote on the notes, flourished his signature. He turned to address Pearson again. 'You'll need the stitches out in ten days.' He moved across the room, picked vinyl disposable gloves out of a box by the sink. 'Your local practitioner nurse can do that for you, or you can make an appointment to return here. You've a waterproof covering over it, but don't get it wet, stay out of the shower until the stitches come out.' He snapped the gloves onto his hands, stretching his short, square fingers into them. 'You can have a bath if you're careful.' He took hold of Pearson's hand and gently persuaded the canula out. 'There you go. That'll save you waiting for a nurse.' Dr Morris pressed a small white gauze to the exit wound and taped it down before he glanced at his watch and winced. 'Sorry, got to get a move on. Is there anything you need to ask me?' He whipped the gloves back off and dumped them in the bin.

Stunned, Pearson gave a vague shake of his head. As his eyes dulled with pain, he turned his gaze on Jenna. The strong desire to laugh at the way he'd been railroaded by the overworked doctor had her grinning as she shot him a fast wink.

Dr Morris jotted notes down and then slipped the clipboard back into its cradle. 'He's good to go.'

Mason closed the door behind him and approached the bed as DI Taylor made himself comfortable in the green, high back chair, making it fart again as he settled into it.

Jenna and Mason stood either side of the bed. While Jenna let Mason take the lead, he pinned Pearson with a hard, flat look.

'Mark? Mark Pearson?'

He grunted.

'I'm sorry, could you confirm that you're Mark Pearson?'

'Yessss.'

Good. With that confirmation, Mason continued. 'Mark, can you tell me what happened on the night of Tuesday, 11 February?'

Mark rolled his head from side to side on the crisp white pillow. 'I don't know. I can't remember.'

'What were you doing at 45 Alexandra Terrace?

A hard edge crept into Pearson's expression. 'I don't know.'

'Okay. Mark, did you know the resident of 45 Alexandra Terrace?'

He blinked several times, his gaze sliding to glance out of the window. His voice when it came was filled with weary resignation as though he already knew they had him. 'I don't know. I can't remember.'

'I'm sure the doctor never mentioned anything about amnesia.' Mason's sarcasm appeared to have no effect on Pearson. 'Something bad happened at 45 Alexandra Terrace that put you in this hospital bed.' He waved his hand over the bed. 'Can you tell me anything about it?'

Mark stared at the ceiling and gave a soft roll of his head again. 'Nothing.'

Jenna wanted him to look at Mason, to connect, just for a glimmer of... she didn't know. Something. Remorse, shame, fear, regret. Anything except this hollowness.

Mason leaned in to try and catch his attention. 'You mentioned there was another one?'

Pearson's breath caught in his throat, but he remained silent.

'What did you mean?' Mason pressed.

A rusty chuckle came from deep within Pearson's chest, but he still never took his gaze from the ceiling and never replied.

The urgency of the situation elevated Mason's voice above the laughter. 'Mark, have you hurt someone else?'

The gurgle rumbled out, louder.

'Is there another body you'd like to tell us about?'

The laughter reeled off Pearson until it turned into a hawking cough that whipped the breath from him and left tears rolling down his face.

Aware Mason would get no further with his line of questioning, Jenna pursed her lips as she swiped up the plastic jug on the side table and filled Pearson's cup with water before she handed it to him.

'Mark, how did you lose your front teeth?'

The cough lodged in his throat as he stiffened. Jenna took instant advantage of a way in.

'Did someone get the better of you?'

He rolled his head so he could look straight at her, a glint of anger in his swollen-closed eyes.

She leaned in, bringing her face closer to his. 'Did she fight back? Mark, did you get far more than you bargained for when you entered 45 Alexandra Terrace?'

His bloodshot eyes flashed with fury.

'You weren't expecting her to be there, were you? She took you by surprise.' She waved her hand over the top of the bed. 'You never expected to have the living daylights beaten out of you by a woman.'

Pearson reared up in bed, his swollen face puce as he spat out, 'Fuck you, bitch! It wasn't me who died.'

Jenna whipped her head back to avoid contact with him and snapped out between bared teeth. 'Detective Sergeant bitch.' She shot him a sharp smile. He'd supplied her with precisely the information she needed for an arrest. 'Mark Pearson, I'm arresting you on suspicion of murder.'

They had a whole day ahead of them to question him and confirmation from the doctor that he was fit for discharge.

She glanced at the time, not bad for a morning's work.

44

He narrowed his eyes and peered through the thicket into the clearing to grab a better view. This would be fun. Not just the act, but the whole package.

There wasn't another person in the world who knew.

They all thought they were safe.

McCambridge. His psychopathic tendencies would ruin him. It would drive him insane to think he'd lost control and Pearson wasn't the only copycat.

Pearson. McCambridge should never have indoctrinated him. He was a poor choice. He was a convicted rapist, not an executioner.

The police. It would send them into a frenzy. The mere thought that there was another one out there.

Pleased with himself, his smile spread until it stretched across his cheeks.

He'd make this his last. This was pure pride. Carla couldn't be allowed to get away with it. She couldn't beat him.

One more and he was done.

He could walk away. The control was all his.

He checked his watch. It was all a matter of patience.

He glanced up and she was there. A creature of habit.

He'd known. Of course he had. He read people. Observed them. Defining their characteristics to get to know them.

With a superior smile, he watched. He'd known she couldn't resist returning – revisiting the place where fear had beaten her. And she wasn't one to be beaten easily.

He tugged at his bottom lip with his teeth. He'd enjoy beating her, breaking her spirit before he broke her body. His grin turned evil.

She'd probably pissed her pants.

Pitiful woman.

But she'd come back as he knew she would. Spine of steel, or so she believed.

He indulged in a silent chuckle, his chest chugging as he held the noise in. Spine of steel indeed. That's what she'd posted on Facebook. Naïve of her. As though she didn't realise he'd be watching and waiting. She'd posted it, out there for all the world to see. Her challenge to him.

Stupid, stupid woman.

She'd left him with no other option when she issued that provocation.

Excitement surged through him, stuttering in his chest, and he swallowed the laughter bubbling in his lungs until it burned. He clasped his hands against his flat stomach as a flood of heat seared his skin.

She was here.

He had her.

He ignored his racing heartbeat as she halted at the end of the road and jogged on the spot to keep her muscles from stiffening in the damp of the miserable morning.

All he needed to do was step into her path as she came by. He practised his surprised look, his recognition from the one coffee date they'd had. Tilted his head to one side. Smiled. *Fancy seeing you here. It's been a while. Shall we do coffee?*

He slipped his gloves from his pocket, slid them over his fingers, enjoying the snap across his wrists, ensuring a snug fit. He tempered his breathing, pulled it in through stressed nostrils and out again past pursed lips, while he indulged himself in the sizzle and spark of power as he waited.

She turned, her long ponytail whipped in the wind as she ran towards him. It swayed from side to side with her building rhythm. A perfect pendulum, bright auburn even in the dull light. A beacon. Good enough for him to use as a weapon against her.

He'd wrap his hand around it, give it a good, hard yank. Not hard enough to snap her neck, but sharp enough to stun her. A blow to send her reeling while her eyes turned desperate.

He grinned, stepped forward.

'Hey, Carla.'

He staggered back, frozen, scenting the air like a wild animal as a small pearlescent white mini pulled up beside the runner, its engine noise drowning out his voice so Carla turned without hearing him.

Fear clutched his chest. Fuck it. He needed to be more careful. He'd not even heard the car. He'd been too preoccupied, too tied up in his own excitement to notice its approach.

Not until it was too late.

Almost too late.

He didn't need that kind of slip-up in his life.

He shrank back, allowing the thicket to swallow him. He bowed his head, raised his hands and dug his fingers deep into his scalp until his eyes watered. Why? Why did she have such luck? Twice now she'd escaped him.

Anger churned low in his belly. Unable to kill it off entirely, he settled for restraining it. Patience. She was his. She'd not escape him a third time.

45

Carla wiped the sweat from her brow as she accepted the lift and laid her head back against the headrest, relief pulsing through her veins. Spine of steel. Spine of steel. What a load of nonsense.

She could barely catch her breath and she'd laughed. Laughed with her colleague who'd picked her up.

Janice.

Janice was such a lovely lady. Quiet, unassuming.

Carla huffed again while she glanced behind her out of the window.

No one.

There was no one there.

She pressed her hands against her hot face as the mini zipped along the lane, coming out at Wellington centre in no time. Not time enough to control herself. Not time enough for her to not beg to stay in the car.

God, oh, god.

Her whole being quaked hard enough to rip her apart from the inside. She'd sensed him. Felt his presence.

She swiped at the thin sheen of sweat on her cheeks with the back of her hand and then ran trembling fingers through her hair.

'You okay?'

With the best will in the world, Carla could do nothing other than nod at Janice. Perhaps she should hug her, kiss her, thank her on bended knee, but it was too much to ask. Too much to admit she'd been shit-scared.

'Here will do nicely, thanks, Janice.'

She let out a pained groan as the car drew alongside the pavement and Janice's concerned stare whispered over her.

'I'm okay. No worries.' At the doe eyes, compelled to reassure her, she could do nothing but blurt out, 'Really, I've had a bit of a tough time lately. But I'm okay.'

She scrabbled for the door handle, desperate not to have to explain. Grateful for Janice's help, she wanted nothing more than to escape. Run back to the safehouse and disappear.

She burst from the car, glanced over her shoulder at the shocked woman who'd saved her without even knowing. 'Thank you. I'm sorry.'

'Wouldn't you like me to take you home?'

Home? God, no. Home was the last place she needed to be. Home was where evil lurked, waiting to kill her.

She should have known better. Known he'd be waiting.

She should never have gone running in the same place. The evilness of it pervaded the soul, touched her as no other. Just as he'd touched her with his sinister stare, stroked it over her as he hid somewhere beyond her vision. But she'd felt him. Revulsion skittered over her flesh, raising goose bumps as her sweat turned cold.

In her mother's house, she clung onto the bathroom sink while nausea ripped through her and tears tracked down her cheeks, gathering at the edge of her lips as she hiccoughed out her pain.

The silky touch of Saskia winding her way around Carla's legs had her drawing in her breath and holding it. If she couldn't control herself, she was in trouble. Her mum was working until late. Decisions had to be made. She needed to think. She needed a plan.

She scooped Saskia up into her arms and took comfort from snuffling into the thick black pelt while Saskia rumbled her contentment against Carla's neck, transferring her calmness. The warmth of the cat soaked through to defrost Carla's icy fingers as she massaged them through her fur.

Her breathing slowed, her pulse rate lowered.

She wandered into her bedroom to sit on the bed and snuggle the cat, stroking Saskia as she circled around on Carla's knees, sharp claws flexing into her skin, and then flopped onto her back so Carla could rub her stomach. She wasn't falling for that. Saskia would tempt her and then grab her with her talons and rip little strips from her flesh the moment she touched her belly.

With the bedroom light off, Carla stared out of the window as thick, black clouds rolled in and darkened the day prematurely to night.

A delicate shiver pebbled her skin with goose bumps.

If she phoned her mum, she'd only panic her. There was no sense in that. There was nothing she could do for her. Her mum couldn't rush home from work simply because Carla imagined someone watching her.

She curled her fingers in Saskia's fur while she chewed the inside of her cheek.

Only it wasn't her imagination.

The police would think she was stupid if she reported it to them. Paranoid. Every woman in Shropshire would be on high alert, cluttering up the phone lines. It would sound so lame. *I think I'm being watched, convinced of it. Yes, I've only felt this way since the nurse was murdered – Marcia, yes, that's the one. In fact, that's exactly the time I started to sense a presence. With my extrasensory perception.*

Ridiculous!

Carla jiggled Saskia on her lap as she lifted her up to dig in her back pocket for her phone.

From the information she'd caught on the news, another woman had been killed. A third, but the police hadn't released much data about it, and it sounded more like a domestic as both a male and a female had been rushed to hospital.

As Saskia gave up her attempt to entice Carla to tickle her stomach, she rolled onto her side and Carla bowed forward to put her face against the cat's shoulder, sucking in all the comfort she could from her feline friend's closeness.

No matter how stupid she felt, she still couldn't shrug off the sensation that crawled over her. When she was running, she'd felt him, the sinister stroke of his gaze. The same feeling she'd had in her own house. Since she'd arrived at her mum's, she'd felt safe. It wasn't far from her own house, though, and now she wasn't sure. Did he know where she stayed with her mother?

She stared out of the window again at the deepening shadows of people passing in the street.

He must. He was waiting.

Carla raised her hands and smudged the dried tears from her cheeks. She needed someone to talk to. Someone who could help.

She swiped her phone open and barely hesitated before she tapped in a message and hit send.

Calmer, she skimmed her fingers through Saskia's fur and smiled as the cat writhed off her lap and onto the bed, pleasure in every move.

Carla pushed up from the bed and stepped to one side of the window before she drew the curtains, unwilling to be seen by anyone. She snapped on her little bedside lamp, so a golden glow filled her bedroom.

She checked her phone to see if she'd received a message back. The one she'd sent hadn't even been read. She blew out a breath and rubbed her hands against her aching thighs. He could be working. She touched the screen as though that alone would tempt him to open the message and read it.

Lost, she glanced around her bedroom. The sanctity of her old room stemmed her panic. It was okay, everything would be all right. He wasn't here. She could no longer feel his presence, his gaze resting on her. Not the way she had when she was out running.

She stared at the phone again as the screen faded to black with still no answer. She'd give him an hour and text again.

To occupy herself, she'd get changed. Just in case.

46

Ryan's phone pinged as a second message came through from Carla as he stepped out of the station. He wasn't really interested, she'd stood him up once before, she'd probably do it again. Too knackered to care, he peered at the screen, his eyes tired from staring at the computer for the past eight hours. He'd have rather gone with Salter and Wainwright on enquiries or with Jenna and Mason to the hospital, but he'd been assigned research, sitting under the close eye of the duty sergeant all day, and he was damned bored.

He didn't want to go on a date.

All he wanted was to go home.

He slipped into the Suzuki Swift, his knees almost to his chest as he started the car and glanced at the screen again. He couldn't ignore it, it wasn't in his nature to be mean. This time he swiped right on the message and it opened up.

Hey Ryan, I'm back. Do you fancy meeting up for a drink?

Still peed off with her, he tapped a sharp reply, letting her get the message that he had no time to mess around.

When?

He shoved his car in first gear. He could go home via his mum's and she'd feed him. Probably some lush stew and potatoes. His stomach let out a grumble and he placed his hand on it as bubbles rose to the surface. He was bloody starving.

Surprised at how quick her reply came back, he took the car out of gear and picked up the phone from the middle console.

How about now, if you're free?

Tempted by her offer, he stared at the backlit screen. Dinner at his mum's, or drinks with a hot nurse? There really wasn't a choice, although his stomach made its protest known as he punched in his reply.

He put the car in gear once more and chased out of the police car park, swinging the little car around the tight curves in the road as he made his way to their agreed meeting place. One drink and then he was out of there. Straight to his mum's before his dinner had a chance to turn cold.

47

He recognised her immediately, the moment he walked into the almost empty cocktail lounge. Vibrant auburn hair bounced in ringlets around her shoulders. Her back turned to the door, she spoke in soft tones to the barman while he constructed a cocktail for her.

Ryan lost his breath as she turned, her warm golden gaze meeting his. She slipped to her feet from the stool, a broad, genuine smile stretched across her face as she reached out a hand to shake his.

'Ryan?' Mellow whisky tones ribboned her voice.

'Carla.' He barely recognised his own voice as it deepened to gravelly huskiness. Struck speechless by her beauty, he could do nothing other than accept her cool fingers in his and stare into her eyes.

Most people lied on the app, but she'd sold herself short. Far prettier than her photograph, it was more her physical presence that vibrated with attractiveness.

Her broad smile dimmed as she withdrew her fingers from his and he stumbled to apologise.

'I'm sorry, I hadn't expected you to be quite so beautiful.' Heat burnt his cheeks at his stumbling awkwardness.

She tipped her head back to laugh, her milky white throat exposed in all its silky glory. 'I'm not beautiful.'

It wasn't coquettishness but, it appeared, a genuine sense of unworthiness of his compliment.

Overwhelmed by her, Ryan stepped towards the bar. 'Can I buy you a drink?'

Everything about her felt like she was comfortable with him as she joined him at the bar, slipping back onto the barstool so her olive-green jumpsuit hitched up to expose shapely ankles.

If he died now, he'd already be in heaven.

'What are you having?' He nodded at the barman as the man poured a drink from the shaker into a prepared glass.

'A Boulevardier.' She grinned, an apologetic smile kicking up one side of her mouth. 'I thought I might get a taxi home.'

'I'm driving.' He swiped up the mocktail menu, scanned it quickly and made a choice. 'I'll have a...' he grabbed onto the first one on the list. '... An Arizona sunset please.'

She cocked an eyebrow. 'You know your mocktails?'

'Not at all.' He shrugged as he pushed the small card menu back onto the bar. 'I'm normally more of a cider man myself.'

'Yeah, I like white wine, but I'll give this a go.'

Her friendly welcome relaxed him, and he slipped onto the barstool beside her.

'How are your family?'

From the blank look on her face, she'd lied. Disappointed at her response, he gave her a moment while he turned to the barman, handing over two ten pound notes.

'Oh, let me go Dutch.' She made a grab for her handbag and he reached out, placed his hand over hers. It didn't feel wrong to touch her and she didn't recoil, so he couldn't have made the wrong move, could he?

'It's okay. You get the next one.'

She placed her small handbag on the bar in front of her and picked up her drink to salute him with.

'Cheers.'

He tapped his glass to hers and took a sip, taking in the overpowering sweetness of his drink. He'd have rather had that pint of cider, but he'd never risk his job on a drink driving charge.

Carla stroked her hair back from her cheek and drew his attention to her flawless, creamy skin. When she took a sip of her own drink, her lips pouted and made his knees weak.

Her direct gaze met his. 'I told a lie. It wasn't a family emergency.'

He had no idea why she wanted to confess now, but he let her continue. Less than twenty quid of the Sarg's money it had taken to establish the woman had baggage. He sighed. One drink and he'd be out of there.

He took another sip and resisted screwing up his nose. There was sweet, and there was unbearably cloying.

'I didn't lie about leaving, nor that it was an emergency.'

'Okay.' He could do nothing other than nod.

Instead of sipping, she took a long swallow of her drink and then pinned him with an expression so intense, he couldn't look away. 'I'm sorry, I shouldn't do this because I really don't appreciate people asking me to diagnose their kids with chicken pox when I'm not actually working and this is exactly what I'm doing to you, but really I feel so worried, and stupid. Really stupid.'

He doubted she was that, but he didn't have a clue what she was talking about. Who the hell had chickenpox and why did it involve him? He didn't really care, but from the passion pulsing from her, she did. 'It's okay. Go ahead.' He might as well let her get it off her chest and then he could go home to his mum for that hot meal. He resisted glancing at his watch as he sent her a reassuring smile.

She leaned forward and pressed a hand against his thigh, sending him into paroxysms of pleasure, so her next words took several beats to sink in. 'It's all this talk of women being killed. One of them a nurse, I heard. And my cat being fed when I wasn't in the house, and I didn't think to ask my mum if she'd popped by, but then she hadn't. She wouldn't have been there so late. Why would she? But there were empty packets of cat food I hadn't put in the bin, in there anyway. And my coffee cup was missing...' she stuttered to a halt, her stare burning into his as though he had the answer, when he hadn't.

Confused by her ramblings, Ryan raised a hand to his head. 'Hold on, Carla. Back up.'

She froze, drew in three short, sharp breaths through her nose and raised her glass to take another drink. Her fingers trembled as she placed the glass back on the bar. She turned back to him. 'I'm sorry. Perhaps I should go. This was unfair of me.'

He took her hand in his, the police officer kicking in, so he looked beyond the beauty at the tortured soul who desperately needed help. 'Start at the beginning, tell me what happened.'

She jiggled her shoulders. 'It's okay, it doesn't matter.' Her fingers twitched in his hand as she tried to disengage them. 'Forget I mentioned it.'

'No, really. Tell me.' He gave her fingers a light squeeze before he released them, so she didn't feel trapped. The woman was obviously disturbed, his gaze locked with hers and he bobbed his head to encourage her. 'I'd like to know. I may not be able to help, but perhaps talking about it will make you feel better.'

She pushed her bright ginger hair back from her face. 'It's my imagination, I'm sure.' She laid both her hands palm down on her thighs. 'Last week when that nurse was murdered...' She closed her eyes for a brief moment and blew out a breath, rubbing her thighs, distress vibrating from her.

'Yes?'

'That's when it started.'

'What started?' The fear in her eyes sent a chill over his skin.

'Things. I thought it was my imagination at first, but I'm convinced it wasn't. Then the second murder happened. I know it's not connected, and I know the first is probably her boyfriend, but...' She closed her eyes. 'I could feel him. Feel someone watching me. In my house.' Her eyes fluttered open. 'Strange things happened. Someone fed my cat. I felt him in my house. Touching my things.' She blew out a breath. 'You're going to think I'm mad. But the other day I went for a run up near the base of the Wrekin, past Ercall Wood. I was going to run up The Wrekin. He followed me. Whispered my name.' Tension radiated from her. 'It wasn't my imagination. I heard him. I ran and ran and when I got home, I knew he'd been there, so I grabbed my cat and left. I went to my mum's.' She moved her hands from her legs and twisted her fingers around each other.

Concerned at the frantic worry etched across her features, Ryan placed his glass on the bar and looked directly at her to try and ease her fear, imagined or not. 'Carla, I know it's a scary time at the moment, especially if you're female.' He didn't dare mention specifically if she was a nurse, that piece of information wasn't yet in the public domain, nor being a ginger, and they needed to keep it that way until they'd finished interviewing their suspect.

He made a quick survey of the quiet room and then leaned forward to speak with her, his voice barely above a whisper.

'Carla, I shouldn't tell you this, I'd get a right bollocking...' a quick rush of heat burnt into him as he choked on the inappropriate word to use in front of her. 'Sorry, I'd be in trouble.' She gave a weak smile with no hint that she'd taken offence as he continued. 'Whatever this is, whether real or imagined, you have nothing further to worry about.' At her sharp intake of breath, he nodded, his own relief at knowing the man he'd identified as Mark Pearson was under lock and key. 'We have the suspect in custody. You can rest easy now.'

'You've caught him?'

'Yes. Yes, we've caught him.'

'Thank God.' Visibly shaken, her fingers trembled as she raised them to her lips. 'Thank God.'

An uneasy doubt shimmered through him.

48

Jenna stared at the image on her screen while she tapped her fingers on the open file on her desk. Paperless office was terminology that would never be used on this Force.

The quiet of the office was all she needed with most of the administration staff already departed for the day. She raised her head to see who else was left, but the main office was empty except for Donna in the far corner, the reflection of her computer screen lighting up her face.

With a groan, Jenna closed her weary eyes and scrubbed her hands over her face. There was something. Something she just couldn't put her finger on. And it bugged the hell out of her.

'Boss?'

She dropped her hands from her face and frowned up at Ryan. He reached out and placed an extra-large disposable coffee cup on her desk and she automatically drew open her top drawer and handed him a tenner. He slipped it into his pocket with no attempt to give her any change. She needed to see about that. She couldn't keep tipping him so much. She needed to have a word about his entrepreneurial enterprise.

He delved into his jacket pocket and fished out a paper-wrapped packet, the savoury waft of warm food reached her belly, which let out a cheerful song loud enough to make him smile.

'I thought you might be hungry?'

'Might be.' There was no doubt about it, she hadn't eaten since lunchtime and, as far as she was concerned, she completely forgave him for being an entrepreneur. He could continue in that vein as long as he wanted, provided it was her he was entrepreneuring for. 'Do I owe you more?'

'Nah, not this time. That about covers it.' He slipped his coat off and draped it over the chair opposite, then melted into the seat next to it, his gangly arms and legs sprawling out as he sipped at his own drink, his keen gaze focused on her. A little too keen.

She took a bite of the panini and guessed at sundried tomato, mozzarella and pesto. The boy definitely was in touch with his feminine side. 'What are you doing back again? I thought you'd finished for the day.'

'Yeah, I had a date.'

Confused, Jenna stared at him over the rim of the cup she raised. He was back for a reason. Ryan did nothing without good reason. He'd get to it. 'Didn't it work out?'

'Yeah, it did. It was only a drink date. See if we like each other on first sight. You keep it short and sweet the first time, then you don't have to have an exit plan.'

'Exit plan?' There was nothing about this dating business she liked.

'Yeah, you know. If she turns out to be a dog...' Jenna whipped her eyebrow up at him and he flushed a mottled puce. 'Sorry, but if you don't like her, you need to think of an excuse to leave.' He jiggled his bony shoulders. 'Girls do it too. This way, you both leave happy, but you have time to decide whether you like each other enough to bother again.'

'Sounds like pretty damned hard work to me.'

His colour refused to turn back to normal, ratcheting up another shade. 'I think I'll ask her out again. She's nice.'

'Nice?' Jenna smiled at him, her heart softening. He may not be that much younger than her, but he was a baby. He brought out all of her protective instincts.

'Yeah. She's really nice.'

'So, you're still using your dating app?'

He nodded, took a swig of his latte and placed the cup on the edge of the desk next to the file. He'd come back for something, but until she knew, she'd poke at him for a little while longer.

'And red-haired nurses? Are they still your date of choice after all of this?' She swept her hand over the desk to include the computer.

Ryan leaned back in the chair, a vague smile curved his lips. 'Not necessarily, but the woman I just met for a drink has beautiful auburn hair, and she's a nurse. We've been speaking online for several weeks. We started before the murders happened.' He nodded at the file. 'Carla.'

'Carla. Pretty name.'

'Yeah.' Pleasure sighed from his lips. 'She let me drop her off home.'

Jenna let the silence hang between them as he reached for his drink again, but he paused with the cup halfway to his mouth.

'Are you happy with the outcome?'

Thrown by his change in direction, she leaned her elbows on the desk and linked her fingers together in front of her face. She knew he'd circle around the reason he'd returned. 'Happy? In terms of what? That we caught the culprit?'

'Yeah.' He poked his tongue in his cheek. 'Did we, though?'

She dropped her hands down to the desk and leaned on them, bowing forward, his idle sense of curiosity prickling at the nerve endings she'd tried to convince herself were just dancing because of her own misgivings.

'Did we catch him? Of course we did. He's in the holding cells right now. We questioned him for almost seven hours on and off, Ryan. Not that much questioning time, as it happens, because his lawyer kept demanding damned breaks every time we got into the flow of things. He kept pulling the "my client has just come out of hospital" bloody card.' She squinted at Ryan. That trickle of doubt feathered its way along the length of her spine until she gave a little shudder. 'We'll question him again at six in the morning. Chief Superintendent Gregg's given authorisation to carry on beyond twenty-four hours as Pearson's solicitor claimed mental and physical exhaustion for his client.'

Ryan settled himself deeper into the chair. 'Just his client?'

She grinned. 'Yeah, and probably the bloody Law Society Annual Dinner had some influence. I could bet this month's salary he'll roll up drunk in the morning, not having been to bed.'

'Won't he send someone else?'

'No. He's functioned like this for years. Got banned from driving years ago, realised it was a good wheeze to have a chauffeur and has carried on with that ever since.' She ran her fingers over the top sheet of paper on the file. 'We have his DNA, you know, Ryan. We've confirmed it's a match. There's no disputing it and Pearson almost bloody confessed.'

'Pearson. Yeah.'

Jenna placed her panini on the desk next to the coffee and steepled her fingers in front of her as she frowned at Ryan while her thoughts still niggled. A worm of discomfort heating her stomach 'Why do you ask? Why wouldn't we have the right person?'

Ryan rubbed his fingers over his lips. 'I don't know. Something just doesn't fit. You know.'

She did know. She knew exactly what he meant. She felt it herself, but she couldn't find the right thread to pull.

She leaned forward, her gaze searching his in the hope she could extract whatever the hell it was they were both looking for. 'What, Ryan? Tell me.'

Frustrated, he slapped his hand on the arm of the chair and surged to his feet. 'I don't know, for God's sake. Something isn't right.'

Jenna flicked her gaze up as Donna raised her head and then pushed away from her desk to saunter across the room just as Mason returned. 'Mason.'

'What's going on?'

'Ryan's not happy that we have the right suspect in custody.' She threw him to the wolf in the hope that Mason would wipe all of their doubts away in a blinding moment of reality and pragmatism.

'I didn't say—'

'Okay.' Mason lowered himself into the chair Ryan had just vacated and surprised her by not immediately reeling off all the reasons why their arrest was correct. He leaned forward, rested his elbows on his legs and dangled his hands between his knees. 'So, what is it you're not comfortable with?'

Donna leaned her backside on the desk as Ryan paced away and then back again, his blue eyes bright and tortured as the name burst from him. 'Marcia.'

Jenna crossed her arms over her chest and let Mason continue. 'Tell me about Marcia.'

Ryan's bright mind, once released, churned out his doubts. 'It's not the same.'

'In what way?'

'The MO. It's supposed to be the same as McCambridge – a clever emulation of his past murders. A copycat.'

Mason nodded. 'It is.'

'Exactly.' Ryan shot a finger out at Mason. 'But the others aren't. They're supposed to be. Again, it's supposed to have been a great imitation of McCambridge's murders. Like McCambridge instigated them, engineered them himself. But they're not. None of the others bear any resemblance to the first. They're bungled. There's no traceable DNA at Marcia's, as though he was too clever, too thorough.' Ryan scratched his forehead as he paused. Brow pulled low over his eyes, he searched Jenna's face. 'If we take Marcia Davies out of the equation, pretend her murder never happened, what have we got?'

Jenna flicked open her file and removed the photograph of Marcia, lining the others up for everyone to see.

'A mess. That's what we've got.' Mason stabbed his forefinger on each of the photographs. 'He's right. The lad's right.'

The fine thread started to unravel.

Donna turned around and Jenna pushed up from her chair as all four of them leaned over the desk to study the photographs.

Jenna pointed at each victim in turn, Karen, then Eleanor. 'Neither of these worked. Usually a killer improves, just like McCambridge did, each one becoming cleaner, tidier, as he worked towards his perfection.'

'Exactly.' Mason swiped up her coffee and took a swift gulp, not even affording her an apologetic grin as he would normally, so absorbed in the information in front of them.

Ryan slipped Marcia's photograph back on top of the others. 'This was his perfection. The first one. An exact replica of McCambridge's fourth victim.' He placed that photograph by the side and traced his finger over the outline of each victim. 'Each one intended to be a nurse. Throat slit, make-up applied, major DNA clean-up carried out, body posed like a mannequin. No rape.' He screwed his eyes closed for a moment, then relaxed as the revelation washed over him at the same time it hit Jenna. 'This is the work of a psychopath.' He pointed at McCambridge's fourth victim. And then to Marcia Davies. 'This is the work of a psychopath. Perfection.' He gathered the photographs and pushed them to one side to expose the most recent victims. 'This is a rapist who happens to kill.'

Jenna fell back into her chair, slapping her hands over her face. 'Ah shit. Ryan's right. I knew it! It didn't add up.'

Horror struck her.

'There are two of them. We've got a second copycat on our hands.'

49

'Oh, you clever girl.'

He took time to clean the blade he'd swiped from her mother's knife block with her dishcloth and bleach. Sterilised it so there was nothing to contaminate his handiwork. This one would be absolute perfection. His pièce de résistance. The press would go wild. The police would rip their hair out and the public would scream their panic.

Better still, it would tip the balance with McCambridge. He'd be ripped apart. Emotionally, psychologically. It would be interesting to observe.

He chuckled to himself. The thought that someone else could mimic McCambridge, improve upon the original and gain far more police and public awareness than ever McCambridge had would send him over the edge.

His own omnipotence vibrated a warm heat from his centre outwards, pulsing with growing power. He'd bested the original. It hadn't been difficult. Wicked laughter burst from his lips at the irony. McCambridge would never know. He'd taught him everything, but the man would never have the pleasure, the glory, of knowing who had bettered him. It would drive him insane.

Just one more, and he was done. He had the strength to stop. The superiority of his skill etched for all time on the minds of the police and the heart of Paul McCambridge.

Empowered, he turned to face Carla, knife in hand. 'Clever girl. Not clever enough though. You thought you'd escaped me.'

Deep satisfaction rumbled through him as her eyes went wide and blinked in panic-stricken fear. The small, desperate squeaks from behind the brown sticky tape he used on her served to thrill him more. If he whipped away the tape, would she scream for him?

Cool control stayed in place and he restrained himself. Keep the tape on her mouth, the restraints on her wrists and ankles. That was the way it needed to be. Take no risks, let the thrill be about the control.

'You did escape. Initially. But just like everyone I deal with, you became over-confident. You couldn't resist the boast. This is the trouble with the human psyche. It has to be nurtured, massaged. And you massaged your ego in public.'

With the knife in hand, he hunkered down in front of her, close enough to notice the thin, spider veins popping in her eyes. It hadn't been difficult to gain access to the house. He gave the young guy who dropped her off three minutes to get away and then knocked on the door. She'd thought it was her date come back. Stupid woman, just opened the door wide, and he stepped in.

'You challenged me.' He circled the knife around, amused to see how long she could hold her breath. As she snorted it out through her nose in a panic-infused exhalation, he touched the tip of the knife to her throat and made her hold her breath again, 'You should never have challenged me.' Interested by the white of her face in contrast to the blood building under the skin of her neck, he narrowed his eyes. As it suffused over her face, he leaned back on his heels. McCambridge had his own reasons for choosing redheads, but it suited his needs too. They were a perfect barometer of feelings. Every one of them displayed over features unable to hide a single emotion.

Satisfied, he reached out to skim a light finger over her naked leg.

As a fresh burst of terrified squeaks erupted from her throat, he patted her knee. 'Have no fear of that, my darling.' He gave a slight squeeze. 'I'm not interested in your sexual favours.' Her body went completely still, every twitch and shake halted as she stared at him, her eyes speaking volumes. 'Oh no. If I want sex, there are plenty of women I can have sex with. Look at me. Believe me, I don't have a problem in that department, my lovely.' He shifted to make himself more comfortable and pushed a gloved hand through his thick, blond hair. 'I'm not a rapist.' Her neck contracted on a hard swallow. 'I know. People believe if you commit one crime, you're capable to committing any crime.' He bestowed her with a soft smile as he stroked a finger along the peachy skin of her cheek. 'That's where McCambridge made his mistake, you see, he looked for the wrong personality. He engaged a rapist to carry out a psychopath's job.' Unable to bear the burn in his thighs any longer, he came to his feet and stretched out his legs to get the blood flowing back into them. 'I don't rape.' The brief flicker of relief was short lived, much to his satisfaction. 'I kill.'

With a deliberate move, he placed the knife on the small wooden kitchen table in perfect line next to the smaller knife he'd already cleaned. He made a soft humming noise of satisfaction in the depth of his throat.

Unable to resist, he picked up the smaller knife, held it in front of his face.

'I think the serrated edge would make a lovely pattern. What do you think?' He slanted her a sharp smile, one he reserved especially for women. He flicked his left eyebrow up in question.

The breath whistled in through her nose and her frantic gaze flashed up to the wall clock.

'Oh no, mummy won't be home for a while yet. I watched her go earlier after I followed you home after the lady in the mini dropped you off in Wellington. I had no idea you lived so close to mummy. She's on half-nights, I believe.' He pointed the knife towards the long, thin cat calendar beside the fridge 'She doesn't finish work until two in the morning. Plenty of time for us to play.' He sent her another smile, this time indulgent. 'Like mother, like daughter. Who'd have known she was a nurse too? You followed in your mummy's footsteps.' He pointed the knife towards the hallway walls littered with photographs of the two of them, proud mum and daughter. 'In more ways than one. You look so like her.' He reached out and fondled one of her long, auburn locks. 'Especially your hair. Although, hers is a little faded.' He came closer and bent at the hips so he could stare into eyes, frantic with fear, enough to send delight skittering over his flesh. 'You led me to her. And now I'll have all night with you, and all day with her.'

Terror wrenched an animalistic howl from her throat, and she shook her head, rocking her body back and forth as hard as possible on the spindle-backed chair while she growled out her fury at him.

He closed his eyes, tipped his head back onto his shoulders and breathed in the air, cleansing his soul, the sharp knife held in his left hand.

'Oh, now this is going to be fun.'

He slashed the knife down with a vicious slice across her chest and joined Carla's muffled scream with his laughter as blood splattered over the clear plastic matting he'd laid out. This time there would be no mistakes.

50

Ryan's breathing came fast and erratic.

'Oh God. What do I do?'

Confused, Jenna gawped at him as he almost tore his hair out while he completed a full circuit of the office.

'I dropped her off. I dropped Carla off after everything she told me, and I said she'd be safe.' Intense blue eyes wide and frantic met Jenna's. 'Sarg, I told her she'd be safe. I said we'd caught him.' He thumped his chest with both fists.

With panic lacing through her own veins, Jenna banked her emotions and took firm control. 'Ryan. Stop.' He froze. 'Listen to me. What did Carla tell you?'

His breath juddered into a heaving chest. 'She said she thought she was being watched. She said he'd been in her house. Her house. But she'd left and taken the cat and gone to stay with her mum a couple of miles down the road.'

'Okay. What else?'

'She thought it was her imagination, that she was tired and over-stressed. She thought someone had fed her cat, taken a favourite mug, moved things, ahhh...' He blew out a long breath. 'I can't remember everything she said, she was stoked, you know. I told her to come in tomorrow morning and we'd take a statement, because I thought we had him and any information she had would be important. We do have him.' His eyes turned glassy. 'But the wrong him for Carla.' He ground his knuckles into his eyes. 'She said he was there today when she went for a run. Watching her. She said she could feel his gaze on her. That it was evil. And I told her she'd be safe. That we'd got him. But we haven't'

'Right. Where is Carla now?'

He sucked in a breath. 'Her mum's house. I dropped her off just before I came back in.'

Relief almost swallowed her. 'You have her address, Ryan?'

He gave a wobbly nod.

'Good.' She swiped up her handbag and looked around at the other two, injecting a false lightness into her voice, 'Anyone fancy a trip out to see Ryan's new girlfriend?'

51

In the pitch dark of the pouring rain, the four of them stood on the doorstep of Carla's mum's house.

Silent. They listened.

Jenna's heart pounded so loud, no other noise could be heard above it other than the steady thrash of rain.

As she frowned into Ryan's face, Jenna reached for a small torch, something she always carried since Fliss's disappearance. Always prepared. Just as she'd learned to carry a warm coat and a pair of gloves for those unexpected moments.

She touched her finger to the on switch and Mason stayed her hand. 'Sssh.'

'MIAOW!'

The shrill, piercing screech shot Jenna's heart into her throat as a huge, wet black cat wound its way through her legs and let out loud pleading screeches to be let into the house.

'Fuck's sake!' Mason clamped a hand on her shoulder. 'Nearly shit myself.'

As her heart settled down, Jenna squatted to stroke the cat. 'Where's your mum, kiddo?'

'It's Carla's cat. It's got to be. She talked about her, how someone else had fed her.' Ryan reminded her as he hunkered down next to her. 'The house is completely dark. That's just weird. I dropped her off less than an hour ago. I watched her go in, she turned on lights in there straight away.'

'Maybe she's in a room at the back.'

'I'll go around back and check,' Mason volunteered.

As they waited for Mason to negotiate his way to the back of the house, Donna peered over Ryan's shoulder at his phone. 'Did she respond to your text?'

'No.'

'What should we do, Sarg?' Donna asked.

'We'll give Mason a moment to get around to the back, then we're going to ring the doorbell and see if we can rouse up some response.'

Donna nudged in between them. Soaked through, she shuffled closer under the porchway. 'She's probably in the bath with a glass of wine. I would be.'

'She's going to think I'm a right headcase,' Ryan mumbled.

The cat let out another plaintive yowl just as Airwaves kicked into vivid life with Mason's voice yelling, 'Go, go, go. He's got her in there. He's got a knife. Holy shit, the fucking security light's come on. He's seen me!'

Jenna's heart skipped a beat as she grabbed the door handle and pushed. Unexpectedly unlocked, the door exploded inwards and she shot through the box hallway straight into the galley kitchen.

Shock flashed through the horror as Jenna's wet shoes skidded over the smooth black and white tiles, sending her into an treacherous skid halfway across the small kitchen, her shoes bunching up a transparent plastic sheet on the floor.

Staggered, her heart squeezed tight in her chest as her eyes widened in disbelief while Donna and Ryan almost ploughed into the back of her.

In an explosion of glass and splintering of old wood, Mason burst through the French windows, straight through the small open-plan dining area and froze halfway across the floor.

Breath soughing in her chest so hard, she hadn't the ability to speak. Jenna barely absorbed the evil intent in the man's frenzied gaze as it clashed with hers. Blue eyes, blond hair and a handsome face twisted with menace. Recognition paralysed her.

With a flash of a grin, he fisted a handful of red hair, wrenched Carla's head back to expose the delicate, creamy flesh of her neck.

'This one's for you, Jenna. Just for you.' He brought his knife up in a smooth move to slash Carla's exposed throat wide open.

Jenna flung up one hand. 'Denton, stop! Don't!'

With a split second to register the sheer terror radiating from Carla's eyes, Jenna knew with certainty that Denton Harper had no intention of surrendering, just as he knew none of them stood a chance of reaching him before he killed his next victim.

She went with her instinct, whipped her hand around the strap of her handbag and lobbed it underarm across the room.

It smashed into his hand, flicking the knife in an upward spiral.

Disbelief registered in the hollowness of his eyes a moment before he pulled back his lips and exposed his perfect white teeth in a savage snarl, his handsome face turning ugly in an instant.

When she thought he would launch himself at her, mania flashed across his face and instead he wrapped his hands around Carla's neck. Her reddened eyes popped wide as she gasped for air through her nose while he squeezed, his arrogant gaze firmly locked on Jenna's in a vicious challenge.

Jenna raced forward, but Ryan beat her to it.

In a straight-arm manoeuvre, he smacked the heel of his hand into Harper's jaw to send him reeling backwards up against the kitchen sink as the young nurse leaned forward against her restraints and dragged in a desperate lungful of air.

With both hands cradling his jaw, fury still flashed in Harper's eyes. He pushed himself away from the countertop and, ignoring Ryan, centred his attention on Jenna, then launched himself straight at her.

Heart clawing at her chest, Jenna pushed the panic to one side and stood her ground.

Dark eyes focused, he came for her. She raised her fists and struck out, catching nothing but thin air as the blow from her right sent him careering onto the slippery floor covering to land in a crumpled heap at her feet.

Mason flexed his fist, his lips curling with regret as he hissed in air. 'This is becoming a painful habit.'

Jenna's lips kicked up in a bitter twist as she leaned over Harper's inert body to check for signs of life. Thick blond eyelashes fluttered as she pressed her fingers against his neck. The man was proof positive that beauty was only skin-deep.

"You know, Mason, just once I'd like to be allowed to hit someone myself.' With a thin, rapid pulse that confirmed he was still alive, Jenna stepped back. 'Cuff him. Read him his rights, DC Ellis.'

Mason heaved a sigh. 'More bloody paperwork. Why can't the kid do it?'

She glanced over her shoulder at Ryan, a weary smile on her lips.

'Because DC Downey has his own work cut out.'

On his knees, Ryan crouched at Carla's side, his tone low and gentle as he peeled the brown tape from her mouth, allowing her hysterical sobs to escape. As tears streamed down her cheeks, Ryan wrapped his arms around her and rocked her gently while his crooning voice soothed her.

Grateful for Donna's cool, calm presence as she stood in the doorway of the hall and spoke into Airwaves, Jenna watched while Mason cuffed Denton Harper, the dull drone of his practised Miranda reading voice zoned out.

Donna's soft tones zoned in again. 'We have everything in hand here. I confirm we do need paramedics and CSI.'

'Juliette Alpha 77, please clarify. Do you need us to dispatch Firearms?'

'Negative, Control, we do not, repeat, *not* need Firearms,' Her dark brown eyes danced with amused relief. 'Sergeant Morgan used her handbag.'

52

'He played us.'

Jenna let out a disgusted snort. 'He didn't play us, Mason, that would indicate we had some kind of awareness of what he was doing. No, he manipulated us. Directed every minute move we made.' She recalled when she met Denton Harper in the supermarket, felt the lurch in her stomach. The texts. The brush with fate. Only it was never fate. It was Harper.

He'd planned it. Every moment of it. Even the packet of spaghetti. He'd left none of it to fate.

The slow build of embarrassment heated her skin.

When they went to court, it would all come out.

She stroked her fingers over her phone. Only it wouldn't all come out. No one would ever know the passing temptation he'd presented her with. Evidence was all that counted. Anything circumstantial held no water in court. And the evidence she was obliged to turn over showed nothing of her feelings, her fleeting indecision. Her temptation.

Oblivious, Mason slanted her a look. 'Don't be so hard on yourself. He manipulated everyone. For years. He managed to manoeuvre himself into a position of trust nobody questioned. He had access to everything, Jenna. Everyone. He pulled people's strings.'

'He did.' She agreed. Bitterness filled her soul. 'Not least of all, mine.'

53

As the day bled away, Jenna leaned her shoulder against the back door-frame of her home and tilted her head up to admire the ribbons of magenta and lavender streaking across the cool blue sky. A slow smile stretched across her face as she stared at it with optimism in her heart. It could only get better. The nights were getting lighter. Spring couldn't be so far away.

She flexed her naked, aching toes into the carpet of icy grass and sighed her pleasure. Peace settled on her.

Soft, padded footsteps stole to her side and Domino burrowed his cold, wet nose into her hand. With an automatic move, she slipped her fingers along his muzzle to rest her hand on his head, appreciating the special satin texture only Dalmatian fur has.

She drew the cool evening air into her lungs.

Aware of another presence, she turned her head as Fliss stepped outside, a glass of white wine in each hand. As Jenna accepted the proffered glass, she curved her lips into a contented smile.

'I thought you were seeing Mason tonight.'

Fliss smiled back and leaned shoulder to shoulder with her, stealing her dog's loyalty away from Jenna. 'Not tonight, he said he was going home to sleep for a week.'

'Ah.' She felt the same herself. It wouldn't be long before she slipped under her own duvet.

'What about Adrian? We haven't had chance to speak. How did your date go?'

Jenna allowed herself a slow, soft smile, the memory of his seductive kiss still a wisp of a taste on her lips and the huge bouquet of yellow roses an elegant reminder.

'Good.' She took a sip of her wine. 'It went very well.' She sighed as Fliss leaned into her and took a sip of her own wine.

'Mason and I—'

Jenna jerked back. 'Stop!'

'But...'

'I don't want to know. Keep it to yourself.' Jenna wrapped one arm around her younger sister. She'd seen the stunning white longiflorum lilies he'd sent, the house was overflowing with flowers. She gave Fliss a swift kiss on her temple. 'Keep it to yourself.'

Jenna tilted her head up and stared at the clear night sky. Sometimes it was too precious to share.

ACKNOWLEDGMENTS

Thanks as always to my daughters, Laura and Meghan, who give their undying support.

My husband, Andy, who loves this book more than the first. Any errors in techniques and law are totally my own.

My sister, Margaret, who believes in me.

Although I have used real place names to give my story authenticity, all characters and their names are entirely fictitious.

Once again to the Boldwood team for putting their trust in this series. Particularly my editor, Caroline, who whips me into shape to produce stronger and better storylines.

MORE FROM DIANE SAXON

We hope you enjoyed reading *Some One's There*. If you did, please leave a review.

If you'd like to gift a copy, this book is also available as an ebook, digital audio download and audiobook CD.

Sign up to Diane Saxon's mailing list for news, competitions and updates on future books.

http://bit.ly/DianeSaxonNewsletter

Explore the DS Jenna Morgan series:

ABOUT THE AUTHOR

Diane Saxon previously wrote romantic fiction for the US market but has now turned to writing psychological crime. *Find Her Alive* was her first novel in this genre and introduced series character DS Jenna Morgan. Diane is married to a retired policeman and lives in Shropshire.

Visit Diane's website: http://dianesaxon.com/

Follow Diane on social media:

facebook.com/dianesaxonauthor

twitter.com/Diane_Saxon

instagram.com/DianeSaxonAuthor

bookbub.com/authors/diane-saxon

ABOUT BOLDWOOD BOOKS

Boldwood Books is a fiction publishing company seeking out the best stories from around the world.

Find out more at www.boldwoodbooks.com

Sign up to the Book and Tonic newsletter for news, offers and competitions from Boldwood Books!

http://www.bit.ly/bookandtonic

We'd love to hear from you, follow us on social media:

facebook.com/BookandTonic

twitter.com/BoldwoodBooks

instagram.com/BookandTonic

Printed in Great Britain
by Amazon

83123703R00200